His Girl Next Door

JESSICA STEELE

Published in Great Britain 2015
by Mills & Boon, an imprint of Harlequin (UK) Limited,
Eton House, 18-24 Paradise Road, Richmond, Surrey, TW9 1SR

HIS GIRL NEXT DOOR © 2015 Harlequin Books S. A.

The Army Ranger's Return, *New York's Finest Rebel* and *The Girl From Honeysuckle Farm* were first published in Great Britain by Harlequin (UK) Limited.

The Army Ranger's Return © 2011 Soraya Lane
New York's Finest Rebel © 2012 Trish Wylie
The Girl From Honeysuckle Farm © 2009 Jessica Steele

ISBN: 978-0-263-25235-4

05-1015

THE ARMY RANGER'S RETURN

BY
SORAYA LANE

Writing romance for Mills & Boon is truly a dream come true for **Soraya Lane**. An avid book reader and writer since her childhood, Soraya describes becoming a published author as "the best job in the world", and hopes to be writing heart-warming, emotional romances for many years to come.

Soraya lives with her own real-life hero on a small farm in New Zealand, surrounded by animals and with an office overlooking a field where their horses graze.

Visit Soraya at www.sorayalane.com.

For Hamish, my husband and real-life hero.
You have always believed in me, and in my writing,
and this book is for you.

CHAPTER ONE

Dear Ryan,

It feels like we've been writing to one another forever, but it's only been a year. When I say only, a lot has happened in that time, but it makes our friendship sound insignificant somehow.

Of course you can come to see me. It would be weird not to meet you, after getting to know you so well, but strange in the same way to put a face to the name. When you are discharged, write to me, or maybe we could use more modern forms of communication once you're back in civilization.

Stay safe and I'll see you soon. It's unbelievable that you could be back here and we'd pass one another in the street without even knowing.
Jessica

JESSICA MITCHELL STARED out the window and started pacing, eyes never leaving the road. She'd been like this for almost an hour. Stupid, because it wasn't even time for him to arrive yet, and he was army. He would be exactly on time.

She knew that. Jessica knew he was punctual. She knew he would be knocking on her door at twelve-noon bang on.

She knew just about everything about him.

Ryan McAdams.

Up until now, he'd just been a name. A name that made her smile, that made her run to the mailbox every morning. But that's all it had been. Innocent letters, two people confiding in one another. Pen pals.

And yet here she was, pacing in her living room, waiting to meet the man in the flesh.

Jessica looked down and watched her hands shaking. They were quivering, her whole body was wired, and for what? He was her friend. Nothing more. A friend she'd never met before, but a friend nonetheless.

So why was she still walking obsessively up and down? She could just make a cup of coffee or read the paper. Take the dog for a walk and not worry if he had to wait on her doorstep for a few minutes.

Because she wanted this to be perfect. There was no use pretending. His letters had helped her through the last year, had stopped her from giving up when she could have hit rock bottom. And she wanted to say thank you to him in person.

The phone rang. Jessica pounced on it, her pulse thumping.

"Hello."

"Is he there yet?" her best friend asked.

Her heart stuttered then restarted again. She let out a breath. It wasn't him.

"Hi, Bella."

"I'm guessing the hunk hasn't arrived then."

Why had she ever told her friend about Ryan? Why couldn't she have kept it to herself? It was stupid even making a fuss like this. He was her *friend*.

"Jess?"

She flopped down onto the sofa.

"I'm a wreck. A nervous wreck," she admitted.

Bella laughed. "You'll be fine. Just remember to breathe, and if you don't phone me with an update I'm coming around to see him for myself."

"He could be overweight and unattractive."

Bella snorted down the line. Jess didn't even know why she'd said it. Since when did she even care what he looked like? Whatever he looked like didn't change the fact that his friendship had meant a lot to her this past year.

"Bella, I— Oh, my God."

She listened to the thump of footfalls on the porch. Heavy, solid men's feet that beat like a drum on timber.

"Jess? What's happening?" Bella squawked.

A knock echoed.

"He's here," she whispered. "He's *early.*"

"You'll be fine, okay? Put down the phone, close your eyes for a few seconds, then go to the door. Okay? Just say 'okay.'"

"Okay." Jessica thought her head might fall off she was nodding so hard.

She placed the phone down without saying good-bye.

He was here. Ryan was actually here.

Waiting outside her front door.

How could she know this man almost as intimately as she knew her best friend, yet be terrified of meeting him?

She looked at the letter on the table, reached for it, then tucked it into her jeans pocket. She didn't need to open it to know what it said. She remembered every word he'd ever written to her.

Jessica squared her shoulders and shook her head to

push away the fear. Ryan was here, waiting for her, and she had to be brave. It felt like she was about to meet a lover she was so nervous, but it made her feel queasy even thinking that way. One of her closest friends was standing at the door, and for some reason she was paralyzed with fear.

Bella had gotten her all wound up in knots, and for what? She wasn't interested in meeting a man in *that* way, especially not now. And she didn't want Ryan to be anything more to her, no matter what he looked like. What she needed in her life were good friends, and he had proven that he was there for her when she needed someone.

Another knock made her jump.

This was it. There was nowhere she could go but forward, down the hall.

Unless she escaped out the back window...

A flash of brown streaked past her and she groaned. Hercules. She'd put him out the back with a bone and hoped he'd stay there, but he must have squeezed through the doggie door when he'd heard the knock.

At least he'd be a good distraction.

Ryan wondered if it were possible for fingers to sweat. His were curled around the paper-wrapped stems of a bunch of white roses, clenching and unclenching as he tried to figure out what to do with them. Out in front seemed too contrived, behind his back looked ridiculous and hanging at his sides just seemed more ridiculous, like he was trying too hard. Why flowers? Why had he felt the need to complicate things by bringing flowers?

He was going insane. He'd survived the trauma and heartache of years serving his country, and now a stupid bunch of flowers was tying him in tight coils. He was a United States Army Ranger. Practised, strong and unflappable. He'd never have made the special ops unit with nerves like this.

Clearly he was losing his touch.

Perhaps he should throw them into the garden? He looked over his shoulder, beyond the porch, then listened as the door clicked and a small dog started barking.

He was out of time. Ryan slowly, cautiously turned back toward the house. He wanted to squeeze his eyes shut, walk back down the steps and start all over. Without the flowers dangling awkwardly from one hand, and instead standing at ease on the doorstep in front of her.

Ryan spun around as the door swished open.

"Jessica."

He exhaled the word as if he'd been waiting a lifetime to say it. In a way he had.

Ryan was pleased he'd never asked her for a photograph. It couldn't have done justice to the reality of her features. Hair the color of rain-drizzled sand was tucked behind her ears, eyes the shade of the richest dark chocolate peeked out beneath dark lashes. She smiled like she was greeting her first date—nervously, expectantly, unsurely.

Worried. Just like he was.

After so many months of writing one another, meeting in person was kind of surreal.

He went to move and something tiny hit him in the knees and almost made him fall. By the time he looked down a small dog was doing laps around his feet, before disappearing back into the house with as much speed as he'd arrived with.

Ryan laughed then looked back to the woman waiting to meet him.

"Jessica." When he said it this time it made him smile naturally, rather than feeling like a word-stuck teenager. "It's so good to finally meet you."

She grinned as he walked toward her, then opened her arms to him.

"Ryan."

Even the way she said his name did something to his insides, but he pushed past it. He was a soldier. He was trained to deal with difficult situations.

"I'm really glad you made it, Ryan."

He let the flowers drop to the porch as he opened his own arms to hold her. Jessica stepped into his embrace as if she'd been made to fit there, firm against his chest, arms tight around him. She hugged him like someone who cared about him.

Like he hadn't been hugged in a long time.

It had been years since his wife had died. Years since he'd felt the genuine embrace of a woman, one that wasn't out of pity, but out of something deeper, warmer.

Ryan inhaled the scent of her—the tease of perfume that reminded him of coconuts on a beach. The soft caress of her hair that fell against his neck as she tucked into him.

It felt good. No…even better than good. It felt *great*.

He cleared his throat and stepped back, not wanting to make her uncomfortable by keeping hold of her too long. Jessica leapt back from him like a bear from a nest of hornets, her face alternating between happy and concerned.

"I…"

"We…"

They both laughed.

"You first," he said.

Jessica grinned at him and rocked back and forth, arms crossed over her chest.

"I don't remember what I was going to say!"

Ryan shook his head and laughed. Laughed like he thought he'd forgotten how to, cheeks aching as he watched her do the same.

He bent to collect the fallen flowers.

"These are for you."

She blushed. When had he last seen a grown woman blush? It made a goofy smile play across his lips.

"Me?"

He nodded.

"It's been a long time since anyone gave me flowers."

Ryan watched as she dipped her nose down to inhale them, her eyes dancing along the white silhouette of each rose.

It had been a long time since he'd *given* a woman flowers.

"Do they give me passage inside?"

Jessica looked up at him with an expression he'd only seen once before. His wife had looked up at him like that from her hospital bed, full of hope, happiness shining from her face.

He clenched his jaw and stamped the memory away, refusing to go there. This was Jessica, the woman who had made an effort to write to him when most Americans seemed to forget what U.S. troops were facing overseas. This was not a time to dwell on the past.

"Yes." She looked sideways, away and then back, but he didn't miss the twinkle in her eyes. "Yes, it does. So long as you're prepared to meet Hercules properly."

"I take it Hercules is the small fur-ball who almost bowled me over."

Jessica reached out to Ryan and grinned. "Maybe if I'd given him a more insignificant name he wouldn't be quite so full of self-importance."

Ryan took the hand she offered and let himself be led inside. It felt too normal to touch his skin to hers, too casual, but when she looked over her shoulder at him and smiled, her fingers trailing away from his until she was just a woman walking ahead of him, he felt the loss of her touch like a limb had just been torn from his body.

The shock of doing normal things was something hard to get used to, after months being surrounded by other men in the desert. Each day started to merge with the next one…and home seemed like just a scene on a postcard.

Being back here wasn't something he had looked forward to, it was something he'd feared and wished he didn't have to confront again. But Jessica had been there for him, eagerly writing him back so he'd had something positive to concentrate on.

When everything else was gone, snatched away from him, Jessica had been there.

She'd come into his life when he'd been losing his way. When he'd almost felt as though his soul had been defeated, like he had lost his purpose. It was Jessica who had held each piece of him together when he could have lost hope.

Maybe she could help him now he was home, too.

Because nothing else had fallen into place since he'd returned.

A man could only hope.

Jessica set the flowers to rest in a vase on her bench and turned back to her guest.

"Shall we have lunch here or go out for something?"

Ryan shrugged. "I don't mind."

"But…?"

She laughed as he squinted at her.

"How did you know there was a *but?*" he asked.

Jessica tapped her nose. "You'd be surprised what I know about you."

Ryan flopped down on the sofa and crossed his legs at the ankle. He looked at home here, comfortable in *her* home. Aside from her brother, she wasn't used to seeing men in her space.

She didn't want it to bother her, but it did. Having a man around had become foreign to her. It felt too intimate, being so close, seeing him so…at ease.

Funny, she had expected being back in America to be hard for him, but it seemed like she was the one struggling.

"Okay, you got me." He gave her a smile that made her almost want to look away, but she didn't. The way his mouth curved, his eyes creasing gently at the corners, was exactly as she'd imagined he would look. Hoped he might look.

Her stomach twisted, as if her organs had been flipped then dropped. She wasn't meant to be thinking about him like that. Not now, not ever.

"The sun's shining, the ground is still wet from the rain last night and I'm desperate to be outside in the open. You've got no idea how good it feels—smells—outside here," he said.

Jessica beamed at him. She was still nervous, but the quiver in her belly felt as if it were less from worry than excitement. A day out with someone with whom she could just be herself was exactly what she needed.

Besides, it would be easier being around him on neutral territory. Even if he was just a friend, she wasn't ready to see a man in her house, on her sofa, like that. Not after Mark. Not after what she'd gone through this last year.

It sent a shiver down her spine just thinking about the last twelve months.

"Give me five minutes, I'll get my handbag and we'll go to the park."

"I'm guessing we have to take the mutt?" he teased.

Jessica cringed as she heard paws racing on the timber floor in the kitchen. Hercules was like a missile, as if he'd known exactly what they'd been talking about.

He sprung through the door and leapt onto Ryan's lap, tongue frantically searching out his victim's face.

"Hercules! No!"

Ryan grabbed him and held him at a safe distance.

"Five minutes?" He raised an eyebrow, ignoring the wriggling dog.

She nodded. "Sorry about him."

Ryan stood, eyeing Hercules. "I'll start the clock now."

She turned sedately and walked toward her bedroom as slowly as she could manage. She wanted to run, to sprint to her room and grab her things and not miss a moment of being in his company.

Ryan. His name was circling her mind over and over, like a record she couldn't turn off. Ryan.

He was everything she'd imagined he would be and more. When they'd first started writing, he was just a soldier. He was a man serving their country and she felt good giving support to him. But when they'd realized they had grown up within ten minutes of one another, something had started stirring within her. Then when he'd made noises of coming back home to California, to Thousand Oaks, she'd started wondering. That despite her insecurities, despite her worries about herself, she had a connection with this man. A man who understood her and wanted to meet her. But a man she only knew on paper, who wouldn't feel pity for her or treat her like an almost-broken doll because of what she'd been through.

And he was hardly a disappointment. In the flesh, he was even more commanding than he was on paper. Well over six feet and built like a man who could protect her on a dark stormy night in the meanest streets of Los Angeles. A man with dark cropped, slightly disheveled hair that begged to be touched, ice-blue eyes that seemed to pierce straight through her body. And beautiful lips that, despite all he'd seen and experienced, still hovered with the hint of a smile as he spoke.

Jessica scolded herself. Smiling over mental pictures of him while she was alone was exactly what she *didn't* need to be doing. Ever. Until she reached the five-year mark, until she knew she was in complete remission, men were strictly off her radar.

Jessica stole a quick glance at herself in the mirror as she passed and fought the urge to cross her arms over her chest. She was still self-conscious, but it was getting better. After all they'd said to one another, all they'd shared, she hadn't told Ryan. Couldn't tell him. Not yet. It was still too fresh for her, too raw, to share with anyone.

And she wanted him to just like her for herself. Treat her like she was normal and not a fragile baby bird in need of extra care.

She picked up her purse, squirted an extra spray of perfume to her wrist and reached for a sweater. She didn't know why, but today felt like a fresh opportunity, a new chance. She wasn't going to let her insecurities ruin it. Not when she had a man like Ryan waiting to spend the day with her.

Even if she was scared to death.

She utterly refused to let her past ruin her future. Not now, not after all she'd been through.

Today was about starting over.

CHAPTER TWO

Dear Jessica,
I've become desensitized to what we have to see
over here. I wait for my orders, I no longer cringe
when an explosion echoes around me, and I au-
tomatically squeeze the trigger to take down the
enemy. Does it make me a bad person that I no
longer feel? I'm starting to think I like being here
because it means I don't have to face reality. I
can pretend my wife didn't die and that my son
doesn't hate me. But I'll be coming home soon,
after all this time, and I'm not going to have any
more excuses.
Thanks for listening, Jessica. You don't know
how much it means to me to be able to write to
you, to be honest like this. I can't talk to anyone
else, but you're always here for me.
Ryan

"So HOW IS it you've managed to stay away for so long?"

Ryan shrugged and turned his body toward Jessica as they walked. He made himself look away from Hercules racing up and down the riverbank so he could give Jessica his full attention.

"I guess I became good at saying yes, and the army were pleased to have me wherever I was needed."

"What about this time?"

Ryan chuckled. After so long being in the company of men, he wasn't used to the way a woman could just fire questions. So candidly wanting to know everything at once.

"What's so funny?" she asked.

Jessica was…what? Pouting? No, not pouting but she was definitely pursing her lips.

"You're very inquisitive, that's all."

She gave him a nudge in the side and rolled her eyes. Ryan tried not to come to a complete standstill, forced his feet to keep moving. He wasn't used to that, either. Someone touching him so casually, with such ease.

He'd definitely been away too long.

"I write to you for months, and you can't tell me where you are or why you're suddenly coming home on such short notice. So spill," she ordered.

He followed Jessica toward the edge of the lake, the water so still it looked like the cover of a postcard. The park was beautiful, much more attractive than he'd remembered it being, but after so long seeing sand and little else, everything about America seemed beautiful. The smell of fresh rain on grass, the softer rays of sunlight, not burning so hot against your skin that it made you sweat. Things you took for granted until they were snatched away.

"I can't tell you where we've been, you know that, but what I can say is that our last, ah, assignment was successful."

Jessica waited. He'd give her that. She could talk his ear off, but she knew when to stay quiet. Seemed to sense that he needed a moment.

"I'm a marksman, Jess." He paused and watched her, made sure she didn't look too alarmed. "I entered the special forces as an expert in my field, and it's why I've been deployed so long."

"But you didn't want to come home," she said softly. "What made you come back now?"

Ryan sighed and looked out at the water. It was so much easier just keeping this sort of stuff in his head. But he didn't have to tell her everything. It wasn't like he'd planned to come home, more like his hand had been forced.

If he'd had it his way he would have stayed away forever. That's what he *had* done until now. Now he was home and he had to deal with being a single dad for real. Not to mention the fact his son didn't want to know him.

He didn't like admitting something was impossible, but repairing that relationship could be like trying to bring someone back from the dead. It was his own fault, his own battle to deal with, and he'd been a coward to wait so long before confronting the problem.

But one thing he'd promised himself was that he was going to be honest with this woman. She'd done something generous for him, helped him from the other side of the world through her constant letters, and he owed it to her to be real and candid with her now.

"I had an injury a while back and it never healed quite right." He moved to sit down on the grass, needing to collapse. It was hard being so open, just talking, and he couldn't go back. Couldn't put into words what had happened to him then, that day he'd realized he wasn't invincible. "I've had a lot of pain in my arm, so I had surgery in Germany on my way back home, and the army wants me on rest until the physio gives me the all clear."

Ryan gritted his teeth and forced his eyes to stay open as his memory tried to claw its way back. The smell of gunpowder, the pain making his arm feel like it was on fire, and not being able to stop. Making his arm work, pushing through, pulling the trigger over and over until his body had finally let him down.

He clamped his jaw down hard and looked at Jessica. She was sitting, too, right beside him, legs tucked up under her as she stared at the water. As if she was the troubled one. He could see it on her face. That she was either reacting to his pain, or harboring her own.

"Jess?"

She turned empty eyes toward him, bottom lip caught between her teeth.

"That means you're going back at some point."

He raised a brow. Had she thought he was home for good? Had he made her think he was staying by something he'd said?

"Ah, all going well, I'll be deployed wherever they need me," he confirmed.

It was wonderful being back here in some ways, but it was also extremely difficult. He'd do his best, try to make amends, but he was a soldier. That's what he did. What he was good at.

She nodded, over and over again, too vigorously. "Of course, of course you're going back. I don't know why I thought you wouldn't be."

"I'll be here a couple months at least, then I have to figure out what to do. I'm eligible to be discharged, they've offered me teaching positions, but I'm just not ready to walk away from my men. I don't know where

I'll be deployed yet but it's my job to go wherever they need me."

Sad eyes greeted him when he looked back at her. She smiled, but he could tell something had upset her. He hoped it wasn't his fault. Seeing those bright eyes cloud over was not something he wanted to be held accountable for.

"What about your son?" she asked quietly.

Ryan sighed. His son. George. Now that was a topic he and Jess could talk about all day. Or maybe not talk about at all, as he'd been home a week already and they'd hardly spoken a word to one another.

"I don't know if I'm just not cut out to be a father, or whether he truly wishes I was back with the army."

He didn't say what else he wondered. That maybe his son wished he were dead.

Ryan picked up a stone and stood, then reached his arm back and threw it into the water. He'd meant to skim it, but instead the stone went a little distance then landed with a plop.

He shut his eyes and pushed away the anger. He hated not being capable, losing the function in his strongest arm, but getting angry about it didn't help his progress and he knew it. Sometimes he just forgot about it, and then he'd surprise himself all over again by not having the control he wanted.

He looked down at Jessica, sitting still, eyes fixed in the distance.

"You okay?"

It was as if she had to snap out of a trance before she even noticed he was speaking.

"Yeah."

Ryan watched as she jumped to her feet and brushed the grass off her jeans. "Yeah, I'm fine."

Maybe he'd been away way too long, or maybe he'd just forgotten how sensitive women were. Because they'd only been at the park less than an hour and already he'd done something to upset her.

And he had no idea what.

"You still want to grab some lunch?" he asked.

She smiled at him, this time more openly. Or maybe more guardedly. He couldn't tell which.

"Sure. Let's go."

Jessica couldn't fathom why her stomach was twisting like a snake had taken ownership of it. Why did it even bother her? So he was going back to war? He was a soldier and that's what soldiers did. It was just that she hadn't *expected* him to be going back. When he'd written to her and told her he was coming home she'd thought it was for good.

It wasn't as if he'd promised her something and was now going back on his word. She had no right to even feel this way.

They were friends.

So why was she acting like her lover had come home and lied to her about his intentions? Or maybe she'd just dealt with too much loss to even comprehend the thought of losing anyone else from her life again. She knew firsthand what the consequences were of him not coming home, what the risks were.

"You *sure* you're all right?" he persisted.

Jessica's head swivelled so quickly it almost swung off.

"Me?"

He laughed and she watched as he pushed his hands into his jeans pockets.

"Yes, you."

She felt the flush of her cheeks as he made fun of her. She'd expected him to be the one clamming up and here she was like a nervous bunch of keys being jangled. She hadn't even realized how long they'd been walking in silence.

"I'm sorry Ryan, it's just…"

He shrugged. "I took you by surprise."

This was a man who'd been away from civilization for years, and yet he seemed to have her all figured out. That made a change.

Jessica sighed.

"I understand if you don't want to, you know, hear about war or anything. It's not exactly the most pleasant experience to discuss," he said.

She frowned at the look on his face. It took her a second, because she hesitated, but Jessica reached for his hand to give it a quick squeeze. She was being stupid and he was the one who needed her to act like normal. To listen to him like she had in all their letters. He had no idea why she was affected by what he'd said, and that's how it had to be. She'd lost too much, exposed those she loved to that loss as well, and it had struck a chord with her. But that was one musical instrument she had no intention of playing around him, and that meant she had to deal with it and move on. Fast.

"You can tell me all you like, honestly. I just didn't expect you to be going back there anytime soon," she explained. "It took me by surprise."

Ryan caught her hand before she could pull it away. His hand was strong, smooth. And the touch made a tingle start in her fingertips and ripple goose bumps up her forearm.

"You're the only person I've been able to talk to, apart from the guys, since I left."

She nodded. Words refused to form in her throat. It had been so long since a man had touched her. Since she'd even felt a spark of attraction that had made her heart beat like a hammer was thwacking it from side to side.

"If I can't talk to you, I've got no one," he added.

Jessica couldn't take her eyes off their hands. Ryan followed her gaze and seemed to realize what the problem was, opening his grip and slowly releasing her fingers.

"I'm sorry," he muttered.

"Don't be sorry."

She smiled up at him. Watched the way his eyes crinkled ever so gently at the sides as he smiled back at her.

"Oh, no!" she exclaimed.

Ryan jumped to attention, eyes scanning, like he was looking for an enemy, but Jessica was already moving back toward the park.

"What?"

"Where's Herc?" she gasped.

Her heart had gone from thumping out of desire to banging from terror. How could she have been that distracted? How could she not have noticed that he'd wandered off? Her baby, her best friend, her...

Hercules had been there for her through everything. When she was home recovering, cuddling up by her side as the chemo ravaged her body. Snuggling her when she couldn't force herself out of bed in the morning. Listening to her as she'd sobbed after surgery.

He'd probably just wandered off in search of more ducks, chasing mallards again, but still...

Jessica had huge hot tears that felt like balls of fire fighting to get free of her lashes, desperate to spill, but she gulped them back, moving as fast as she could back the way they'd come.

She jumped as a hand came down on her shoulder. A hand that seemed to distribute calm energy through her body, grounding her, telling her everything was going to be okay.

"I'll run ahead, you keep your eyes peeled." Ryan's deep voice was commanding as he took charge. "I'll get him, you just stay calm."

Jessica nodded. She wasn't capable of doing anything else. Herc always followed along beside her off the lead, but then she wasn't usually so distracted.

She watched Ryan thump gracefully down the sidewalk, his feet beating a steady rhythm as he jogged away from her.

"Herc!" Jessica called as loud as she could. "Come on, Herc!"

Ryan had never felt as if his heart was actually in his throat before. Maybe at the funeral, when he'd had to watch his son cry as his mother was lowered in a coffin into her grave. But that was a different kind of emotion. That was pure agony, mourning like he'd never known he could experience.

This? This was desperation, panic. Determination to find what he was looking for.

He'd settled into a quick steady jog and he was almost back to where they'd come from, searching with his eyes as he moved. The dog had been at their side when they'd left but the little rascal must have skipped off when something caught his nose.

Then Ryan spotted him. A brown bullet barking his head off as he chased ducks back and forth along the bank again. Completely oblivious to the fact he was alone and had found his way back solo.

Phew.

"Hercules!"

The dog ignored him. Ryan kept running, slowing only to scoop the bundle of fur into his arms.

Hercules jumped and wriggled, but Ryan held him firm.

"You gave us a fright, bud."

The dog just wriggled some more, tongue flapping as he tried to contort his little body around so he could lick him. Ryan held him in an iron-tight grip, just far enough away so he could avoid being slobbered all over.

"Come on, let's go find your mom."

He started jogging again, until he spotted Jessica ahead. He would have waved but he was determined not to let the dog go. He was writhing like a slippery fish again.

When she saw them, Jessica's entire face lit up, a smile stretching across her lips.

"Herc!"

Ryan slowed and grinned. "Told you I'd get him."

Now she was crying. Oh, no, he didn't do tears well. He went to hold the dog out but she threw herself into his arms instead, almost making him drop the little animal!

"Thank you, Ryan. Thank you, thank you, thank you."

He gave her a half hug back, the other arm still occupied by Hercules.

Ryan went to move at the same time as she kissed him on the cheek. His face turned too far and she got him on the side of his mouth.

He fought not to turn farther into her, his pulse racing at her mouth on his.

"Oh."

He grimaced. "Sorry."

Jessica was bright red again, like a piece of freshly snapped rhubarb.

"I—"

He stepped back, clipped the dog onto the leash hanging from her hand and put him down.

"How about we head back to your place? Get him out of trouble?" he suggested.

Jessica nodded, still flushed.

He didn't know what was happening here, but one thing he did know was that somehow they weren't behaving like long lost pen pals. When she'd held him before, it had felt too warm. Like someone had shone the sun itself between them. Like they were the only two people in the world.

And if it had been another time and another place, he'd have been tempted to never let her go.

But he was only here for a few months. Maybe less. He'd come looking for her because she'd been such a wonderful support to him. Helped him talk about his feelings, open up.

Without her, he doubted he'd have ever have had the strength to come home, to face his demons once and for all.

There was no chance he was going to stuff this up by letting his emotions get the better of him. Jessica was off limits romantically.

And that was nonnegotiable.

He had to maintain their friendship, repair his relationship with his son and summon the strength to open up to his own parents. Tell them how much he appreciated them and what they'd done for him.

He grimaced at the thought of what the coming months held.

He'd just have to take it all one step at a time.

CHAPTER THREE

Dear Ryan,
I know you feel like you can't come back home,
but that's just fear talking. I'm not going to tell
you that soldiers shouldn't be fearful, because a
soldier is nothing more than a brave human being
and you can't help how you feel. But you need to
repair your relationship with your son while you
can. And you need to face the fact that he will
want to talk with you about his mother.

I don't know what you're going through, but I
do understand pain and loss. I know what it feels
like to grieve, and to want to hide away, but in
the end you have to be honest with yourself. It's
the only way forward.

Remember I'm here for you. If you need some-
one to hold your hand, that person can be me. No
questions asked.
Jessica

JESSICA HAD BEHAVED like a brainless airhead. Since
when could she forget her dog? And the way she'd shut
out Ryan after he'd opened up to her was unacceptable.
He must think she was some kind of a nutcase. Not the

level-headed pen pal who was full of wisdom that he'd come to rely on.

Nothing about today had gone as planned.

Jessica smiled as he walked back into the room. She swallowed away her fear and pinched her hand.

"Ryan, I'm so sorry."

He looked confused. One eyebrow raised slightly higher than the other. "What about?"

She sighed. He was either really good at pretending, or men actually were incredibly good at just letting things go.

"About before. Can we just start over? Go back to when you arrived?"

Ryan chuckled. He actually chuckled, while she stood there all breathless and red-faced.

"Whatever you say."

Argh! Men could be so irritating. He was just like her brother. Or worse. Acting like something hadn't happened when it had. But if he wanted to forget about it then she wasn't going to argue with him. She'd behaved badly and now she had a chance to make things right.

"Okay, how about we actually have a cup of something hot and make some lunch then?"

He grinned and walked right up to her, stopping a few feet back. Ryan held out his hand.

"I'm Ryan, it's so good to finally meet you."

She glared at him and stuck her hands in her pockets.

"Not funny, Ryan." The expression on his face didn't change. It was so serious he almost made her laugh, but she felt like too much of an idiot to shrug it off. "I made a fool of myself back there and it wasn't me. I mean, I don't even know how to explain myself."

He smiled at her again, but this time she didn't feel mocked.

"I thought you wanted to start over?"

Jessica turned away from him.

"Look, I took you by surprise, that's all. Now let's have some food, okay? I'm starving. Unless you want to meet all over again, again?" he teased.

Jessica sighed and walked back into the kitchen. Her face still felt flushed, but she was starting to relax. Lucky this was a friendship where they already kind of knew one another. If it had been a first date she'd have been toast.

"Can I do anything?" he offered.

She shook her head.

"I'll make some sandwiches and meet you outside."

When he didn't move she made herself look up at him.

"Hercules would love to play ball if you're up for a game in the yard," she suggested.

He winked at her and sauntered out the door.

Jessica had to force her mouth to stay shut. It was in grave risk of dropping down and hitting her on the chest.

Something about that man had her all twisted in knots, and that wink hadn't helped. She was all hot, like she needed a fan, but she gulped down a glass of water instead.

And it didn't help her any.

Ten minutes later, and still hot under the collar, Jessica found Ryan sitting back on one of her chairs, eyes closed, basking in the sun. A very put-out-looking Hercules lay nearby, ball neglected between his front paws.

She leant over to put the tray of food and drinks on

the table when Ryan's eyes popped open. He looked lazy, comfortable.

Gorgeous.

She pushed the thought away as he ran a hand through his hair and then down his face, as if to wake himself up.

"You've got no idea how good this is, just sitting here."

"Sandwich?"

He took it happily and started eating. Jessica made herself do the same, even though swallowing was like forcing large chunks through a sieve.

They sat in silence for a bit. Eating. Watching the dog chase his tail then start stalking a bird.

"Don't get me wrong, Jess, but I could have sworn you had something other than my going back to war on your mind before."

This time she actually choked. Had to reach for her coffee and take a big gulp. What had happened to the stereotype of brooding soldier who hardly said a word and wasn't up with the whole feelings thing? She had expected him to be quiet and reserved, but the reality of him was anything but. He'd either come out of his shell big-time, or he was making a huge effort here.

And hadn't they put this behind them and started over?

"Sorry, went down the wrong way," she stuttered.

Ryan didn't look convinced, just reached for another sandwich.

"Whatever you say."

She sighed.

"It's true I've had a lot going on this past year, but I just wasn't expecting to have to worry about you going back on top of it all. That's all."

It wasn't technically a lie. She *would* worry about him when he was gone. But when he'd told her, her mind had wandered. To a place she didn't want to go and shouldn't have let herself be drawn back to.

"Jessica?"

She put on the brave face she had perfected over the months of treatment she'd received and turned back to him.

"I'm fine, honestly. Tell me about you. What do you want to do while you're home? Do you need somewhere to stay?"

She held her breath, hoping he'd say no. There was no way she could deal with him staying here. Not now. It was messing her head up just trying to be normal around him for an afternoon.

"Tempting offer, but no, thanks."

She tucked her feet up beneath her on the seat and turned to face him. It was comforting in a way to watch his face, but off-putting at the same time. Hard to fathom this man sitting here was the author of all those letters, the ones that had kept her going, even through the hard times. Given her something to look forward to and something to focus on.

His eyes softened as he smiled, laughter lines etched ever so slightly into his tanned skin.

"I've been hoping you might have some good advice to throw my way." He paused, taking a sip of his coffee. "On how to deal with a twelve-year-old boy who can't seem to bear the sight of me."

Her heart throbbed for a moment, feeling his pain. But she recovered without him noticing.

"When you say he can't bear the sight of you..."

Ryan grimaced. "I mean that he gets up and leaves the

room the moment he sees me, or suffers my presence at mealtime by sitting silently and not raising his eyes."

Oh. "And your parents?"

That brought the smile back to his face. "Thrilled to have their only son home and desperate for me to reconnect with my own boy."

She thought about it for a moment. The nice thing about already having a relationship with someone, even if it was on paper, was that silent stretches weren't uncomfortable. Or at least they weren't with Ryan.

She unfolded her legs and leaned toward him.

"I know it's going to sound like a cliché, saying that you just need to give him time, especially after all the time you've been away, but I think he'll come around. He's probably angry at you for leaving and staying away so long, and he wants answers. You need to let him know that when he does want to ask you questions you can be there for him, straight up, honest."

Ryan closed his eyes and sat back. She could see this was painful for him, but he was better to get it all off his chest with her.

Besides, talking about him was taking her mind off the fact that she was attracted to him. That his being there, beside her, was making her have feelings she'd long ago abandoned when it came to men. And it also made her push her memories back where they belonged. Locked in a box, out of mind's reach.

He smiled sadly. "You're right, but sometimes I wonder if he'd have been better off if I'd just stayed away."

Jessica shook her head. It wasn't true and he knew it.

"Why don't you practice on me," she suggested, voice soft. "You can pretend I'm George."

He nodded. She only just registered the incline of his head as he moved it.

Jessica took a deep breath. "Okay, I'll start." She paused. "Why did you really go back to war so soon? Why didn't you come home? Stay with me?"

He kept his eyes shut. "I can't answer that."

She sighed and sat back. On second thought she reached for his hand, wanting to give him strength even if it hurt her. "If you can't be honest with me, how are you going to be honest with a boy who wants the truth?"

She watched as Ryan's thumb traced her palm, holding her hand back. It felt so good it hurt, but she didn't dare pull her hand away. Couldn't. The tingle in her fingertips and the pulse at her neck were enough to make her stay put.

When he was ready to talk he dropped his hold and pulled his chair around to face her head-on. She forced herself to breathe, had to concentrate on every inhale and exhale of her lungs.

"Okay, let's do this."

She nodded, still off balance from touching him, from his skin connecting with hers. From wanting him to do it again and hating herself for even thinking about him like that.

Ryan squeezed his eyes shut one more time then focused, looking firmly into hers.

"I left because going away was easier than staying. I was a coward and I should have been here for you."

Jessica gulped silently as tears pooled in her eyes. This was what he'd been needing to say for so long. There was no disguising the pain in his voice.

"Go on," she urged huskily.

"I told myself that you would be better off without

me, and I felt guilty over your mom's death. Like if only I'd loved her more, been here for her more, she could have pulled through. Everyone thought we had this perfect life, and in many ways we did, but then when she got sick everything just went into free fall, and after a while it was easier to just stay away than deal with her death." He paused. "And with you."

Jessica stood and walked away a few steps. She couldn't help it. Tears hit her cheeks and trickled their way down her jaw. She'd known hurt before, known what it was like to be left, but she also knew what it was like to be the one who did the hurting.

"Jess?"

"I'm sorry, it's just…"

"Did I say something wrong?" He sounded concerned.

She reached her fingertips to her face and brushed the tears away. Before she could turn large hands fell on her arms, holding her from behind.

"I shouldn't have said all that, but once I started it…"

Jessica closed her eyes then turned back to face him. She'd tried not to let her own feelings intrude, but it was hard. Impossible even.

"I lost someone once, too, Ryan, that's all. Hearing you say all that kind of brought that back. I don't know why but it did."

His eyes questioned her but he didn't say anything. Instead it was as if a metal guard had been raised, shielding his gaze and putting a wall between them. A divide that hadn't been there before.

Jessica didn't want to think about her past. Probably as much as Ryan wanted to disclose his, if the look on his face right now was any indication. It did give them something in common. Not exactly the common element most people would wish for, but on some level she did understand him. And if she wanted to tell him, he'd probably feel the same about her. But she didn't want to, and the last thing she intended was burdening him with her problems, or letting her mind dwell on what could happen to her.

"You know what? I think maybe it's time for me to go," he said, suddenly looking like a startled animal within sight of a predator. As if he wanted to flee the scene.

"Okay." Now she was the one confused. "Do you want to maybe grab dinner tonight? Do that 'start over' thing again?"

He was smiling but it looked forced. Not like before.

"Can we take a rain check on that? Maybe tomorrow night?"

Ouch. She hadn't seen that one coming. She'd over-reacted, not been able to keep her emotions in check, but she hadn't realized he'd react like that.

"How about you call me when you're free?" she suggested.

He nodded and turned back toward the house. "See you, bud."

At least he'd said goodbye to the dog.

"I'm sorry, Jess. It's just that I need to pick George up from school."

She shrugged. Even she knew that school didn't get out for a while yet. "I get it. We can catch up later."

She followed him back into the house, wondering what she would give to truly start over with him and be the strong girl from the letters. To go back to him standing on her doorstep and make the day turn out completely different.

His tall frame disappeared through the door and he didn't look back, his broad shoulders and dark hair fading from sight.

Jessica stood with her hands on her hips and surveyed the huge stretch of canvas on the floor in front of her. Not her best work, but the colors were brilliant. The organic paint took some getting used to, although if it meant no toxic fumes she had no intention of complaining.

She'd tried to focus on her new piece, but her mind kept wandering. Going to a place she didn't want to go back to but couldn't claw out from.

She found it was easier sometimes to pretend it hadn't happened. When you were surrounded by people who loved you or who had been the cause of grief, it sucked something from you. Pulled you into a world you didn't want to confront.

Like her cancer. She'd dealt with. Fought it. Survived it.

Yet her family treated her like she needed permanent wrapping in cotton wool just to survive each day now. Looked at her in a way that made her uncomfortable. And she hated it.

Was that how Ryan felt? The same way she did when she looked in the mirror and saw the reality of her body? Is that how he felt about being home? About the reality of what he'd gone through and then battled every day? How it was to come home and face something you'd run from for years?

Sometimes she felt like that, too. Sometimes she wished she could run away from what had happened and leave it all behind. But just like Ryan had had to return, so had she. To the reality of life as a cancer survivor.

She let her hand brush over the almost-hard contour of her breast, skimming the side of it, not caring that her fingers were covered in paint. Jessica sighed. She'd always mocked women with implants. Found it hard to fathom why breast augmentation was such an attraction.

She smiled with the irony. When she'd faced the reality of a double mastectomy, the first question she'd asked was what kind of reconstruction they could do. How they could give her her femininity back. Her breasts.

So now she had teardrop-shaped silicone implants that were better than nothing, but that still made her shake her head sometimes. That despite being diagnosed with cancer, facing chemo, knowing there was a chance she could die, all she'd wanted was to feel like a woman again. To know that even though they didn't feel soft when they'd once been natural, she still had her femininity, even if it had meant facing cosmetic reconstructive surgery to obtain them.

Maybe it was the same for Ryan. Without being a soldier, he would feel like less of a man, less of a human being. Maybe that was why he felt he had to go back, had to return to his unit. Had to offer himself up for redeployment.

If she could talk to him, explain to him how she felt, maybe it would help him. Help them both. But she couldn't do it.

She didn't want him to know. Couldn't tell him. Because then he'd start looking at her the same way everyone else did, and with Ryan, she just wanted to be Jessica. Not the girl with cancer. The girl in remission. Or the girl who'd already lost her sister to the disease.

Maybe he wouldn't look at her differently, or treat her like a different person, but she wasn't prepared to risk it. Not when she only had a limited time to enjoy having a friend like Ryan.

Or maybe she was too scared to tell him.

Either way, it was her secret and she had no intention of divulging it.

But after the way he'd left today, like he was fleeing a burning wreckage, she didn't know when they'd be seeing each other again. If ever.

"Jess?"

She looked up as Bella crossed her arms and leaned against the door of her studio. Jess sighed. Today had definitely not gone as planned.

"You have some serious explaining to do," her friend said.

CHAPTER FOUR

Jessica,

I don't know how you know so much about loss or dealing with pain, but you've helped me more than I could ever tell you. Having a friend to write to, someone to just hang out with in the normal world, makes all the difference to me. I love what I do, wouldn't give it up for the world, but sometimes it helps to have someone non-army to talk to.

You do realize I'm gonna owe you big-time when I come home. Dinner, drinks, whatever you want, but you writing to me has given me a boost, and that only makes me a better soldier. I was starting to think I was too old for war, but it's like I've been recharged.

So think about it. When I finally leave this place and come home, my shout. Whatever you want. And I promise not to talk about me or ask you for any more advice. Okay?
Ryan

RYAN SAT IN the car and watched the throng of kids as they spilled out from the building. He couldn't see George, but then that was hardly a surprise. The boy would probably hide in class to avoid having to get in the car with his dad.

But Ryan was patient. He'd wait here as long as he had to. Besides, it wasn't as if he didn't have enough on his mind to keep him occupied.

Jessica.

Today had started out so well and ended so…badly. He closed his eyes and leaned back into the seat. He thumped his hand on the wheel. Ow! Sometimes he forgot he was meant to be recuperating, that he couldn't use his arm like that. It hurt badly sometimes, ached, bothered him when he was uptight or unsure.

He hated not being strong and capable. It wasn't that he was weak, but he'd always been the tough guy, the one who could be counted on physically and mentally in the worst of situations.

And it wasn't like it was only his arm troubling him. His head was messed up, too, especially after his behavior earlier.

Somehow he'd managed to screw today up. Jessica was supposed to be the easy part, the simple meeting of a friend. How wrong he'd been.

Why was being back so hard? He was so good at being a soldier, it came so naturally to him. Ryan swallowed and looked out the window.

Being a dad had come naturally to him once, too.

So had being a husband.

But that felt like another lifetime ago. Like he could just hold on to it as a long-distant memory, but it was starting to fade. Fast.

Ryan jumped at a knock on the car window.

He cursed, then pushed the button to wind down the window and acknowledge George's teacher. "You frightened the life out of me!"

"Sorry." The young man smiled, holding out his hand.

Ryan opened the door and got out, shaking the teacher's hand and leaning against the side of his car.

"It's Shaun, right?"

The teacher nodded. Ryan had only met him once before, on his first day back, but he'd liked him straight away.

"I saw you sitting here and thought I'd see how you were getting on with George," Shaun said.

Ryan shrugged. What did he say to that?

"Not great." There seemed no point in not telling the truth.

"Anything I can do to help?"

"You know, once upon a time I knew exactly what to say to make him laugh, just to be there for him. You know?" he said.

Shaun gave him a kind smile.

"It's not so easy anymore. Figuring out what the right thing to do with him is hard work," Ryan admitted.

"I'm sure you're doing everything you can. Just stick with it and do what feels right."

Ryan nodded, shoulders heaving as he exhaled. He wasn't usually one to open up, to talk to someone about how he felt, but George seemed to genuinely like his teacher. And he appreciated the offer of help.

"I guess I've found it hard to know what to say to him since his mom died. Until now, I've taken the easy way out and let my parents do the hard work."

It had indeed been the coward's way out and he was man enough to admit it. Especially now he could see firsthand the effect it had had on his boy.

"What matters is that you're here now and you want to do something about it." The teacher held out his hand again and patted Ryan on the shoulder with the other.

"You'll get there, and if you need someone to talk to—either of you—I'm here. Okay?"

"Thanks."

Shaun gestured toward the door. "I saw him by his locker before, I'm sure he'll be out soon."

Ryan watched the teacher walk off and got back in the car.

When he'd been redeployed the last time, he was still grieving for his wife. He'd held his son at the airport, hugged him tight and then walked away. Seeing his own mother hold his boy had left an image in his mind that had never faded. An image that told him George would be happier without his dad. That a messed-up, grieving, unsure father was nothing compared to the steady, loving influence of grandparents.

And then every month he'd stayed away it had simply been easier to keep telling himself it was true. That it was better for George, and it was sure easier for him. Because he didn't have to see the similarities to his wife in his son's face on a daily basis. Didn't have to remember what it had been like when they'd been a family, the three of them. Happy and content.

But now… Now George was, well, not a little boy anymore. He'd gone from a sweet nine-year-old to an almost twelve-year-old with a voice on the verge of cracking and an attitude to boot. It was obvious he loved his grandparents, but his feelings toward his father were a whole other matter entirely.

If he even felt anything for his father anymore.

But what had Ryan expected? To come home and pick up where they'd left off? He'd been a fool to stay away so long, but he wasn't going to run away again. He was going to stand up, take it on the chin and accept the fact that he'd failed his son.

The car door opened. Ryan sat up straighter and looked into the eyes of his son.

George scowled at him and slammed the door, school bag on his knee.

"Hey."

George ignored him.

"Good day at school?"

Ryan received a shrug in return before George slumped down low and stared out the window.

He turned the ignition and pulled out into the traffic.

Part of Ryan wanted to explode. To pull over and grab his son and shake him until he listened. To tell him what he'd been through, how much he hurt, what he'd seen during wartime that had made his stomach turn.

"George…"

But he couldn't tell him off. Because his son had done nothing wrong. He was just behaving how any hurt child of his age would. By dishing out the silent treatment. So Ryan clenched all his fingers around the wheel and kept his eyes on the road and his mouth shut.

George didn't seem to have noticed he'd even been spoken to. But a letter every other week and a dad absent for almost two years since his last trip home meant that Ryan deserved the silent treatment. The short time he'd spent with him between deployments the last time had been strained and emotional, but George had been a lot younger then. More accepting and so excited to have his dad back.

So right now he needed to wait it out, or figure out a way to make amends. It wasn't as if he could jump up and down and insist the boy behave. George was on his way to becoming a young man, and if he didn't fix things between them soon, he might lose his chance forever.

But this wasn't the army. And George wasn't his subordinate.

He was a dad and he had a lot to prove before he deserved the title. Being a father wasn't something you could write on a name tag and lay claim to. He'd been anything *but* a dad these past few years, and it was embarrassing. Ryan had grown up in a loving family, his parents had been married thirty-seven years and his own father had been a shining role model.

Ryan felt his knuckles harden, like he was trying to squeeze the lifeblood from the steering wheel.

He'd let his own dad down, too, as much as he'd let himself down. After having the best example set for him, Ryan had ignored his instincts, that gut feeling that he was behaving badly. Had left it way too long to make amends.

Which is why part of him wanted to run back to the army and write this entire episode off as too hard. Hide again because it was easier.

But he'd promised himself he wouldn't do that. Because this time he had to face up to his past, to what had happened, and try to move forward. Instead of sticking his head in the sand like a stubborn ostrich.

Ryan flexed his jaw. The kid still hadn't made a noise.

"What do you think about grabbing something to eat?"

George didn't look at him, eyes still trained out the window, like he couldn't think of anything worse than being in an enclosed space with his father, let alone having to communicate with him.

"Or would you rather go home?" Ryan asked.

"Home."

Ryan nodded. At least he'd spoken. But he knew the

drill. They'd arrive home, George would kiss his grand-mother on the cheek and grab a handful of her baking, then head to his room. He'd either push his headphones on and blast music through his eardrums like he was determined to be deaf before his eighteenth birthday, or go square-eyed playing video games.

He had intended on asking George if he wanted to do something tonight, but that clearly wasn't going to happen.

Which meant maybe, just maybe, he should call Jessica.

Jessica.

Now that was one word that was always sure to put a smile on his face. He had grinned like an idiot when-ever a letter had arrived for him with her unmistakable handwriting on the back. And when he'd seen her today, he could barely wipe the smile from his lips.

He'd been rude earlier, hot then cold, and he had no idea why she'd rattled him so bad. Seeing her cry had done something to him, made him remember what it was like to see his wife cry. Years of her being the strong pillar of their marriage had fallen like dust to the ground that day they'd found out she'd had cancer. And seeing Jessica cry today had messed with his head in the same way.

But she had seemed on edge, too, before she'd broken down. Not herself, if that was even possible for him to know when he'd never met her before. But all those letters, all those words they'd shared, they counted for something. And deep down something was telling him that she would be just as annoyed with herself as he was with himself right now.

Which meant there was a glimmer of hope that she'd give him another chance and agree to the dinner she'd suggested before he'd blown cold and fled like a pride of lions was in pursuit of his soul.

Ryan sighed and pulled into the driveway of his parents' house.

He'd already made a mess of his relationship with his son, but he didn't have to ruin the one good thing in his life right now. Jessica was a great friend, *had* been a great friend, and he wasn't going to act like an idiot and face the prospect of going back to war somewhere without knowing her letters would follow him there.

Wherever in the world he'd been, wherever they'd sent him, her letters had always found him. And she had no idea how that had kept him going. Kept him alive when everything else had gone so wrong.

He glanced at George again and noticed his eyes had closed. Great, now he preferred being unconscious to being in the car with his dad.

There was no chance of them spending time together tonight, so he wasn't going to beat himself up about going out on a date.

Ryan clasped the wheel harder and stared straight ahead.

Not a date. Not in any way a date.

He was going to ask a friend for dinner. They'd already discussed it earlier.

Just because she looked incredible did not mean it was a date by any stretch of the word.

He ground his teeth together.

George leaped from the car with the most enthusiasm Ryan had seen from him all day as soon as they were stationary.

Dinner with Jessica was definitely his best option.

* * *

Jessica couldn't stop stirring her coffee. It was the only way she could continuously avoid her friend's stare.

"You can't avoid me forever."

That was the problem. Bella had been her best friend far too long to be put off so easily. But what could she tell her? The truth was she had no idea herself what had happened.

"So what did he look like?"

Jessica took a sip and ignored the way the liquid burned her mouth.

"He was, um, normal. You know? Just a regular guy."

She looked down again. If normal guys had frames that could fill doorways without an inch of fat covering their bones. Sharp blue eyes that made her want to blush every time they were turned her way, or tanned skin that seemed like the sun itself had fallen to earth to kiss it.

"Normal?" Bella didn't sound convinced.

Jess nodded.

And received a punch to the arm in response.

"You're lying." Then Bella poked her, hard. "You know you can't lie to me!"

Jess sighed. "Okay, so he was good-looking, but it doesn't matter anyway."

Bella started to laugh. "Mmm, so the fact that your soldier was hot didn't interest you at all?"

Jessica felt her cheeks burn. They heated up so fast it was as if a fire had been lit in her mouth.

"Bella, we both know I'm not interested. He's a friend, nothing more." She did her best to sound firm. Assertive.

It didn't come naturally to her. Not given the current subject matter.

"Did you like him, though? I mean, if you weren't all hung up on not getting involved with someone…"

Jessica didn't like where this conversation was going. Not at all.

"Theoretically, yes." She held up her hand as Bella got that look on her face. That look that made her appear like an overexcited Labrador dog. "But that's irrelevant because I'm *not* interested in men. Period."

Bella didn't seem put off. "Did you find out if he was being redeployed anywhere?"

Jessica felt her skin prickle, like a hedgehog had rolled over her arms, making goose pimples appear. She didn't want to think about Ryan being sent back to his unit. Wherever in the world that might be, she knew in her gut it would be dangerous.

She nodded. "Yeah, he's going back."

"So let me get this right." Bella grinned and shuffled her chair closer. "You're telling me that the guy was gorgeous, you were attracted to him and he's only here for a short time?"

Jess *definitely* didn't like where this was going. She didn't even bother replying. It wasn't as if Bella was about to start listening to her now. She never had before.

"So can you explain to me why you don't want to jump his bones?"

She sighed. Did that type of question even warrant a response? So she'd thought about him *like that*. He was attractive, yes. He was charming. He was, well, *nice*. Better than nice. Wonderful.

But it still didn't mean she was going to let something happen romantically. She'd promised herself no men, no complications, no romance.

So why would she consider breaking her rules now for him?

"Jess?"

She shook her head. "I'm just not interested in Ryan or anyone else for that matter. Not now."

"You're missing the point, Jess." Bella reached over the kitchen counter and took hold of her friend's hand. "We're talking about a guy who's only going to be here for a short time, *before he's sent miles away.* It's not like it would be something long-term." She paused. "You could let your hair down, forget all about what's happened and just live in the now for a while."

Jessica didn't want to hear this. She wished she could close her ears and sing loudly like a naughty child who refused to listen until her friend shut up. Only they weren't children and Bella kind of had a point. But it didn't matter what she said or how tempting it might sound. She was a cancer survivor. She had to focus on her health. On her future.

On protecting her heart.

And she didn't want to ruin her friendship with Ryan. What they had might be paper-based, but it meant a lot to her.

"Well?"

"No."

Bella rolled her eyes. "Give me one good reason?"

The phone rang. Jessica had never been so pleased for an interruption. Its shrill bleeping made her jump to her feet.

"Hello," she answered.

"Hey, Jess, it's Ryan."

The deep baritone that hit her eardrums sent a lick of excitement down her spine. She could curse Bella for putting ideas in her head!

"Hi, Ryan."

There was a pause. A silence that made her heart pound hard.

"I was, ah, wondering if you wanted to have dinner tonight after all?"

Jessica made the mistake of looking up at Bella. Her friend looked like she needed a paper bag, as if she were on the verge of hyperventilating.

"Is it him?" Bella was mouthing at her.

She nodded then turned her back. "Sure."

Now Bella was flapping her hands. She was in danger of becoming airborne.

"Quiet," Jess mouthed as she turned back, but her friend wasn't listening.

"Shall I pick you up around seven?"

"Sounds great. I'll see you then."

As she hung up Jessica looked at Bella.

"Well?"

Jess gulped. "We're going out for dinner."

"Yaaaaaay!"

She cringed at Bella's high pitch. She should never have told her.

"I can't believe you're finally back in the game." Her friend sighed with satisfaction. "Going out on a date."

Jess wished a hole would open up in the carpet and swallow her. Just suck her up and eat her whole. This was not a date. Absolutely *not* a date. No way.

"What are you going to wear?"

Jess groaned. Who was she kidding? This was absolutely a date. It didn't matter what she tried to pretend, or how she thought about it. She was a girl going out for dinner with a boy, her stomach was leaping around as if something with wings had taken ownership of it, and Ryan had sounded as unsure as she had felt herself on the phone.

Given that she'd promised herself there was to be no dating for five years, she'd broken her one rule pretty fast.

But maybe Bella was right. If something did happen between them, if she did want something to happen, would it be so bad? Ryan wasn't hanging around for long, there was no chance she could have her heart broken or get into something long-term, because he wouldn't even be here beyond a couple of months.

"Come on, let's get you ready."

She looked at Bella and tried not to get excited. Ryan would be here in a few hours. She'd be getting in his car, sitting across from him at a restaurant somewhere, looking into those sparkling blue eyes…

Jess groaned again, even more loudly.

So much for thinking of him as nothing more than a friend.

Jessica wished she could quell the inconsistent thudding of her heart, but she couldn't. It was no use.

She was nervous. Terrified. And for some reason there was nothing she could do to calm her nerves, her fear *or* her excitement.

If Bella hadn't kept insisting it was a date…

Argh. The word kept circling her brain like an eagle hunting prey. It wasn't a date. So why—the more she thought about the word—did it seem she was trying to convince herself of a cold-edged lie?

Jess parted the blinds to look out at the street. She watched as a couple of cars passed. The third one slowed then pulled up outside her house. Her hand dropped away, as if she'd been burned.

It was like this morning all over again.

Except this time she didn't want to run from the scene. This time she wanted to run into his arms.

She growled at herself. She needed to stop listening to Bella.

But despite all her reasoning to the contrary, her promises to herself, the truth was that she was tempted. He *was* going away again soon. And she *was* attracted to him. So if he was interested in her *like that* then didn't she owe it to herself to have a good time?

The logical part of her brain was telling her no. That his friendship meant too much to throw it all away. To even risk the possibility of something happening.

But the other part? That was telling her to have fun. To let her hair down for once. To enjoy the company of a man who didn't know any of her baggage, her past. Who didn't want to treat her as if broken glass was shattered over her skin, like he could hurt her.

That part knew that maybe, just maybe, this was an opportunity to be herself. A woman who wasn't afraid of moving forward and having fun. For the short term anyway.

Jess straightened her shoulders and ran her hands down her jeans. She wasn't going to wait for him to knock this time. Her poor heart couldn't handle it.

It had been a long time since Ryan had felt like he couldn't settle his nerves. His career depended on it. When he was deployed, he always kept calm, had a confidence and calmness that saw him through any scenario.

So when Jessica walked out onto the porch and gave him a half wave, before turning to lock the door, he was taken by surprise. It felt like someone had placed a steady hand around his throat and squeezed, just for a moment, to make him gasp for the next gulp of air. Made his mind scramble, as if he were incapable of utilizing the rational, functioning part of his brain.

Jessica had to fiddle with the lock and it gave him time to watch her. This girl who'd meant so much to him for so long.

He'd known he would feel close to her, but he hadn't expected this. He'd thought she would be a normal American girl, just another person in the world. The kind of girl you'd pass in the street and not necessarily notice.

How wrong he'd been.

Her hair was messy, as if she'd spent hours at the beach to put the wind through it and then played with each strand through her fingers. It was tousled and slightly curly, falling below her shoulders. Her skin was golden, as if the sun had just been allowed to skim it, and… He gulped.

Looking any further wasn't going to help him. The curve of her backside in her denim jeans, the silhouette of her upper half in her summery top.

He swallowed again, hard, when she turned to face him. Jessica was smiling, her full lips pulled back to show off white teeth, eyes slightly downcast as if she was a touch embarrassed.

Any thought of her being "just a friend" fled his mind.

It wasn't because he'd been away serving. It wasn't because he hadn't been around women in a long while.

It was simply Jessica.

She did something to him, scrambled his brain and made his body jump, like he'd never experienced before.

Ryan leaped from the car. He couldn't have moved faster if it had been on fire. It was like his brain and his body were finally capable of acting as one.

"Hey."

Jessica's cheeks were touched with the lightest of pink blushes.

"Hey," she said back.

He walked forward, wanted to kiss her on the cheek, but felt awkward. They stood, watched one another for a moment, before he stepped back.

Idiot.

"Let me get the door." Suddenly he was all nerves, more thumbs than fingers as he walked around to the passenger side.

She walked past him and ducked to get into the car. "Thanks."

He grinned at her, he could feel the goofy smile on his face and was incapable of doing anything to remove it.

Jessica looked up at him, her own face open, expectant.

"Let's go grab some dinner," he said.

She nodded at him, before he closed the door.

Ryan walked slowly back around to the driver's side and tried to pull himself together. He had possibly the most beautiful woman he'd ever met sitting in his car, waiting for him to be charming, expecting the person she'd met on paper, and he could hardly string a sentence together.

Jessica had looked good earlier today, but he hadn't had the chance to just watch her and drink her in.

He got in the car and pulled on his seat belt.

Ryan could feel her, smell her, sense her beside him. He made himself look over at her and smile. Ignored the insistent thump of his pulse, or his heart near beating from his chest and tried to act relaxed.

"We doing that 'start over' thing again?"

He smiled at Jessica's joking tone.

"We don't need to start over." He turned the ignition. "It was just, well, kind of weird meeting after knowing each other on paper for so long. Don't you think? We both sort of overreacted."

Jessica sighed. "Thank goodness we're on the same page."

He laughed at the same time she did. Their eyes met and they laughed some more. It was as if all the worry had vanished, the knot of uneasiness in his stomach had been untied. Just from hearing her laugh, knowing she felt the same way.

"Excuse the pun," Jessica managed to say, when they'd stopped laughing.

Ryan resisted the urge to reach for her hand, to make a connection with her. It was so unnatural for him to even think like that, but with Jessica it felt natural.

"We're going to have a good time tonight."

She leaned back in her seat, body angled to face him. "I think so, too."

Ryan chanced a quick glance at his passenger. She was looking out the window now.

He dragged his eyes back to the road.

Maybe coming home was the best thing he'd ever done.

Jessica smiled. She couldn't have wiped the grin from her face if she wanted to.

This morning, she'd been a bundle of nerves. She hadn't been much better this afternoon. But seeing Ryan again, being with him, something about it felt so right.

They shared an understanding, had a bond that was hard to describe.

And Bella had been right.

She *was* attracted to him.

It didn't mean she wanted something to happen between them. But maybe she did have to listen to her friend. She'd been celibate for well over a year now, had pledged not to put her heart in harm's reach or let someone else suffer because of what she might have to go through in the future.

But if Ryan was only here for a short time, who was she to say no to a romantic fling?

Jessica glanced over at Ryan, watched his strong hands grip the wheel, his jaw strong and angled and freshly shaved.

There was nothing not to like about him.

So if she couldn't get hurt or hurt him in return, what was the harm in admitting it?

CHAPTER FIVE

Dear Ryan,
I still can't believe we grew up so close together.
Not much has changed here since you've been
gone, well at least not that I can think of. I often
wonder about traveling, but I'm such a homebody.
I like being surrounded by family and doing the
same old thing, but sometimes, well, sometimes
I think it would be nice to run away for a bit,
even for a week or two. Step out of my life and be
someone else, just another traveler in a foreign
place.
Jessica

"I THOUGHT YOU said nothing much had changed around here."

Ryan raised an eyebrow as he looked at her before diverting his gaze. He was looking at a new electronics store, which was certainly not the restaurant he'd been expecting.

"Hmmm, maybe I hadn't realized quite how long you'd been away." She bit her lip to stop from smiling.

"I can't believe the little Italian place has gone. It was my favorite." He sighed and put the car in gear again. "When I was away I'd dream of their bruschetta and pasta, or watching their pizzas come out of the oven while we waited."

Now he had her mouth watering.

But, hang on…

"Do you mean Luciano's?"

Ryan's eyes flashed. "Sure do."

Jessica fought the urge to laugh again. The look on his face was priceless. "It might not be as good, but do you mind if I choose where we go?"

Ryan shrugged. "Sure."

"Turn left up here, then keep going straight."

He obeyed, pulling the car back out into the traffic.

"You go to this place often?"

Jessica shook her head. "No, but I've heard about it."

"Up here?"

"Yep, keep going and then pull into any spot past the next set of lights."

When the car was stationary Jessica grabbed her bag and opened the door. She had gotten the hint earlier that Ryan was a little old-fashioned about manners, but she couldn't wait to get out. To lead him to the restaurant. There was no time to wait for him to get her door.

"So where exactly are we heading?"

Ryan had one hand slipped into his jeans pocket. He looked strong, completely unflappable. He had dark eyebrows, and they were pulled together now, as if he was wondering what to say to her. His almost-black hair was tousled, just-got-out-of-bed messy. Not the cropped soldier look she had expected. There were two buttons of his shirt undone, the sleeves were rolled up to expose his forearms, and his tanned, soft skin was doing something to her insides. To her brain.

Jessica forced her eyes from him. Drinking in the sight of him was way too easy to do.

"This way."

He followed. They fell into step beside one another. It was weird, this feeling that she was out with a friend, yet the pair of them behaving somehow like it was more of a date than a casual outing.

"Ryan, can I ask you a question?"

He glanced at her as they walked. "Shoot."

"You've only just come back, but your hair is, well, normal. I thought you'd have a buzz cut."

Ryan laughed. "Not in special forces. Well, not all the time."

Now she was confused. "Huh?"

He had both hands pushed into his jeans pockets now, his long legs going slow so as not to outwalk her.

"We often have to look the part, you know, fit in wherever we're posted."

She liked how comfortable the air felt between them. Like they could talk about anything. That's how it had always felt when they wrote to one another, like they could open up about whatever was troubling them. No matter what.

"Let's just say you wouldn't have recognized me when I was away this time. I had a full beard and my hair was long and shaggy."

"What!"

"We often have to blend in. The last thing you want is your buzz cut marking you as U.S. Army. That way we're in less danger, because we're not likely to create attention. I have to go completely undercover as a sniper sometimes, and that usually means making sure no one notices me."

Jessica giggled. She couldn't help it.

"So you looked like a hobo?"

Ryan nudged her, bumped his arm into her shoulder.

Jessica kept her eyes downcast, was too afraid to look up. His touch, the strength of his upper arm as it skimmed hers, made her stomach flip.

"Slow down."

He did.

Jessica indulged in the pleasure of closing her hand over his forearm, let the warmth of his skin tingle through hers. It had been a long time since she'd touched a man, and even longer since the feel of another human being had made her feel like this.

"We're here."

The restaurant had a full glass frontage, a podium outside with the menu displayed and the unmistakable red-and-white checked tablecloths of an Italian restaurant.

"This isn't…"

Jessica squeezed his arm and dragged him inside.

"Luciano's."

Ryan stopped and stared into the restaurant. She loved the wide smile on his face, the way his eyes were dancing. Seeing happiness in another was something that never ceased to warm her heart.

"Wow."

"Not quite the little old restaurant you remembered, but let's hope the food hasn't changed."

She went to walk inside but Ryan's grip stopped her. Suddenly it was him holding her, his skin possessing hers rather than the other way around.

"Thank you."

Jessica refused to drop her eyes, to look at his hand. She made herself be brave, didn't let her nerves stop her.

Because she wanted this. She didn't want him to think she didn't.

"No problem."

Ryan stared at her, his eyes never leaving hers for what felt like forever.

"Table for two?"

Jessica turned, the spell broken. A waiter stood before them in the doorway, menus in hand.

"Ah, sure."

She felt Ryan follow her, his big body close behind hers.

She glanced at him as they sat at a small table in the corner, tucked near the window. He smiled.

And she knew then that everything had changed.

Because from the look on his face, the way his eyes looked like a storm was brewing but at the same time sunlight was shining through them, made her realize that maybe he was having the same internal battle she was.

That they were supposed to be friends and yet within a few hours the goalposts had moved.

But it wasn't just a new set of rules. It felt like a new game entirely.

One that she hadn't played before. Or at least not in a very long time.

Ryan sat back and studied Jessica.

He was confused. More than confused. He had no idea what he was doing or what he should do, and it wasn't a feeling he was used to.

This woman was doing something to him and he was helpless to stop it happening. In fact, he didn't want to stop it. With everything else that was going on, with his son and his arm, this was a pleasant distraction.

He watched as she glanced up, long lashes hiding her eyes when she quickly looked back down.

She was as nervous and uncertain as he was, there was no mistaking it, and it felt good. He liked that she was unsure, too. He was as confused as a guy could get over what was happening here, so he couldn't have handled her being Little Miss Confident. Her shyness made him want to step up and protect her, but not like it had been with his wife near the end.

He never wanted to feel helpless like that again. Like no matter what he did he couldn't protect the person he loved. That he was useless and not strong enough to make a difference, to save that someone.

With Jessica it was different. He wanted to protect her, the animal within him wanted to growl like a tiger and keep her to himself, but it wasn't because she needed protecting.

Jessica was strong. Healthy. Happy.

All he needed to do was enjoy her company, and humor the alpha inside of him that wanted to be released.

Ryan grinned when she glanced up at him again.

"Seen anything you like the look of?"

He didn't miss the instant flush as it hit her cheeks. "Ah…"

He shook his head. That had come out all wrong. From the look on her face, she liked what she saw as much as he did when he watched her.

"I'm going to go with good old spaghetti bolognese," he said.

Ryan watched as she let out a breath and placed her hands over the menu.

"Meatballs for me, please."

He raised an eyebrow. "Good choice."

They watched one another. For a heartbeat that seemed like forever. Until she spoke, as if scared to just sit there and not say anything.

"How did you get on with George this afternoon?"

Ryan shook his head. "Not great. He's still not talking to me."

She smiled. "You'll get there with him. Have faith."

Faith. He'd kept the faith his entire time away, but at times, well, when he thought about his late wife or the way he'd run from his family, he wondered if he had any at all. What he'd seen away serving, what he'd had to witness, had made him question everything he'd ever known or believed in.

But sitting here with this sweet, charming woman now…it made him want to believe all over again. That he could be the man he'd been before experiencing loss. Before serving his country for so long.

That maybe, just maybe, before he went back the next time to rejoin his unit, he could be the man he'd like to be again in the future.

"Jess, about earlier today…"

"Water under the bridge." She put her hand up. "I asked for a chance to start over already, now you've had one. Consider us even."

He smiled at her; it was all he ever seemed to do when he was with her.

"Seeing you, well, emotional like that, it reminded me of a time I usually try to forget. I shouldn't have reacted like that," he apologized.

She reached out to touch his hand, the softest of touches, but enough to tell him that she was there for him. That she understood. "You mean your wife?"

Ryan swallowed what felt like a solid piece of gum in his throat. It shouldn't be so hard to go back there in his mind, not after all this time, but whenever he thought of the end, of what had happened, it was as if his mind put up an impenetrable shield.

"What I saw my wife go through took something from me." He paused. Jessica's hand was still hovering. "I couldn't ever go through seeing someone I care about experience that kind of pain again. Cancer is like a snake, it sneaks up on you, and once you're in its grip I don't know if you can ever be released."

He watched as Jessica's face froze. Only for a second, but he saw it. Saw something cross her eyes and her mouth, something that he couldn't put his finger on.

Her hand rose then fell back to his again, before she pulled it back entirely. Her face was back to normal but something had made her waver.

"I didn't know your wife died of cancer," she said.

Ryan nodded. Had he never told her in all those letters how she'd died?

"Seeing someone you love battle with it, well, I can't think of anything worse a person could go through."

The smile she gave him was tight, strained, but he'd probably just made her uncomfortable. Bringing up terminal cancer as a subject made people react differently. He should have realized that.

"Ryan, didn't you mention something about bruschetta before?"

His mouth watered. "Sure did."

"Why don't we share it? See if it's as good as it used to be."

Ryan raised his glass, pleased to see the sparkle back in her eyes, that sweet, natural smile back on her lips.

"To old times," he said.

"To friendship."

They clinked their glasses together, before he took a long sip of red wine from his.

It was good. Better than good.

This whole night felt great.

"I'll only say yes to bruschetta if we can finish the night with gelato," he teased.

Jessica sat back, wineglass tucked in her hand. "You're lucky I like my food."

They both laughed.

He'd done the right thing, inviting her out tonight. If they stayed just friends, then he'd be happy. But if something more happened...Ryan took another sip of wine before leaning in closer to Jessica across the table.

If something else happened then he wasn't going to say no.

He'd have to be a stronger man to resist. And after years of not being interested like this in a woman, it felt seriously good.

Jessica smiled at Ryan as he attempted to cut a huge piece of bruschetta, piled high with tomato, onion and basil. Her insides felt kind of fluttery, her brain kept firing her warning signals that she was electing to ignore, but she was still enjoying herself.

Hearing Ryan open up about his wife, hearing the dreaded *C* word...it had rattled her. She knew he'd noticed the look on her face, seen the blood drain from her skin temporarily, but she'd managed to recover fast enough that he hadn't called her out on it.

But still. Cancer? Part of her was pleased she'd never told him. After the way he'd talked about what he'd gone through, talked about what he *never wanted to go through again*, it had been clear he might not be sitting with her right now if she'd been honest from the beginning. He might not have even wanted to write to her if she'd told him.

But her chance to confess, to share what she'd been through, had passed. There had been a moment, a tiny window of opportunity, where she could have stopped him and told him what had happened to her. But she hadn't.

And she had no intention of telling him now. Maybe not ever.

"Jessica?"

She looked up. Ryan was watching her.

"This is delicious."

Jess reached for the large piece of bruschetta he had sliced off for her. The smell of the balsamic alone had her mouth watering. She could feel him watching her as she took a bite, trying to be dainty but struggling given the portion size.

"Mmmmm." She finished her mouthful. "You're right, it is delicious."

When he smiled at her, before finishing what was left on his plate like it was no more than a snack, she knew deep down that she couldn't tell him. If he was only here for a short time, who was she to be the one responsible for turning that happy smile into a frown? Why should her problems—health problems she'd dealt with on her own—be a reason not to have fun with him?

It wasn't like she was embarking on a long-term future with the man. They were friends, and friends kept their secrets sometimes. It just so happened this was one she didn't want to share with anyone who didn't already know about it.

"More wine?"

Jessica internally shrugged off her fears and eliminated all thoughts of Ryan's earlier words.

This was about having fun. Enjoying herself with a handsome soldier who would be back with his unit before the year was out.

"Please," she said recklessly, holding up her glass.

Ryan tipped the bottle of red and filled her glass to the halfway mark.

She took a long, slow sip, and leaned across the table toward him. "Tell me all about the guys you serve with. I want to know what it'll be like for you going back to them."

Jessica twirled her fingers around the long stem of her glass as Ryan sat back, his body relaxed against the chair.

"I don't know how exciting a story it is," he protested.

She shook her head, laughing as he grimaced. "You're not getting off that easily, and we've got all night."

"So gelato, huh?"

Ryan laughed. He seemed to do a lot of that around her.

"Believe me, when you're hot and sticky in the desert, thinking about gelato is like torture."

"And now you finally get to indulge."

He passed her the waffle cone before reaching back for his own. They were only a few blocks from where the car was parked, close enough to walk.

"Good?"

"Mmmmm."

Jessica was too busy swirling her tongue around the Italian ice cream to answer. She just kept making the noise in her throat to indicate how tasty it was.

Ryan gulped and tried to focus on his own dessert. But dragging his eyes from her mouth, from her tongue and the way her eyes were dancing as she watched what she was eating…

She looked up.

Whoops. Caught out like a dog trying to sneak a leg of lamb from the kitchen bench.

He watched in fascination as this time her throat worked slowly, swallowing, running her tongue over her lips then letting her hand drop lower as if she'd forgotten the gelato completely.

Ryan wanted to look away. He tried, he really did. But he found his body moving instead, toward her. The look in her eyes tormented and taunted him, pulled him into her web. He had to fight not to drop his cone to the ground.

Ryan could hear his own breathing, and he could hear hers, too. It was as if there was nothing else in the world around them, like they were the only two people on the street, in this moment.

He raised his arm, high enough to reach out and touch her face, and wiped the tiniest bit of ice cream from Jessica's mouth. Maybe he had imagined it, maybe he'd gently wiped away nothing. Maybe he just wanted an excuse to get closer to her, to be pulled toward her like a magnet to metal.

His arm ached, he felt a dull throb as he held it up, but he didn't care. He'd felt worse, and she was worth it. Touching her was worth any lick of pain, no matter how bad.

"Thanks," she whispered, eyes flickering low then higher again.

Ryan stood there. He gave her the chance to walk away, to move back so their bodies weren't so close. When she didn't he closed in, stepped forward and leaned toward her. She was tall but not as tall as him, the top of her head just higher than his chin.

"Jess," he murmured.

She nodded.

He pushed her arm down slightly, so she had to move her cone away from her body. It allowed him to get closer. Their chests were close, hovering, but not pressed together.

Ryan dipped his head, waited in case she wanted to move away. But she didn't.

Jessica raised her chin, inclined it up toward him.

He took a deep breath, looked at her mouth, couldn't pull his eyes away, then dropped his mouth to hers. Gently, ever so gently, he brushed his lips across Jessica's.

She tasted sweet, intoxicating. Gelato mixed with the warmth of a woman who wasn't sure, who wasn't used to being kissed in the street on a first date.

Ryan couldn't pull away, couldn't force his feet back. Instead he pressed their bodies that little bit closer, and touched his lips to hers again, more firmly this time.

Jessica couldn't breathe. She was finding it hard enough staying upright, let alone making her lungs work.

His lips fell on hers again, brushing, teasing, tasting. She couldn't help the tiny moan that escaped her mouth. Ryan's lips were soft yet strong, gentle yet firm, and it was turning her body into jelly.

He slowly pulled his lips away, raised his head high enough to look into her eyes.

"Hey," he whispered.

"Hey," she managed to reply.

They stood like that, bodies pressed together, neither ready to back away.

Ryan cleared his throat.

"I think your gelato's dripping down my arm."

"Oh!" Jessica jumped back and worked to clean up her cone, to stop the drips.

"Napkin?"

She nodded.

He walked back over to the ice cream vendor and retrieved a handful of paper napkins.

They wiped at their cones and started to eat them again, standing like a pair of teenagers who had no idea what to say to one another after their first kiss.

Jessica's body was singing, talking to her like a record on repeat. Telling her how good that had felt.

She'd just been kissed like she'd never been kissed before in her life. Her body was tingling, her skin on fire, alive. And her lips were tender from the thorough way his lips had danced over hers.

When Ryan grinned at her she couldn't help but do the same back.

"Shall we head back to the car?" he asked her.

Jessica nodded. And when he reached for her hand and took it against his big palm, she didn't resist. His skin was smooth but worn, a testament to the work he did.

Now there was no mistaking it.

This was definitely, without a doubt, one hundred percent a date.

Jessica wondered if it was possible for a heart to beat so hard that it could pump right through a chest cavity.

It didn't matter what she did, hers was heaving away so madly she could barely concentrate. She only hoped Ryan couldn't hear it.

He walked around and opened the door. This time

when he'd pulled up, she'd sat there in her seat, hadn't moved. And now he was towering above her.

Jessica gulped and forced herself to step out. She was torn. Part of her wanted another breathtaking, spine-numbing kiss. For Ryan to hold her in his arms and cocoon her, wrap her tight against him and kiss the breath from her over and over again.

But the other part told her to scurry inside her house as fast as she could. To never look back and to forget what had happened. No letting herself hope. Or think about what he'd said in the restaurant. Because no matter how much she liked him or wanted to take things further, his words had echoed in her mind over and over, reminding her of what he'd been through, telling her to be careful.

Reminding her of what he never wanted to go through again.

And it made her feel like she was deceiving him.

"It was great seeing you tonight, Jess."

Ryan held out his hand and she took it. Tried to ignore the tingle she felt when their skin connected.

He didn't let go.

"I had a really good time." Her voice was failing her, going all soft and breathy, but she couldn't help it.

He twisted her hand gently so their palms fell together and pushed the door shut with his other.

Ryan walked her up the path to her front door, slowly. "Good enough that you don't want it to end?"

"Yeah," she admitted. Only she couldn't ask him in. She wasn't ready for what it might mean or what he might think it meant.

"Can I call you tomorrow?"

Jessica was relieved he wasn't going to ask if he could

come in. She would have been powerless to say no if he'd given her the option.

"Until tomorrow," she agreed.

"Well, I guess it's good night then," he murmured.

Jessica tried not to wriggle. He still had hold of her hand, was turning her palm over so her wrist was facing up.

"'Night," she whispered.

Ryan smiled at her, a lazy smile that made her heart start thumping wildly all over again.

He brought his lips down slowly to her wrist, pressed a kiss there, then turned her hand back over. The touch of his lips, soft and pillowy, left an emotional indent on her skin.

It was one of the most intimate touches she'd ever experienced.

Ryan walked a few steps backward while she stood there. Immobile. She looked up at him and for a moment, words refused to form in her throat.

Then he took her breath away. "You know, I think you might just be better in real life than you were on paper," he said and he laughed as he turned, hand raised up over his head in a wave goodbye.

Jessica laughed until tears sprang into her eyes and she didn't miss the cheeky grin on his face as he winked before driving off. *You are, too,* she thought. *You are so much better in real life than on paper, and I never could have imagined it.*

Tonight had been crazy. Amazing.

But scary too.

Because here she was, standing on her porch, watching the taillights of his car disappear down the road, feeling like she had maybe, just maybe, fallen head over heels in love with a man who wasn't within her reach.

If they'd met under different circumstances, maybe it would have been different. But she'd promised herself time to heal, to not let anyone else in, and here she was wishing things could be different.

And Ryan didn't want this, either. He might think he did, but he didn't. Not if he knew the truth about her.

He had told her what had happened with his wife, she knew how much it had hurt him, the demons it had created that he'd never truly been able to shake. And tonight, he'd made it clear he could never cope with cancer again. Had spoken of it like the hideous disease it was.

But cancer was still as much a part of her life right now as her family was. It wasn't something she could pretend she'd never had or might never have again in the future. She was in the safe zone now, but it didn't mean it wouldn't come back or haunt her again one day. Unlikely, given the fact she'd had an elective double mastectomy, but it still worried her every day.

She knew what losing someone was like—the disease had taken her sister, too. So she couldn't blame Ryan for how he felt.

So would it be lying if she didn't tell him? If she just enjoyed his company while he was here, before he was redeployed? Would that make her a bad person, after what he'd told her tonight?

Jessica wiped tears away as they fell, heavy on her cheeks. This time she wasn't laughing. This time her tears hurt.

She wasn't going to say no to fun, but what had happened tonight hadn't just felt like fun.

It had felt like the start of something great.

Jessica heard shuffling then scratching on the other side of the door. It brought the smile back to her face.

"Hey, Herc."

She unlocked the door and picked her scruffy little boy up, holding him close to her chest. He licked at her face, tucked tightly against her body.

"Hey, baby. Come on, let's go to bed."

Hercules wriggled to get down and danced down the hall, his tiny feet padding on the carpet. He looked up at her, waiting, happy about tucking up in bed beside her.

"At least I'll always have you, huh?"

His tongue lolled out, as if he was smiling up at her.

She felt tears well at the back of her eyes again, and she didn't try to stop them. Life could be so unfair sometimes. Just when you thought you'd been through enough, coped with all you could, something else came along to steal the breath from your lungs and the fight from your soul.

CHAPTER SIX

Dear Jessica,
It's funny what you've done to me. For all this time
I've avoided coming home, and now that I want
to I don't know how long it'll be before I can. If
you believe I can make things right with my son,
then I'll give you the benefit of the doubt. Let's
hope we can sit together and laugh one day, and
you can say I told you so.

Hope you're well and that you're not sick of
writing to me yet. You've got no idea how your
letters bring a smile to this soldier's face. I haven't
had a lot to look forward to for a while, and your
letters make a world of difference.

Here's to seeing you soon.
Ryan

"PUSH UP AS hard as you can then hold."

Ryan felt his mouth twist into a grimace. This was hard. Harder than last time, but then he was making himself work as much as he could physically endure.

The physio pushed down on him, forcing him to exert as much energy, as much power, as possible.

"Okay, and relax," she instructed.

He let his arm drop. The thud started again, the pain

that seemed to shoot through every inch of his skin on that side when he exercised too hard. He'd told her the pain wasn't bad because he wanted to go as hard as he could.

Maybe that hadn't been such a great idea.

Ryan wiped away the sweat that had formed on his forehead.

"You did good today."

He gave the physio what he hoped was an innocent smile. "Why don't we keep going? Another few reps?"

She shook her head, not fooled this time. "You going to tell me again that it doesn't hurt?"

Ryan reached for his workout towel and wiped it over his face. She had him there. Perhaps she'd seen through his bravado the entire time. Seen the pain in his face each time he pushed himself too far.

"I just want to get stronger again as fast as I can."

"And *I* want you to develop your strength slowly, so you can use your arm properly until you're an old man," she said tartly.

Ryan laughed. He couldn't argue with that.

"Can I ask you a personal question?"

He looked up at her. "Shoot."

"I was just wondering why you boys are always in such a hurry to get back to your unit? I get that you're all close, but isn't it nice having an excuse to be home for once?" she asked curiously.

Ryan understood what she was saying. Lots of people seemed to think that way, but they didn't get what it was like to have such an unbreakable bond with another group of men. To feel that closeness and not want to let your team down. The way he felt about his unit was indescribable. He could probably never find words to explain it.

Maybe if his wife was still alive he'd have finished up in the army already, but now...? Well, now the army was his focus, what kept him going.

"It's hard to explain," Ryan said, complying as she flexed his fingers back and stretched his muscles out. "There's something about not wanting to let your unit down, but it's also about wanting to do the right thing."

She smiled, but he didn't think she understood. Not really.

"It's not that I want to be redeployed more than being here, but I'm good at it. It's what I do best."

He was sure better at that than at being a dad.

"So you still want to get fixed up as soon as possible, right? Get back to wherever it is they want to send you."

He nodded. "Yes, ma'am."

She gave him a pat on the back. He could see she didn't truly get it, but his physio was great at her job. And truth be told, not many civilians *could* ever understand the bond and camaraderie a good soldier enjoyed with his unit.

"Same time on Tuesday. And don't leave here until you've stretched out some more."

Ryan watched as she walked away. He sat there, thinking, barely noticing the other people in the room.

He always felt so useless, so powerless when he was here, even though he knew he was making good progress. Because it didn't matter how hard he tried, he was never as strong as he wanted to be.

Ryan took a deep, long gulp of water before moving

to stretch out his muscles some more. He knew he'd be sore in the morning if he didn't do as she'd said.

He couldn't help but think that the only time lately he hadn't thought about his weakness, about what was holding him back physically, was when he'd been with Jessica. Last night he hadn't thought about his arm once. Even when it had ached as he'd lifted it to touch her face, the pain had been nothing.

Or nothing compared to not letting his skin brush against hers.

He liked that she made him smile. That she listened to him.

That she blushed every time they were close, or the way a smile hinted at the corners of her mouth when he spoke.

For a guy who had sworn to never let another woman close again he sure could have fooled himself. Because when he was with Jessica, close to her, beside her, there was no other place he wanted to be. He couldn't offer her a future, anything more than a friendship or short-term relationship really, but he'd been honest with her. He was only back for a short time. No matter how much he liked her, his duty was to his unit, and he would be back serving again as soon as he passed the physical.

Maybe one day in the future they could be something more, but right now he didn't know what his long-term future held. His timing was way off, but he wasn't going to let that stop him seeing her now.

If only he could repair his relationship with his son, he'd feel like he was making real progress being back here.

He stood and tried to ignore the pain as it twinged through his biceps.

Ryan smiled. He might have said no to the pain

medication his doctor had prescribed, but Jessica was purely organic and the best pain relief he could wish for. He dialed her number. He didn't care if asking her out again tonight was too soon. He wanted to see her and it wasn't like he had all the time in the world.

If she was up for some fun while he was here, then he wanted to spend as much time with her as he could. Whether that was just hanging out together or something more.

Jessica stretched back and closed her eyes. The sun felt good on her skin. Like it was soaking through her pores to warm her from the inside out.

Hercules's bark made her open her eyes. He was chasing Bella's daughter, Ruby, around the yard, running alongside her and bouncing up and down.

Jess laughed. "Better than any toy, right?"

Bella agreed. "Nothing makes her giggle like that dog of yours."

"You know it's funny, but I don't think I could ever tire of hearing that little girl laugh."

They both sat back to watch the game between dog and child.

Bella was like her sister. When her own sister had died, Bella had been there for her, unwavering in her support even though it had been a lot for another teenager to cope with. And now Jessica liked to be there for Ruby. It was her way of paying Bella back for all she'd done. In the past and when Jess had been sick, too. Bella had never let her down.

Jessica watched as her brother, Steven, pushed himself up off the grass and stretched out his legs. He'd been lying back, swigging on a beer with Bella's husband, but she figured the barbeque was calling him.

"Are Mom and Dad coming over?"

Steven dropped a kiss to her head as he passed. "Nope. They had some old-folks thing to go to."

They all laughed at him.

"They're not that old."

Steven shrugged. "When you choose bingo over a real night out, you're getting old."

Jessica made a noise in her throat but she could hardly reprimand him. Aside from the fact he was her older brother, Steven didn't mean a word of it. He loved their parents as much as she did.

"You wouldn't get me a beer would you?" he asked.

This time she stood up and thumped him on the arm. "If you weren't so charming I'd tell you to get it yourself."

Steven pouted and made them all laugh again. "Then who'd make you burgers?"

Jess stood up and walked inside. She liked it here. Steven's place was a bachelor pad, not exactly warm and cosy like her house, but it always felt good. They'd had plenty of good times here, fun times with friends and their little family. It was like her second home.

Jessica reached into the fridge for a six-pack of beer just as her phone rang, vibrating and singing in her jeans pocket.

"Ouch!" She hit her head and almost dropped the beer. Darn phone, she thought. "Hello?"

The voice on the other end made her close the fridge and lean against it.

"Hey, Jess, it's Ryan."

She took a moment to catch her breath. Ryan. How could the sound of his voice make her legs wobble like that? Her heart was pounding.

"Hey."

"I was wondering if you were free tonight?"

Heck. She could hardly bail on her brother and Bella, not when they'd been planning to all catch up together for weeks.

But an offer from Ryan was sure tempting.

"Ah, I'm actually out already. At a barbeque."

There was a beat of silence.

"Oh sure, no problem. Maybe another time."

Jess cringed. She didn't want to say no to him. Well, she did and she didn't, she couldn't decide, but right now saying no felt like the wrong answer. Especially after that kiss last night.

She sighed. *Kisses* plural, more like.

"Ryan, I…"

Jessica looked out the window at her brother goofing around, chasing her dog. Bella was sitting on her husband's knee, laughing as her daughter bounced up and down with excitement as she played.

Would it be so bad if she asked Ryan over?

"It's fine, really, we can just catch up some other time."

"No, I mean, why don't you come join me? It's only a few of us. Just casual," she said.

He went silent again. Jessica pressed her ear closer to the phone, harder, willing him to say yes and terrified at the same time.

"Are you sure? I don't want to intrude."

"I'd love to see you again. We're sitting around having a beer and waiting for my—" Jess paused and watched Steven entertain Ruby "—idiot brother to get started with the meat patties."

"I'll see you soon then."

Jessica gave him directions then hung up. She leaned

against the fridge again and tried to steady her thoughts. Had she done the right thing?

Probably not, but she was desperate to see him again. To be near him, to touch him and see whether she'd imagined what had happened yesterday. To see if maybe the connection hadn't been as strong as she'd remembered it to be.

Or whether it was even stronger.

To see whether he was worth the heartache that was sure to come when he left again in a couple of months' time. Because no matter how much she told herself she was okay with his leaving, she'd never allowed herself to get close to a man before without thinking there was a chance at some sort of future.

"You making the beer yourself, sis?"

Steven's call forced her to move her feet, reach back in for the beers and go outside.

He gave her a puzzled look when she walked out again. He dropped his cooking utensil and moved toward her but she put up her hand.

"I'm fine."

He was overprotective. Always worrying about her, especially after the cancer. But he'd already lost one sister, she could hardly blame him for wanting to keep her safe.

"You look like you've seen a ghost."

She waved her hand in the air and tried to relax. "I was just chatting to a friend on the phone." Jess gave Bella a sharp look, but her friend was already smiling. She had guessed exactly whom she'd been talking to.

"Oh." Steven looked unsure but he turned back to the meat.

"He's, ah, going to come over and join us soon, actually."

"He?" Steven growled.

Now Steven was holding his cooking utensil at a scary angle, like he was about to behead someone with it.

Jess gulped. She should have predicted this. "Yes, *he*," she repeated, standing up to her brother. "I think I mentioned that I had a pen pal, a soldier who I wrote to."

The look on Steven's face spelt thunder. There was a possibility he could have summoned a hurricane just with his expression. "And he's coming here? *Now?*"

"He's a friend, Steven, nothing to get concerned about."

He grimaced then turned away from her. Bella was wriggling in her chair, but Jess shook her head. She didn't want this to become a big deal. Right now Ryan *was* just a friend, and the last thing she needed was Steven getting worked up over it.

"His name is Ryan, and he's back for a while to recover. He had surgery and as soon as he's better he'll be back with his unit, so there is *absolutely no reason* to overreact. It's not like he's even here for long," she told him.

Steven shrugged, but he didn't turn around. She could tell he wasn't happy about it. But then given her recent track record, she could hardly blame him.

"And I don't want him knowing about the cancer."

That made him turn. Now he looked like Neptune about to command the entire ocean. "What kind of friend do you have to keep your cancer from?"

She reached for the bottle opener and popped the top off a beer for Steven. She passed it to him.

"The kind of friend who doesn't need to know. Okay?"

He took the beer and tipped it up, draining a third of the bottle. "If he hurts you, I'll deck him."

She had no doubt that he'd try. Her only issue was that even with a less than perfect arm, Ryan could probably kill her brother with his bare hands.

Bella waved her over and Jess went to sit beside her.

"He only wants to protect you," Bella said quietly.

Jess knew that, she did. And she liked that he was always there for her. After what her ex had done to her, she couldn't blame her brother. She'd been left heartbroken, facing surgery and serious chemotherapy on her own. One moment she'd been looking forward to a wedding, and the next she'd been fighting for her life without the man she'd once loved by her side.

Ryan was different though. He'd been there for his wife, by her side, and she'd lost her battle. He might not want to go back to that dark place ever again, but it wasn't something she could fault him for. He was a different kind of man. Honorable. Dependable.

"Is it so bad that I don't want him to know?" she asked Bella in a low voice.

Her friend squeezed her hand and shook her head. "No. No, it's not."

"He's not going to be around long enough for it to matter, right?"

Bella sighed then shrugged. She didn't answer; it was a hypothetical question, anyway.

"You were right yesterday," Jessica told her. "It's time I let my hair down, enjoyed being in remission, being alive, and being in the company of a man." She took a tiny sip of beer and tucked her feet up under her on the chair. She liked Ryan. She didn't have to pretend otherwise. So why was she still trying to convince herself he was just another friend?

Because after what had happened last night, she knew that they were way beyond friends now.

Ryan pushed the button on his key to lock the car and walked toward the house. It was stupid, being nervous about meeting Jessica's friends, but it had been a long time since he'd done normal stuff like this.

And his latest argument with George was playing on his mind. Hard to ignore.

His son had finally found his tongue, but the words coming out weren't pretty. Ryan grimaced. Maybe George did genuinely hate him. And if he did, what on earth was he going to do about it?

He knocked at the door, sternly pushing back thoughts of his son. It swung back and Jessica grinned at him from inside.

"Hey, Ryan."

The warmth that spread through him, the smile he couldn't help but give her in return, somehow took away all the pain.

She was like his ray of sunshine on the gloomiest of days.

"Hi," he answered.

She beckoned with her hand. "Come on in."

Ryan hesitated for a second too long. He should have kissed her on the cheek, touched his hand to her arm, anything. But he'd waited too long. Now it would just be awkward. It was the second time he'd managed to do that and he vowed not to miss his chance again.

"So this is a friend's place?"

She shook her head. "My brother's."

Oh, dear. He'd walked in on a family do or something.

When she'd said her brother was on burger duty he hadn't realized it was his house.

"I don't want to intrude, if you're doing the whole family thing."

She laughed and tucked a strand of hair behind her ear, her expression shy. "It's just my brother and another couple of friends."

"If you're sure."

This time she was braver in reassuring him. This time she reached out and touched his arm, so lightly he could have missed it if he wasn't watching the way her skin connected with his.

"It's really nice to see you again."

Ryan felt the warmth spread through him, just like it had when he'd arrived. He'd thought of little else but her since last night, except for when he was trying to deal with his son, and being with her again, right now, sure seemed right.

But then maybe he'd been away so long he wasn't sure what he was feeling anymore.

"Come and meet everyone," she urged.

Ryan stepped out into the yard and looked up. But the smile fell from his face in an instant, leaving him cold. That warmth that had spread through him like cookies just taken from the oven died like ice had been poured on them.

It wasn't hard to pick out her brother. He was the one looking like he'd crush every bone in Ryan's body, given half a chance. He stood up straighter, lifted his chin. He understood protective. If he had a sister like Jessica he'd probably be the same. But she was a grown woman and she'd invited him over. And he wasn't the kind of guy easily intimidated—even if he did respect the big-brother macho act.

"Ryan, this is my friend Bella, and her husband, Bruce," Jess said, making the introductions.

Ryan turned his attention to the petite blonde sitting with a little girl on her lap. Her double-wattage smile made up for the deathlike stare of the brother. He took the few steps to shake her husband's hand.

"And little Ruby, of course."

He smiled at the pudgy-armed child wriggling to get down.

Jessica moved closer to Ryan when she turned to face her brother.

"And this is my big brother, Steve." He felt her stiffen as Steve walked over. "I promise he won't bite."

Ryan extended his hand and regretted it the moment the other man clasped it. His grip was tight, viselike, and his dodgy arm was barely up to matching his strength.

He tried not to scowl as pain shot up his arm. He was used to being the strongest, never losing an arm wrestle. Ryan clamped down his jaw and took the pain, refused to give in to it. Didn't let it show even though he was burning inside.

"Nice to meet you, Steve."

Jessica smiled sweetly in Ryan's direction before taking a step closer to her brother and kicking him in the shin.

"Ow!" Steve dropped his iron grip and stepped back.

"He can be a pain in the backside." Jessica smiled as her brother glared at her then went back to the barbeque. "It's not until we have company over that we realize how barbaric he really is."

Ryan smiled, but it was hard. His arm hurt like hell,

scorching hot. He hated the ache that was thumping under his skin.

"So, Ryan, Jess tells us you've not long been back."

He took the beer Jessica passed him and sat down in the nearest seat, looking over at her friend as she spoke.

"I'm home for a bit of rest and recovery, then hopefully back with my unit."

Jessica sat down on the grass nearby. He moved to stand, to give her his seat, but she shook her head and crossed her legs, Hercules tucking in beside her.

It was hard not to watch her. Not to ignore everyone else and just drink her in. The way her ponytail fell over one shoulder, her tanned skin soft against the white of her T-shirt. The scoop neck showed him just enough cleavage to make it hard to swallow his beer.

And that smile. The way she cast her eyes downward when her lips curved up. It made him wonder what he'd ever done to have that look directed his way. To deserve her attention.

"So you're not tempted to stay here, now you're home?"

Ryan forced his eyes from Jessica and focused his attention back on her friends. "Tempting, but no." He watched as Jessica played with a blade of grass, not looking up. "I need to be back with my unit."

Steve appeared next to him then. "So you're definitely leaving?"

Ryan nodded. Had he not made that clear?

Her brother gave Ryan what he guessed was a smile. It should have been easy to tell but it wasn't. Unsaid words hung between them. Was Steve wondering why he was bothering with Jess, because he was leaving?

"How are those burgers coming along?" Jessica asked, breaking the silence.

Steve turned back to the meat, putting his hands up like he was surrendering.

Ryan took another swig of beer.

Maybe staying home with George would have been easier than facing off with the brother.

Jessica went out to Ryan's car with him. It had been an interesting evening.

The fact it was only nine and the night was over told her it probably hadn't been that successful. But then she'd pushed her luck hoping it would be.

It had reinforced a few things in her mind, though.

Her brother was an idiot sometimes, but he loved her and did his best to protect her. Even if it annoyed her intensely sometimes, she got it.

The other thing she'd learned was that Ryan was the kind of guy she wished she'd met years ago. Instead of wasting all her time on her idiot ex. Ryan had stood up to her brother with ease, and he was up-front and honest.

Bella had been right. What harm was there in having a little fun with a nice guy, when there was no chance of having her heart broken or breaking his? If he was only here for a short time, they could have a blast, enjoy one another and say goodbye as friends.

They were only a few steps from his car.

Jessica willed her body to cooperate and took a deep breath. She fell back one step and reached for Ryan's hand, catching his wrist then letting her fingers glide down to his palm as he turned.

"Ryan, stop."

She registered the surprise in his eyes as he faced her, but she didn't let herself think about it. She'd been waiting to do this all night, wishing she had the courage. Jess kept hold of his hand and pulled him closer. His body obliged. Then she reached her other hand to cup his cheek, standing on tiptoe to kiss him.

"Jessica…" he murmured against her mouth.

She shook her head. "Just kiss me."

His lips met hers as if they'd been made to touch. But he only let her feather-light kiss brush him for a moment before he pushed closer to her, deepened their embrace and slipped his hand around her waist, pressing her gently against him.

His hold was tender but his kisses became more insistent, his mouth moving firmly over hers, his breath hot against her skin when he pulled away, before crushing her lips against his again.

Jessica sighed into his mouth, head cloudy, as if she was being swept away on a wave of happiness, floating with the tenderness of his touch and the way he'd responded to her.

"I'm not usually brave enough to do things like that," she whispered.

Ryan smiled down at her, touched his forehead to hers, still holding her, both his arms around her waist now. He raised a hand and oh, so gently let his fingers skim her face, caress her cheek.

"Well lucky me then, huh?"

When she smiled at him, her lower lip caught between her teeth, he spun her around, one arm tight around her back, then pressed her against the car. Almost rough, but she knew he wouldn't hurt her. That he wouldn't even think one bruise on her skin was acceptable. And then he was kissing her again. This time harder, more urgently.

Jess let her head dip back as he pressed into her, his

body hard against hers, fitted snugly against her shape. She moaned as he left her lips and traced a row of kisses down her neck, stopping with the last touch against the indent of her collarbone.

When he raised his eyes again, held her face with both his hands, she couldn't help but giggle. A tiny gurgling noise that rose in her throat.

"What's so funny?" he asked.

She smiled then sighed, letting her lower body press into his, as he moved his upper body back slightly to accommodate her.

"It's just…"

He nodded. "I know."

She wondered if he did. If he understood how conflicted she felt.

And still they stood there, bodies locked together.

"Can I make it up to you and cook you dinner this weekend?"

Ryan raised an eyebrow. "I must be missing something here."

"What?"

He dropped a kiss to her nose then took a step back. Jess shivered. She hadn't been ready to let any air between them yet, could have stood like that all night. Against his rock-hard, strong body, and melted against that soft, pillowy mouth of his all evening.

"What do you need to make up to me?" he asked.

"For the way my brother was. The way tonight turned out."

He caught her hand and traced a finger across her palm. "Believe me, sweetheart, you more than made up for his frostiness."

Jessica's entire body felt hot, clammy. She wasn't used to being so bold, and she certainly wasn't used to talking about her actions. "He's, well, protective over me. We lost my sister a few years back, and he's made it his personal mission to keep me safe."

She wasn't lying. The fact they'd lost their sister had made Steven protective. Her ending up with the same cancer had made him worse, spurred his "big bad wolf" routine into action, but keeping that part from Ryan wasn't the same as not telling the truth.

"I've met my share of tough guys, Jess, and your brother doesn't strike me as anything other than worried about his little sister making a bad choice. He just wants to keep you safe, right?"

She liked the kindness on Ryan's face, the way he looked so open. It was not how she'd expected him to be. The soldier who'd seemed so tortured on paper was surprisingly unmessed-up in real life. Or else he was just really good at disguising it.

"I still want to make it up to you."

He grinned. "I'd like that."

Jessica didn't know where to look. His eyes were shining at her, suggesting things she wasn't sure about. Things she might want but maybe wasn't ready for. Yet.

"So dinner Sunday night?" she offered.

"Yeah." Ryan squeezed her hand and opened his door. "Maybe you could tell me about your sister."

Jess felt a shiver trawl her spine, her pulse suddenly thumping. She didn't want to go there. Didn't want to tell him how her sister had died, without being able to admit what she'd been through.

It was too close. Still too real for her to open up to him. And if she told him the truth, about her sister dying and then her getting the same disease, he would know she'd been lying all this time. That she'd listened to him talk about his wife, listened to him say he didn't ever want to be in that position again, and pretended she was fine. When she hadn't been fine, and still might not be.

"Maybe."

He didn't seem put out. Relief washed through her as he casually shrugged. "I'll see you Sunday."

She pushed his car door shut when he put down the window.

"Sunday," she affirmed.

Ryan pulled away slowly from the curb.

She watched him for a moment, then walked back to the house. Even though she felt a little guilty, that she should have just told him from the very beginning what had happened to her last year, about the breast cancer, it was so nice that he didn't know.

Would he hold her the same if he knew? Or would he think her as breakable as a tiny bird? Would he want her so bad if he knew what she'd been through? Especially when his wife had battled something similar and lost. From what he'd so honestly told her, she already knew the answer to that.

Jessica looked up and found Steve leaning in the door frame, his body filling the space. She glared at him.

"How long have you been standing there?"

He shrugged, not even caring he'd been found out, that she'd caught him as good as spying on her. "Long enough."

She gave him a shove in the shoulder and walked past him.

Once upon a time he would have shoved her back, grabbed her and made her beg for mercy, the way they'd been as kids, play fighting at every opportunity.

Tonight he just shut the door and followed. "You really like this guy, don't you?"

"He's only here for a couple of months."

He grabbed her shoulder, his fingers firm enough to stop her. She didn't turn.

"That wasn't my question."

Jess spun around. "So what? So what if I do?"

His eyes crumpled, the creases at the side of his eyes, the ones that hadn't been there before she'd battled her cancer, appearing. Jessica hated seeing the way he'd aged.

She relaxed against his touch. "I'm sorry, I didn't mean to snap at you. I've just got a lot on my mind."

"I was going to say that he actually seemed like a nice guy."

Jessica let out a shuddering breath. "He is."

"And I can tell he likes you."

She closed her eyes, embarrassed. Had Steve seen the way she'd kissed him? "But...?"

"But he's going away soon and I don't want you to get hurt."

Argh. There he went again. Just when she was starting to think he wasn't going to interfere. But he was only telling her what she already knew.

"I know what I'm getting myself into, Steve."

She turned to walk away again, but his words made her stop.

"But does *he*?" Her brother paused. She could feel him behind her but he didn't touch her this time, didn't try to stop her from walking away. "You need to tell him, Jess. He needs to know."

Tears filled her eyes then, but she forced down the choke in her throat. Wouldn't let it take hold of her. "Or what?"

His voice softened. "I just don't want to see you get hurt, okay?"

Too late for that. Her heart had already been broken before, shattered into so many pieces she'd wondered if it could ever recover. She was in no danger of Ryan doing that to her.

"I don't want him to treat me any different, Steve. I just want him to like me for me."

Steve moved closer, touched both his hands to her shoulders, waiting until she spun around to face him. "He'll still want you, Jess. If he's half-decent it won't scare him, but you need to tell him."

"I can't," she whispered.

Steve couldn't understand, because she didn't want to tell him the whole story. The truth about Ryan's wife's death. And it wasn't her story to tell anyway.

"Come here." Steve pulled her into his embrace and held her as she cried. As the tears soaked the shoulder of his T-shirt.

He might be an ass sometimes, an overprotective oaf, but when she needed him he was always there for her. She leaned heavily against him, safe in his arms.

"He's not Mark, you know," he told her, holding her tight. "The way he looked at you tonight, the way he was around you, I can just tell."

She nodded against his shoulder and closed her eyes until the tears stopped.

"What if I want to be the old me for a little while? What if I want to enjoy his company and have fun while he's here? Does he really need to know?" she begged.

Steve stepped back. "You're not that kind of girl, Jess. If you were, your ex leaving you wouldn't have hit you so hard."

It was true. She'd never been interested in casual

relationships, but this was different. This was getting outside her comfort zone with a man who wasn't making her any promises, who was only here for a short time. Was it so bad that she wanted to be with him while she could?

"I don't want him to know, Steve. It's more complicated than I can explain."

"I'm not saying anything if you're not. It's your choice."

She kissed her brother on the cheek. "So if you liked him so much why were you so hard on him?"

That made him grin. "I had to test him. No point letting him off easy."

Jessica rolled her eyes. "You're terrible."

He linked arms with her and they walked back into the kitchen. "Nope, I'm your big brother. And it means I'm allowed to be the tough guy."

As much as she moaned about him, there sure was something nice about knowing she had Steve around to protect her.

Ryan sat on his bed and toyed with his dog tag. It comforted him, the weight of it, reminded him of all those nights he'd lain awake on the other side of the world. Thinking about what he'd done, what he should have done and what the future held.

Part of him was itching to be back with his unit, but the other part was feeling settled. Happy to be back home on American soil.

And spending time with a girl he was going crazy about.

But it wasn't helping him with his son. Jessica had helped him, plenty, but his feelings for her weren't making things right with George. Instead he was showing her the person he wanted to be without proving the same to his son.

Something was weird about being back under the same roof as his parents. About having his son down the hall yet not feeling brave enough to go into his room to try to talk to him.

When he'd gone back to war after his wife died, he hadn't had a choice. He had been granted emergency leave when she'd been diagnosed, and the army had been understanding when he'd kept extending it. But the reality was that he'd owed them more time, and even though it had been hard going away again after all that had happened, he'd done it.

Back then, he'd told his parents they could move into his house, to keep things less traumatic for George. Besides, their place had been small, and the home Ryan had shared with his wife was comfortable and much bigger.

Ryan had felt like his paying the mortgage, making sure his parents and son were financially okay, was enough. But it hadn't been enough and until a couple of weeks ago he hadn't truly understood that.

Jessica was helping him to clear his head. To realize what it meant to be a real father again. Somehow her letters and her compassion, the way she made him feel when they were together, were reminding him of the man he'd once been.

Because right now the man he was around her wasn't the same man he was around his son.

And it was fear holding him back. Because when his son refused to talk to him, he wasn't telling him he hated him. Ryan could still pretend that one day things might be okay again.

But unless he did something about it, he might lose his chance forever.

He smiled as he thought about Jessica. About the way she'd fallen into his arms tonight and kissed him like he'd almost forgotten how to. It had been a long time since he'd held a woman, and with her he felt like himself again.

It spurred him into action. If he was going to be that guy, he had to be him in every aspect of his life. And that meant making things right with George.

Now.

No more excuses.

He got up and opened the door, then walked down the hall. Light was still spilling out from beneath his son's door, even though it was late.

Ryan knocked softly. There was no response, so he opened it.

George was lying on his bed, earphones in his ears, iPod resting on his chest. The lamp was still on, even though he'd fallen asleep.

He stood there, towering over his boy as he slept. His face was so young in slumber. There was no trace of the sulky preteen, almost a hint of the face he'd known years ago, when they'd been so close.

Ryan bent to pick up the iPod and gently reached to take the earphones out.

George stirred. Then opened his eyes.

Ryan froze.

His son went to say something, went to move, but Ryan put his hand against George's chest and slowly bent his legs until he could sit on the bed. George didn't say a word.

There were questions in his son's eyes. Questions he

wished would come out in the open so he could tell him the truth, could tell him how sorry he was.

George pulled the cord so his ears were free. Then glared at him. Ryan went to move, to stand up again, but his son grabbed his hand. Made him stop. Then George burst into tears, his entire body shaking from the sobs deep in his chest.

"Come here." Ryan took his boy into his arms and held him, held him so tight he hoped he wasn't hurting him, and fought the emotions that were running through his own body, thrumming through him, desperate to escape. His eyes were burning, body tense as he held his son, the boy suddenly feeling so young and vulnerable in his arms. "Shhh, it's okay."

"You left me," George managed to say between sobs. "Why did you leave me?"

"I'm sorry," he said, holding him even tighter, never wanting to let him go. "I'm so, so sorry."

"Grams told me," George sobbed, "she said you would be leaving again soon."

Ryan squeezed his eyes shut and did his best to force away his own tears, to push them away and be strong for his son. It was like his heart was being pulled from his body to beat in the unforgiving heat of the desert sun. Left to wither, exposed to the world.

"I'll never leave you like that again, ever." Ryan said the words into his son's hair. "I promise."

"But you are going back?"

George pushed away from him to sit upright. His eyes full of hurt, questioning his father.

"I am going back," he said, knowing he had to be honest. There was no point in pretending otherwise. But it was also time for him to be honest with himself. He wasn't done with the army, not yet, and he'd already agreed to another term. But it was time to prioritize, and he'd given his country years of service. Had been a dedicated and loyal soldier.

Now maybe it was time to put that same amount of energy into being the father he'd once been. The father he'd always wanted to be. Maybe it wasn't just about his duty to the army anymore.

"This time will be my last tour," he said, knowing he was speaking the truth, even though he'd never decided, until right now, that it was going to be his final stint away. "I will go away one more time, then I'll be done. And this time I'll be there for you even though I'm away—we'll stay in touch properly, okay?"

George looked unsure, hesitant, but Ryan didn't care. Tonight had been a major breakthrough. And all it had taken was some courage on his behalf to take the first step. His son might not believe his words yet, but Ryan would see his promise through and show his son he could be trusted. It was up to him to give George a reason to trust in him.

"You promise?"

He nodded and pulled his boy in for another hug. "I promise, kid. I'm not going to let you down again."

George held him back hard, clinging on to his father, and Ryan sent a silent prayer skyward. He wouldn't trade anything for this moment. The pain in his arm, the hurt of his memories, nothing would be worth sacrificing for knowing his son was close. For feeling like forgiveness was possible.

For remembering what it was like to be a real dad again.

CHAPTER SEVEN

Dear Ryan,
I guess you might be wondering just how I un-
derstand what you've gone through. Maybe you
haven't thought about it, but I feel like we're close
enough now that I need to tell you something—
that I've gone through what you have. Lost some-
one close. Battled with my own health and my own
demons. That I've had…

JESSICA SAT OUTSIDE, one hand raised to shield her eyes from the sun. Hercules lay at her feet, her constant companion. She ran the toes of one foot across his fur, the touch comforting her.

She couldn't stop thinking about the letter she'd almost sent Ryan. The one in which she'd tried to tell him everything. The one that was her opening her heart and telling him what had happened in her past, and what she was scared might happen in her future.

But then she'd scrunched it up into a ball and thrown it out. Forgotten about it. Except for last night, when the words of that letter had played over and over in her mind. She hadn't even realized they'd be in her memory bank still, but they had been. Every single word. Keeping sleep from her and haunting her thoughts.

Maybe her brother was right. Maybe she should tell Ryan. Maybe it was the right thing to do.

But she wasn't going to. If she did, she'd have to end their romance. Right now. Or more likely he'd end it straight away before she had the chance.

If she didn't? They could continue on, enjoying themselves, and Ryan could go back to his unit oblivious to what she'd been through. And why should he know? He had enough of his own problems to deal with.

Jess stood and stretched. She needed to get back into her studio and paint, unwind and enjoy her creativity. There was no use worrying over something once you'd made a decision, and she had.

It didn't matter how many times she went over it.

Ryan wasn't going to find out, she wasn't going to tell him, and that was the end of it.

"Come on, mister."

Hercules yawned and padded after her.

They had Bella coming around to visit this afternoon, and she'd be able to talk the subject to death if she wanted. Right now, it was time to paint.

And there was going to be no thinking about the past or the future. It was about time she learned to live in the now.

Ryan knew he had Jess to thank for reconnecting with his son. They had a long way to go, but they'd made progress. When he'd left George's room last night, he'd felt lighter somehow, like the burden he'd carried all this time had been a weight on his shoulders, pushing him down, trying to cripple him.

Even his arm felt better, despite the pummelling it had taken last night when Jess's brother had nearly crushed his hand.

But it was all worth it. Having George on speaking terms with him again, listening to his son talk and watching him smile, it was the best reward he could ever have wished for.

And all it had taken was a little courage.

"You want to walk down for an ice cream or something?"

George looked up and put down the video game control. "Yeah, okay."

He was going to have to get used to those kind of responses. Kids didn't seem that enthusiastic over anything these days. But he wasn't complaining. Not while his son was actually talking to him.

"Let's go."

They stood up to leave. George walked close to him, but Ryan resisted the urge to sling his arm around his son's shoulder. They might have made progress, but it was going to be slow and he didn't want to push it.

Jessica sat at the café, Hercules's lead around her ankle. She couldn't stop laughing at Bella. Her friend was in a particularly entertaining mood. Even though Bella had left her daughter at home with her husband, she was all they talked about, and it made Jess feel good.

"You know, Mr. Soldier Stud and you would make beautiful babies, if I do say so myself."

Jess almost spat out her mouthful of coffee. "Babies?"

How had the subject swung around to her all of a sudden?

"Oh, come on," Bella said as she swatted her hand through the air. "Don't go telling me you don't want a family of your own one day."

Her heart seemed to twinge, like a small knife had

been thrown into it. She had always dreamed of being a mother, but the chance of that happening seemed less and less likely these days. It wasn't even the kind of thing she'd let herself think about this last year.

"Maybe, Bella, but not with Ryan."

Her friend snorted. "Why not Ryan? He's gorgeous, funny, buff, did I mention gorgeous?"

It wasn't like Jess didn't agree, but it just wasn't a possibility. "You forget that he's a widower, a father, and oh, that's right. A soldier. Who's returning to his unit soon."

"Okay, so I get the soldier part, but that's doable. Heaps of soldiers are great husbands." Bella paused. "The fact that he's a widower doesn't mean he can't fall in love again, and so what if he already has a son?"

"I know it sounds lame, but…"

There was no way Ryan would consider a relationship with her if he knew the truth, and she didn't want to get serious. She wasn't ready to trust someone like that again. To put all her love and dreams into another person only to have them sucked away forever. And she didn't intend on putting anyone through her getting sick again. It was unlikely, but not impossible, and she'd rather be alone until she at least hit the five-year remission mark.

Bella gestured at her to continue.

"It's nothing. Let's just talk about something else, okay?"

Her friend just laughed. Not the response she'd expected.

"Well, well. Look who's walking toward us."

Jess glanced up and didn't see anyone. "Where?"

"Over your shoulder." Bella smirked. "It's the stud himself."

Jessica scowled at Bella before turning. "You seriously need to get out more. You're getting tragic."

But she felt her own heart start to race—the flutter in her belly that started whenever she was around Ryan began tickling her over and over.

Ryan hadn't seen them. He was walking with a young boy, clearly his son, and they were talking. Talking!

The nervousness she'd felt at him walking toward her disappeared as she watched the two of them smiling and chatting. Something major must have happened last night.

He'd be over the moon to be spending time with George.

Jessica felt her cheeks ignite. She hoped the smile on his face still had something to do with their kiss, too. It sure had her heart racing again just thinking about it.

Bella kicked her under the table. "Well? Get up!"

She glared at Bella before rising. She raised one hand, hesitantly. An even wider smile crossed Ryan's face when he saw her. She watched as he touched his son on the shoulder and directed him their way.

"Hi, Ryan," Jessica called out as they came nearer, swallowing away her nervousness.

"Hi." He gave her a beamer of a smile back and put his hand back on the boy's shoulder. "Jess, I'd like you to meet my son, George."

The kid gave her an awkward smile. "Hey."

"Hi, George. I've heard so much about you."

"And this is Bella," Ryan said, gesturing toward her friend.

George nodded in Bella's direction.

"So where are you two off to?"

Ryan stepped back slightly from his son. She wanted to reach out and touch him, to reassure him that he was doing a good job, but she didn't dare move any closer. They were only friends, and his son didn't need any confusing messages sent his way. Not when he was finally on speaking terms with his father.

"We're going to grab an ice cream then walk back home."

She was dying to know what had happened. "Sounds like a plan. I'd invite you to join us but you two probably want to spend some time alone together, right?"

George was shuffling his feet, head down, awkward. She felt sorry for him.

"Yeah," said Ryan, obviously picking up on his son's discomfort. "We had better get going."

That made George look up.

"Nice to see you, Ryan," Jess said.

"Yeah, you, too. See you, Bella."

Bella waved and grinned back at him.

"Great to meet you, George. Have a nice afternoon," Jess said.

The boy met Jessica's gaze, and she wasn't sure what she saw there. A touch of happiness perhaps, but more uncertainty than anything. She wished she could help him, talk to him maybe, but Ryan would find his way with him. It looked like they'd made some good progress. And it wasn't about how they got there, it was about how well they connected along the way. Ryan was his father and no matter how hard he was finding it, George was his son and deep down he would want to let his dad in. No child wanted to feel alone.

They started to walk away, father and son, before Ryan turned back. His large frame against George's slight one brought a smile to her face all over again.

"We still on for tomorrow night?"

Jess nodded. "I'll see you around seven."

Ryan gave her a wink and turned away again, but she hardly noticed it. It didn't make her heart palpitate like it usually would. Because it was George's last look at her over his shoulder that registered in her brain. The look of horror that passed through his eyes, the disbelief, said it all.

She wanted to run after them, explain she was only friends with his dad, tell Ryan that he needed to talk to his son about them. But it was too late.

She could have been wrong, but from the extra distance now between them, and the despairing stoop of George's shoulders, she knew she was right.

He had gone from happy to be out with his father to wondering if his dad was trying to replace his mom. And if he thought Ryan had come home for her and not for him, his son, then they'd end up right back at square one all over again.

"You all right?"

Bella pulled her back to reality.

"Why does everything have to be so complicated?" Jess asked.

Hercules moaned at her feet, a big sigh that made her wish she could do the same, whinge then put her paws over her eyes to block out the world.

Bella had no idea what she was talking about, and Jessica didn't want to discuss it. The last thing she needed was something else to panic about.

"Tell me more about Ruby, okay? Just make me smile."

Bella frowned but didn't push the point. Sometimes even her best friend knew when not to pry.

Ryan was starting to feel like there was a pattern developing as he drove toward Jessica's house. His palms had started to clam up and he was getting nervous again. Not alarmingly nervous, but it was there, and it wasn't something he was used to feeling.

Today had been good, and yesterday had been even better. George had gone a little quiet on him after they'd bumped into Jess, but they'd had fun, hung out and started to get to know one another again.

And now he had something else to look forward to. An entire evening with Jess, at her place.

He grinned to himself as he drove. Even though he had his arm resting on the open window ledge, and it was throbbing with a hint of pain, he didn't care. There were too many good things going on his life to worry about something he had no control over. His physio had told him he was progressing well, there were no indications of it being a long-term problem, not after the surgery going so well, and he just needed to keep up his exercises.

So having fun with his son, and with a woman like Jessica, was something he could enjoy before he had to go back to work. As hard as it would be to return this time, he was looking forward to being with the guys again, and now that he'd decided it would be his last tour, he had to make the most of being back with his unit.

Ryan pulled onto her street.

He didn't know what exactly it was about her, but something about spending time with Jessica felt so right. After his wife had died, he'd never wanted to be close to another woman again. Never wanted to feel so helpless again, so weak. And until recently he'd thought he'd feel like that for the rest of his life.

But Jessica was quickly changing his feelings. He didn't know what she wanted, if she felt the same way as he did, but this was starting to feel real. Part of him wanted to take it slow, to stay as friends yet something more, but then he also wanted to make things happen more quickly. To make the most of his time back home and see if something special could happen between them.

Because in the span of a week, Jessica had gone from pen pal and good friend, to meaning a whole lot more to him than any other woman had since his wife.

And he liked it. Liked the way she made him feel, the effect she had on him. Whether she felt the same was another matter entirely, but from the way she'd kissed him the other night, he liked to think he could hope.

More than hope.

He liked to think he was in with a real chance.

If he was going to be coming back for good soon, then maybe that meant a chance at a future together.

Jessica fluffed around in the kitchen, knowing she had no purpose, yet not being able to stop herself from moving. It was just a casual dinner at her place, not exactly some grand dinner party, but she was like a ball of wool writhing to untangle. On edge.

She'd put together a simple pasta dish, lots of fresh ingredients tossed with olive oil and lemon juice in a pan, so there was hardly anything culinary to worry about. And dessert was a cake she'd made earlier in the day, but she still felt panicky.

The knock at the door came while she was eyeing up her glass of wine and deciding whether or not to drain it for courage. She was leaning on the counter, staring at it.

Jessica turned away from the glass. She didn't ever

drink more than a couple of glasses, and the last thing she needed was to make a fool of herself.

"Come in!" she called, hoping Ryan would hear her.

Hercules went bounding down the hall and a second later the door clicked.

Jess took a deep breath, ran her hands down her jeans, then stepped out to greet him. This was ridiculous. She'd seen Ryan a handful of times now. First-time nerves were one thing, but there was nothing to panic about tonight.

"Hi, Ryan."

He was crouched down giving Herc a scratch. When he looked up she temporarily lost the ability to move. His eyes locked on hers, bright blue, serious yet laughing, drawing her in as if she'd never be let back out again.

"Hi." He stood and they both watched as Hercules took off down the hall again. "You look great."

Jess looked down and felt awkward. She was only wearing jeans, an embellished T-shirt that dressed her outfit up and a pair of heels. Her cheeks were flushed, she could feel the heat in them—and her hands could have been shaking. She was so off balance she wasn't even sure.

She went to turn down the hall, but he stopped her with a hand to her wrist.

"Hey."

When she turned Ryan took a step forward and pressed a kiss to her cheek before putting space between them again.

"You act like no one ever gave you a compliment before."

His voice was low, almost a whisper, and it made a shiver lick its way down her spine. She swallowed, hard.

"I'm not."

The last compliments she'd had had been from a man who told her what he thought she wanted to hear, but there'd never been any substance to his words. The reason she was embarrassed now was because from the look on his face, Ryan meant what he said.

"I don't say what I don't mean," he assured her.

She didn't doubt that. "I know, it's just…"

"Jess?"

She felt uncomfortable being scrutinized.

"I find you not receiving compliments by the bucket-load hard to swallow," he said. Ryan tucked his fingers beneath her chin and smiled down at her, his eyes locked on hers, body so close. "You look beautiful tonight and you need to believe it."

Jessica fought against the urge to pull away from him. Instead of giving in to her instincts she made herself smile, forced herself to behave like the grown-up woman she was. "Thanks," she whispered.

He grinned and let his fingers fall from her skin. "Much better."

She turned before he had the chance to do anything else. She was nervous, scared.

Exhilarated.

So much for telling herself this was going to be a casual dinner with a friend, that there was no need to panic. She doubted there was much *friend* left in the equation between her and Ryan anymore. Part of her had hoped he would want more, and the other part told her that friend was as good as it got. Even after their kisses.

Now she wasn't so sure she was ready for the something more.

Ryan was a hot-blooded male who had suddenly, just from looking at her, from touching her, made his intent very clear.

The way her body was reacting told her she felt the same, no matter how much she wanted to deny it.

Maybe that glass of wine hadn't been such a bad idea after all.

Jessica didn't taste a mouthful of her food. She opened her mouth, forked spaghetti in delicate twirls and forced herself to swallow. But the only sense she had was of the man sitting across from her.

She'd forgotten everything else. Had no control over her other senses. Or maybe she did and they were too overloaded on Ryan. She was drunk on the sight of him, the feel of him, the look of him.

The taste of him.

She remembered only too well what his lips felt like on hers, how her body had felt when she was tucked against him, wrapped in his embrace. And after the way he'd touched her in the hall before, the way he felt had been the only thing she'd thought about since.

"This is great."

At least Ryan seemed to be enjoying the food.

Jessica took another sip of wine. She was going to tell him not to be silly but she remembered only too well what he'd said earlier about taking a compliment.

"Thanks."

She wished she could say more, could come up with something more savvy and chic, but her brain just wasn't cooperating. Her tongue was swollen like it was bee-stung, not letting her communicate properly.

It was stupid. She was a confident, capable woman and there was no excuse. She had to get a grip. Jessica cleared her throat and set down her fork. "So tell me about George. You two looked like you were having a good time yesterday?"

Ryan's entire face seemed to light up.

"We had a fantastic time. It's like we've really connected."

She smiled. It was good to hear.

"But I have to thank you, you know."

Jess gulped. Her? "Why me?"

Ryan put his own fork down and reached for her hand across the table. "Because you gave me the confidence to make it happen. I don't think I could have done it without you."

Jessica forced herself to look up and meet his gaze. His hand over hers was doing something to her, making her body feel hot all over, every inch of it.

"I don't think I did anything, Ryan. I was just honest with you."

He squeezed her hand, his eyes never leaving hers. She could gaze into them all night, lose herself in the ocean-blue depths of them, become mesmerized. She wondered if anything had ever looked so beautiful before. The way he was looking at her, the softness she saw there.

The honesty.

All this time, she'd thought it would be impossible to ever truly trust a man again. Told herself it couldn't happen.

But the way Ryan was watching her, the genuine feeling he conveyed through his gaze, the way the skin around his eyes crinkled ever so lightly in the corners when he watched her, his smile upturned to match his expression: all of these things told her that trust and honesty *was* possible with a man.

She'd just chosen the wrong one before. And let herself believe that he represented the entire male population.

"I went to him, Jess. I went to him because you told me to, because you told me I had to confront the past and be honest with him."

She looked down, unable to match his stare any longer. "I told you what anyone else would have."

Ryan shook his head. "That's the problem." He dropped the contact with her hand and raised it to her cheek instead, his fingers resting against her skin.

Jess pushed in, lightly, toward his touch. Fought the urge to close her eyes and sigh into his caress.

"I've never told anyone else what I told you in my letters. You're the first person I've been honest with in a long while."

She glanced up at him again, her breath catching in silent hiccups in her throat.

"It started because I trusted you on paper, and now I know I can trust you in real life, too."

She didn't know what to say. But when Ryan kept the contact with her face and raised his body, leaning over the table toward her, she knew exactly what to do.

Jessica raised her face to meet his, parted her mouth for his kiss. For the brush of his lips that she knew were coming.

Ryan took her mouth, gently at first and then with a hunger that scared her. She was barely conscious of him standing, of the way he had moved closer, until he pulled away and left her lips tender and alone.

She stifled the moan that fought to be heard deep within her throat.

But Ryan didn't leave her alone for long. He stalked around the table like a big game animal on the hunt. His large frame towered above her, then he dropped to his knees in front of her. She parted her own knees slightly so he could move closer to her. He was so tall that even with her sitting on the chair he wasn't much lower than her.

Jess just watched him—the rise and fall of his chest, and the way his eyes fell to her lips. She tried not to think about the what-ifs. Fought against the voice in her head that told her to take things slow, to stop now before it went too far.

Because Jessica knew they had already crossed that line. They'd already gone too far and she was powerless to do anything about it.

"Ryan."

He circled his arms around her waist, making her feel safe. Wanted. She slowly raised her hands and let them flutter to his shoulders, not sure where to touch him, and then they found his hair. Jess ran her fingers through the soft strands then stopped, fingertips on the back of his head as she bravely urged him forward.

He waited for her. Hardly let out a breath as he watched her and waited. Like he was leaving it up to her, wanted her to tell him it was okay.

And she didn't disappoint him, was powerless to do anything but make the next move. Jessica kissed him like she'd never kissed a man before. Kept her hands on him, drawing him to her, pressing herself closer to him as their lips danced, his arms still wrapped around her.

She only dropped her hold when she knew he wasn't going to pull away, to run her hands down his arms, drawing in a sharp inhale as she found bare skin.

His lips became more insistent on hers. Teasing her. Showing her how much he wanted her. And oh, did she want him, too. More than she'd ever wanted to be close to a man before.

"Ryan," she said his name again. "Are you sure…"

He just kissed her more deeply, ignoring her words. She took his lack of reply as a yes.

Jessica let her fingers keep exploring, reached the hem of his T-shirt and pushed it up, letting one hand discover the contours of his hard stomach, muscles firm against her touch.

His belly quivered, but he didn't move. Only moaned against her mouth.

She took it as encouragement.

Jess tugged, breaking their kiss to pull his T-shirt over his head, and Ryan didn't resist.

He shrugged out of it in a second and had his arms back around her before she could properly drink in the sight of him.

But she pushed him back, lightly.

"You have a tattoo," she whispered.

Wow.

"Yeah." He shrugged.

If the sun-kissed golden skin and hard muscles weren't enough, hadn't already taken her breath away, the tattoo came as even more of a shock.

She'd never dated a guy with a tattoo before. Had always thought they were for bad boys, and she'd never gone for that type. But on Ryan? It looked incredible.

"You're staring." His voice was low, husky.

Jess gave him a sideways look and smiled. Shyly. "Does it mean anything special?"

The black ink carved out a beautiful eagle, wings open, covering his entire shoulder and down his upper biceps. She'd never liked the idea of a tattoo, but this was something else. Made him look even stronger, tougher. Exciting.

His response was another shrug. She hoped she hadn't made him self-conscious about it.

"It's a special forces thing. I got it after my initiation with all the other snipers."

She leaned forward, bent to touch her lips to his shoulder, kissing down every inch of the inky black image. She let her fingers trail over the small, dark pink scar that showed where his keyhole surgery had been.

Ryan moaned and tightened his hold on her. It made her smile, pleased that he liked it, that he wanted her touch.

"Jess."

The way he said her name made it sound like a warning. He tugged at her hair, gently, to pull her had back up. She ignored him, slowly running her lips up his neck, making him wait before she returned to his mouth.

She stopped, hovered her lips beside his before kissing him.

Ryan didn't hold back at all this time. He took her face in his hands, kissed her again, and then stood, lip still tangled, arms around her body.

He only had to look at her to ask her the question. To tell her what he wanted.

The way he watched her, touched her, caressed her, told her everything she needed to know. Left only one question between them.

"Yes," she whispered, tugging his hand.

He dropped a feather-light kiss to her lips. "Are you sure?"

She tucked in tight against him, nuzzled her mouth

to the tender spot between his shoulder and neck, before taking his hand and leading him to the stairs.

No, she wasn't sure. Showing her body to a man again had been something she'd feared since her operation. All she knew was that she wanted to be with this man, right now, more than anything else in the world.

And that meant swallowing her fears and taking a big step forward. Maybe he wouldn't notice the difference? she found herself wishing…

Ryan felt as if his whole body was on fire. He wanted this woman like he'd never wanted a woman ever before.

And he was too weak to do what he most wanted. To scoop her up into his arms and carry her to her bed, to make her feel light and wanted in his embrace. He hated not having the strength in his arm, but then if he hadn't been injured he wouldn't be here right now. And he knew where he'd rather be, given the choice.

But even though he couldn't lift her like he wanted to, he could enjoy the weight of her hand in his and the promise in her eyes as she sent a shy glance back over her shoulder at him.

He'd never been nervous before, not with a woman, not like this. But it had been a long time since… He tightened his jaw and pushed the thoughts away. Now was not the time to think about the past.

The problem with Jessica was that she wasn't just another girl. A one-night stand. He hadn't been with a woman he felt this serious about since his wife.

She was rather like his wife—not physically, but the same type of woman. He didn't want to hurt her in any way, do anything that might compromise what they had. Because she meant too much to him. But right now he was powerless to stop what was about to happen, and it was too late to start thinking about why this was a bad idea. He was the one who'd started it, and he certainly wasn't going to not follow through.

Jessica stopped at what he presumed was her bedroom and dropped his hand. She touched the door frame, looked over her shoulder and gave him an even shyer smile than before.

"You joining me?"

Ryan gave Jessica a brave grin back. "Yes."

It seemed to settle her, looked like relief crossed her eyes, softening her face.

He was going to ask her again whether she was sure, whether this was what she really wanted, but then she disappeared into the room. Ryan hesitated for a moment before following her in.

Jessica was standing, waiting for him, like she didn't know what to do. He hated seeing her look unsure, uncertain and nervous, but he knew what he could do to make her feel better. To make sure she knew how much he wanted her.

Ryan tried not to but he knew he stalked her across the room. He wrapped both arms around her, sweeping her to him, before walking her backward until her legs touched the base of the bed.

"Ryan…" His name caught in her throat, and it made him smile.

"Yes?" He arched an eyebrow before taking up on her neck again, where he'd last kissed her, letting his lips tease her skin.

She didn't say another word.

He already had his shirt off but Jessica was fully clothed. He tipped her back and gently let her fall, before moving to cover her, to lie half above her.

She blinked and kept her eyes downcast, but he tipped

her chin up and kissed her lightly on the nose then on her lips. At the same time he touched his other hand to her T-shirt, curling his fingers around it and raising it, pausing to give her the chance to say no.

Jessica responded by wriggling to rid herself of the top.

His gaze fell from her face to her skin, eyes dancing over her lacy red bra, the way her breasts filled it to almost overflowing.

"The light," she whispered.

Ryan shook his head. "No."

He stopped when he saw the panicked look on her face.

"Please." Her voice held urgency, desperation.

"Okay," he said as got up again, crossed the room and flicked off the switch. "Your call."

It didn't matter how much he wanted to watch her, to drink in the sight of her, he would do as she asked. He wasn't doing anything to compromise what was happening between them.

He stopped, in the dark, letting his eyes adjust.

Before using all of his willpower not to rush across the room and pin her down to devour her, piece by piece.

Jessica felt like she was blushing all the way down to her toes.

She wanted to stop him, to tell Ryan she couldn't go through with it, but if she told him that she'd be lying to herself.

She wanted him.

She just didn't want to know his reaction when he realized her breasts weren't natural.

It was the first time she'd been intimate with a man

since her reconstruction, since she'd gone through her treatment, and it scared her. She hadn't wanted him to see them bare, didn't want to see his reaction, either, but as soon as he touched them he'd surely know. They weren't soft and natural as they'd once been. Now there was the undisguisable firmness of silicone, and she was embarrassed about it.

Ryan's hand skimmed her arm then trailed slowly down the edge of her breast.

She took in a deep breath. This was it. The moment she'd dreaded for almost a year.

"You're beautiful."

Jessica closed her eyes and tried not to cry, fighting happiness and tears at the same time. As confused as she'd ever been.

She tried not to shake her head. Thank goodness the light was off so she didn't have to see the look on his face when he realized.

"You are. You're more beautiful than I ever could have imagined you'd be."

Jessica wanted to tell him she wasn't, admit what he'd find when he took off her final layer, but she held her words in, too scared to say them out loud.

Ryan stopped, as if he were questioning her, but Jess responded by staying still, waiting for him.

She held her breath. Terrified.

When his hand touched her bra, her entire body went stiff, rigid.

She couldn't do it.

"Stop."

His hand hovered then fell.

"I can't, Ryan," she whispered, distraught.

He dropped his hands to hers, and lowered himself to rest beside her. "Tell me what's wrong."

Jessica closed her eyes and pushed away the pain. Tried to figure out what exactly she could tell him.

"I have, well…"

He brushed the back of one hand gently across the side of her face, touching her cheek with the softness of a feather.

"We don't have to do anything you don't want to do."

Jessica smiled bravely at him. She did want to, that was the problem, but she didn't know how to deal with the embarrassment of what he was about to find.

Because even with the lights out, without being able to see, he would be able to feel. The scars were minor, the surgeon had done a great job, but the evidence was real and he would notice. There was no way not to.

She took a deep breath.

"Ryan, I have scars. I don't want…"

"Shhhh." He bent forward and kissed her, lips hovering over hers. "You don't have to explain anything to me."

She shook her head. "I do. My breasts, they're…"

He waited, fingers stroking her hair.

"I have scars because I had surgery. My breasts aren't real," she finally blurted out.

Ryan didn't say anything. He dropped another kiss to her lips before trailing his way down her neck, delicately across her collarbone, until he reached the lacy edge of her bra.

He paused and looked up at her. She could make out his face even in the dark.

"You're beautiful, Jessica, and I don't care what you've had done or about any scars."

With an incredible sense of relief exploding inside her, her body felt like it had turned into a marshmallow.

Her fears faded, and her body responded to his touch again. By his lack of reaction, he obviously just thought she'd had a breast augmentation. Realizing she'd managed to put off telling him the truth for a little longer, she trembled. Right now, he didn't need to know why she'd had cosmetic surgery. If he didn't care, then why should she?

Her body still thrummed with tension as he slipped off her underwear, but she forced herself to enjoy his touch. She couldn't help but stiffen when he kissed first one breast then the other, his fingers gliding softly over her skin.

"See, they're beautiful, just like I knew they'd be," he whispered. "Just like the rest of you."

Jessica finally relaxed into his touch, closed her eyes and sighed as his hands explored her body.

Tonight was about feeling good and enjoying herself. Losing herself in the moment. All this time she'd been terrified of showing someone her new body shape, worried what the reaction would be and if she'd even want to be intimate again.

But this—this was what she'd needed. To feel loved and wanted by a man like Ryan. A man who made her feel like she was the most beautiful woman in the world, like he truly wanted her.

Even if it was only just for tonight. Or until he went away again. Because if the light had been on, she could have looked into his eyes and seen his honesty, his integrity. Yet what she couldn't see in his eyes, she could feel in his touch.

When Ryan inched his way back up her body and started to kiss her again, she pushed away her barriers, made herself think of nothing but the way he was touching her. The way his fingers felt against her skin, and the way his lips brushed hers in a motion she'd never tire of.

If this wasn't heaven, then she didn't know what was.

CHAPTER EIGHT

Dear Jessica,
It's funny, now I know I'm coming home for sure
and that we're going to meet. I should have asked
you for a photo, but then we probably don't look
like either of us expects.

You know, I've enjoyed this life for so long, but
now the thought of coming back and sleeping in
a comfortable bed, of not having to get up at the
crack of dawn, sounds pretty appealing. I can
hardly imagine what it will be like not to be with
my unit, here in the desert, because it's been so
long. But I'm sure looking forward to meeting
you.

I'll see you soon.
Ryan

RYAN WOKE WITH a smile on his face. It had been a long
while since he'd woken up grinning, but then it had also
been a long time since his arm had been taken captive
by a beautiful woman.

Jessica lay in the crook of his arm, face turned into
him, cheek against the edge of his chest. Her mouth was
slightly parted, her long hair falling over his skin and
spilling out onto the white pillow.

He didn't move, hardly let himself even breathe. Ryan could have stayed there forever, watching her. Content in what had happened between them. In the way his trip home had turned out after so many months of dreading it, after years of denying himself the luxury of returning. Of putting up barriers and refusing to confront what he'd left.

When he'd promised his son that this tour of duty would be his last, it had been a decision he'd made as a father.

But now? Deep down, he knew that part of that decision had been influenced by how he felt about Jessica. He wanted to come back for his son, but he also wanted more from this woman lying in his arms. Part of his decision had been because he wanted a real chance at making a future with her, too.

And that meant he had to let her in. A week ago, he'd have never thought it possible, but now he wanted to open up to her. To tell her the final chapter he'd kept behind lock and key from everyone but himself until now.

Jessica stirred. He shifted his body to face her, looking at her face as she started to wake.

Her eyes opened slowly, fluttered, then her head dropped slightly as she realized he was watching her.

"Hey, you," he whispered, stroking his thumb across her cheek.

She smiled, but he could tell she was shy. "Hey."

Her voice was so low he only just heard her.

"What do you say I rustle up something for breakfast?" he offered.

She tucked her head down and snuggled against him, hair tickling his chest as she buried into his body and pulled the comforter farther over them in the process.

Jess planted a kiss to his collarbone and sighed into his skin.

He lay with her in his arms for a few minutes then dropped a kiss to the top of her head and wriggled back.

His stomach growled. Loud.

"As much as I want to stay like this, I think my body needs some fuel."

Jess laughed and rolled over.

"What's so funny?"

He propped himself up and looked down at her. She was still trying to hide from him, face partially covered, but she didn't look nervous any longer.

"Jess?"

She groaned then turned back toward him. "I probably shouldn't tell you, in case you change your mind."

He raised an eyebrow and watched her.

She groaned again. "You're the first guy to offer me breakfast in bed, okay?" She let her eyes meet his. "Here I was worried you'd make an excuse and bolt, and instead you offer to feed me."

Ryan leaned forward to kiss her, brushing the hair from her face so he could see her better. He liked that her trademark pink blush was starting to cover her cheeks again.

"I don't recall saying anything about breakfast in *bed* exactly, but it can be arranged. Although if I remember correctly, you never actually gave me dessert last night."

She responded by pushing him away and throwing a pillow at him. He caught it and grinned.

"Okay, okay! Your wish is my command."

He stood up and walked across the room. Most of his clothes were in a heap near the foot of the bed, but it was her silk robe hanging on the back of the door that caught his eye.

"Mind if I borrow this?" He plucked it from the hanger and held it up.

Jessica was blushing all over again but she nodded, sitting up with the sheet clutched to her chest.

He grinned and put it on, just managing to secure the pink satin with the flimsy tie. It barely covered him but it made her smile, laugh even, and right now he'd do anything to see those lips of hers upturned, those chocolate-brown eyes sparkling.

Even if he did have to make a fool of himself.

He was about to turn around and make a joke when he heard a phone ringing.

"Yours?"

She shook her head. "Nope. Your cell?"

It *was* his. He took off down the stairs and looked around for where he'd left it. Nowhere. He scanned the room and found it just as it stopped ringing.

When he flipped it open he saw he'd missed a few calls. All from the same number.

Ryan gulped.

His parents. Or his son. He hoped everything was okay. After so long being used to only thinking about himself, he should have at least phoned to tell them he wasn't going to make it home last night. Not that his parents would be worried, but George might be. He was going to have to change his habits if he was going to gain George's trust again.

He hit redial.

"Hello."

His son picked up almost immediately.

"Hey, George, it's your dad."

There was silence for a moment, before his son cleared his throat.

"I thought something had happened to you."

Ryan felt as though someone had reached into his chest and stuck a knife through his heart. If he was going to get this dad business sorted, he was going to have to start acting like a father, not a bachelor with no responsibilities.

"I, ah, ended up staying at a friend's place. I should have phoned."

There was silence on the other end.

"George?"

"Are you coming home soon?"

Ryan looked down at the pink robe, at his hairy legs poking out, and then turned to look at the stairs. He wanted to see his son, to be there for him, but he also didn't want to hurt Jess, and if he left now she'd think he'd used her. That he was as bad as the last guy who'd clearly broken her heart by not caring enough.

She deserved better than that. But then so did his son.

"I'm going to be a bit longer." He paused, cringing at the silence down the line. "But I'll be home soon, then we should grab some lunch, okay?"

"Yeah."

Ryan hated the way he felt when George hung up. Like he was being torn in two different directions. Yanked one way in his heart, then the other.

He sighed and put down the phone. Fifteen minutes ago he'd been on cloud nine, had felt like everything was going to work out perfectly, and now he was all messed up in his head again. He needed to do something to make things right, and that might mean talking to his boy about Jessica. Somehow.

"Is everything okay?"

Ryan turned to find Jessica standing nearby. He was pleased he'd put down the phone because it would have dropped from his hand and hit the floor.

She was wearing his T-shirt and what looked like nothing else. It only covered her down to the top of her thighs, and she had her ankles crossed, legs together, hair all mussed up and falling around her face. She must have found it while he was on the phone, which meant he'd missed seeing her walk into the room naked.

"Ryan?"

He realized he was standing there like an idiot, mouth hanging open. Her face was like an open question mark, eyes showing her confusion. He didn't like it. He liked what he saw, her big brown eyes watching him, so much skin on show apart from what was hidden beneath his shirt, but he hated that she was unsure of him.

Ryan crossed the room and wrapped his arms around her, smiling as he realized that she now smelled like his cologne. He kissed her neck, then her cheek, then her lips, hands buried in her hair.

"Everything is fine."

She pressed her face against his chest, fingers teasing his bare skin where her dressing gown didn't stretch enough to cover him.

"So where's breakfast then?"

He growled and slapped her bottom. Jess shrieked and jumped away from him.

"Any more naughty business and I'll take a photo of you like that," she threatened.

He followed her across the room, teasing her. "Oh, really?"

She giggled, darting away, one hand holding down his T-shirt. He couldn't help but smile at her modesty.

After the night they'd just had, here she was still innocent enough not to want him to see her bare in the daylight.

When she moved again he pounced, grabbing her wrists and pinning her against the wall.

"You win." She wriggled but didn't put up much of a fight.

Ryan held her, restrained her, taking the chance to kiss her before backing away.

"If I win, that means I get a prize."

He let go of her wrists and walked into the kitchen, taking a look in the pantry. Jess followed him, but she stopped to fill the jug.

"Coffee? That can be your reward."

He shook his head, reaching for a loaf of bread and the maple syrup.

"French toast?" he asked.

Jessica nodded.

"And my prize is that you say yes to lunch with me today."

She leaned back against the counter, eyes slanted slightly like she didn't believe him. "What's the catch?"

"My son's joining us."

Jessica gulped and watched Ryan's face. He wasn't kidding.

"Are you sure that's a good idea?"

He looked around. "Eggs?"

She went to the fridge and pulled out a tray, still waiting for him to respond.

Ryan nodded, but she could tell he was teetering on being unsure about it.

"I don't know if it's a good idea or not, to be honest.

But I'm not here long and I don't want to feel torn between the two of you. I want to enjoy you both and that means not keeping us a secret."

Us. She took a silent, deep breath.

She had no idea what that even meant. What they even were to one another. Last night had only further complicated her jumbled thoughts.

This was supposed to be fun, something casual, but it was starting to feel a whole lot more serious than that.

"When you say *us*…"

Ryan looked up as he cracked eggs into a dish.

"Jess, you mean a lot to me." He paused, before opening a drawer and reaching in and rummaging, emerging with the whisk. "I want George to know how much you helped me when I was away, and I don't know why I should have to keep that a secret. If I'm going to make things right with him, I need to be honest. About everything. And I think it might help to open up to him."

Okay. That sounded better. More like introducing her as a good friend.

"So when I meet him you'll tell him we're…"

He smiled. "Close friends."

Right. "I just don't want you to push it with him. If he thinks I'm your girlfriend it might make things difficult for you."

Ryan dipped the first slice of bread into the bowl and gave her one of his double-wattage grins.

"I'm not going to make this difficult for him. But I have to be honest about what's going on in my life if I want him to let me back in. Trust me again. I'll talk to him beforehand, explain myself so he understands." He paused. "I'm doing this for him. If I thought it wouldn't be the right thing for him, I wouldn't even suggest it."

Jessica sighed. She knew what he meant, she just

wasn't convinced, personally, that his son was ready to meet her.

"Do you have any fruit?"

Jessica moved back to the fridge again. He seemed set on them meeting, and she wasn't going to hurt his feelings by saying no to the lunch. But she hadn't missed the look on George's face the other day, and something told her it might not be the right thing to do. Even if Ryan was doing his best to evade her questions right now, they had to tread carefully.

But he sure was good at changing the subject. "Go back up to bed," Ryan told her, pausing and leaning toward her to plant a kiss on her forehead. "I'll bring breakfast up when it's ready."

Ryan watched as Jessica's fingers played across his chest as they lay side by side. Breakfast had been started and then somehow quickly forgotten about, but he wasn't complaining.

He sighed as she snuggled in closer to him.

"What?"

Ryan propped himself up on one elbow, looking down at her. She was so beautiful it took his breath away. So innocent and giving, so kind.

He wasn't sure if this was the right time to bring this up, but he needed to tell her. Needed to be real with her, be honest if they were going to have a chance at that future he was starting to think about.

"I'm scared, Jess."

She tucked even closer into him and kissed his jaw. "Why? What do you have to be scared of?"

He tried not to frown. He had everything to be scared of. That was the problem.

"Because part of me wonders if I can do this being a

normal person thing. I don't know if I can forget what I've seen, and forget what I've thought and just be a human being again."

"You've always been a human being, Ryan. You've just seen things that most of us would be too scared to confront," she said.

"Sometimes I wonder if being in the army, serving overseas, takes the humanity from you and makes you into some sort of machine. It stops you from feeling, it makes it okay to just treat each day as a new opportunity. But in real life, you need to look back, too. You need to remember."

"See this?" Jessica let her fingers dance along his cheek to wipe at a tear. "This makes you human."

He smiled, just, from the corner of his mouth on one side.

She kissed his lips, softly, so he could only just feel it. He leaned forward as she pulled away.

"That makes you human, too." She rolled over and reached inside her bedside table and pulled out a letter. "See this?"

He would recognize it anywhere. One of the letters he'd sent her. "You kept them?"

"Every one. My drawer is full of them."

He reached for it but she pulled it away and tucked it back again.

"I don't even know which letter that was, or why it was on the top of the pile, but those letters? Each one told me you were a man who knew how to love and how to lose. That you were a man who could help save our country, who could help his men, and now here you are at home trying to be a man and a dad and a civilian."

"And?"

"And now I know that you can do it."

"Why?"

She pressed her face into his chest. He had no idea why she had so much faith in him, but it gave him a strength he'd worried he didn't have.

"Because now you're helping me and it's working," she told him, her voice muffled by his skin.

He smiled and puller her closer. "You do know that whatever I'm not sure about, whatever I'm worried about, doesn't mean I'm not absolutely sure about what's happening between us, right?"

Jessica sighed as she lay in his arms.

Ryan nudged at her breast with his finger, circling over her skin and tracing back up to her face. It was as if he couldn't stop touching her, and she felt the same about him.

One day he'd ask her about her scars, what had led to her cosmetic surgery, but he didn't care. Plenty of women enhanced their breasts, and she had obviously had her reasons.

"You're my second chance, Jessica."

She pulled up so her head was resting on her hand, propped by the pillow. "I wasn't aware you needed a second chance."

He needed to tell her now. Take that step to let her in completely. "You're my chance to make things right."

"It wasn't your fault your wife died, Ryan."

He smiled, sadly. He hoped she'd understand. "No, but I didn't love her like she deserved to be loved. She was my best friend in school, and I loved her like only a best friend can."

He didn't say what he really wanted to. Tell her how he felt right now. Because it seemed too soon, too fast.

Now he knew what true love really felt like.

"Did she feel the same way?"

Ryan shook his head and played with her hair, his arm resting on her shoulder. This was the part he hated to admit, even to himself. Why he felt guilt like a crawling parasite over his skin sometimes. He'd always wondered if maybe he hadn't loved her enough to save her.

"She loved me deeply, I'd always known it. I could see it in her eyes every time she looked at me, even when she was in hospital with machines bleeping every time she so much as blinked."

He stopped and she just watched him. Ryan wished he could tell what she was thinking. "I never lied when I told her I loved her. We got married when we were eighteen, she was already pregnant with George, and we were happy. We never argued, and I told her every day that she meant the world to me. And she did."

"But?"

He leaned forward and kissed the tip of her nose. He wanted to ask Jessica if it made him a bad person for thinking he was so pleased to have met her. That finding her meant he could finally forgive Julia for leaving him. But he didn't. Because part of him wasn't ready to admit that out aloud yet. And he had a feeling that maybe Jessica wasn't ready to hear it.

But what he was sure about was how he felt about her. The last twenty-four hours had proven to him how special she was. "There's no but. I just want to say thank you, Jess. For everything."

She smiled as a tear escaped from the edge of her own eye. He kissed it away as she whispered back to him.

"You're welcome."

CHAPTER NINE

Dear Ryan,
I know by now that you probably torture yourself
by thinking over things you should have done, but
there's no point dwelling on the past. Especially
on things you had no power to control. Before you
come home, I think you need to forgive yourself,
and let yourself move on.

Focus on what you have to do, stay safe and
promise me that you'll write to your son more
often. Even if you don't have much to say, just
put pen to paper.

We write to one another so often now that
you don't have any excuses not to write to him.
Okay?
Jessica

JESSICA COULDN'T HELP the sigh that escaped her lips.
She'd thought waiting for Ryan to arrive last night had
been nerve-wracking. How wrong she'd been. Waiting
to meet his son was far worse. The only consolation was
that she wasn't meeting his parents, too.

She walked into the park, clutching Hercules's lead
and telling herself it was worth it. They'd had a great
time last night. Make that super. And if he needed her to

meet his son, to keep things open and honest, and help to repair his relationship with George, then she didn't have much choice other than to go along with it.

But she was already feeling messed up in her head about what had happened. Not the physical side, but the way he'd opened up to her. She was starting to think that maybe he wanted more from her than she'd expected from him. The way he'd talked to her, the things he'd told her…

She'd told herself this thing with Ryan was meant to be casual. He was leaving soon. She was not available to the idea of anything serious, and yet it felt like they had gone from friends to something very serious, very fast.

Jess pushed her hair behind her ears and tried to shut off the voice in her brain telling her to run. No matter what happened today, she had to remember it was worth it. Ryan had made her feel incredible last night. He had made her realize that she could be wanted and loved again. Just because he was going away did not mean it wasn't worth every moment. Because it was.

She'd been so scared of showing a man her body, of opening up again and putting her heart out there. But Ryan had helped her through something she had thought was impossible to recover from. Once she'd gotten over the initial shock of him seeing her breasts, she hadn't thought about it again all night. After months of worrying, he'd made her thoughts vanish in less than a heartbeat.

Just thinking about him like that put a smile back on her face. Until she spotted them. And her anxiety came back like a troop of butterflies playing in her stomach.

Ryan raised a hand to wave. They were walking along

by the pond. She could see his son smiling, then watched as his face fell when he saw her. She wanted to run. But it was too late to back out now.

Instead she sucked up her courage and bent to let Hercules off the lead. The least she could do was let the dog have fun, chase some ducks while she tried not to find a hole to crawl and hide in.

"Jess!" Ryan called out and she mustered up a big smile again. Forced it on her face.

She waved back and watched as Hercules bounded up to them, before taking off to do laps back and forth along the water's edge.

"Hi, guys."

Ryan walked toward her and kissed her on the cheek. She tried to enjoy it, to experience that magical breathlessness she usually felt when his lips touched her. But instead all she saw was the flush of George's cheeks as he looked the other way.

"I was telling George what happened with your dog the last time we were here," Ryan said.

The boy nodded, face still stained a patchy red.

Jess shook herself out of the slump she was in. She was the adult here, the least she could do was make it as easy on George as she could.

"Little Herc means the world to me," she said, taking a step away from Ryan, needing the breathing space as his boy watched them. "I can't believe I was so caught up in getting to know your dad that I almost lost him."

"Why did you start writing to my dad?" The boy's face flushed a deep red just asking her.

"Well…" She paused and looked at Ryan. He nodded at her to continue. "I wanted to show that I cared about what our soldiers were doing for us, for our country. I heard about a pen-pal program that was being run with the army, and somehow I ended up writing to your father, out of all the soldiers serving overseas."

Ryan moved closer to his son, hand on his shoulder. "When I told you that Jess made a huge effort to write to me, I meant that she wrote to me all the time. Every week. She helped me to see why I needed to come back home."

George took a few steps back then turned to face the water again. "What did she tell you?"

Jessica didn't know what to say. She was uncomfortable being made to feel like she was somehow a surrogate mother for the day. It wasn't a role she wanted to fill. She wasn't ready to face that kind of commitment.

"She guided me through dealing with my problems, we talked about everything and it gave me the strength to face what I'd left behind," Ryan explained.

"Did you talk about Mom?" George asked.

Jessica wanted to back away but she couldn't. She just stood there, feeling like an intruder.

"Yeah, about you and your mom."

George turned away, like he didn't want to talk about it anymore. It hadn't gone down that badly, but it hadn't exactly been great, either.

"Lunch?" She made the suggestion as the air became stale between them all.

Ryan looked at her gratefully. "Yeah, good idea."

She sat beneath a nearby tree on the grass and Ryan did the same. George didn't move.

Jess didn't want to be here any more than she guessed the boy did. It felt like she was intruding on something she had no right to be a part of.

"I hope you like sushi."

She nodded. At least lunch was going to be good. "Show me what you've got."

Ryan gave her a relieved look, reaching out to squeeze her hand before calling to his son. "You joining us, George?"

He slowly turned toward them, his eyes telling his entire life story. They looked sad, haunted almost, and Jess fought the sudden tug deep inside her that made her want to hold him, to comfort this boy who was so confused.

He just shrugged, but she knew he probably wanted to cry. To yell at her and ask his dad why he had to meet her at all.

"Hey, George, why don't you go get Hercules for me?" she suggested.

There was a small light in his eyes as she gave him the Get Out of Jail Free card.

"Either throw sticks into the water for him, or just get hold of him and bring him back," she told him.

George went off straight away and Ryan reached for her knee, his hand closing over it. "Thanks for that."

She took a deep breath. "I don't know if meeting George today was the best idea."

Ryan grimaced. "I know, but I did have a big talk with him before we came. Explained why I wanted him to meet you." He paused. "Sometimes the hardest thing is the best thing to do, even if it doesn't feel like it at the time, right?"

"I think him having to deal with me when you guys are only just starting to sort things out is too much." But part of her felt dishonest—because maybe, just maybe, it was just too much for *her* and yet exactly the right thing for George.

Ryan shook his head, jaw suddenly clenched a bit tighter, making him look more determined. His hand hovered then came to rest on her cheek.

Jess sighed at his touch.

"You mean something to me, Jess, and I don't want to keep things from him."

She turned her face to kiss his palm, wishing things could be more simple between them. That he wasn't going away, and that she didn't have to keep huge secrets from him.

"Ryan, you're going away soon." Jessica paused. "There's no need to cause complications when they don't even need to exist."

Now it was Ryan shaking his head. "I should have told you that I'm not leaving for good, Jess. If I didn't think we had a chance, that this didn't mean something, I wouldn't have let things go this far between us."

She swallowed, hard.

"In fact, I've already decided that this will be my last tour."

Silence hung between them.

Oh, my.

Was he serious?

She hadn't seen this coming. He'd been so determined to continue on with his career in the army, had made that so clear to her in his letters, it was the only reason *she'd* let things go this far. He'd even told her as much that first day they'd met.

Ryan was being so honest with her, and here she was keeping guilty secrets from him. All this time she'd thought it was men she couldn't trust, yet right now she was the one lying by omission. Who wasn't being up front about what she wanted and what she had to give. And now he was telling her that maybe they had a chance at a future. The one thing she'd thought he didn't have to offer her.

"Ryan..."

She didn't know what to say.

"Do you really think I would have jeopardized our friendship by making love with you if I was going to walk away and never look back?" She saw a flash of anger, of disappointment in his eyes. "You've done so much for me, the last thing I want to do is hurt you."

And yet from the sound of it, she was going to be the one doing the hurting.

Did that mean he wanted more from her? That he thought this was going to develop into something she hadn't possibly thought it *could* turn into?

Tears stung, pricked at the back of her eyes, but she fought them. She was used to putting on a brave face, to keeping her emotions to herself.

She wasn't emotionally available for a relationship. And she'd lied to him. If she'd just told him about the cancer in the first place, things would never have gotten to this point. It was her fault and no one else's.

"I think what you need to do is focus on your son," she said instead.

Ryan's eyebrows knotted as he drew them together. "Without you I wouldn't even *have* a relationship with my son."

She disagreed. He would have found a way to reconnect with George even if she hadn't been there for him. She looked up as Hercules landed in her lap. She cleared her throat as George appeared.

"Hey, buddy." She swatted at her dog as he tried to kiss her.

Ryan stayed silent.

"Thanks, George, he can be a handful sometimes."

The boy smiled at her and sat down. Hercules went straight over to him and had him laughing within seconds.

Ryan looked back at her, confusion in his eyes. She gave him a tight smile back. There was a lot unsaid between them, and from the look on his face, she'd hurt the one man who had given her a glimpse of what she might one day have in the future. An honest, caring, kind man who deserved better than what she could give him right now.

When he found out what she'd kept from him, he'd be hurt beyond belief. So the only thing she could do was make sure he never, ever found out. Which meant she had to make a decision and stick to it. Maybe it was time to walk away. Either that or she had to brave up and give him the chance to accept her for who she really was. The very thought made her shiver with fear.

"Sushi, right?"

Ryan gave her a confused smile and took three trays out of the plastic bag he'd been carrying.

She smiled back, but inside she was crying a thousand tears. He'd opened up to her, and she'd let him, because as his friend she owed it to him to listen and be there for him. What she hadn't realized was that when he'd told her this morning that he hadn't loved his wife *enough,* that just maybe he'd been trying to tell her something else.

Except she wasn't ever going to put him through that kind of heartache ever again.

CHAPTER TEN

Dear Ryan,
Have you ever thought about coming home for
good? I know you love what you do, but I often
wonder how long a person can live away from
their family. From their normal life.

Don't you miss being home? Or are you so
focused on your task over there that you don't
even let yourself think about what you're missing
out on back here?

Whatever happens, even if we don't end up
meeting, I want you to know that I think about
you and your unit every day. And I pray for your
safe return home one day soon.
Jessica

AFTER TOYING WITH her phone for what felt like forever,
Jessica put the key back in her car's ignition and gripped
the steering wheel.

Things hadn't gone well this afternoon. Not well at
all.

Somehow the perfect morning, waking in the arms
of a man like none other she'd met before, had turned
into the most dismal afternoon on record.

And no amount of grocery shopping or busying herself at home had helped the way she was feeling.

She needed to deal with this properly.

Finally she'd met the kind of guy she'd always dreamed of. Enjoyed the company of a member of the opposite sex, had a night that she would remember forever and had a man open up to her and tell her that she meant something to him.

Yet she was the one who'd managed to blow things. She wasn't ready for a relationship, had never thought whatever it was she had with Ryan could even have the chance of turning into something serious. Not when she'd expected him to be away serving again for goodness only knew how long.

So she either had to hurt him by coming clean and telling him about her past, and break her own heart in the process, and convince him that she liked him back but that nothing could happen, or call things off right now.

But in all the hours that had passed since she'd left him this afternoon, she hadn't figured out what to do. She cringed and put her foot down on the accelerator a little harder.

The way she felt around him was…indescribable and made her *want* to tell him the truth about her past. Yet would calling things off now be easier on him than telling him the truth? It would certainly prevent her from ever hurting him again like he had been over his wife's death, if he wasn't around to see her in the event that she became sick again.

If she wasn't driving she'd have banged her head against the wheel. It was all such a mess. Even without the added complication of his son, it was too much, too soon. Yet here she was, looking for his house, determined to do *something* to make the afternoon turn out better than it had so far.

She owed it to both of them not to leave things like this.

Jess scanned the numbers on mailboxes until she saw 109. Phew. His car was in the driveway. And it appeared to be the only one in residence. He'd mentioned that his parents were away for the night, had gone off to visit friends. And his son was to be at a friend's place, too, or so he'd said earlier.

That meant it was now or never.

Jessica stepped from the car and walked up the path. It was a nice house, nothing flashy, but modern and solid. A small family home. She guessed it had been Ryan's when his wife was still alive. He'd told her that he owned it, but his parents lived there and took care of the place while he was gone.

Jess knocked on the door.

"Coming."

His voice hit her in the chest, pierced her in the gut.

Suddenly the idea of calling things off was definitely not an option. That left her with one possibility on her list: she could leave it up to him, tell him the truth and let him decide if he could face the possibility of the pain of cancer again.

The door swung back.

"Jess?"

She stood there, awkward, handbag clutched under her arm. Unsurprisingly, Ryan looked unsure. She'd bolted from the park straight after lunch, so he was probably wondering why she was even here.

"Can I come in?" she asked.

His face relaxed and he held out his hand. "Come here."

She softened at his touch, let him draw her in, hold her. Comfort her. Even though she didn't deserve it.

"I'm sorry about earlier," she mumbled against his chest.

Ryan kissed her forehead and stepped back. "My fault, not yours. It was too much, too soon, right?"

She nodded, eyes cloudy with tears. It felt so right to be tucked against him, to find comfort from his body, but she knew what she had done was wrong. For once she had to admit that her brother had been right. If she'd been honest from the start she wouldn't be in this position right now.

"George is out?"

Ryan took her hand and led her down the hall. "Yep, at his friend's house. He looked pleased to get out of here."

She relaxed. It was just the two of them. Time to finally clear the air and come clean.

She followed him into the living room, toying with her bag, before sitting down on the sofa. He sat down, too, falling beside her, knees knocking hers, thigh brushing against her own.

Jessica felt rotten. The look on his face was so open, so kind, and she was about to bring up something that she'd wanted so badly to keep hidden.

And in the process she was going to hurt him.

But when she looked at him, saw the honesty there, remembered the way he'd treated her last night, she owed him nothing less than the truth.

"Ryan, I need to talk to you about something."

"Sounds serious." He grinned and took her hand, fingers circling her palm.

Why did this have to be so hard?

"It's ah, about your wife. Sort of."

Ryan's hand fell away from hers. She wasn't sure if he was angry or just plain unsure.

"You told me that you couldn't go through that again. That what happened with your wife…"

His face had gone from soft to hard. Like steel, braced for impact. "Is this about what I said earlier? I'm sorry if I scared you off, I just wanted you to know how I felt, that I wouldn't be doing this, misleading you, if I didn't think we had something special between us."

Jessica sighed. She didn't even know if she was doing the right thing now. Had no idea how to continue. But she had to try. Maybe she hadn't completely ruined what chance they might have had at a future together. Maybe he would understand.

"You opened up to me this morning, Ryan, and I think I owe you an explanation. I need to tell you something."

Ryan was a soldier. His life was all about walking away from his own personal issues and fighting for a greater cause. And yet he'd been brave enough to talk to her, to tell her the truth.

There was only so long she could run and hide from what had happened.

"You can tell me anything, Jess." He smiled at her so genuinely she wanted to cry. "Whatever you need to say, you can."

Jessica gripped his hand harder. Her eyes locked on his.

"I know what it's like to keep things hidden inside. I…"

He held her hand back, tight. "You do?"

A noise startled them both.

Jessica turned at the same time as Ryan. And came face-to-face with his son.

"George?" Ryan said, startled.

George looked at them and walked through the room and into the kitchen.

Jessica felt her heart sink to her toes. From the way they were cuddled up close on the sofa George probably thought he'd walked in on something he shouldn't have.

"Jess, can we…"

She smiled. There was nothing else she could do. Except maybe fall in a heap and sob her heart out. "Where's your room? I'll go and give you two some privacy."

He pointed down the hall. "Third on the left."

She touched his arm and walked away. "Take all the time you need."

Jessica opened the door to Ryan's room and stepped in. She could hear the sound of his voice as he spoke, but it was muffled and she didn't return to hear anyway. Whatever he needed to say was between him and his son, and she had enough on her own mind than needing to stick her nose in where it wasn't welcome.

It was weird being in Ryan's own personal space, and there was something disturbing about being there for the first time on her own. It made her think about what she hadn't managed to tell him. What she'd come here to say.

What she didn't want to tell him but had to.

Ryan was like a huge grizzly bear with a heart of gold, a man who'd known heartache like she could only barely understand, despite what she'd been through. A man who could kill an enemy with his bare hands yet was prepared to admit that he'd been a bad father in the past, and be honest with her that he couldn't face losing another person he loved again.

A man she wanted to love so bad, but was too scared of being honest with. It had been so much easier writing letters, when she could imagine that one day they could meet, that maybe he'd like her.

But she'd never considered that he'd be the kind of man she could fall in love with.

And deep down she knew she had already.

The reality of what she was feeling was harder to deal with. The reality of Ryan was a man who could cocoon her in his arms and make her feel safe. Make her think he could protect her from anything, maybe even from cancer. A man whose smile could make her forget every worry she'd ever had in her mind.

A man she could imagine having a life with.

So why hadn't she just been honest with him from the start? Why hadn't she told him when he'd opened up to her about losing his wife that first night over dinner?

Jessica sat on Ryan's bed, waiting for him. It seemed silly to be hiding out in here while he tried to deal with his son, but he was the parent. He was doing his best and she wasn't exactly helping the father-son relationship any. In fact, if they were both honest about it, her being in his life was probably the only remaining wedge stuck between him and his son.

But for some reason they had a connection that meant he was prepared to cause himself further heartache, to allow something to develop between them. And that only made her feel worse.

She'd been dishonest. And she knew that whatever he told her, as honest as he'd been with her, he'd probably still run away once she told him the truth. And if, by some miracle, he didn't run, at the very least he'd be angry…no, furious with her.

Jessica fought the urge to lay back and cry. Instead she sat up straight and looked around her. Pushed her thoughts away. His scent was in the room, the bed still crumpled from where he'd slept the night before, but it wasn't a personal room.

Jessica stood and walked to the dresser. She let her eyes wander over a photo of George and a very old wedding photo of a Ryan she didn't recognize. It felt like she was already intruding, looking over his things like this, but she didn't stop. At least it was taking her mind off the way she'd behaved.

She moved to his wardrobe and stood in front of the door, fingers itching to open it. She listened. Just faintly, she could still hear the echo of voices in the living room.

Jessica looked at the closet, considering it as if it was a living, breathing thing. She opened the door so fast she couldn't change her mind, then staggered back, stumbling over her own feet.

Oh, my.

Ryan's U.S. Army camouflage pants and shirt hung from a thick, sturdy hanger. It was as if it was a person, the way his clothes hung with such a presence. The way they managed to steal the breath from her lungs, just hanging there like that. The uniform looked back at her like it had a soul of its own.

It was a part of Ryan, as much a part of his life as anything. It was the uniform he had worn when he'd been on tour last, what he'd no doubt been wearing when he'd sat and written to her. Maybe he'd even been wearing it when he'd read the letters she'd sent him.

It was a Ryan from another life, not the man she knew here.

Jessica wriggled her fingers, flexing them, before touching the fabric. Her fingers skimmed the strong, rough cotton of the camouflage shirt, nails tracing the nametag. McAdams. His name played in front of her eyes.

She touched down the legs. Same fabric, same feel. His boots, black and shiny, stood forlorn beneath the hanging uniform.

Jessica stepped closer, inhaling as she moved. It was clean, but not freshly laundered. She pulled it closer, hoping he'd never wear it again, then wishing she could stop herself from thinking that.

Tears stung her eyes. It was like a lump of wood was jammed in her throat, making swallowing impossible.

Why had it taken seeing his uniform to truly make her realize? The problem wasn't that she didn't want to be with Ryan, didn't want a future with him.

What she was scared of was losing him.

She'd never wanted it to be just a fling. To start with, she'd convinced herself that a few weeks or months with him was all she wanted. But from the moment they'd met…no, from the moment she'd felt the power of his words, she'd let herself hope that what they had could develop into something special.

She'd just been too scared to admit it to herself.

Deep down she didn't want him to go back at all. To leave her for even a moment. She wanted him to stay here, safe, to look after her instead of her country.

To protect *her*.

Something crinkled. Jessica let go and watched as the uniform swung back into place, like it was trained to hang straight, with perfection, like the way a soldier stands to attention. She looked over her shoulder, making sure she was still alone, then reached forward. Her hand connected with the front pocket of his shirt, and she heard the rustle again.

Something made her open it. Made her curious. Something told her she had to see what was there.

She undid the button and reached inside. It was a letter. Someone else might not have realized straight away, but she knew. Just like she knew instinctively that it was a letter for her.

After months of writing one another, she knew his handwriting almost as well as she knew her own. Even the way he folded his letters was precise, although this one was rumpled, like he'd been carrying it a long time.

The only difference was that this one wasn't in an envelope that had her name scrawled across the front. But when she unfolded the sheet, it had her name at the top of it.

She closed her eyes, wishing she could walk away from it, put it back and not read it. He hadn't given it to her, it felt wrong to look at it like this, but she couldn't *not* read it.

Turning away would be like denying a bee its pollen.

It was okay. If he didn't want her to read it, he wouldn't have been carrying it in his pocket, right? He'd probably just forgotten to post it, then he'd arrived home and he'd probably already told her what was written inside.

Or maybe not.

Either way she had to know what it said.

CHAPTER ELEVEN

Dear Jessica,
I've been sitting here since before sunrise, and now it's almost midday. There's only one thing I want to tell you. One thing I've been wanting to tell you, so I'm just going to come out and say it.

I think I love you, Jessica. I know I've never met you, I know it's impossible to say this when I could pass you in the street at this exact moment and not know you. But one day, when we do meet, I know I'll look at you and still feel the same.

A stranger might say that when we meet it won't be the same, but something tells me it will be. That there's a reason we managed to find each other even though we're on opposite sides of the world. I want to come home, and I think the reason is you.

I love you, Jessica.
Ryan

JESSICA CAREFULLY REFOLDED the letter. She couldn't breathe. She couldn't blink. She could barely move.

She forced herself to put the letter back in his

breast pocket, fumbled with the button, then closed the closet door.

No.

He couldn't love her. He couldn't.

Now that he'd met her, did he still feel that way?

Could he truly feel that way about her now?

Love her?

But in her heart, she knew the answer to that. Just like she knew that, without a shadow of doubt, she loved him back with all her heart. She'd fallen in love with him about the time she'd been released from hospital. When she'd realized that his letters were what had helped her pull through. Had given her the strength to recover.

All this time she'd been denying it, telling herself she was okay with a casual fling, with him going away again when she'd been in love with him since before he'd even arrived home.

But he couldn't love her back. He couldn't. And she wasn't going to wait around to find out.

He'd made it clear he couldn't live through the pain of losing a wife again. And even if he accepted what had happened to her, what she'd hidden from him, it wasn't fair to put him in that position again when even she didn't know what was going to happen to her.

Jessica grabbed her sweater and tried not to run. She walked out of his room, moving as quietly as she could, and made for the back door. He'd be better off forgetting her. If he knew the truth he'd be devastated, and he deserved better. If she left now, before things went any further, he'd hurt less than finding out the truth later on. A slightly broken heart was better than him knowing she had cancer and having to deal with what might happen to her in the future. What could reoccur.

She should have ended things before they got this far.

Should never have considered telling him about what she'd battled. It would be better for both of them, her leaving.

So why was it so hard walking away?

Tears fell down her cheeks like oversize raindrops falling from the sky to touch her. Shudders ran back and forth along the planes of her skin. Her bottom lip quivered like it was an instrument being played. But she kept on walking, until she was outside, and she didn't stop until she got in the car.

It was over. It had to be.

She only wished she could have said goodbye to him first.

When she walked back into her house, even the smile and waggy tail that Hercules threw her way couldn't make her happy, not even for a heartbeat.

"Come here."

She hardly had to whisper for Hercules to come to her. It was like he knew the power of his fur, knew how much she'd come to need him, to crave the warmth of his little body and the way he cuddled into her when she held him.

Jessica scooped him up and pressed him tight to her chest, her face falling to kiss his little head.

She tried not to think about Ryan but no matter what she thought of, his eyes were in her mind and the words of his final letter to her were ringing in her ears.

"Who's been phoning us, huh?"

She smiled at her loyal companion through her tears, walking with him in her arms to hit the flashing light on the machine.

"Hey, sis, haven't heard from you in a while. Call

around for a drink tonight if you're free, or whenever. See you later."

Jess smiled and hit delete. Steven might be overprotective and overbearing sometimes, but he was a great brother. And she knew that no matter what happened, how right he might have been, that he'd never say *I told you so*.

There was one more message.

She leant back on the counter and snuggled Herc.

"Ah, Jessica…"

She jerked forward, almost losing Hercules in the process. She would know that voice anywhere. It was her doctor.

"I'd hoped to speak to you in person but I haven't been able to get hold of you. Your test results came back and we're going to need to do some follow-ups. Please don't worry, it might not mean anything but as you know we need to be overcautious."

Jessica hit delete immediately.

She gently placed Hercules down on the ground and let her shaky hand reach for the glass in the sink. She turned the faucet on and filled the glass, drinking a few mouthfuls, before turning the water back on to let the cool liquid run over her wrists.

This couldn't be happening.

She eyed the telephone and wished she didn't know the doctor's number by heart.

Jessica sat down at the table, pen in hand. It didn't matter how she felt about Ryan, but what she wanted to say, it was just so hard to get it out, to make the words form in her brain and force them out in the open. The only way she truly knew how to communicate with him was on paper.

The words ran like the credits of a movie over and over, around and around in her mind, a well of dialogue she couldn't deny. Writing to Ryan came so naturally, usually, but no other letter had ever been so hard to write.

The doctor was right, it might be nothing, but she still had to tell Ryan. She owed him more than a lie now. She hoped he wouldn't think that he had to be there for her, that he couldn't walk away, even if he really wanted to. That somehow her cancer was his problem, too, when it wasn't.

Because unlike her ex, Ryan would probably feel obliged to be there for her now, if something was wrong, and she didn't want to be a pity case.

She needed to tell him the truth, and there was only one way she knew how to.

Jessica started to write.

Dear Ryan,
I don't know how we got here, or what we did to deserve this, but there's something you need to know about me that I never told you. Something that will no doubt make you want to run and never see me again.

When I started writing to you, I was in the hospital. I should have told you, but then I never thought I'd actually ever meet you. I never thought you would have to be the one supporting me. You were the soldier, the man away at war, and help-ing you made me feel better. You were the only person in my life who didn't treat me like a bird with broken wings. I could be myself, talk to you, laugh, without any strings.

But something happened when you arrived

here, into my life. Suddenly you weren't just a soldier, a faceless person who needed a friend. You were a man and I was a woman. So I didn't tell you about my cancer.

Before you, cancer was all I thought about. Then I thought I'd beaten it. Maybe I still have, but I don't know for certain yet. Either way I owe you an explanation for why I ran out on you earlier today, and why I'm going to disappear from your life forever.

I need to go back and see my specialist, Ryan, and so I think it's best we don't see each other again. You have George to deal with, and my being with you was complicated enough even before I plucked up the courage to tell you about my past.

You mean so much to me, but I can't put you through this, not after what you've seen. What you've gone through in the past with your wife, and what you made so clear you could never cope with living through again. I should have come clean then, been honest with you, but I was scared you'd walk away, and I wasn't ready to lose you so soon after meeting you. I wanted to enjoy your company while you were here, enjoy our friendship, although I can see now that was selfish of me.

Please know that I love you, Ryan. If we'd met in another lifetime, maybe we could have had something amazing together. I'm sorry, for what it's worth, and I will never forget you so long as there is breath in my body.

Yours always,
Jessica

Jessica wiped at the tears falling in a steady stream down her cheeks, but one still managed to plop onto the paper. It didn't matter. In her heart she knew he'd probably shed his own tears when he found her note, and she deserved to feel bad over what she'd done to him.

What she'd kept from him.

She picked up the letter, folded it, then placed it in an envelope. Jessica scrawled his name across it and picked it up, her bag in the other hand.

Earlier he'd phoned, telling her he wasn't sure what had happened before but that he'd be around later tonight to see her. To make sure she was okay.

Jessica dialed her brother's number.

"You okay?"

She smiled into the earpiece. Her brother meant the world to her. "The specialist has agreed to see me in the morning."

"You want me to come with you?"

"No, I'll be fine." She hoped. "If it's okay with you I'm going to come over soon with Herc so he can hang out with you tomorrow while I'm gone."

"You want to stay here the night?"

She tried not to cry. "Yeah, if that doesn't mess up your evening."

"Get in the car, sis, I'll have dinner waiting."

She hung up and picked up her keys.

Hercules was at her heel and followed her outside. Jessica only paused to lock the door and tape the envelope to the timber, just below the handle. She was glad she wasn't going to be around to see the look on Ryan's face. Just walking away from what she'd written was like a stake was being forced through her heart.

* * *

Ryan held his son tight and gave him a pat on the back. Man-to-man kind of stuff.

George smiled when he released him.

He hated that Jessica had had to leave, that his heart-to-heart with George had taken so long, but he'd have time to explain himself to her tonight. What mattered was that he'd been honest with George about his feelings for Jess, and now he had to be honest with her about them, too.

"You sure you don't mind if I leave you here for a bit?"

George shook his head. "Nah, go see her."

"Because if you'd rather me stay here I will."

His son rolled his eyes. "I get it. Just go, all right?"

Ryan gave him another slap on the back and stood, feeling good about how things were turning out. Finally.

"Guess I need to stop running for good, right?"

George just watched him.

"It's time for me to put down my roots again here, son. You know I meant it the other night when I said this would be my last tour, didn't you?"

He received a nod in return. Ryan gave George one final look, to reassure himself he'd be okay, then pulled on his jacket and found his car keys.

He'd finally found out what it meant to be a father again, and he wanted to be there for George. Had spent the better part of the afternoon opening his heart up to him and making sure he understood what his priorities were. Made sure he knew that his bringing Jessica into their lives was because what he felt for her was real. And what she'd done for them, the way she'd helped him man up to his son, was why he was prepared to fight for his right to be in both of their lives.

If there was one thing this injury had taught him, it was that he wasn't invincible. Or immortal.

He was desperate to speak to Jessica now. Whatever she'd been upset about telling him couldn't change his mind, even if she was nervous about getting something off her chest.

Opening his soul to her had been less painful than he'd thought, and after having a long talk with George, he had no intention of mucking up a future with Jess. Not now that his son understood what she meant to him.

It was now or never.

Ryan pulled up outside Jessica's house and walked up the path. There were no lights on inside and the curtains weren't drawn.

Maybe she hadn't got his message? His stomach flipped, anxiously. He hoped nothing had happened to her.

Ryan decided to go and knock anyway. She could be taking a nap, reading in her room without the light on. He wasn't going to back down now, not when he'd mustered the courage to open up to her. To tell her what she needed to know about him, and to admit how he really felt about her.

As he neared the door, he saw something white moving ever so slightly in the breeze. He squinted. It was almost dark, but he could tell it was an envelope. He'd waited for enough of them over the last year to know the exact size of the stationery she used.

Ryan stopped a foot from the door and reached out to touch it. Jessica's soft, scrawly handwriting stood out and beckoned him, called to him as it always did.

He'd loved receiving her letters when he was away, had treasured every one, but this one felt different.

This time when he saw his name, it made him want to drop it. Why would she have left him a letter? She could have called or waited for him, or scribbled a note on the door telling him when she'd be back.

The formality of this one felt all wrong. His name on the outside. The envelope. The darkness of the house in contrast to the white of the paper.

Ryan pushed his thumb beneath the seal and slowly took the letter from it. He walked back to the car so he'd have enough light to read it. There was no point knocking on her door, she'd clearly left this for him, and she wouldn't have pinned it there if she'd been inside.

He opened his car door and dropped into the driver's seat, feet still firmly planted on the road. He flicked the interior light on and held the note up.

Ryan felt the kick of betrayal, of pain, the moment he read her words. They hit him like a heavy man's fist to his stomach.

Jessica had lied to him.

She'd lied to him and she didn't even have the guts to tell him to his face.

He finished her words, eyes first skimming then rereading more slowly what she'd written. What she'd written on paper rather than tell him to his face.

Ryan dropped the letter then bent to retrieve it, screwing it up into a tight ball and throwing it out onto the sidewalk, not even able to bear having it in the car with him.

He sat, he couldn't do anything else.

Why? Why hadn't she just told him? What had he done to make her think she had to hide herself from him? To think she had to deal with all his problems yet not share her own?

Ryan tried to calm himself down. Tried to put his training in place and stay collected, to keep his mind settled.

But he couldn't. Fury charged within him like a tornado that built itself up to rip homes from the ground and spit them out again all torn and broken. His face was burning hot, fists clenched at his sides.

No! He was *not* going to let her just walk away like this. He'd finally opened up, acted like the man he so wanted to believe he was, and she'd just disappeared.

Ryan swallowed, over and over, trying to fight something he hadn't felt in so long. Sadness. Gut-wrenching, heart-breaking sadness. Guilt and pain like he'd thought he'd never have to experience again.

Tears stung in his eyes but he was powerless to stop them. They wet his cheeks then streamed down his jaw. He wiped at them, furious, but he couldn't stop the way he felt, or the way his body was reacting.

He wasn't the kind of guy who cried, for heaven's sake!

Ryan pulled his arm back and made a fist, pummelling the steering wheel. His fingers and wrist exploded with pain upon impact, his upper arm and shoulder throbbing within seconds.

His physio was going to kill him, but he didn't care.

What he cared about right now, right at this moment, was the woman who'd run from him. Who'd thought he wasn't man enough to deal with her past, when she'd been so caring about his.

He hung his head, nursing his arm against his chest, and ordered himself to stop crying.

He couldn't lose her. Not now. If she didn't want him, if he didn't mean to her what she did to him, then fine. But he was not going to lose another person he loved, however long they might have together. He wasn't going to live with any regrets this time. *If* her cancer had returned, if she was that sick, then he was going to suck up his memories and his pain and deal with it. He was going to be there for her.

Now all he had to do was find her and tell her that.

Ryan got out of the car, slammed the door shut and wiped at his face. His hand and arm still hurt but he didn't care. He stood, fists clenched, trying to figure out what to do.

He didn't care if she'd had cancer. He didn't care how angry he was, or how much he wanted to shake her and tell her how stupid she'd been. He no longer even cared that she'd lied to him. He realized she had thought it was the right thing to do, just like he'd thought staying away from home so long was the right thing to do.

He would do anything for Jessica, and even if it meant facing his biggest fear, he would be there. This was his chance to prove himself to her once and for all.

He had two options. Find Bella. Or turn up at her brother's place.

Bella was the easier option, and probably the more logical one, but if confronting her brother was what he had to do, then he'd turn up on his doorstep and not leave until he had an answer. He didn't care what it took. What he had to do. Even if her brother gave him a black eye for upsetting her and making her run.

Ryan was going to find her and tell her how he felt.

Whatever the consequences.

CHAPTER TWELVE

Dear Ryan,
Everything is fine here. Nothing really to report.
Your letters are always so much more interesting
than mine! I'm just busy with my painting and
life in general, sorry I can't entertain you with
anything more exciting.

Not long now until you're home, right? You
must be so looking forward to stepping off that
plane.
Jessica

JESSICA KNEW WHY she was feeling guilty. She knew
why she had had to run, because she was scared of feeling like she had once before.

In love. With no power over her future.

Scared.

She couldn't deal with feeling like that, not now. Her
focus had to be on healing herself, on *protecting* herself. And that's why she'd had to spend the night at her
brother's place. She didn't have the strength to deal with
being back here at the hospital and facing Ryan, too.

It was like she was only half the woman she'd been.
The cancer had done that to her. Stripped away her
hopes and dreams for the future and made her question

her every move. It had taken away the part of her that made her feel like a woman. And she just didn't want to put another human being through what she'd seen her family go through.

Yes, Ryan had made her realize that her cosmetic concerns were unfounded, but the reality of him dealing with her past, with her *cancer,* meant she'd had no choice other than to leave him.

To see the look in another person's eyes that said they thought they were going to lose her was more than she could deal with. And to cry herself to sleep with another person in her mind who she couldn't bear the thought of never seeing again—that was what she was truly frightened of.

If the cancer came back.

Every day she lived with that. The worry that slowly ate at her brain and her thoughts like a termite gnawing on wood. She was a cancer survivor, she'd beaten the odds once, but there was always the chance that it could come back.

Since Ryan had stepped into her life in all his physical glory, she'd almost forgotten, almost felt normal for the first time in what seemed like forever. But then reality had come crashing down.

Her family would be heartbroken if she'd relapsed. No, they were already heartbroken that she'd gone through what she had. It would shatter their entire beings piece by piece if it had come back.

Jessica walked faster, moving as quickly as she could—as if doing so would make her heart heal. Or her mind forget the man she'd just walked out on last night. But the reality that confronted her was a sterile waiting room, and the smell of hospital that she'd grown to hate.

She should have brought someone with her. Bella. Her brother. Anyone. No matter how strong she tried to be, there was nothing worse than being alone.

Ryan felt like his head had been in a car crash. It was pounding, throbbing with a pain all of its own. He should have stopped to get a sling for his arm, too, but instead he'd swallowed a couple of pain relief pills he had in the car from the physio, and he was driving like a madman.

Bella had been a pain in the backside last night, refusing to tell him where he could find Jessica, but when he'd turned up at Steven's place this morning and told him the truth about how he felt, her brother had told him everything.

He was almost at the hospital.

Ryan had gotten over the fact that she'd written him a letter instead of telling him to his face. He'd gotten over the fact that she hadn't trusted him enough to tell him, to really let him in. He knew why she'd done it. He'd told her himself that he never wanted to see a loved one battle cancer, that he was scared of being truly heartbroken again, not knowing how much his words would have pierced her to the core. The last thing he wanted was to deal with her being sick, with anyone close facing something like cancer, but he certainly wasn't going to turn his back on Jessica. It wasn't her fault she'd been ill.

Once upon a time he'd thought he couldn't be strong enough to be there for someone again like he'd had to be there for his wife, but it didn't mean he wouldn't pull himself together for Jessica. Given the choice, he'd help her battle anything if it truly meant a future with her. Even just the chance at a future.

Maybe she was right not to have told him before. Maybe he would have run if he'd known about her cancer that first day he'd come back. To be honest, he probably would have avoided getting close to her at all, even via letters, had he known about her illness.

But this was *Jessica*. The woman he had now grown to love through letters and in person, who meant so much to him, that he couldn't be without her for however long they had together.

He pumped the accelerator a little harder, increasing his speed. If she told him to leave, he would. But he wasn't giving up without a fight. Without at least proving to her that he deserved a chance to be with her. To love her.

Jessica walked down the corridor. They wanted to keep her for a few hours, do some tests, and she needed to retrieve some things from the car. She knew how long these things could take, and she wanted to grab her book and sketch paper to draw on.

Heavy footsteps echoed out behind her but she didn't bother to turn. The hospital was full of noise, and even though she hated the place she felt safe here. So long as she didn't see too many cancer patients being pushed through the wards.

"Jessica!"

She stopped. Her feet actually stopped moving at the command, even though she didn't want them to. She squeezed her eyes shut for a nanosecond then started walking faster.

Ryan. She would know that voice anywhere and it was not one she wanted to hear. Not now. Maybe if she didn't turn around he'd figure it wasn't her. How had he found her anyway?

"Jessica!"

His voice was deep, strong, even more commanding this time.

She kept moving, head down. She wasn't going to let herself turn. Couldn't deal with him right now.

"Stop! Just stop."

The footfalls were right behind her. Running away wasn't an option. She had to stop. She forced her feet to a halt. Her shoulders heaved.

Why now? She didn't have the strength to deal with Ryan. Couldn't face him and see the hurt she knew she'd find there. The betrayal she knew he must be feeling. Why had he come?

"Jessica, look at me."

His voice was still commanding, but it was starting to crack.

"Look at me."

It was a whisper this time, barely audible. She still didn't move, not until his hand curled around her forearm and made her turn.

She could feel his big body behind her, so close all she wanted to do was lean back into him, to seek comfort from him.

But she couldn't. Not now. Not after what she'd done to him. If she'd just been honest from the beginning, instead of enjoying the fact that she could correspond with a friend who never asked her how she was coping, never reminded her of what she'd been through, she never would have had to face this kind of pain right now.

If she hadn't kept writing to him and pretending everything was normal, when she was actually in hospital and recovering…

Ryan's fingers traced up her arm, across her shoulder

and cupped her chin to make her turn properly. He gently tilted her face to look up at his.

Jessica opened her eyes, let him see her as the damaged, emotional mess she had become.

"Jessica, I love you."

His words almost made her crumple to the ground. No. He couldn't love her. Not after what she'd done, the way she'd deceived him, what she'd told him in her letter. He was saying it because he felt sorry for her, because he felt he had to care for her after what she'd been through.

The only thing worse than a man running out on you when you thought he loved you, was a man who was so honorable he felt he had to stay.

"Did you hear me?" Ryan's eyes flickered, searching her gaze. "I love you, Jessica."

She shook her head. "It's not enough." Her voice wobbled.

"Not enough?"

He stepped back, his hand leaving her skin to run through his hair. He looked like he was going to turn and storm off, like he didn't know what to do, but instead he propelled himself forward. She stepped back but he grabbed her, held her in place.

"I've been waiting for you my entire life, Jessica." His voice dropped as he reached both hands to her cheeks, holding her face. "It's like I've been living in slow motion, like my life has been building to this moment, like I've been waiting to meet you, to be with you, every day of my existence."

Tears started falling again, beating down her cheeks and curling into her mouth, their salty taste making it even harder to swallow. To say anything at all back to him.

She couldn't believe him.

"I don't want to hurt you." She stuttered the words out.

"Don't want to? Or are you afraid to let me in?"

She'd never seen him like this, so intense. One moment he looked broken, the next like the soldier he was. The powerful man she knew he must be when he was on duty. In uniform.

"I know what hurt is, Jessica." He stepped back again, like he needed distance from her to regain his strength. "I've seen men die, I've pulled triggers and thrown grenades and done plenty of things to hurt myself and others. I watched my wife die, in a hospital not unlike this, and I've had my heart break into so many pieces that I thought it would never heal."

Her tears ceased. She stood, arms hanging at her sides, face angled toward him. After pushing him away, and hoping he wouldn't come back, now she wanted to grab him and never let go.

"Despite everything I've already been through, do you know when I realized that I'd never truly known hurt before?" he asked.

She shook her head.

"When you told me in a letter you loved me, but then ran away from me. When I thought that maybe you might die, and I wouldn't be at your side to help fight it with you."

"Ryan."

"No." He put his hand up and started walking backward down the corridor as she followed him. "Don't pity me, or tell me you're sorry. Just don't."

He stopped when she did. Jessica wiped at her cheeks and took a deep breath. She'd tried to save him the pain of her problems and instead she'd done the opposite. His eyes were like the pathway to his soul. Big blue pools that blazed with hurt and betrayal. His skin was pale, so unlike its usual sun-tanned gold. Like all the blood had drained away.

There was only one thing she could tell him. And that was the truth. There was no point hiding behind her pride or her fear any longer. If he was prepared to put his own heart on the line, could honestly tell her that he felt for her so deeply that he'd face any battle with her, then she had to be honest with him in return.

If he was brave enough to deal with her cancer, then she owed it to him to face her own fears. To take a chance. To risk her own heart.

"I love you, too, Ryan." She only whispered but he'd heard her. Of course he'd heard her. "I'm sorry and I love you."

He didn't move. His feet were planted shoulder-width apart, like he was awaiting orders, and his face was frozen.

"Ryan?"

He blinked and looked back at her. "I think I fell in love with you before we even met."

Jessica started to cry again as she ran the distance between them. He opened his arms as she propelled herself forward, catching her as she landed against his chest. His hands circled her waist and hoisted her in the air, legs winding around his torso as she clung on to him like she'd never held anything in her life before.

The words from his letter, that last letter she'd found, played through her mind. It still seemed too good to be true, but she couldn't fight the way she felt any longer.

"I love you, Ryan. I love you so much it hurts."

Why hadn't she given him the chance to be here? To

hold her and protect her? Why had she not let it be his decision?

He pulled his face away from her neck, buried against her hair, to look at her. She leaned back in his arms, safe in his strong hold.

"Promise you'll never leave me again. Promise you'll never walk away again," he said urgently.

She nodded. "I promise."

Ryan watched her eyes, his now filled with tears, just like her own. He tipped her forward until their foreheads touched, before a big smile made his mouth twitch.

"We can fight anything together, Jessica. I promise."

She didn't have the chance to say it back. To tell him that she agreed. His lips searched for hers, his smooth skin whispering across hers as she clung on to him so hard her fingers dug into his shoulders. Ryan pulled her tighter against his body, one hand holding her, the other pressed into the back of her head as his lips continued their hungry assault on hers.

He was right. It was as if they'd been waiting their entire lives for one another.

And this was only just the beginning.

CHAPTER THIRTEEN

Dear Jessica,
Do you ever think about how your life turned
out? If you've made decisions, done things that
you should maybe have done differently? I often
wonder how it was I ended up here, whether I was
always destined to this life, even though I love
what I do. Maybe it's just my injury making me
think things like this, because I'm already sick of
being laid up and waiting for surgery.
Anyway, see you soon, okay? Maybe it's our
destiny to meet, or maybe I'm just getting carried
away. You decide.
Ryan

JESSICA LOOKED UP at Ryan as he cocooned her in his arms. They were sitting on the grass as Hercules played his duck-chasing game. She leaned back into Ryan, her body fitting snugly between his legs so she could rest on his chest.

"What are you thinking about?" Ryan asked, nuzzling her neck, his lips making goose pimples appear on her skin.

"I'm wondering how neither of us realized that

we were writing love letters all this time," she said, smiling.

He wrapped his arms around her tighter. "Maybe we did and we just didn't want to admit it to ourselves."

She turned her body to face him, arms circling him as she sat between his legs still but pressing her chest to him now instead. She wrapped her legs around him, too.

"Have you told George about my cancer yet?"

Ryan dropped a kiss to her forehead. "Yeah."

She sat up straighter. "What did he say? What did you tell him?"

Ryan pulled her closer. "I haven't told him all the details yet, but I told him that you were in remission." He paused then sighed. "It was tough telling him, but he asked me a few questions and I did my best to answer honestly."

"Maybe I should say something to him. Talk to him about it."

Ryan shook his head. "No, I think *we* can talk about it as a couple with him. Make sure he understands how unlikely it is that it could come back, explain about the mastectomy, cover everything."

Jessica nodded.

"The last thing I want is for him to be scared of losing his future stepmom, too."

She snuggled into his shoulder, but Ryan pulled her back.

"What's wrong?"

Jessica squeezed her eyes shut before looking up at Ryan. Worry lines covered his face, brows pulled together.

"I'm scared about you going away again."

He closed his eyes as she tucked her face back into his neck.

"I have to go."

It sounded like the words were painful for him, like he didn't want to admit that he was going to be leaving her.

"I know, it's just…"

Ryan held her away from him and leaned back, his eyes searching hers. "I've got a lot to live for. Nothing's going to happen to me. I'm going to be back here before you know it, okay?"

She admired his bravery. "Okay."

"Your letters kept me alive on my last tour," he reminded her.

Jess laughed. "Yeah?"

"Yeah." Ryan pulled her back into him, his lips covering hers. "I'll be back here in a few months. Any sooner and you'd probably be sick of me."

Jessica just shook her head and pulled him closer. She doubted that could ever happen. "Just shut up and kiss me."

Ryan tipped her back onto the grass and pinned her down, hands above her head. He leaned over her, his shoulders blocking the sun from her eyes.

She giggled as he growled, his mouth moving closer to hers.

"You should know better than to give orders to a soldier."

Jessica sighed against his lips. If this was her punishment, she intended on ordering him around more often.

EPILOGUE

Dear Jessica,
I can't believe it's been six months since we were
last together. Would you believe me if I said they
were the longest six months of my life? Every day
I think of you, not a day goes past when I don't
think about what I have to come home to.

Not long ago, the word home *scared me. Now*
it makes me smile. Have I told you that you saved
me? I know you'll say I saved myself, but you've
made me whole. You gave me the strength to fight
for what I believed in, what I wanted in my life,
and somehow I managed to fight hard enough for
you too.

Before you ask, my arm is fine. But I'm not cut
out for this any more. My heart's not in it, and for
the first time in my life I'm looking forward to a
desk job.

I promised you this would be my last tour, and I
had the papers through today to confirm it. When
you see me next, I'll be yours forever. I promise
I'll never leave you again.

All my love, now and forever.
Ryan

* * *

JESSICA COULDN'T STAND still. She shifted her weight from foot to foot, gripping George's hand tight and grinning as he squeezed back.

"That kind of hurts."

She laughed. "Sorry. It's just…"

"I know."

Jessica watched as the first of the soldiers came through the gate. Her mouth was dry, heart hammering so loud she was struggling to hear herself think.

She had hated Ryan being away, but it had been good in a way. Jessica pulled George against her and his arm found her waist. He was as nervous and excited as she was. But he was also her friend. All these months with Ryan away had brought them closer, made them develop a bond that she knew would never be broken.

She couldn't wait to see the look on Ryan's face.

"Jess, do you…"

Suddenly she couldn't hear what George was saying. Her eyes were transfixed, body humming as she recognized the man walking through the gates and toward them.

Tousled dark hair, shorter than before he'd left, but unmistakably his. Tanned skin, broad shoulders, eyes that could find hers in any crowd.

Ryan.

She knew George had left her side, that he'd already seen his dad. But she was powerless to move. She didn't know whether to leap in the air and squeal with excitement or cry her eyes out that he was actually here. Alive. Whole.

She drunk in the sight of him in his combat uniform. Camouflage pants and shirt, the same uniform she'd seen hanging in his closet that day. He looked good enough to eat and he was almost standing in front of her now, his son by his side.

"Hey, baby," he said.

She couldn't move. Words stuck in her throat.

But he didn't care. His smile lit up his entire face as he dropped his bag and grabbed her around the waist, swinging her up in the air and kissing her so hard she almost lost her breath.

"Ryan…" His name came out a whisper, like she couldn't truly believe he was back.

He kissed her again, his lips soft against hers this time, like he was whispering back to her. He only pulled away to put his other arm around his son.

"I've been waiting for this day for six months, and I'm never leaving either of you again. Okay?"

George nodded and all Jessica could do was grin up at him, feeling giddy with the sight of him before her, with the strength of him beneath her touch.

"Welcome home, Dad."

She reached for George and the three of them hugged, snuggled up close together.

"I'm so lucky to have you guys as my family." Jessica almost choked on her words but she had to say them. She *was* lucky. To have a man like Ryan by her side and a boy like George in her life.

"We're the lucky ones, right, bud?" Ryan asked his son.

George laughed and stepped back, quickly rubbing at his face to hide his tears.

But Jessica knew better. She was the lucky one.

She'd fought cancer, she'd faced heartache and loss, and yet she'd still managed to find Ryan. He'd made everything right again.

Today was like the start of their new life together.

He'd returned home safely from war. She'd passed all her tests with flying colors. And George had finally accepted her like they'd known one another all their lives.

"Shall we go home?" she asked.

Ryan laughed and George nudged him in the side.

"You got it?" Ryan asked his son.

George blocked Jessica and gave his father something from his pocket.

"What's going on?" she asked curiously.

Ryan passed his son his kit bag and they grinned at one another, before he turned to face her, reaching for one of her hands.

"This time when I was away, I wrote to George, too, as often as I wrote to you."

Jessica nodded. She knew that already.

"So that's how I knew all your tests had gone fine, and that George was coping okay. That he wasn't scared of losing you, too, now that the two of you had become so close."

She wasn't sure where this was going. "I know, Ryan. George and I talk about everything, we don't have any secrets."

George laughed.

She turned to glare at his cheeky response but he just shrugged.

"There is something he's been keeping secret." He paused. "In one of my last letters, I asked George a question." Ryan smiled over at his son again, before dropping to one knee.

Suddenly the noise of the airport, the hustle and bustle around them, disappeared. She could hardly see straight, could only focus on Ryan on one knee before her. Surely not?

Her heart started to thump. Hard.

"I know it's tradition to ask the bride's family for permission first, but in this case I thought it was George's permission we needed."

Oh, my. Her mouth was dry, she couldn't move. Bride? Had she heard him right?

"Jessica, will you do me the honor of becoming my wife? Of becoming George's stepmum?" Ryan asked huskily.

Jessica couldn't help the excited squeal as it left her lips. "Yes!" She grinned as Ryan rose. "Yes, yes, yes."

He leaned in and kissed her, touching his nose to hers, his forehead pressed against hers.

"Are you sure?" he whispered.

"I've never been more sure of anything in my life."

Ryan stepped back and held up her left hand, opening his other palm to reveal a ring. She watched as he raised it and placed it on her finger. A single solitaire on a platinum band.

"I can't believe you were in on this." Jessica turned to George, who was blushing from ear to ear. He just shrugged, obviously thrilled to have surprised her.

Jess turned her attention back to the ring, holding it up to the light to watch it sparkle.

"Do you like it?" Ryan asked anxiously.

She reached for him and held him tight, never wanting to let him go. "I love it."

He kissed her on the top of her head and took her hand.

"Let's go home, family."

Jessica reached for George's hand with her free one as they walked from the airport.

Home had never sounded so good.

NEW YORK'S FINEST REBEL

BY
TRISH WYLIE

Trish Wylie worked on a long career of careers to get to the one she wanted from her late teens. She flicked her blonde hair over her shoulder while playing the promotions game, patted her manicured hands on the backs of musicians in the music business, smiled sweetly at awkward customers during the retail nightmare known as the run-up to Christmas, and has got completely lost in her car in every single town in Ireland while working as a sales rep. And it took all that character-building and a healthy sense of humour to get her dream job, she feels—where she spends her days in reindeer slippers, with her hair in whatever band she can find to keep it out of the way, make-up as vague and distant a memory as manicured nails, while she gets to create the kind of dream man she'd still like to believe is out there some-where. If it turns out he is, she promises she'll let you know. . .after she's been out for a new wardrobe, a manicure and a make-over. . .

To my lovely editor Flo, fellow member of the
"I heart Daniel Brannigan" fanclub.

CHAPTER ONE

'Every girl knows there are days for heels and days for flats. It could be a metaphor for life if you think about it. Let's all make today a heels day, shall we?'

SIREN red and dangerously high, they were the sexiest pair of heels Daniel Brannigan had ever seen. Silently cursing the amount of time it took to haul the cage doors into place, he watched them disappear upstairs.

He *really* wanted to meet the woman in those shoes.

Punching on the button until there was a jerk of upward movement, he tried to play catch-up in the slowest elevator ever invented. After the first of three endlessly monotonous trips, he knew the stairs were going to be his preferred mode of travel in the future. But until he had all of his worldly possessions—few that they were—carted from his truck to the fifth floor, he didn't have a choice.

A flash of red appeared in his peripheral vision.

Target acquired.

Turning in the small space, he assessed each detail as it came into sight. Thin straps circled dainty ankles, the angle of her small feet adding enough shape to her calves to remind him that he was overdue for some R & R. If she lived in the same apartment block he was moving into, it was a complication he could do without. But if the effect her shoes had on his libido was anything to go by, he reckoned it was worth the risk. He hadn't earned the nickname Danger Danny for nothing.

The elevator jarred to an unexpected halt, an elderly woman with a small dog in her arms scowling pointedly at the boxes piled around his feet. 'Going down?'

'Up,' he replied curtly. Rocking forward, he nudged the button with his elbow.

Don't disappear on me, babe.

The adrenalin rush of pursuit had always done it for him, as had the kind of woman it took to wear a skirt so short it made him stifle a groan when it came into view. Flared at mid-smooth-skinned-thigh, the flirty cheerleader number lovingly hugged the curve of her hips before dipping in at a narrow waist. He glanced at the fine-boned hand curled around handles of bags labelled with names that meant nothing to him, mouth curving into a smile at the lack of anything sparkling on her ring finger. On the floor below his, she turned to speak to someone in the hall. To his frustration it meant he couldn't see her face as the elevator creaked by. Instead he was left with an image of tumbling locks of long dark hair and the sound of sparkling feminine laughter.

Fighting with the cage again when the elevator stopped, he did what he had done on his previous trips and nudged a box forward to fill the gap. In the following moment of silence, footsteps sounded on the stairs. A trickle of awareness ran down his spine as he turned, gaze rising until he was looking into large dark eyes. Eyes that narrowed as his smile faded.

'Jorja,' he said dryly.

'Daniel,' she replied in the same tone before she tilted her head and arched a brow. 'Didn't occur to you anyone else might want to use the elevator today?'

'Stairs are good for cardio.'

'That would be a no, then.'

'Offering to help me move in? That's neighbourly of you.' He thrust the box in his arms at her, letting go before she had an opportunity to refuse.

There was a tinkle of breaking glass as it hit the floor between their feet.

'Oops.' She blinked.

Oops, his ass. The fact she'd obviously made interesting changes in wardrobe while he was overseas didn't make her any less irritating than she'd been for the last five and a half years. 'No welcome-home banner?' he asked.

'Wouldn't that suggest I'm happy you're here?'

'You got a problem with me being here, you should have made it known when my application came up in front of the residents committee.'

'What makes you think I didn't?'

'Clue was in the words *unanimous decision*.' He shrugged. 'What can I say? People like when a cop lives in the building. Makes them feel secure.'

She smiled a saccharine-sweet smile. 'The elderly woman you ticked off two floors down is the head of the residents' committee. I give it a week before she starts a petition to have you evicted.'

Daniel took a measured breath. He had never met another woman who had the same effect on his nerves as fingernails down a chalkboard. 'Know your biggest problem, babe?'

'Don't call me babe.'

'You underestimate my ability to be adorable when I set my mind to it. I can have the poodle lady baking cookies for me inside forty-eight hours.'

'Bichon.'

'What?'

'The dog. It's a Bichon frise.'

'It got a name?'

'Gershwin.' She rolled her eyes when she realized what

she was doing. 'And I'm afraid that's my quota for helpfulness all used up for the day.'

Bending over, he lifted the box at their feet, held it to his ear and gave it a brisk shake. 'You owe me a half-dozen glasses.'

'Sue me,' she said as she turned on her heel.

As he followed her down the hall Daniel's errant gaze lowered to watch the sway of her hips before he reminded himself who he was looking at. He had done some dumb things in his time but checking out Jorja Dawson was stupid on a whole new level. If she were the last woman left in the state of New York, he would take a vow of celibacy before getting involved with her. He even had a list of reasons why.

Casually tossing long locks of shining hair over her shoulder, she reached into her purse and turned to face him at the door to her apartment. 'I don't suppose you're considering showing your face at Sunday lunch once you've unpacked? Your mother would appreciate it.'

Number six on his list: *Family involvement*.

He looked into her eyes. 'Will you be there?'

'Never miss it.'

'Tell them I said hi.'

'Are you saying you don't go because I'm there?'

'Don't flatter yourself.' He moved the box in his arms to dig into a pocket for his key. 'If I rearranged my life around you I wouldn't be moving into an apartment across the hall from you. But just so you know—' he leaned closer and lowered his voice '—you'll move before I do.'

'You've never stayed anywhere longer than six months,' she stated categorically. 'And even then it was because the army sent you there.'

'Navy,' he corrected without missing a beat. 'And if there's one thing you should keep in mind about the Marines, it's that we don't give up ground.'

'I've lived here for more than four years. I'm not going anywhere.'

'Then I guess we'll be seeing a lot of each other.'

Something he could have done without, frankly. Not that he was likely to tell her, but she was the main reason he'd debated taking the apartment. She was a spy who could report back to the rest of the Brannigan clan in weekly discussions over a roast and cheesecake from Junior's. But as far as Daniel was concerned, if his family wanted to know how he was doing they could ask. When they did, he'd give them the same answer he had for the last eight years. With a few more recent additions to throw them off the trail.

He was fine, thanks. Sure it was good to be home. No, he hadn't had any problems settling back into his unit. Yes, if the Reserves called him up again he would go.

They didn't need to know more than that.

'You know *your* problem, Daniel?' She angled her head to the irritating angle she did best. 'You think your being here bugs me when to be honest I couldn't care less where you are, what you're doing or who you're doing it with.'

'Is that so?'

'Mmm-hmm.' She nodded. 'I'm not one of those women you can turn into a gibbering idiot with a smile. I just hope your ego can handle that.'

'Careful, Jo, I might take that as a challenge.'

There was a low burst of the same sparkling laughter he heard on the stairwell, making him wonder why it was he hadn't recognized it before. Most likely it was because she didn't laugh much when he was around. The second it looked as if she would, he'd say something to ruin her mood. He'd been good at that long before he'd started to put any effort into it.

'I had no idea you had a sense of humour,' she said with enough derogatory amusement to tempt him to rise to the bait.

Before he could, she opened the door to her apartment

and stepped over the threshold. She turned, her gaze sliding over his body from head to toe and back up again; her laughter louder as she swung the door shut.

Daniel shook his head. *Damn, she bugged him.*

Damn, he bugged her.

Leaning back against the door, Jo took a long breath and frowned at the fact her heart rate was running a little faster than usual. If taking the stairs in heels had that much of an effect, she might have to consider taking a gym membership.

Granted, a small part of it could probably be chalked up to frustration at her inability to hold a conversation with him without it turning into a verbal sparring match. But she hadn't been sparring alone. To say they brought out the worst in each other would be the understatement of the century.

Heading across the open-plan living area to her bedroom, she resisted the urge to hunt out fluffy slippers and a pair of pyjamas. If he drove her into ice-cream-eating attire on his first day there wasn't a hope she could survive the next three months. When her cell phone rang an hour later, she checked the name on the screen before answering.

'I still can't believe you've done this to me.'

A smile sounded in Olivia's voice. 'Which part? Moving out, putting you in a bridesmaid dress or telling Danny about the apartment next door?'

'I think you know what I mean,' Jo smirked sarcastically. 'I need a new BFF; my ideal man could have moved into that apartment if you hadn't mentioned it to Mr Personality.'

'Since when have you been looking for an ideal man? And anyway, he won't be there long. Short lease, remember?'

'If he renews I'm making a little doll and sticking dozens of pins in it.' Leaving the mirror where she had been staging a personal fashion show in front of hyper-critical eyes, she headed for the kitchen. 'But just so you know, he's determined I'll move first.'

Since everyone who had ever lived in Manhattan knew what their apartment meant to a New Yorker, she didn't have to explain how ridiculous it was for Daniel to think she was going anywhere. The apartment she'd shared with Olivia—and from time to time still did with Jess—was a few hundred square feet of space she could call her own.

She hadn't worked her butt off to end up back in a place she'd sworn she would never find herself again.

'You saw him already? Is there blood in the hall?'

'Not yet. But give it a few weeks and only one of us is leaving this building intact.' Lifting the empty coffeepot, she sighed at the heavy beat coming from across the hall. 'Can you hear that?'

She held the phone out at arm's length for a moment.

'My brother and classic rock go together like—'

'Satan and eternal torture?' Jo enquired.

'Probably not the best time to mention he's agreed to be in the wedding party, is it?'

'I am *not* walking up the aisle with him.'

'You can have Tyler.'

Good call. She loved Tyler Brannigan. *He* was fun to be around. 'I thought he was determined he wasn't wearing a monkey suit. How did you talk him into it?'

'Danny? The same way we got him to his niece's birthday party last month. Only this time Blake helped...'

Meaning he'd lost a bet. Jo smiled a small smile at the idea of Liv's new fiancé tag-teaming with the rest of the Brannigan brothers against one of their own on poker night. She spooned coffee granules into the percolator. *Go Blake.*

'How did he look to you?'

The question made Jo blink, her voice threaded with suspicion. 'Same as he always looks. Why?'

'I take it you haven't watched the news today.'

'No.' She stepped into the living room and pointed the remote at the TV screen. 'What did I miss?'

'Wait for it…'

The report appeared almost instantaneously on the local news channel. Unable to hear what was said without racking the volume up to competitive levels, she read the feed across the bottom of the screen. It mentioned a yet-to-be-named Emergency Services Officer who might or might not have unhooked his safety harness to rescue a man on the Williamsburg Bridge. If it was who she thought it was Jo could have told them the answer. The camera attempted to focus on a speck of arm-waving humanity among the suspension cables at the exact moment another speck closed in on him. For a second they came dangerously close to falling; a collective gasp coming from the crowd of gawkers on the ground. At the last minute several more specks surrounded them and hauled them to safety.

A round of applause sounded on the screen as Jo shook her head. 'You got to be kidding me.'

'I know.' Olivia sighed. 'Mom is climbing the walls. It was tough enough for her when he was overseas…'

'Did you call him?'

'He's not picking up.'

Jo glared at the door. 'I'll call you back.'

In the hall, she banged her fist several times against wood before the music lowered and the door opened.

'Call your mother,' she demanded as she thrust her cell phone at him.

'What's wrong?'

Ignoring what could have almost been mistaken for concern in his deep voice, she turned her hand around, hit speed-dial and lifted the phone to her ear.

'You're an inconsiderate asshat,' she muttered.

The second his mother picked up she thrust the phone at him again, snatching her hand back when warm fingers brushed against hers.

'No, it's me. I'm fine. Someone would have called you if

I wasn't. You know that.' He took a step back and closed the door in Jo's face.

Back in her apartment, she froze and swore under her breath at the fact he had her cell phone. Her life was in that little rectangle of technology. Hadn't stopped to think that one through, had she? Marching back to the kitchen, she lifted the apartment phone, checked the Post-it note on the crowded refrigerator door and dialled his sister's new number.

'He's talking to your mother now.'

'What did you do?' Liv asked.

'Told him exactly what I thought of him.'

'To his face?'

Picking up where she'd left off, Jo hit the switch on the percolator. 'I've never had a problem saying what I think to his face. You *know* that.'

There was a firm knock against wood.

'Hang on.' When she opened the door and her gaze met narrowed blue eyes, she took the phone from him, replacing it with the one in her hand. 'Your sister.'

Lifting the receiver to his ear, he stepped across the threshold. 'Hey, sis, what's up?'

Jo blinked. How had he ended up in her apartment? Swinging the door shut, she turned and went back to the kitchen. If he thought it was becoming a regular occurrence, he could forget it. She wanted to spend time with him as much as she loved the idea of having her fingernails pulled out. Glancing briefly at the room that seemed smaller with him in it, she frowned when he looked at her from the corner of his eye.

His gaze swept over her body, lingering for longer than necessary on her feet. What was *that*?

Jo resisted the urge to look down at what she was wearing. There was nothing wrong with her outfit. If anything, it covered more than the one she was wearing last time he saw her. Personally she loved how the high-waist black pants made her legs seem longer, especially when accompanied by a pair of deep purple, skyscraper-heeled Louboutins. Five feet six inches didn't exactly make her small. But considering the number of models towering over her like Amazons on regular occasions during working hours, she appreciated every additional illusionary inch of height. She shook her head a minute amount. Why should she care what he thought? What he knew about fashion wouldn't fill a thimble. His jeans were a prime example.

Judging by the way they were worn at the knees and around the pockets on his—

She sharply averted her gaze. If he caught her looking at his rear she would never hear the end of it.

The man already had an ego the size of Texas.

'It's my job,' he said with a note of impatience as he paced around the room. 'The line didn't reach... There wasn't time... I knew they had my back. You done, 'cos I'm pretty sure your friend has three more calls to make...'

Unrepentant, Jo grabbed her favourite mug and set it on the counter. She hoped Liv gave him hell, especially when he had just confirmed his stupidity. What kind of idiot unhooked his safety harness that high up? Hadn't he heard of a little thing called gravity?

Turning as the coffee bubbled, she leaned her hip against the counter and folded her arms, studying him while he paced. His jaw tensed, broad chest lifting and lowering beneath a faded Giants T-Shirt. He looked...weary? No, weary wasn't the right word. Tired, maybe—as if he hadn't slept much lately. Not that she cared about that either, but since Liv asked how he looked, apparently she felt the need to study him more closely than usual and once she'd gotten started...

Okay, so if injected with a truth serum she supposed she would admit there were understandable reasons women tended to trip over their feet when he smiled. Vivid blue eyes, shortly cropped dark blond hair, the hint of shadow on his strong jaw… Add them to the ease with which his long, lean, muscular frame covered the ground and there wasn't a single gal in Manhattan who wouldn't volunteer their phone number.

Not that they'd hold his interest for long.

'Well, you can stop. I'm fine. Don't you have a wedding to plan? Said I would, didn't I?' His gaze slid across the room. 'She'll call you back.'

Before he hung up, Jo was across the apartment and had swung the door open with a smile. But instead of his taking the hint, a large hand closed it, his palm flattening on the wood by her head. His body loomed over hers. If they'd been outside he would have blocked out the sun.

'We obviously need to talk,' he said flatly.

No, they didn't. Jo gritted her teeth together, rapidly losing what was left of her patience. She was contemplating grinding a stiletto heel into one of his boots when he took a short breath and added, 'Butting your pretty little nose into other people's business might be okay with other folks. It's not with me.'

'Try answering your phone and I won't have to.' She arched a brow. 'Is the fact your family might think you have a death wish so very difficult for you to grasp?'

'I don't have a death wish.'

'Unhooking your harness is standard procedure, is it?'

'Go stand on the chair.'

She faltered. 'What?'

'You heard me.'

When she didn't move, he circled her wrist with a thumb and forefinger. The jolt of heat that travelled swiftly up her arm made her drop her chin and frown as he led her across the room. Now he was *touching* her? He never touched her. If anything it had always felt as if there were a quarantine zone around her.

'What do you think you're doing?' she asked.

'Staging a demonstration…'

Her eyes widened when he released her wrist, set his hands on her waist and hoisted her onto an overstuffed chair. 'Where do you get off—? Don't stand on my furniture!'

Feet spread shoulder-width apart on the deep cushions of the sofa, he tested the springs with a couple of small bounces before jerking his chin at her. 'Jump.'

'What?'

'Jump.'

That was it, she'd had enough. She wasn't the remotest bit interested in playing games. What was he—*five*?

But when she attempted to get down off the chair, a long arm snapped around her waist and she was launched into mid-air. The next thing she knew, she was slammed into what felt like a wall of heat, a sharp gasp hauled through her parted lips. She jerked her chin up and stared into his eyes, the tips of their noses almost touching. What. The. Hell?

'You see…' he said in a mesmerizing rumble '…it's all about balance…'

Surreally, his intense gaze examined her face in a way that suggested he'd never looked at her before. But what was more disconcerting was how it felt as if there weren't anywhere they weren't touching. The sensation of her breasts crushed against his chest made it difficult to breathe, the contact sending an erotic jolt through her abdomen. How could she be attracted to him when she disliked him so much?

When she was lowered—unbearably slowly—along the length of his large body, Jo had no choice but to grasp wide shoulders until her feet hit the cushions. She swayed as she let go. For a moment she even felt light-headed.

'I knew what I was doing.' Stepping down, he lifted her onto the floor as if she weighed nothing.

Taking an immediate step back, Jo dropped her arms to her sides. Her gaze lowered to his chest. She should be angry,

ticked off beyond belief he had the gall to touch her and—
worse still—have an effect on her body. She liked her world
right-side-up, *thank you very much*, and if he knew what he
had done to her...

Folding her arms over heavy breasts, she lifted her chin
again. 'The giant footprints you've left on my sofa make us
even for the half-dozen glasses.'

'If you've got nothing better to do with your time than
talk about me to my family, try taking up a hobby.'

A small cough of disbelief left her lips. 'I have plenty of
things to fill my time.'

'Dating obviously isn't one of them,' he said dryly.

'Meaning *what*, exactly?'

'Meaning I may have forgotten why it is you've stayed
single for so long, but after an hour it's starting to come back
to me.' He folded his arms in a mirror of her stance. 'Ever
consider being nice from time to time might improve the
odds of getting laid?'

'Since when has my sex life been remotely in the region
of any of your business?'

'If I had to guess, I'd say around about the same time my
relationship with my family became yours.'

Reaching for the kind of strength that had gotten her
through worse things than an argument in the past, Jo smiled
sweetly. 'Try not to let the door hit your ass on the way out.'

'That's the best you've got?' he asked with a lift of his
brows. 'You're obviously out of practice.' He nodded firmly.
'Don't worry, we'll soon get you combat-ready again.'

Jo sighed heavily and headed for the door. She didn't
look at him as he crossed the room. But for some completely
unknown reason, just before he left, she heard herself ask,
'Don't you ever get tired of this?'

Where had *that* come from?

Daniel stopped, turned his head and studied her with an
intense gaze. 'Quitting on me, babe?'

She frowned when the softly spoken question did something weird to her chest. 'Don't call me babe.'

When he didn't move, the air seemed to thicken in the space between them. Stupid hormones—even if she was in the market for a relationship he was the last man—

'You want to negotiate a truce?'

She didn't know what had possessed her to ask the question in the first place and now he was asking if she wanted them to be *friends*? She stifled a burst of laughter. 'Did I give the impression I was waving a white flag? I'm talking about you, not me. You look tired, Daniel.' She pouted. 'Is the energy required pretending to be a nice guy to everyone else finally wearing you down?'

His eyes darkened. 'Questioning my stamina, babe?'

The 'babe' thing was really starting to get to her.

Taking a step closer, he leaned his face close enough for her to feel the warmth of his breath on her cheeks.

'Bad idea,' he warned.

Ignoring the flutter of her pulse, Jo stiffened her spine. Since childhood she'd had a code she lived by; one she still found hard to break, even for the tiny handful of people she allowed to occupy an equally tiny corner of her heart. Show any sign of weakness and it was the beginning of the end. The masks she wore were the reason she had survived a time in her life when she was invisible. At the beginning of her career they gave the impression professional criticism never stung. So while her heart thudded erratically, she donned a mask of Zen-like calm. 'Am I supposed to be intimidated by that?'

He smiled dangerously in reply. 'Keep challenging me and this is going to get real interesting, real quick.'

'Seriously, you're hilarious. I never knew that about you.' Raising a hand, she patted him in the centre of his broad chest. 'Now be a good boy and treat yourself to an early night. Can't have those good looks fading, now, can we?'

She flattened her palm and pushed him back to make enough room to open the door. 'What would we use to fool members of the opposite sex into thinking we're a catch if we had to rely on our personality?'

'You tell me.'

Moving her hand from his chest, she wrapped her fingers around a muscled upper arm and encouraged him to step through the door with another push. When he was standing in the hall and looking at her with a hint of a smile on his face, she leaned her shoulder against the door frame and angled her chin. Her eyes narrowed. It felt as if he knew something she didn't.

She *hated* when he did that.

'Admit it: you missed this.'

Lifting her gaze upwards, she studied the air and took a deep breath. 'Nope, can't say I did.'

'Without me around there's no one to set you straight when you need it.'

'You say that as if you know me well enough to know what I need.' She shook her head. 'You don't know me, Daniel. You're afraid to get to know me.'

'Really,' he said dryly.

'Yes, really, because if you did you might have to admit you were wrong about me and we both know you don't like to admit you're wrong about anything.' She glanced up and down the hall as if searching for eavesdroppers before lowering her voice. 'Worse still, you might discover you *like* me. And we can't have that, can we?'

Rocking forward, he lowered his voice to the same level. 'I don't think there's any danger of that.'

Jo searched his too-blue eyes, suddenly questioning if he even remembered how the war between them began. Looking back, she realized she didn't; what was it that made him so much more difficult to get along with than every other member of his family? Everyone got to a point where they started to try and make sense of their life. She was at peace with a lot of the things she couldn't change. But since Daniel was the only person she'd ever been immature around in her entire life, she couldn't help but wonder why. Apparently he wasn't the only one in need of a good night's rest.

She rolled her eyes at the momentary weakness. 'Whatever you tell yourself to help you sleep at night.'

'I sleep just fine,' he said tightly. 'You don't need to worry about me.'

'I wasn't—'

'Just do us both a favour and stay out of my business. If you don't, I might start poking my nose into yours.'

'I have nothing to hide,' she lied. 'Do you?'

'Don't push me, babe.'

She managed to stop the words *or what?* leaving her lips, but it wasn't solely the need to strive for maturity. There was something else going on; she could *feel* it. It was more than the chill in his gaze, more than the rigid set of his shoulders or the unmistakable edge of warning in his deep voice. What *was* it?

As if he could read the question in her eyes, Daniel frowned and turned his profile to her. A muscle tensed on his jaw, suggesting he was grinding his teeth together. But even if she had the right to ask what was wrong, before she had the chance, he turned away. When she ended up staring at his door again, she blinked and shook her head.

Well, Day One had been great.

She couldn't *wait* for Day Two.

CHAPTER TWO

'Is it just me or does coffee taste better when they make those little love hearts in the foam? It's funny the things that can make a difference in how we feel.'

JORJA DAWSON had breasts. Considering he was a man and she was a woman, part of Daniel's brain had to have always known that. Fortunately, in the past, they had never been pressed against his chest in a way that made them difficult to ignore.

It was the kind of intel he could have done without.

Judging by the way the tips of those breasts were beaded against the material of her tight-fitting top before she hid them beneath folded arms, the spark of sexual awareness had been mutual. She should just be thankful he had an honourable streak. If she ever found out he'd been as aware of her as she was of him, she would have a brand-new weapon at her disposal. One that, were she foolish enough to use it, would leave him no choice but to launch a counterattack with heavy artillery until she offered her unconditional surrender.

In terms of fallout, it would be similar to pulling the pin on a grenade he couldn't toss to a safe distance.

Number two on his list: *sister's best friend.*

Since every guy on the planet who didn't have long-term plans knew to avoid that minefield, it wouldn't matter if she wore nothing but lacy underwear to go with the shoes he would have been happy for her to wear to bed. She could have pole-danced for him and he would still resist the urge to kiss her.

'Whatever you tell yourself to help you sleep at night.'

When the echoed words led directly to the memory of the unspoken questions in her eyes, he pushed his body harder in the last block of a five mile run. She'd hit a nerve but there was no way she could know he wasn't sleeping. Or that he was sick of waking up bathed in a cold sweat, his throat raw from yelling. It had to stop before he did something stupid in work again or was forced to look for another apartment. He would damn well *make* it stop.

But distracting himself from the problem with thoughts of Jorja Dawson's breasts wasn't the way to go about it.

Slowing his pace to a walk, he shouldered his way into a busy coffee shop and pushed back the hood on his sweatshirt. After placing his order, he looked around while he waited for it to arrive, his gaze discovering a woman sitting alone by the windows. It was exactly what he needed: *another woman.*

Questioning if he was forming a fetish, he started his assessment with her shoes—a pair of simple black patent heels with open toes—before he moved up the legs crossed elegantly beneath the table to a fitted skirt that hugged her like a second skin. *Nice.* Continuing upwards, he was rewarded with a glimpse of curved breast between the lapels of a crisp white blouse as she turned in her seat. Then his gaze took in the smooth twist of dark hair at the nape of her neck in the kind of up-do that begged to be unpinned so she could shake her hair loose. She was even wearing a pair of small, rectangular-framed reading glasses to complete the fantasy.

But when she turned again, he shook his head. Used to be a time he was better at sensing the presence of the enemy.

She looked up at him when he stopped for a paper napkin at the condiment station beside her. 'Are you kidding me?'

'I can't buy a cup of coffee now?'

'You can buy it somewhere else.'

'This is the closest coffee shop.'

'You can have the one two blocks down. This one is mine.' She returned her attention to her computer screen. 'It's my work space every Monday, Wednesday and Friday morning.'

'I must have missed the notice on the door,' Daniel said as he pulled out the chair facing her and sat down. He smirked when she scowled at him. 'Good morning.'

After an attempt to continue what she was doing while he looked through the window at the steady build of people headed to their offices, she sighed. 'You're going to be here every Monday, Wednesday and Friday, aren't you?'

'Not a morning person, I take it.'

'This is your plan?' She arched a brow when he looked at her. 'You're going to be there every time I turn around until you wear me down and I move? Wow…that's…'

'Effective?'

'I was going to say adolescent. I can't tell you how reassuring it is to know the city is in the hands of such a mature example of the New York Police Department.'

When her fingers began to move across the keyboard again, Daniel realized he didn't have the faintest idea what she did for a living. He wondered why. Hadn't needed to know was the simple answer. Though it did kind of beg the question of why it was he needed to know *now*.

Know your enemy and know yourself and you could fight a hundred battles, as the saying went. With that in mind he took a short breath. 'So what is it you do anyway?'

She didn't look up from the screen. 'It's the first time you've been tempted to ask that question?'

'I don't have a newspaper to pass the time.'

'They're on a stand by the door.'

'It's an internet thing, isn't it?'

Long lashes lifted behind her glasses. 'Meaning?'

'You're one of those people who reports their every move every five minutes so the universe can know how much time they spend doing laundry.'

'Yes, that's the only thing people use the internet for these days.' She reached for her coffee. 'It's because working on-line isn't a physical job, right? Anyone who isn't lifting heavy objects or doing something with their hands instantly earns a low ranking on your Neanderthal scale of the survival of the fittest.'

'You might want to slow down on the caffeine intake. I think you're close to the legal limit already.'

Setting the cup down, she breathed deep and went back to work. 'I write a blog.'

'You can earn a living doing that?'

'Among other things,' she replied.

'What's it about?'

'Don't you have somewhere you need to be?'

'Nope.'

'Fine, then. I can play the "get to know me better" game until you get bored and leave. It shouldn't take long with your attention span.' Lifting her coffee again, she leaned back in her chair and looked him straight in the eye. 'I work for a fashion magazine and as part of my job I write a daily blog on the latest trends and the kind of things twenty-something women might find interesting.'

'You're as deep as a shallow puddle, aren't you?'

'Not everything is about the meaning of life. Sometimes it's more about living it. For some people that means finding joy in the little things.'

'Like spending money on the kind of clothes that will put them in debt?'

'Like wearing things that make them feel good.' She

shrugged a narrow shoulder. 'I assume it's how someone like you feels when they wear their uniform of choice.'

'I don't wear a uniform as a fashion statement.'

'You're saying you don't feel good when you wear it?'

'It's a matter of pride in what I do.'

'And doesn't that make you feel good about yourself?'

She was smart, but *that* he'd known. Trouble was she wasn't entirely right. 'It's not as simple as that.'

When her head tilted at an obviously curious angle, he lounged back in his chair. Since she'd given him the opening with the topic of conversation, he openly checked her out. 'I take it the librarian look is in vogue now.'

'It's better than the mugger ensemble you're wearing.'

Lowering his chin, he ran a large palm over the faded U.S.M.C. lettering on his chest. 'I've had this since basic training. It has sentimental value.'

'Wouldn't that suggest you have a heart?'

'Bit difficult to walk around without one.'

'As difficult as it is to survive without sleep?'

Daniel stared at her without blinking.

'Thin walls…' she said in a soft tone that smacked too much of sympathy for his liking before she shrugged. 'Try falling asleep without the television on, you might get more benefit from the traditional eight hours—especially if you're watching something with that much yelling in it. What was it—horror flick of the week?'

'You're worried about me again? That's sweet.' Feeling sick to his stomach at how close he'd been to humiliation, he got to his feet. 'Now I know you spend your nights with a glass pressed to the wall I'll try and find something on the nature channel with whale song in it.' When his trip to the door was halted by the brush of cool fingers against his hand, he looked down at her. 'What?'

Dropping her arm, she avoided his gaze and shook her head. 'Forget it.'

'You got something to say, spit it out.' He checked his watch. 'I have an appointment with my boss in an hour.'

The statement lifted her chin again. 'Because of what happened yesterday?'

'Hardly the first time I've had my ass hauled across the coals for breaking the rules.'

'You saved a man's life.' She shrugged her shoulders and looked away. 'I'm sure that counts for something.'

She was reassuring him?

'Not that you don't deserve it for doing something so asinine,' she added. 'You could have placed other members of your team in danger.'

That was more like it. It was also pretty much exactly what he expected to have yelled at him in an hour. 'We all do what we gotta do when the situation calls for it.' He lowered his voice. 'You should know that better than most.'

She looked up at him from the corner of her eye. 'And there you go thinking you know me again.'

'Did it ever occur to you that you don't make it easy for people to do that?'

'People who want to make an effort.'

'And how many tests do they have to pass before you talk to them like they have an IQ higher than a rock?'

'Stupid is as stupid does,' she replied with a smile.

'I take it back. If you're quoting *Forrest Gump* at me you obviously need more caffeine.' He placed an apologetic look on his face. 'I'd get you some before I leave but I'm not allowed to buy coffee here.'

'You're the most irritating person I've ever met.'

'See you later, babe.'

'Not if I see you first.'

'Still rusty.' He shook his head. 'Keep practising.'

* * *

'How's the challenge coming along?'

'Hmm?' Jo blinked at her erstwhile roomie, a second night of interrupted sleep catching up with her.

He must have moved his bed after the conversation in the coffee shop. The yelling had been further away but, like the first time, when it came it was torture. She doubted anyone could hear a human being in that much pain and not feel the effect of it emotionally.

'The challenge the magazine gave you?' Jess prompted. 'The one where you wear outfits from the centre pages to discover if different images change how people see you? I'm assuming that's why you look like a French onion seller today. Not that the beret doesn't work for you.'

Yes, she liked the beret. It was the kind of thing she'd have chosen herself, especially when it had a little touch of France to it. But since she wasn't supposed to wear anything the magazine hadn't chosen for her...

Lowering her chin, she idly rearranged the crumbs on her plate with the prongs of her fork. Wasn't as if he would tell her what had caused the nightmare if she asked him, was it? That part of not pushing the subject she got. Where it began to get weird started with the fact she hadn't felt the need to talk it through with his sister. His family cared about him. If he was struggling with something that happened when he was overseas they would want to help in any way possible. Not that he would make it easy. Trouble was she couldn't forget how the colour drained from his face when he'd thought she knew.

It felt as if the man she had known and disliked so much hadn't come home and someone new had taken his place. Someone she could empathize with and wanted to get to know better.

It was just plain *weird*.

'Earth to Jo...'

'It's going fine,' she replied as she speared another piece

of cake with her fork and popped it into her mouth. 'Mmm, this one...'

When she risked a brief glance across the table at the only person who knew when she was hiding something, Jo was relieved to find amusement sparkling in Liv's eyes.

'You said that about the last two.'

Jo angled her head. 'Remind me again why we're doing this with you instead of Blake?'

'Because he's more interested in the honeymoon than the cake we have at our reception.'

Fair enough. She reached for a second sample of chocolate cake. 'I lied, it's still this one.'

'You know chocolate is a substitute for sex,' Jess commented. 'It's an endorphins thing.'

'It's more than that,' Jo replied. 'You never have to worry if chocolate will call...it never stands you up...and it doesn't mind keeping you company during a rom-com on a Friday night.' She sighed contentedly as she reached for another sample. 'Chocolate is *better* than sex.'

Jess snorted. 'The hell it is.'

'She's young.' Liv nodded sagely. 'She'll learn.'

'If she tried having it occasionally she'd learn a lot quicker.'

'She scares them off.'

Jo waggled her fork in the air. *'Still in the room...'*

It wasn't her fault guys found her intimidating. With the kind of life experience that went beyond her twenty-four years, she was self-sufficient and hard-working with her focus fixed firmly on her career. If there was overtime available, she took it. Holidays people with family commitments didn't want to work, she volunteered. But regardless of her career, she was also very open about the fact she wasn't interested in getting involved, even if she wasn't prepared to explain why. Put everything together it was difficult for guys to envisage her needing them for more than one thing.

Though in fairness there were plenty of them who wouldn't see that as a problem.

There was a short debate on the merits of vanilla cream before Jess asked, 'How's our new neighbour?'

'In order to be "our" new neighbour wouldn't you need to be there more than once a week?' Jo smiled sweetly.

'You need reinforcements, you just have to yell.'

'You *like* Daniel.'

'Everyone but you likes Danny.' Jess shrugged. 'He is what he is and doesn't make any excuses for it. There's a lot to be said for that.'

'There's nothing hidden with him,' Liv agreed. 'When we were kids his bluntness got him into trouble, but honestly? We all kind of relied on it.'

Jo was beginning to wonder if anyone knew Daniel as well as they thought they did but she didn't say so out loud. She couldn't. Not without telling them there were *some* things he kept hidden.

'You could try taking the high road,' Jess suggested.

'I get nosebleeds.' Jo frowned.

The chocolate cake was gone and how had they got from the subject of her sex life to Daniel in the space of two minutes anyway? Apart from spending time with the friends it felt as if she hadn't seen much of lately, part of the appeal of the cake tasting had been the opportunity to take a break from him.

'You make a decision on the cake yet?' she asked.

'I'm swaying towards different layers of these three.' Liv pointed her fork at the emptiest plates.

'What's next on the list?'

'Flowers.'

The conversation swayed back towards wedding plans as they left the bakery and made their way past the public library to the nearest subway station. Jess glanced at the steps in front of the large Grecian columns where several men in helmets and bulletproof vests were gathered around one of the stone lions.

'Isn't that Danny?'

Oh, *come on*.

Reluctantly—as Olivia and Jess headed towards him and she lagged a step behind—Jo had to admit the uniform was sexy in a badass/mess-with-me-and-die kind of way. But then she'd always known Daniel had an edge to him. While he could attract women with a smile, he could make grown men cower with just a look. She had seen that look once. When was it? Tyler's thirtieth, which his younger brother deigned to make an appearance at? Yes, she thought that was it. A giant with a brain the size of a pea was foolish enough to manhandle his girlfriend within Daniel's line of sight. All it had taken was that *look* and a quietly spoken *'show the lady some respect'* and he'd backed down with a string of mumbled apologies. When it was over Daniel had simply continued what he was doing as if nothing had happened.

Jo wondered why it had taken seeing him in uniform for her to remember she'd been impressed by that.

'Ladies.' He nodded once in greeting.

Gathering herself together, she stepped forward and gave the answer everyone expected. 'Officer Moron.'

'Really?' he questioned with a deadpan expression. 'When I'm holding a gun?'

'What can I say?' She shrugged. 'Guess I must like living on the edge.'

While she cocked her head in challenge, he shot a brief downward glance at what she was wearing. It lasted less than a heartbeat, was immediately followed by a cursory blink and then his intense gaze locked with hers, leaving her feeling suddenly…exposed. Whether it was because she'd never noticed him looking at her before or because she was more aware of when he did, she didn't know. But neither option sat well with her. Particularly when she suspected the momentary sense of vulnerability she'd experienced stemmed from the sensation he knew she was remembering things she'd chosen to forget.

Jess chuckled at the interaction. 'Hey, Danny.'

He turned on the charm with the flick of an invisible switch. 'Hey, gorgeous.'

Jo inwardly rolled her eyes at her friend's reaction to his infamous smile before allowing her gaze to roam over the crowd. If she focused on something else, with any luck, she could try and pretend he wasn't there. All she needed was something to take her mind off—

Her stomach dropped to the soles of her strappy heels. 'I've got to go.'

'I thought we were going to look at flowers?'

Looking into Liv's eyes, she used the tone that translated into a hidden message. 'I'll call you later.'

'Okay.'

She didn't look at Daniel as she left, but Jo could sense his gaze on her as she merged into the crowd. How it made her feel helped explain the secret she kept from his sister. Only someone with a shadowy secret of their own could understand what it meant to bring it into the cold light of day. Gaze fixed on the figure she could see moving into the park, she shut down emotionally in preparation.

It was the only way she could deal with it.

The dream began a handful of hours before dawn. New faces—a different scenario—but the outcome was always the same. As he jerked back into reality, pulse racing and heart pounding, Daniel wondered why he was surprised at the latest additions. There was nothing the damn thing loved more than new material.

At times he swore he could hear scaly little demon hands being rubbed together with glee.

Grabbing the sweatpants on the end of his rack, he hauled

them on and swore when he stubbed his toe on a box on his way to the kitchen. As he reached for a light switch he froze. The second he yanked open the door to the hall she jumped and dropped her keys.

'Damn it, Daniel!' Jo exclaimed.

Leaning a shoulder against the door frame, he folded his arms across his chest. 'Late night or early start?'

It was a question that didn't require an answer; the outfit she had been wearing outside the library said it all. With considerable effort, he dragged his gaze away from the perfect rear poured into tight black trousers that ended halfway down her calves.

'Who made you the hall monitor?' Keys in hand, she stood up tall and turned to face him.

'I'm a light sleeper.'

A brief frown crossed her face before her gaze landed squarely in the centre of his naked chest. The former should have bugged him more than the latter, especially when it was dangerously close to the kind of look that had forced him to move apartments over the years. Instead he was more bothered by the jolt of electricity travelling through his body from the point of impact. The fact she continued staring didn't help. If anything it aided the flow of blood that rushed to his groin in response.

'Isn't it usually the guy who sneaks home after the deed is done?' he asked as if bringing up the subject of her sex life again would distract his misbehaving body. When her gaze lifted sharply, he changed the subject. 'Didn't occur to you that having a cop for a neighbour might involve him greeting you with his service weapon if he hears you creeping around in the dark?'

'The lights are on,' she argued.

'It's the middle of the night.'

'I don't have to answer to you.'

'Do you have any idea how much paperwork I'll have to fill out if I accidentally shoot you?'

She arched a brow. *'Accidentally?'*

'That's what I'll call it.'

A lump appeared in her cheek as her gaze searched the air. 'That's twice in twenty-four hours you've threatened to shoot me. I wonder if that's enough for a restraining order. Remind me to ask your sister.'

'He tossed you out of his apartment, didn't he?'

'What is it with this sudden obsession with my sex life?' She looked into his eyes. 'If I didn't know any better I might think it's been a while for you.'

Longer than he cared to admit, but it wasn't as if he could share a bed with a woman for long. He could guarantee his complete and undivided attention while he was there; took a great deal of pride in that fact. But when it came to leaving them satisfied, there was just as much emphasis on the word *leaving*. Preferably before he was dumb enough to fall asleep and risk making a fool of himself.

'Worried I might be lonely, babe?'

She scowled. 'Don't call me babe.'

'If the shoe fits…'

'You know by saying that you're saying you think—?'

'You don't have to like someone to think they're hot.'

'I… You…' When her mouth formed words that didn't appear she clamped it shut, took a short breath through her nose and snapped, 'What are you doing?'

Damned if he knew but the fact it had flustered her worked for him. 'Isn't he a little old for you?'

Something unreadable crossed her eyes before she blinked and lifted her chin. 'Who are we talking about?'

'The guy you were with in Bryant Park.'

'What guy?'

Nice try, but Daniel had never been known to give up that

easily. 'The one you argued with before you dragged him into the subway station.'

'You were spying on me?'

'You think when I'm dressed like that I'm supposed to ignore what's happening around me?'

She sighed heavily and turned away. 'I don't have the energy for this.'

'It's Wednesday. We'll pick it up in the coffee shop.'

'No, we won't.'

As her door opened he saw her shoulders slump as if she'd been putting considerable effort into disguising how exhausted she was and the proximity to home allowed her to relax. Most folks were the same at the end of a long day but Daniel knew it was more than that. If he hadn't, he would have got it when she glanced over her shoulder.

Long lashes lifted and for a split second what he could see in her eyes made him frown. He recognized it because he'd seen it in the eyes of men in combat and guys who'd been on the job as a cop for too long. Given no other choice he might have admitted he had been avoiding looking for it in his own eyes in the mirror of late.

If a person's eyes were really the windows to the soul, part of hers was close to giving up the fight.

He took a step forward before he realized he was doing it, compelled by the need to say something, but unable to find the words. With the men he had worked with they were never needed. There was a silent understanding, an empathy born from shared experiences. A nod of acknowledgement could say as much as a hundred words. Cracking jokes or discussing something inane was more welcome. But someone as full of life as Jo shouldn't—

When her door closed with a low click, Daniel made a snap decision. It wasn't as if he had much choice. If she was in trouble and his family knew he hadn't done something, they would make the roasting he got from his captain look like a weekend barbecue. Taking a long breath, he stepped back and closed the door. In order to prepare for battle he was going to need a few more hours of—hopefully uninterrupted—sleep.

Come daylight he was venturing into enemy territory.

CHAPTER THREE

'We all know a new outfit can lift our spirits. But how often do we look at the person wearing one and wonder if it's a hint of something bigger happening inside?'

'COME on, Jack, pick up.'

Jo rubbed her fingertips across her forehead to ease the first indications of a massive headache. Touching the screen to turn the phone off, she set it down on the table beside her computer. She was going to have to go over there. It was the only way she could be certain where he was.

Sighing heavily, she reached for her coffee cup only to frown at how light it was. If she was going to get a day's work done in half the time she was going to need a constant supply of caffeine.

'That his name, is it?'

The sound of a familiar deep voice snapped her gaze to another coffee cup being held out towards her. She blinked at the large hand holding it. 'Eavesdrop much?'

'Let's call it an occupational hazard.' Daniel rocked his hand a little. 'You want this or not?'

Her gaze lifted, lingering for a moment on his chest when she remembered what it had looked like naked: taut tanned skin over muscle and a six-pack to make a girl drool. Frowning at the memory, she moved further up until she was looking into too-blue eyes and asked, 'Why are you buying me coffee?'

'You looked like you could do with it,' he replied.

'You don't even know how I take it.'

'Since you're a regular, I surmised the guy behind the counter would. Turns out I was right.'

Jo's gaze lowered to the temptation as she weighed up the risk involved with accepting it. Not that he would wait for an invitation to join her, but apart from the fact she wasn't in the mood to get into a verbal sparring match with him—

'Your loss.' He shrugged. Setting it down on the opposite side of the table, he pulled out the empty chair and sat down.

'There are other tables in here, you know.'

Daniel didn't say anything, his steady gaze fixed on hers as he took the lid off his cup.

'We're not picking up where we left off last night, if that's what you're thinking,' she said.

'Technically it was this morning.'

'I've stayed out of your business.'

'Glad to hear it.'

'How about you return the favour and stay out of mine?' She smiled sweetly, determined not to look at the abandoned coffee on the table in front of him.

Daniel brought his cup to his face and took a deep breath. 'Nothing quite like a cup of Joe to kick-start the morning...'

While her eyes narrowed at the innuendo, he lifted his other arm and tapped the lid of the abandoned coffee cup with a long forefinger. 'Sure you don't want this? Seems a shame for it to go to waste...'

'What do you want?'

'Suspicious, aren't we?'

'I've met you.'

'And still not a morning person.' He inclined his head towards the cup. 'Another shot of caffeine might help.'

Jo fought the need to growl. She wanted that coffee so

badly she could taste it on her tongue. Despite her strong-willed determination to stop it happening, her gaze lowered to watch the tip of his forefinger trace an almost absent-minded circle around the edge of the plastic lid. It was one of the most sensual things she had ever seen, adding a new dimension to the temptation, which had nothing to do with caffeine. For a moment her imagination even wondered what the movement would feel like against her skin...

Reaching out, she waggled her fingers. 'Give.'

His hand moved, fingers curling around the cup to draw it back towards him. 'How much trouble are you in?'

Her gaze snapped up again. 'What?'

'Answer the question.'

'Why would you even care if I was in trouble?' She arched a brow. 'I'd have thought the idea of my body lying in an alley somewhere would have made your day.'

'Is there a chance that might happen?'

'Not like it would be the first time.'

'That's not funny.'

'No, but I have dozens of jokes from that period of my life if you need them.' Angling her chin, she pulled one at random from the air. 'You know the best part about dating a homeless chick? You can drop her off wherever you want.'

Daniel didn't laugh. 'Do you owe him money?'

'Owe who money?'

'Jack.'

'No.'

'Then what's going on?'

A short burst of laughter left her lips. 'I'm supposed to confide in you because you bought me a cup of coffee?'

'If you're in some kind of trouble, tell me now and—'

'You'll help?' The words came out more sharply than she intended and, when they did, she felt a need to soften them by adding, 'You can't, and even if you could you'd be the last person I'd go to for help.'

Great, now he was never going to leave it alone.

She might as well have dangled a scented cloth under the nose of a bloodhound.

'I'm aware of that,' he said flatly.

'Then why are you doing this?'

When she thought about it, she realized it was simply what he did. All she was to him was another citizen of the city of New York. One he probably felt pressured to help because of her connection to his family. She shook her head. She didn't need this, least of all from him.

'Tell me what's going on.'

The tone of his deep voice inflicted more damage than anything he'd said or done in five and a half years to get to her and she hated him for it. Mostly because the rough rumble was accompanied by a softening of the blue in his eyes, which made it feel as if he understood. As always when there was the slightest danger someone might see through one of her masks, Jo fought fire with fire. 'I'll tell you what's going on when you tell me why it is you can't sleep.'

To his credit he disguised his reaction better than he had before. But the second the softer hue of his eyes became an ice-cold blue, Jo regretted what she'd said. She shouldn't have thrown it in his face. Not to get at him. It was *low*.

'What makes you think I'm not sleeping?'

Jo wavered on an indecisive tightrope between familiar ground and freefalling into the unknown. 'You were awake in the middle of the night. And you still look tired.'

'I work shifts. And it's not always easy to adjust,' he replied without missing a beat. Stretching a long arm across the table, he set the coffee beside her computer. *'Your turn.'*

It would have been if he'd told her the truth.

'You've been a cop for, what, eight years now?'

'More or less.' He nodded. 'And can have your every move reported back to me if I have to. Your point?'

'How long does it take to adjust?'

'I was overseas seven months. I've been back one.'

'What happened when you were over there?'

'We got shot at.' Lifting his cup to his mouth, he took a drink without breaking eye contact. 'Avoid the subject all you want, but we both know if I want to find out what you're hiding I can do it without your co-operation. I'll start with Liv.'

It was an empty threat. Jo reached for the coffee he had given her. 'Your sister won't tell you anything.'

'Meaning she knows what it is.'

'Meaning she wouldn't betray a confidence.'

A corner of his mouth tugged upwards. 'You know my family. They'll organize an intervention if they think something is wrong. If you've never been on the receiving end of one I can tell you they're a barrel of laughs. Nothing beats a little quality family time when it's five against one. And I did say I'd *start* with Liv…'

'What makes you think you're not the only one who doesn't know?' she asked.

'If I am you've just made it easier for me.'

The message blood was thicker than water was clear. But she wasn't so far removed they wouldn't rally to her aid if she needed help. Jo had known that for years. They were all cut from a cloth threaded with loyalty, honour, integrity and at least a dozen other positive attributes she'd had absolutely no experience of in a family until she met the Brannigans. To Jo, they were everything a family should be. It was part of the reason she'd never understood why Daniel didn't appreciate them more. But the comment he made about family interventions explained a lot. It was an insight into why he was fighting his demons alone.

She lifted the coffee cup to her lips. 'When you speak to them you should mention the problems you're having adjusting to shift patterns. Your brothers might be able to offer some words of advice.'

'Maybe you should just tell me what's going on before this starts to get ugly,' he smirked in reply.

'We could do this all day.'

'Next round's on you. I take mine black.'

She sighed. 'You're not going to back down, are you?'

'Not my thing.'

'Which brings us back to why you need to know. Correct me if I'm wrong, but I don't think you've answered that yet.'

When he didn't reply, she set her coffee down and went back to work, answering some of the comments on her blog while he reached across to the next table and lifted an abandoned newspaper. They sat in silence for a while until Jo could feel a tingle along the back of her neck. Without lifting her chin, she looked up from beneath her fringe to discover him studying her intently. 'What?'

'Were the glasses a fashion accessory?'

She focused on the screen again. 'I get headaches if I work at the computer for too long.'

'So where are they?'

'I left them in the apartment.'

'Other things on your mind…' he surmised.

'I can make the print bigger on the screen if you're so concerned about my eyesight.'

There was another moment of silence, then 'Just out of curiosity, what look is it you're aiming for today?'

'It's called Gothic chic.'

At least that was what the magazine had called it. Of all the outfits she had worn during the challenge it was the most outlandish. But since she'd awoken with a need to face the world with a little more bravado and it was the kind of outfit that required confidence to carry it off…

'Might want to remember vampires aren't supposed to walk in direct sunlight before you step outside,' he said.

'Are you going to tell me to avoid holy water, garlic and crosses too?'

He nodded. 'And teenage cheerleaders with wooden stakes...'

Turning in her chair, Jo stretched her legs and pouted. 'You don't like the boots?' she asked as she looked at him. 'They're my favourite part.'

Daniel leaned to the side to examine them, a small frown appearing between his brows. 'You can walk in those things?'

'Women don't wear boots like these for comfort.'

Bending forward, she reached down and ran her hands over the shining leather, tucking her thumbs under the edge at her thigh and tugging as she lifted her foot off the ground. Her hair fell over her shoulder as she turned her head and smiled the kind of small, meaningful smile she'd never aimed at him before. 'Didn't we talk about how people wear things because of the way they make them feel?'

The glint of danger in his eyes was obviously intended to make her stop what she was doing before she was any deeper in trouble. *Foolish man.* He really didn't know her at all.

Daniel gritted his teeth together as she repeated the motion with her hands on her other leg and tossed her hair over her shoulder as she sat up. When she smiled across the room, his gaze followed her line of vision to the barista who was smiling back at her.

The one who had known how she took her coffee.

The second his gaze shifted, Daniel glared at him. But the guy who immediately went scurrying back to his coffee beans wasn't the source of his annoyance. Neither was the fact his plan to purposefully avoid looking at her feet as he approached the table had backfired on him, though, with hindsight, forewarned might have been forearmed. What got to him was how well her diversionary tactic had worked.

There wasn't a male cell in his body that hadn't reacted to those boots and the strip of bare skin below another sinful short skirt. He had spent every moment since he'd sat down with her consciously stopping himself from looking at the

straining buttons on her black blouse and once again she'd
got him with footwear. But if she thought it would distract
him from his target for long, she was mistaken.

He was a Marine, for crying out loud; the phrase 'courage under fire' was as good as tattooed on his ass.

Watching with hooded eyes, he saw her slide her computer
to one side before resting her elbow on the table. Setting her
chin in her palm, she leaned forward, feigned innocence with
a flutter of long lashes and asked, 'Something wrong?'

'You done?' he questioned dryly.

'Done with what?' Amusement danced in her eyes. 'You
might need to elaborate.'

If he didn't know what she was doing, he might have been
tempted to play along. But if he did, Daniel knew what would
happen. He would play to win.

'Tell me what's going on.'

When she rolled her eyes, he set his forearms on the table
and leaned closer, his gaze locked on hers while he waited.
Up close she did have pretty spectacular eyes. A little large
for her face maybe, but they were so deep a brown it was
difficult to tell where the irises began.

He'd never noticed that before.

After studying him for a long moment, she lowered her
voice. 'What if I told you it was private?'

'I'd tell you I won't share it with anyone else,' he replied
in the same low tone.

'Why should I believe you?'

'A man is nothing without his word.'

'Tell me why you need to know.'

He wondered when she thought he'd handed over control of the negotiation. Dragging his gaze from mesmerizing eyes, he considered what to tell her. She was right; they
could do this all day. Until one of them bent a little nothing
would ever change. Of course knowing that meant he had

to ask himself if he *wanted* their relationship to change. But since it felt as if it already was…

'I recognized what I saw in your eyes before you closed the door this morning.' He looked into them again as he spoke. 'I've seen it before.'

'What did you see?' she asked in a whisper, forcing him to lean closer to hear her.

'Resignation.'

She stared at him and then blinked as if trying to bring him into focus. 'If you knew me as well as you like to think you do, you'd know…'

'I'd know?' he prompted as she frowned.

'Why I don't want to talk about it.' Dropping her palm from her chin, she leaned back and swiped a strand of hair behind her ear. 'People keep secrets for a reason.'

When she reached for her computer, Daniel felt the lost opportunity as keenly as he sensed she wasn't just talking about herself. But if she knew the reason he wasn't sleeping, why hadn't she pushed the advantage? Lifting his coffee cup, he looked out of the window and questioned what he would have done if their places had been switched. The exact same thing was the honest answer. It was what he was doing already. He knew there was something wrong and was giving her an opportunity to tell him. In turn, she was refusing to open up.

Number four on his list: *nothing in common*.

So much for that one…

'You want another coffee?' she asked.

He looked at her cup from the corner of his eye. 'What did you do, inhale it?'

'Figured if you were planning on digging in, I may as well top up on supplies.'

Since sitting still for any amount of time inevitably led to reminders of his sleep deprivation, Daniel shook his head.

'Think I'll head down to the station and look through mug-shots for Jack before my shift starts.'

Jo sighed heavily as he stood up. 'Dig all you want. I'm telling you now there's only one way you'll find out and that avenue isn't and never will be open to you.'

'And there you go challenging me again…'

Taking a step forward, he set his coffee cup hand on the table by her computer and the other on the back of her chair. As her chin lifted he leaned down, smiling the same kind of small, meaningful smile she'd aimed at him when she'd pulled her little stunt with the boots.

'When I want something, nothing gets in my way,' he told her in a deliberately low, intimate tone. 'Make it difficult for me, I'll want it more and work twice as hard to get it. So feel free to keep doing what you're doing, but don't say you weren't warned.'

When her eyes widened he leaned back, lifted his hands and turned away. She could interpret his words any way she liked. If she came to the conclusion he was talking about more than the secret she was keeping, he wasn't certain she'd be wrong.

Gothic chic was either going to be the death of her or get her arrested. For starters, her feet were killing her, but if she'd known she would end up walking the length and breadth of her old neighbourhood looking for Jack she would have changed. When it came to getting arrested, she might be grateful. Even if the charge was related to standing still for too long on a street corner as she tried to get her bearings, she could take comfort from the knowledge she was safe in the back of a squad car. When she looked over her shoulder and thought she could see someone moving in the shadows, her pace quickened.

If Daniel saw where she was, she could imagine the lecture she'd get on personal safety. There hadn't been a single

set of flashing lights she hadn't looked at twice or an echo-
ing siren that hadn't turned her head. Every time it happened
she would find herself thinking of him and what he'd said
before he left the coffee shop.

He couldn't possibly have meant what she thought he
meant. But what was worse was her reaction. Instead of
being outraged or angry or laughing in his face, she had
been turned on, *big time*. Her breath had caught, her pulse
had skipped, and her breasts had ached. She'd even had to
press her thighs together. No man had ever had such an immediate erotic effect on her.

That it was *him*?

A shiver ran down her spine, forcing her to look over her
shoulder again. Ridiculously she wished he were there, but
in her defence she was starting to get seriously creeped out.
The presence of a six-foot-two police officer could have made
her feel better, even if they argued every step of the way.

Taking a breath, she shook off her paranoia. She could
take care of herself. Harsh truth was, until Liv, the only person she had ever been able to depend on was herself.

Tugging the edges of her long black coat together in an attempt to hide what she was wearing, she stopped and looked
up at the neon sign before opening the door. If Jack wasn't
in there she swore he was on his own this time.

'Well, *hello, gorgeous*! You want to come over here and—'

Jo glared at the man who stepped in front of her. 'I have
pepper spray and I'm not afraid to use it.'

She didn't, but he didn't know that.

'Mikey, leave the lady alone,' a voice called from behind
the long wooden bar. 'She's *way* out of your league.'

She smiled when she got there. 'Hey, Ben.'

'Hey, Jo,' he beamed in reply. 'How's my best girl?'

'She's good. He here?'

Ben nodded. 'Back room.'

'He run up a tab?'

'Made a deal with you, didn't we?'

'Thanks, Ben.'

Jo made her way through the crowd, regretting how much time it had taken to get through her work so she could begin the search. If she'd got away earlier, not only would it not be dark outside, it wouldn't have got to the point where she had to attempt to carry Jack home. She sighed heavily.

Ahead of her was the inevitable debate about whether or not it was time to leave. She knew exactly what he would say, the excuses he would make, how many random strangers she would have to be polite to while she gritted her teeth. It was a scenario she'd experienced countless times.

No matter how far she managed to get from her past, she could always rely on Jack to remind her of her roots.

The thought of Daniel being able to do the same thing...

She rolled her eyes. *Enough with the thinking about him, already!* It was getting to the point where it felt as if he were with her wherever she went.

Daniel leaned back against the wall and frowned. Any guilt he might have felt about tailing her had disappeared within five minutes of arriving at her destination.

What the hell had she got herself into?

Judging by the number of times she did a double take at passing police vehicles or lifted her chin when she heard a siren, it wasn't anything good. He waited to see if she spent the same two minutes in the eighth bar as she had in the other seven. When she hadn't reappeared after twenty minutes he was contemplating crossing the street. Then the doors opened.

The man staggered back a step as she helped him get his arm into the sleeve of his coat. He had obviously been in the bar for a lot longer than she had. Placing his arm across her shoulders, she wrapped one of hers around his waist before steering him along the sidewalk.

What was she doing with a guy like that? Apart from the fact he was twice her age, she shouldn't be with someone she had to go searching for in bars. Daniel was disproportionately disappointed in her considering their relationship. He might have made several digs about her sex life, but a woman who looked as she did, who was as smart as she was and could turn a guy on the way she'd—

Grinding his teeth together hard enough to crack the enamel, he thought about finding the nearest subway station. Why should he care what she was doing when she plainly didn't? But before he could leave the man staggered sideways, slammed Jo into a wall, and something inside Daniel snapped.

Reaching a hand beneath the neck of his sweater to pull out the badge hanging on a chain around his neck, he checked for traffic and jogged across the street. Once he'd caught up to them, he set a firm hand on the man's shoulder and pushed him back a couple of steps. 'NYPD—you, over there.' He pointed a finger at Jo. 'And *you* stay right where you are.'

Her eyes widened in disbelief as he turned towards her. 'You're following me now?'

'Cop, remember? What did you think I was gonna do?'

'You're *unbelievable*!'

'And you're damn lucky you had a bodyguard for the last couple of hours considering where you are. What the hell did you think you were doing coming out here alone? Do you have any idea the number of shots-fired reports we get from this neighbourhood?' When her companion staggered forward, Daniel glared at him from the corner of his eye. 'I wouldn't if I were you, buddy. I'll tell you when you can move.'

The man lowered his chin, his words slurred. 'You can't talk to my—'

'Shut up, Jack,' Jo continued, frowning at Daniel. *'How dare you—?'*

'Oh, I dare,' he replied. 'What's more, you're going to tell me exactly what's going on and you can do it here or you can do it at the nearest precinct. *Your call.*'

'You can't *arrest me.*'

'Wanna bet?'

'I haven't *done* anything!'

Daniel nodded. 'Okay, then, I'll arrest him. Seems to me he could do with a night in a cell to sober up.'

When he turned, a hand gripped his arm.

'Don't.' The dark pools of her eyes sparkled as she let go of his arm, gathered control and lowered her voice. 'I just need to get him home.'

Going to the nearest precinct felt like the better option to Daniel, but something stopped him. She was still angry—he could feel it radiating from her in waves—but he had been in enough situations to know when there was more to the story. It made him wish for better light so he could search for a clue. If he'd had a flashlight he would have aimed it at her eyes.

Taking a long, measured breath, he gave *good old Jack* the once-over while making his decision. 'How far?'

'Four blocks.'

'And you were planning on carrying him there?'

'Daniel—'

'You lead the way, I'll bring him, and when we get there we're having a long talk.'

'You *think*?'

Crossing his jaw as he watched her turn and walk away, Daniel reached out a hand and grabbed hold of a sleeve before the man next to him fell over. 'Throw up on me and I'm still arresting you.'

The journey took twice as long as it would if all three of them had been able to walk in a straight line. Most of which an impatient Daniel spent shutting the guy down every time he tried to start a conversation. Once they got there Jo ushered the older man into the bathroom of a sparsely furnished one-bed apartment. Daniel paced the small living room while he waited. Then something caught his eye.

Stopping in front of a set of bookshelves, he reached out and picked up a framed certificate that had been presented to Jorja Elizabeth Dawson for perfect attendance in the sixth grade. Lifting his chin, he then discovered a photograph propped against a pile of books further in. It was a younger Jack standing in front of what looked like a Ferris wheel, his arms around a skinny kid with long, dark pigtails and a huge grin that revealed two missing front teeth.

Daniel realized his mistake in an instant and the second he did felt like the biggest jackass on the face of the earth. Glancing at the hall from the corner of his eye he found Jo watching him in silence.

'He's your father,' he said with certainty.

'Yes,' she replied.

'You should have told me.'

'If I'd wanted you to know, I would.'

After placing the certificate back on the shelf, he turned towards her and shoved his hands into the pockets of his jeans. 'How long has he been drinking?'

'It would be quicker to tell you when he wasn't.' She shrugged a shoulder and damped her lips with the tip of her tongue as she avoided his gaze. 'It's worse one month than the other eleven. This just happens to be that one month.'

When she looked at him, Daniel experienced a sensation he'd never felt before. Inwardly squirming didn't quite cover it. Not when it felt as if his internal organs were trying to crawl away and find a place to hide.

He took a deep breath. 'Jo—'

The door behind her opened and Jack appeared, taking an uneven path from wall to wall until he stopped and swayed on his feet. As Jo turned towards him Daniel stepped forward and freed his hands.

'I owe you an apology for the misunderstanding.' He held out an arm and shook her father's hand. 'Daniel Brannigan. I'm a friend of your daughter.'

There was a soft derisive snort from his right. 'Bit of an exaggeration, don't you think?'

'I was worried about her.'

'Since when?'

Considering he deserved whatever she tossed at him, Daniel sucked it up and looked her straight in the eye as he added, 'I thought she was in some kind of trouble.'

'Not my Jo,' Jack slurred. 'She's a good girl.' He dropped his chin and squinted. 'You're a cop?'

'Yes.' Swearing inwardly, Daniel reached for his badge to tuck it away. 'Emergency Services Unit.'

'People need help they call 911.' Jack grinned. 'Cops need help they call the ESU.'

'That's us.' Daniel nodded.

'You want a drink?'

'Good luck finding one,' Jo interjected. 'I cleaned you out last night.'

Daniel shook his head. 'No, thank you. I'm just gonna see your daughter home safely if that's okay with you.'

'That won't be necessary,' she said tightly.

He looked into her eyes again, his tone firm. 'It's the least I can do.'

'Okay.' She smiled sweetly. 'We can have that talk you wanted on the way back. While I get Jack settled, how about you have a *good long think* about the things you want to say to me?' Scrunching her nose in mocking delight, she placed an arm around her father's waist. 'Come on, Jack, let's go.'

As they left Daniel dropped his head back, stared at the ceiling and took a deep breath.

It was going to be the longest subway ride of his life.

CHAPTER FOUR

'Don't you love it when you find something you forgot you bought in the sales? It's true what people say: look closely and you might be surprised what you find.'

'You know what this reminds me of?'

Daniel's gaze shifted to tangle with hers from across the compartment. 'We're talking now, are we?'

'No. I'm talking. You don't get to speak yet.'

As the train slowed he glanced out of the window behind her. Jo had a sneaking suspicion he was counting down stations in the same way an imprisoned man might mark off the days of his sentence on a wall. But if he thought she'd forgive him because he'd had the sense to keep his mouth shut since they left Jack's place…

'It reminds me of the number of times I've heard my best friend complain about her brothers running background checks on every guy they ever saw her with.' She angled her head in thought. 'I used to think it was funny, now not so much…'

'We were looking out for her,' he said flatly.

'Why can I hear you?'

When he breathed deep and exhaled in a way that suggested he was running out of patience, she folded her arms.

'Beats me why you didn't put one of those tracking anklets on her.'

'If you mean a tether, we considered it.'

It was exactly the kind of opening he should have known not to give her. 'What gives you the right to interfere in other people's lives?'

'It's called concern.'

'It's called harassment.'

'I'm not going to apologize for following you.'

Her brows lifted. *'Excuse me?'*

'While you were giving me the silent treatment, I had time to think it over.' Stretching long legs, he spread his feet a little wider and shrugged. 'Considering where you ended up I'm not sorry I followed you. From now on, if you have to go there at night, I'll be going with you.'

Oh, no, he wouldn't. 'I'm not your sister.'

'I'm more than aware of that,' he replied tightly.

'You can't tell me what to do.'

'No. But I can tell you how it is.' Briefly glancing at the other passenger in the compartment, he brought his legs back towards him. Leaning forward, he rested his elbows on his knees and lowered his voice. 'Something happens to you I won't have it on my conscience. It's crowded enough already.'

When she frowned he leaned back, his profile turned to her and the muscle working in his jawline. Jo wanted to stay mad at him, still hadn't forgiven him and refused point-blank to be told what she could and couldn't do. But at the same time—much as she'd prefer if it didn't—the insight softened her a little, especially when telling her had obviously cost him something. It was his way of making amends, wasn't it?

Drumming her fingers on her arm, she tried to decide if she felt like being reasonable. On the one hand, she'd been conscious of the fact she was alone at night in an area where she was likely to get mugged, or worse. On the other, she'd grown up in that neighbourhood, could take care of herself and wouldn't have been so creeped out if she hadn't been *followed*.

It wasn't that she didn't appreciate the concern for her safety—as unexpected as it was coming from *him*—or that he'd apologized to Jack and shown respect to a man many people would at best have pitied. It was just, if she was honest, it stung that he knew.

Everyone had things they weren't comfortable with other people knowing. As he'd been when he told her something he had to know would leave her more curious than before...

Darn it, she really didn't want to be reasonable.

But he wasn't *forgiven*.

As the train rocked along the tracks she thought about the last time she had to deal with someone who'd learnt about Jack. Difference was with Liv she had been in control what she chose to divulge. Liv hadn't pushed. Liv would never have followed her. But even after six years and with a traumatic experience to bond them together, Jo knew she held things back. It was what she'd done for the vast majority of her life. She didn't think she would ever change.

As he looked out of the window behind her Daniel stood up. 'We change here.'

Jo grimaced when she got to her feet. Determined not to reveal she was suffering in the name of fashion, she grabbed hold of one of the vertical metal bars while they waited for the train to stop and the doors to slide open. Walking with an enviable ease to the other side of the platform, Daniel looked over his shoulder and stilled.

'What's wrong?'

'Nothing,' she answered through gritted teeth.

Turning, he studied her feet while she focused on the bench in the middle of the platform. 'Would kill you to ask for help, wouldn't it?'

'They're blisters, not broken legs.'

As she sat down he turned to check the tunnel for signs of an oncoming train before pushing his hands into the pockets of his jeans. Since he took a good long look at her boots when he turned around, Jo leaned back on the bench and allowed her coat to fall open. Resting her palms on the plastic beams, she crossed her legs. When his gaze shifted sharply to the extra inches of thigh the move revealed, she stifled a satisfied smile. Knowing she could get to him had always helped, even if the rash impulse to discover just how much she affected him in *that way* probably wasn't the best idea she'd ever had.

With a single blink, his gaze snapped to attention and locked with hers. She jerked her brows in reply.

It earned an almost imperceptible shake of his head. 'I'd heard women don't wear boots like that for comfort.'

Goosebumps erupted on her skin when she heard his voice. Deeper, rougher, it conjured up the kind of thoughts her self-preservation was forced to stamp with 'CENSORED' before her imagination provided the images to go with them.

'These boots definitely weren't made for walking,' she mused as she rocked her crossed leg.

'Begs the question of why you didn't think to change.'

Jo angled her chin. 'You have a real problem with what I'm wearing, don't you? Don't tell me you prefer your women in crinolines. Carrying a parasol maybe? Someone who will drop her handkerchief and swoon as you pass by...who'd be *eternally grateful* when you come to her rescue...'

'You really gonna go there?'

It would seem so. She shrugged a shoulder. 'It's half your problem with me. Neanderthal man meets modern-day, independent woman and he doesn't know what to do with her.'

The smile was slow, deliciously dangerous and steeped in heady sensuality. 'You have a lot to learn about a man like me, babe. When you're ready to find out, let me know.'

She would have called him on the 'babe' thing again if the

invitation hadn't felt like six-foot-two of blue-eyed Death by Chocolate. But there was no way she was letting what he'd said slide. 'Is that supposed to scare me?'

'What makes you think that's what I was aiming for?'

'You think I can't take you on and win, Danny?'

He smiled again. 'I'm Danny now, am I?'

An answering smile formed on her lips before she realized it was happening. When it came, his smile grew.

Thought he had the upper hand, did he? Well, in that case, she might have to give in to the impulse to find out how much of an effect she had on him. Rationalizing it as the need to know what she had to work with, she lifted her chin, stretched her arms out to her sides and arched her back. Purposefully pushing her breasts forward in a way she knew would strain the buttons on her blouse to the breaking point, she parted her lips and took a deep breath. To top it off, she shook her hair off her shoulders, caught her lower lip between her teeth and let it slowly slide free. When she was done she looked at him.

A burning gaze travelled the length of her body and back up. It lingered on her breasts for a moment, making them swell against the decadent lace of the bra she'd forgotten she had until she went digging in a drawer for the kind of underwear befitting her outfit.

When his gaze found hers, he nodded. 'You do like living on the edge.'

There it was again: that deeper, rougher voice…

It was beyond tempting to ask what he planned to do about it. But before she could weigh up the risk the opportunity was lost to the sound of an oncoming train.

Stepping over to the bench, he held out a large palm and jerked his chin. 'Up.'

Jo stared at his hand as brakes squealed and a rush of air whispered strands of hair against her cheeks. But she couldn't back down, not after her show of sexual bravado. Sliding her palm across his, she felt the same jolt of heat travel up her arm she had experienced the first time he touched her. By the time long fingers closed around hers and he tugged her to her feet, it was spreading over her entire body. Drawing a long breath, she avoided his gaze by looking over a wide shoulder at the train. As it stopped she took a tentative step forward and grimaced when her ankle turned.

The grip on her hand tightened. 'You got it?'

The question raised a small smile. 'You tell me.'

Threading his fingers through hers, he stepped forward to push the release button on the train doors. Holding them open with his arm to allow her to step inside, he leaned closer to inform her, 'I know what you're doing.'

'Do you?' she questioned over her shoulder as the doors slid shut behind them.

'Mmm-hmm,' he replied with a firm nod, his too-blue eyes darkening as she turned and looked up at him.

When the train jerked into motion, she rocked forward, a low gasp hauled through her lips when her breasts made contact with his chest. If it felt as good as it did with layers of clothing between them the thought of skin-to-skin was enough to form a moan in the base of her throat. She tried to take a step back, but a long arm wrapped around her waist, holding her in place as he lowered his head and spoke into the hair above her ear.

'How close do you want to get to that edge?'

Jo's heart kicked against the wall of her chest, her blood transformed into liquid fire.

Turning his hand against hers, he made enough room to rub his thumb against her palm, the long fingers of his other hand splayed possessively over her hip. 'If you're curious what's on the other side, I can take you there.'

His low, rough voice made the words *take you* sound like a promise of ecstasy. A distant whispered *yes* echoed inside her and made her slide her lower body across his. When

Daniel tensed in response and the fingers on her hip pressed tighter, a surge of feminine empowerment washed over Jo.

Turning her head, she lifted her chin and spoke in an equally low tone into his ear. 'This would be working a lot better if you *stopped talking.*'

'Someone who makes a living with words should know what they can do.' The hand at her hip slid dangerously close to the curve of her rear. 'Only takes a few and our minds fill in the rest.'

Jo took a breath of clean, masculine scent and resisted the urge to rub her cheek against his jaw. 'It takes the *right* words.' She smiled languidly. 'And I think you'll find I have the advantage there...'

'Lay a few on me and we'll see.'

What they were doing should have felt weird but didn't. If anything it felt like an adult version of the 'fun' she needed to draw her back from the past. She glanced at what she could see of his face. Instead of fighting her attraction to him the way she knew she should, she decided to enjoy the ride. Just for a little while. She'd never had a male playmate before but it was an exhilarating experience. Especially with a Marine-turned-cop she could go toe-to-toe with on equal terms...

The movement of the train rocked their bodies while his thumb traced circles in her palm. His head moved a fraction, the millimetres of space between her cheek and his jawline tingled with static. 'Chickening out on me, babe?'

As if. Lowering her voice to an even more intimate level, Jo carefully enunciated each word. 'Anticipation...longing... *desire*...' Lifting her hand, she set her palm on his upper arm, curling her fingers around the dark material of his jacket and the tight muscles underneath. 'Heighten...intensify... quicken...' She sighed breathily as her hand moved up his arm and across a shoulder to the rigid column of his neck. 'Tighten, strain, grasp, reach—' She gasped, held her breath for a second and exhaled on a blissful sigh. 'Release.'

'Jorja.'

The growled warning made her lean back so she could see his face. What she'd done might have ended up doing more for *her* than she'd planned, but it was obvious it had done just as much for him. His eyes were as dark as storm-filled skies. Waves of the kind of tension that could only be eased with physical satisfaction rolled off his large body, seeped into hers, and made her ache for the satisfaction to be mutual. When his gaze lowered to her mouth, it elicited an unintentional swipe of her tongue in preparation.

She wondered what kissing him would feel like…

Okay, that was enough. She really needed to snap out of it. She couldn't hand him a victory like that when he would never let her forget it. Daniel equalled arch nemesis. Any *other* guy who had the same effect on her equalled candidate for the kind of sex she obviously needed more than she'd realized.

Dropping her chin, she looked up at him from beneath heavy lashes. 'I have another word for you…'

'Trouble?'

'Disappointment. I'd learn to live with it if I were you.' Adding a sweet smile, she dropped her hand from his neck to his chest and pushed as she looked over a shoulder. 'Look at that, it's our stop. Doesn't time fly when you're having fun?'

Stepping onto the platform ahead of him, Jo held her arm out to her side to regain her balance before she let go of his hand. Without warning he yanked her back towards him. As she stumbled a large hand wrapped around the back of her neck and the world as she'd known it came swiftly to an end.

Firm lips crushed hers in a bruising kiss that rocked her back on her heels. She squeaked in surprise, blinked wide eyes and grasped hold of his shoulder to stay upright. But when he canted his head, she closed her eyes. As it always had in every other aspect of their relationship, her competitive streak kicked in. He couldn't light up her body like a roman candle on the fourth of July without repercussions.

Absorbing the intensity of the kiss, she bundled it into a fist in her chest and tossed it back at him. Her lips parted. His tongue pushed inside, duelling with hers. It was angry and messy and uncoordinated and without a doubt the hottest kiss she'd ever experienced and Jo *hated him* for that. She didn't want to spend the rest of her life comparing every kiss to one and have the rest fall short. Not when it was obviously meant to punish her for what she'd done to him on the train. He just couldn't back down and let her win one, could he?

He didn't know *how*.

When the kiss ended as suddenly as it began, Jo's eyes snapped open, the sound of ragged breathing making her realize the train had left. She stared up at him. To her surprise he didn't look at all victorious. If anything he looked as angry as she felt. Without saying anything, he released her, turned and headed straight for the exit. She gritted her teeth and followed him to give him a piece of her mind, frowning with frustration when her feet wouldn't allow her to match his long stride. As he reached the turnstiles Daniel glanced over his shoulder. When he turned and marched right back towards her, Jo froze. What was he—?

She was swept off her feet before she had time to figure out what he intended. 'Put me down!'

'We go at your pace we'll be lucky to get back before Thanksgiving,' he said tightly.

'I can still *walk*.'

'The expression on your face that suggests it's over broken glass says otherwise. Stop squirming.'

Lifting her higher, he turned sideways and pushed his leg against the turnstile. His gaze was fixed firmly ahead, his jaw set with determination; she knew there wasn't a hope in hell he would put her down any time soon. *Fine, then*, he wanted to carry her for two blocks, he could go right ahead. She hoped he strained something while doing it. Sighing heavily, she placed an arm around his neck. When they hit the sidewalk and a passer-by smiled, she pointed at her feet.

'Blisters,' she explained before the woman got the idea what she was seeing was anywhere in the region of romantic.

'Ah,' the woman said in reply.

Having started, Jo found the prospect of talking to random strangers infinitely preferable to talking to *him*.

'Lovely evening.'

'Yes, it is.'

She swung her legs a little and tried to ignore the fact a large hand was wrapped around her knee. 'Enjoying the city?'

A couple wearing the obligatory 'I heart New York' T-shirts lifted their gazes from the map they were poring over. 'Yes, thank you. It is wonderful.'

'Wait. Go back,' she demanded before craning her neck to look at the tourists. 'Are you lost?'

Daniel sighed impatiently before turning, remaining silent while the couple held the map out. Jo offered directions and tips for places to visit. Smiling brightly, she then enquired where they were from and said she hoped they enjoyed the rest of their trip. She even got to try out some conversational—if a little on the rusty side—French. They were a lovely couple.

'You going to do this the whole way back?' Daniel asked as he started walking again.

Jo ignored him and looked around. 'Hi, how are you?'

'I'm good, how are you?'

'I have blisters.' She pouted.

When he finally shouldered his way into the foyer of their apartment building, he headed for the stairs.

'If we'd taken the elevator you wouldn't have to carry me any more,' she pointed out after the second flight.

'We rescued two people stuck in an elevator yesterday. It occurred to me at the time if I ever got stuck in that ancient contraption the guys would never let me hear the end of it.'

'Two people stuck in an elevator.' She pondered. 'I wonder what they did to pass the time...'

'Two *men* stuck in an elevator.'

'I wonder what they did to pass the time...'

He glanced at her. 'Forgiven me for following you yet?'

It didn't escape Jo's attention he hadn't mentioned any forgiveness for kissing her. But either way her answer was the same. 'No.'

Eight flights later and—to her great irritation—without Daniel so much as breaking a sweat, they were at her door.

'Key,' he ordered.

'You can put me down now.'

'*Key.*'

Tugging on the strap across her breasts, she removed her arm from around his neck to unzip the small bag at the end of it and dig for her keychain. Lifting it in front of his face, she jangled it for effect. 'Happy now?'

'I will be when you put it in the door.'

'And how exactly am I supposed to do that from way up here?' When he simply leaned forward, she muttered under her breath, 'Planning on tucking me into bed too?'

'That an invitation?'

'I can't believe you just said that out loud.' Swiping her hair behind her ear, she focused on getting the key into the lock and turning it.

Daniel carried her inside, waited for her to hit the light and then kicked the door shut. Unceremoniously dumping her on the cushions of the sofa, he sat down on the chest she used as a coffee table and raised a palm. 'Give me your foot.'

Jo wriggled up the cushions, swiping her hair out of her eyes. 'You're kidding me, right?'

'I'm not leaving till I see how much damage you've done. Give me your foot.'

'Sure you're not trying to sneak a feel of the boots? You know you can get therapy for that, right?'

'It's amazing to me you've lived this long without someone strangling you.' He waggled long fingers. 'The sooner you give me your foot, the sooner you can get rid of me.'

'Well, when you put it *that* way…' Raising her foot, she set it on his knee, her pulse thrumming while she waited for the opening she needed to slap him.

Daniel ran his palms along her boot. When he got to the top Jo pressed her lips together at his expression. He didn't deserve a smile for the hesitation.

'Problem?' she asked.

'No.'

'The zip is at the back.'

'I know.'

'Do you also know in order to take it off you're going to have to touch me?' Seemed to Jo it hadn't been an issue before he dumped her on the sofa.

His gaze lifted and locked with hers as a heated palm set against the back of her thigh drew a gasp through her lips.

'It doesn't go any higher than that,' she warned.

A low rasp sounded as he opened the zipper. Slipping long fingers under the edge, he pushed the leather down her leg and lifted her foot with his other hand. As the boot descended his hand smoothed over her skin, distracting her from the sharp sting at her ankle with an excruciatingly gentle caress.

Despite how mad she was at him for kissing her, there wasn't an inch of her body that didn't ache for that touch. But since it was Daniel, she still couldn't wrap her head around it. Her heart hammered erratically. Had he changed or had she? Heat seeped into her skin and travelled back up her leg. When had it happened? *How* had it happened? Her pulse sang with intense pleasure. Who cared when it felt so good?

Setting the boot aside, he lowered his gaze and ran his palm up her calf. Jo swallowed in an attempt to dampen her dry mouth, caught her lower lip between her teeth to stop another moan from escaping. She really should put a stop to what he was doing. In a little minute, she vowed she would.

Leaning to the side as one hand smoothed over the top of her foot, he used the long fingers curled around the back of her calf to lift her leg so he could look at her ankle. 'Is the other one as bad as this one?'

That deep, rough voice again…

Jo silently cleared her throat. 'Probably.'

Oh, good, now *her voice* sounded different.

'Let me see,' he demanded.

One. More. Minute.

Setting her foot on the floor, she raised her other leg and held her breath while he repeated each slow move. With a second opportunity to take everything in, the way his hands touched the leather felt reverent, the way they smoothed over her skin more decadent. She should have been prepared for the effect it had on her knowing what he could do with a kiss, but she wasn't. Jo doubted anything could have prepared her for what felt like tenderness, especially from a man like him. If he added tenderness to a kiss, would it still be as hot? She should *not* want to know the answer to that question as badly as she did.

'You have a first-aid kit?' he asked.

'Mmm-hmm.'

His gaze lifted, a smile forming in too-blue eyes when she didn't say anything else. 'Want to tell me where it is?'

'Bathroom.'

'I'll find it. You stay here.'

Once he stood and walked away, Jo hauled a breath into

her aching chest and exhaled it with puffed cheeks. Time seemed to be slipping from her grasp along with her sanity. That minute was bound to be up. Her eyes widened when she remembered what the first-aid kit was sitting beside in her bathroom cabinet. He'd better not think *that* was an invitation.

But when he reappeared, Daniel simply set the first-aid kit on the chest, sat down and reached for her foot again.

'I can do that,' Jo said when she found her voice.

Selecting what he needed, he ripped open a small white package and curled a hand under her calf. 'As appreciative as I am of your footwear, you should consider flats from time to time. This might sting.'

'*Ouch!*'

A corner of his mouth lifted as he reached for a Band-Aid. 'They're blisters, not broken legs.'

'And now he's funny again.' She frowned as he swapped one foot for another. 'Could you get a move on?'

'Almost done.'

She gritted her teeth. After he smoothed a second Band-Aid in place, she snatched her foot back.

''*Night, Daniel,*' she hinted heavily.

He pushed upright, but instead of standing straight he leaned over her, his gaze locked with hers. Jo's eyes widened when he laid his hands on the cushions at either side of her hips. What was he doing? Her stupid, errant tongue damped her lips in preparation as his face angled over hers.

He couldn't seriously... She shouldn't want... She lifted her chin an unconscious inch. But instead of kissing her, Daniel stilled and a devastatingly sexy smile formed on his mouth.

''Night, babe,' he said in *that* voice.

Jo blinked as he crossed the room and she heard the door

close. Now he knew what he did to her, he would use it every opportunity he got. Reaching to her side for a throw cushion, she pressed it tight to her face and screamed in frustration.

CHAPTER FIVE

'Much as I adore summer, I love the rich colours of the fall. Breathe deep right now and even in the city you can sense the approach of something spectacular.'

SHE started it. Hardly the most mature response, but, since he had spent every waking hour replaying the hottest kiss of his life over and over in his mind, Daniel didn't care.

Even the fact she was who she was didn't make a difference any more, particularly when he took into consideration how he'd reacted to the box that had greeted him directly at eye level as he opened her bathroom cabinet. It wasn't that he didn't think it was sensible to have them there. It wasn't as if she'd been unfaithful to him or he'd been a saint since the day they met either. But for a split second it had been hard to resist the urge to bring the box back with him, toss it in her lap and demand she told him who she'd used them *with*.

As it was, he had slammed the cabinet shut and swore there was only one man she would be using them with in the not-too-distant future. She might have unwittingly caught his interest with a pair of red stilettos, but she knew exactly what she'd been doing on the train. Just as he knew exactly what would happen if she discovered he was attracted to her and used it against him.

Unfortunately, when he'd rolled out the heavy artillery, he'd discovered he was dealing with guerilla warfare. She'd hit him hard and fast, disappeared behind the woman who'd bugged him with very little effort, then hit him again when he attempted a temporary ceasefire by doing something *nice*.

Those boots had a lot to answer for.

He liked to think he'd launched an effective counterattack before he'd left her apartment. She was angry he had kissed her. Most likely wasn't any happier she'd kissed him back. But she had made it obvious she was open to it happening again. The way Daniel saw it, considering there hadn't been a whole heap of finesse involved in their first kiss, his next step was to right that wrong.

Taking a stealth approach, he entered the coffee shop by the door furthest from her table. While waiting for his order he did a little reconnaissance. She wouldn't catch him out the same way twice. Starting with her hair—since it was as far as he could get from the danger zones—he discovered a sleek ponytail. His gaze moved lower to discover a white dress and what looked like a low scooped neckline—needed to be ready for that one, then. Lower still and he frowned as he wondered if there was a worldwide shortage of skirt material. When he remembered how soft her skin was at the back of her thighs he tore his gaze away. He wasn't convinced he could handle what was on her feet. Not when his body was primed for a lot more than a kiss.

'Figured it was too good to last,' she muttered as he set a coffee cup beside her computer and sat down.

'Miss me?'

'How about you disappear for more than thirty-two hours and we'll see if it helps any? A decade might do it.'

Easing the lid off his cup, Daniel stared at her and waited to see how long it would take for her to crack under pressure. To her credit she lasted longer than he expected. In the end it took a yawn she covered with the back of her hand to break the silence.

'Did you go see Jack again last night?' he asked. Since she didn't reply, he took it to mean 'yes'. 'I thought we'd agreed you wouldn't go there alone.'

'Don't remember agreeing to that.'

He reached out a hand. 'Give me your cell phone.'

The demand lifted her gaze. 'Am I grounded, too?'

'No,' he replied. 'But you're about five seconds away from a curfew. *Phone.*'

'What do you want it for?'

'I'm going to put my number in it. The next time you have to go there at night, you'll call me.'

'No, I won't.'

Daniel rested his elbow on the table while he took a drink of coffee.

'You can hold your hand there till you get cramp. I'm not giving you my cell phone.' She focused on her screen again. 'I don't need a bodyguard and you work shifts. Not like you can drop everything and come running to my aid if you're working at night, is it?'

'If I'm on duty, Tyler will go with you.'

'Again, don't need a bodyguard—but if I did I have Tyler's number on speed-dial.'

Daniel frowned when his mind decided to make a connection between his brother and the box in her bathroom cabinet. 'I'm not kidding around here, Jo. Give me the damn cell phone.'

The sharp tone lifted her gaze again. Whatever it was she discovered when she searched his eyes softened her voice. 'I can take care of myself.'

'Humour me,' he replied with more control.

'Not something I'm usually prone to do…'

'Make an exception this time.' He used a beckoning motion with his fingers. 'If it helps tell yourself just because the number is there doesn't mean you'll use it. We can argue that one later.'

Angling her chin, she pouted and thought it over. 'I don't suppose you'll consider going away once the number is there?'

'Not till I drink my coffee.'

She brightened. 'Can you drink it faster?'

'Any particular reason you're uncomfortable with me being here?' he enquired.

Avoiding his gaze, she shrugged. 'No more than usual.'

Daniel smiled. Now he knew what to look for, she sucked at lying. 'If you don't give me your cell phone I can make this cup last all day.' He purposefully lowered his voice. 'There's a lot to be said for taking things slowly…'

Frowning, she lifted a pile of papers, produced her cell phone and reached out to drop it in his hand. Wasn't prepared to risk touching him, was she?

His smile grew. 'See now, was that so difficult?'

'Pushing your luck,' she said as she looked at her screen and lifted her fingers to the keyboard.

Daniel entered his number, sending a text to his phone so he had hers. When he was done, he held his hand up, her phone dead centre in his palm.

She glanced at it. 'You can put it on the table.'

'You want it, come get it.'

'With lines like that I can see how you're the equivalent of catnip to the ladies…'

With a small sigh, she reached out. When her nails scraped against his skin, every muscle in his body jerked in response. His fingers closed around hers. Full lips parted, her breasts rising on a sharp inward breath as she looked into his eyes.

'Tell me you'll call me,' he said.

'You said we'd argue about that later.'

'That was a couple of minutes ago.' When she tugged on her hand he tightened his hold. 'Say it.'

'Daniel—'

'Why did I follow you, Jo?'

She arched a brow. 'You know if you keep reminding me what you did it's not going to help me forgive you any quicker.'

'Why do you think I did it?'

'You told me why.'

'That I wouldn't have it on my conscience if anything happened to you—still true—but I told you that *after* I saw where you were.' Relaxing his hold a little, he brushed his thumb over the soft skin on the back of her hand as he lowered his arm to the table. 'Now ask yourself why I followed you in the first place.'

'It's what you do.' Her gaze was drawn to the movement of his thumb.

'Not with everyone. Not enough hours in the day…'

'Not what I meant. You're a cop and a Marine, your whole life is based on a sense of duty towards others. You figured you had to get to the bottom of it because of my relationship with your family.'

Daniel nodded. 'That's what I told myself.'

She slipped her hand free and lifted her chin. 'It's not that I don't appreciate your concern—'

'Concern would be part of it,' he allowed as he set her cell phone down. 'Same kind of concern you felt for my safety when I unhooked my harness on the bridge that day.'

'That wasn't concern for your safety.' She scowled. 'It was incredulity at your stupidity and anger at your lack of consideration for the people who care about you.'

'You'd have been fine if I fell.'

'Wasn't the fall that would have done the damage, it was hitting the water that would have got you killed.'

Daniel kept pushing. 'You'd have been okay with that?'

'Of course I wouldn't have been okay with it. You *know* what it would have done to your family.'

'But you'd have been fine.'

'I'm not having this conversation any more.' Grabbing her cell phone, she slammed it down on the pile of papers before flicking her ponytail over her shoulder and aiming the scowl at her screen. *'Go away.'*

Daniel took a breath. 'We may have been arguing since the day we met, but we've known each other for almost six years. It's difficult *not* to care about someone who's been there that long. Something happens, you notice the gap left behind. Might take a decade for you to miss me, but I like to think you'd get round to it if you knew I wasn't coming back.'

Fine-boned fingers stilled on the keyboard as her gaze focused on an invisible point in the air a couple of inches above the screen. During the following silence Daniel tried to figure out if he regretted what he'd said. He probably should, if for no other reason than the fact it explained her second appearance in his nightmare.

'Why are you telling me this?'

The question was asked in so low a voice he almost missed it in the ambient noise of the coffee shop. While he reached for the lid of his cup, he considered the answer.

Getting them to the point where they both accepted the inevitable conclusion of their volatile attraction was one explanation. It was certainly the one at the forefront of his mind. But the fact he wasn't firing on all six cylinders might have had something to do with it. If he hadn't been driven by the need to pick up where they'd left off, he could have tried grabbing some sleep before he went looking for her.

Too late now...

It was bound to happen at some point. Focus was the first thing to go, swiftly followed by hand-to-eye coordination; the latter of which probably explained the reason he was having so much damn difficulty putting the lid back on his cup.

He frowned at it in annoyance.

Resisting the need to yawn when she yawned had been more than a natural reflex. It was a reminder his body could only run for so long on adrenalin alone. His work provided regular top-ups. As did spending time with Jo with the electricity of their attraction constantly crackling in the air between them. But strip those things away and Daniel was bone-tired, off his game and a shadow of his former self.

'You asked if I ever got tired of this…' It was as close as he could get to the heart of the problem without giving too much away. 'Maybe you were right.' When he managed to slot the lid into place, he stood up. 'On that note, since I covered half of someone's shift this morning and I'm back in at four, I better get some sleep.'

He was at the door when she stopped him.

'Danny?' She turned in her seat to look at him.

'Yes?'

'If I need help, I'll call.' The concession was followed by a lift of her brows to indicate it was his turn.

'You won't go there alone at night.'

She shook her head. 'I can't make that promise.'

'You'll change before you go and you'll be *careful*.'

'I'm always careful.'

'Flat shoes, loose clothes.' He waved a hand up and down. 'The kind that cover you from head to toe…'

The smile in her eyes wavered on her lips. 'Should I put a bag over my head?'

'A ski-mask would probably help you blend in more easily in that neighbourhood.' When she rolled her eyes, he fought a smile of his own. 'First sign of trouble, you call.' He nodded his head at her cell phone. 'My number's under *H*.'

'I've said I…' She blinked. 'Why is it under *H*?'

Cutting the smile loose, he reached for the door. She was checking her phone as he passed the window, what looked like a burst of laughter leaving her lips before she shook her head.

He might have ended up saying more than he'd intended, but he was definitely gaining ground.

Of course she would notice if he were gone for ever. Did he really think she was so detached from her fellow human beings?

She would probably have got mad at him if he hadn't caught her off guard. It was his voice to begin with—the words laced with sincerity. But what got to her was the slight tremor to his hand when he put the lid back on his cup. While he frowned at it, she studied him: the lines of tension at the corner of his eye, a slight hint of grey beneath his tan. Added to the secret she kept for him, they lent a deeper meaning to the question she'd asked the night he moved in. Jo would dare anyone not to stop and think about how they felt after that. Even if they weren't convinced they wanted to know the answer.

Closer to the top of the well of memories she'd chosen to forget, she remembered how he looked the last time she saw him before he went overseas. It was one of the rare occasions he'd made an appearance at Sunday lunch and the last time he sat in his place opposite her at the table. She remembered how laid-back he'd been while an underlying note of tension in the room had said everything about his family's concern for his safety.

Had she taken the time then to think about what it would be like if he hadn't come home? If the chair opposite hers had remained empty for as long as his father's before the family moved around the table? She would like to think she had. But she couldn't remember worrying beyond keeping an eye on the news reports, wondering where he was if anything happened to a Marine. It was the same thing anyone would have done if they knew someone in a war zone. But when it came down to it she'd assumed how she would feel if something happened to him would be attached to his family. If they were hurting, she'd hurt for them. Grieving, she would feel grief for their loss. Part of the trouble was she'd never been able to remove his family from the equation. She still didn't.

But for the first time she thought about how she'd feel if it was just Danny and Jo and then Danny wasn't there any more...

She *would* miss him. Who would she argue with the way she argued with him? But it couldn't be anything more. Jo knew all about the gap a person could leave behind and what it did to people who loved them. She could never allow herself to care about someone so much she disappeared into that hole.

Not after she'd watched it happen to someone else.

Having spent a good portion of her time in the coffee shop staring into space, she returned to the apartment. An entire day at home during the week was a rare luxury when more often than not she was running all over Manhattan by mid-afternoon. So after checking in with the office to discuss images for her assignment and catch up on the gossip, she settled down with some freelance work. The first time she thought she'd heard something, her gaze lifted from the computer. Shaking her head when she found nothing but the usual city soundtrack running in the background, she went back to work.

There it was again.

Pushing back her chair, she walked to her bedroom door where it was muffled, but louder. When it stopped, she held her breath and waited, heart twisting the second it started again. It was no less torturous during daylight hours than it was at night. Did he *ever* sleep? She glanced across the room at the large clock on the kitchen wall. It was almost three. Hadn't he said he had to be in work at four? The dilemma made her waver on her feet. He would *hate* that she knew.

A text to her 'Hot Neighbour' wouldn't be any better than

turning up at his door. Either way there had to be a reason she knew he was there and might be late for his shift. She could say she hadn't heard his door close but then he might think she was listening for his movements. Up until, well, a few hours ago, if she was honest, she'd rather have poked red-hot needles in her eyes than allow him to think that.

The second hand on the clock sounded a 'Don't. Let. Him. Be. Late.' with each tick in the silence broken by an agonized cry from beyond the wall.

Okay, that was it. She was going over there.

When the door yanked open, the sight of a naked muscled chest made her breath catch—forcing her gaze sharply upwards. What she found didn't have any less of an effect, albeit in a different, more worrisome way. His eyes were red, his jaw was tense and he frowned as he blinked her into focus.

It did something to her heart she had to ignore.

Lifting an arm, he rested a large hand on the edge of the door by his head. 'What?'

'You said you had to go to work at four.' She held out a mug. 'You're going to be late.'

A brief glance at his wristwatch was swiftly followed by a low expletive before he lifted his gaze and his eyes narrowed. 'How did you know I was still here?'

'I didn't,' she lied with a shrug. 'Thought I'd check…'

His frown darkened. 'You shouldn't do that when you're not any good at it.'

When she didn't say anything, his gaze searched the hall. Suddenly slicing through the air, it slammed into her, driving the air from her lungs.

'Since the first night?' he asked grimly.

Jo nodded.

A shadow crossed his eyes, revealing something she never expected to see. Coming back at him had always been easy when he was cocky and in control; tossing jibes the equivalent of bouncing pebbles off an armoured tank. He knew who he was, what he was capable of, was calm under pressure and unwavering when it came to what he wanted. She supposed there had always been something she found sexy about that, even when they argued.

But the tiny crack in his control, the mere hint of a vulnerability that made it feel as if he desperately needed something he hadn't found? It echoed deep inside Jo where she kept her own vulnerability hidden. Unlikely as it would have once been, she wanted to be the one to give him that missing something. She just wished it didn't feel as if the one thing he needed was the one thing she could never give him.

'Thanks for the coffee.' He reached out and took the mug from her hand. 'And the wake-up call.'

Jo took a step forward when he stepped back. 'Danny—'

'Don't.' A large hand nodded once in a 'calm down' move she suspected wasn't solely for her benefit. He took a deep breath, crossed his jaw, looked anywhere but at her, and then used his forefinger to emphasize each word. 'Just...*don't*...'

When the door swung shut in her face, Jo stared at it for a long time without moving. Whatever headway they had made in the coffee shop disappeared like early morning mist. Crossing the hall had been a mistake. Why couldn't she have left it alone?

The answer was simple: She *did* care.

Probably more than she should.

'Damn it!' Daniel threw his gloves at the truck.

'We can't save them all,' his partner said flatly.

'Two inches, Jim.' He demonstrated the distance with a gap between his thumb and forefinger. 'All I needed was *two inches* and I could have put pressure on the artery.'

'And once we'd freed his leg he could have gone into shock and died anyway. You know that. Let it go.'

Except he couldn't let it go, could he? Not so far away there were scaly little hands rubbing together in glee. Didn't take a genius to work out what he would see in his night-mare the next time he closed his eyes, did it? Daniel's gaze sliced through flashes of red and blue neon reflected on rain-soaked surfaces to the collapsed wall several ESU squads had been working on. The man who had died had gone out for a carton of milk, walked past an abandoned building at the wrong time and that was that. Game over.

When they had arrived at the scene Daniel had volun-teered to crawl inside a narrow space deemed unsafe for a paramedic. He'd been there for three hours as he talked to the guy to try and keep him conscious while they dug him out. Mike Krakowski, forty-three, wife, two kids, somewhat ironically—possibly because the universe had a sick sense of humour—a construction worker. Mike had lost conscious-ness a half-hour ago and when his pulse stopped beating there hadn't been a damn thing Daniel could do about it.

His partner slapped his shoulder. 'Walk it off, brother.'

Pacing around the emergency vehicles, he tried to roll the tension out of his shoulders and neck. He *hated* that Jo knew. The thought she knew because she had heard him yell-ing made it worse. There was only one thing he wanted to see in her eyes and sympathy wasn't it. So much for gaining ground...

He wondered how the residents' committee felt about sub-letting on a short-term lease. Moving from hotel to hotel the way he had after he landed stateside wasn't an option Daniel favoured, having tried it. Wasn't as if he could spend a night on someone's sofa either and he sure as hell couldn't go home. A handful of hours in the room he shared with Tyler growing up and keeping his distance from his family would have been a complete waste of effort.

Not for the first time, he missed the respite of being over-seas. Turned out the scaly-handed little sucker hadn't liked the background noise of bullets firing and exploding shells. Frightened of losing its plaything, Daniel assumed, since a lack of sleep could have led to a fatal error a lot faster out there. So while many of the men he shared sleeping quarters with would toss and turn on their racks, he'd slept like a baby. He'd been paying for it with interest ever since.

Heading back to the truck to help pack away the equipment, he decided avoiding Jo for a few days was the only option open to him. Much as beating a retreat went against every instinct the Marine in him possessed, he didn't have a choice.

The next time he faced her, if there was so much as a *hint* of sympathy in her eyes…

Remind him of how much less a man he felt compared to the way he used to be and he'd be honour-bound to prove her wrong. Strong as she was, he doubted she was ready for the full force of that, especially when it had been held inside him for so long. The thought of what was involved got his juices flowing and reminded him how primed he was for more than a kiss, but she was still *Jo*. He wouldn't do that to her. The very fact he reacted the way he did to her knowledge was dangerous enough.

Let her get any closer…

Bending down, he picked up his gloves and tucked them in his back pocket. *Game over.*

CHAPTER SIX

'There's nothing quite like rearranging a closet to make a girl feel she's in control. The smallest of moves can have a domino effect on our lives.'

WHAT did he think he was going to do—assume a new identity and move to another state? It was something he might want to consider, because by Monday—when he hadn't shown up in the coffee shop—Jo was good and mad at him.

It felt as if her body were tuned in to him; didn't matter what time of night it was or how quiet he was on his way into the apartment. Once her subconscious assumed he was restless, she got restless. Before she knew it, she was blinking into the darkness, waiting. When the yelling came, as it inevitably would, for Jo it felt worse than before.

Each night he was shredding a jagged little slither off her heart and his answer to the fact she'd kept her mouth shut to protect his secret was to *avoid her*?

She was going to kick his ass.

Halfway up the second flight of stairs in their apartment block, she heard a familiar deep rumble. Picking up the pace, she arrived—a little breathless and ready to spit nails—at the top of the sixth flight. Rounding the corner she discovered he was talking to the head of the residents' committee.

Heart thudding erratically and unable to blame it *entirely* on the stairs, she gave him the once over. As usual he was in the prerequisite jeans, presently matched with a dark round-necked sweatshirt and a charcoal sports jacket. She had seen him in similar clothes a hundred times, so what was it that suddenly made him more of a feast for the eyes than before? No one had the right to look that good when they hadn't slept in as long as he hadn't so her singing pulse could just *shut up.*

She glanced at the bag in his hand. 'Are those cookies?'

'Freshly baked…' Daniel smiled his infamous smile at their neighbour who behaved liked a giddy schoolgirl in response.

'Danny confessed to a sweet tooth,' she explained. 'Have to look after our boys in uniform when they're away from home, don't we?'

'Yes.' Jo nodded. 'It's a long way to Staten Island.'

Daniel leaned forward and turned on the charm. 'Still too far away from home baking, right, Agatha?'

She patted his arm. 'Let me know when you run out.'

'You're too good to me.'

'Yes, she is.' Reaching out to ruffle woolly white ears, Jo crooned, 'Isn't she, Gershwin?'

When her hand dropped Daniel replaced it with his.

'Bye, little guy. Look after your mom.' As their neighbour left, he tilted closer to her and lowered his voice. 'Did I mention this is the second batch she's baked for me?'

Jo didn't say anything as they waved goodbye but as soon as the door down the hall closed, she swung on him. Aiming a brief glance over a wide shoulder, she grabbed a fistful of dark sweater and backed him into the elevator.

'Stay,' she ordered before turning to close the cage door.

Just once was it so much to ask the stupid thing to close without having an argument first?

'Need a hand with that?' a deep voice enquired.

'Don't make me hurt you.' It took several angry attempts

to achieve her goal before she pressed the button and turned on him again.

Leaning against the back of the cage, he reached into the bag before tilting it towards her. 'Fresh-baked cookie?'

'I hope you choke on them.' She folded her arms over her breasts. 'How long are you planning on avoiding me?'

'That's what I'm doing, is it?' Taking a bite of toffee pecan, he leaned his head back and frowned as he studied the creaking mechanism above their heads.

Jo was too mad at him to play games. 'You think you're the only one losing sleep since you moved in across the hall? But did I say anything? No. What I did was make sure you weren't late for work. Thanks for that, Jo. No problem, Daniel. That's all it would have taken. We could have gone on pretending I didn't know. Instead you asked, I answered and now you've decided to punish me for not lying when *apparently* I wasn't any good at it to begin with.'

When his gaze locked with hers, a warning sparkled in his too-blue eyes.

She sighed. 'Our apartments wrap round the building. We share a wall. How long did you think you could hide it?'

Daniel tossed what was left in his hand back into the bag. When his gaze lifted to the appearance of their floor—despite the speed of the elevator—Jo could sense she was running out of time. What would it take to get through to him?

'Why do you think I didn't say anything, Danny?'

It was a question she would prefer not to answer, but even the softening of her voice wasn't enough. His shoulders lifted a very visible inch and the knuckles of the hand holding the bag went white. Ridiculously, it felt as if she was losing him.

As the elevator shuddered to a halt he stepped forward and looked her straight in the eye.

She lifted her chin. 'I'm not moving.'

Setting his hands on either side of her waist, he simply

lifted her out of the way and set her down at the back of the elevator. When he did Jo dropped her arms and lost it.

'You can't avoid me *for ever*!'

As if it knew not to mess with him, the cage door moved with one sharp tug. The second he stepped into the hall, he turned and yanked it shut again.

Her eyes widened. 'What are you—?'

Reaching through the cage, he hit the button to send her back to the ground floor.

Forget kicking his ass. She was going to *kill him*.

If he'd been in a better mood the expression on her face as the elevator descended would have made him laugh out loud. Instead he turned and walked away.

He didn't get far before her voice sounded.

'Go ahead and avoid me for the next fifty years. Up until a few days ago you could have gift-wrapped that for me and it would have been the best present I've ever been given!' There was a pause he presumed was to allow her to take a breath. But when she spoke again he could hear something new threaded in her voice. 'I'm not angry you don't want to talk about it. I get that part. Probably better than you think. But they'll be selling ice cream in hell before I try talking to you again.'

Daniel stilled and took a long, calming breath. It wasn't what she said, what got to him was the note in her voice that almost sounded...*hurt*.

Shaking his head, he headed for his apartment. He'd been tossing pointed verbal spears at her for years without leaving a mark but a silent response had hit the target?

How did *that* work?

He'd braced himself for several things when he laid eyes on her again. With hindsight the stand-to-attention greeting from his body should have been higher up the list. But when it came to the things he knew he would struggle with most like sympathy, pity—hell, even being *nice* to him would have done it—there hadn't been one. Instead he got the kind of response he should have known to expect from her. Not only had she called him on what he was doing and set him straight, she kicked him to the kerb for punishing her for something that wasn't her fault. It was the note of hurt in her voice and his answering guilt for causing it that said the most about the change in their evolving relationship.

Stepping out of the hall, he closed the door and found his gaze drawn across the room to the item on the kitchen counter.

By the time she made it to the top of the stairs he was leaning on his door frame, ankles crossed and a hand held out in front of him. Gauntlet casually swinging on his forefinger, he watched from the corner of his eye as she glared at him before pointedly focusing on her destination. When she came to a halt in front of him she pressed her lips together, took a breath and looked at his finger.

'Is that my mug?'

He let it swing a little harder. 'Yes.'

'I hate you.'

'I know.'

Snatching the mug, she fitted her key in the lock, stepped inside her apartment and slammed the door. Daniel stayed where he was and waited. *Four, three, two...*

The door swung open again.

'You know what I hate most?' she snapped.

'That you didn't think of the elevator trick first?'

'I *hate* that you can make me this mad.'

He nodded. 'It's a talent.'

'I'm normally pretty Zen about the universe, despite everything it's thrown at me. But you—*you* bug the hell out of me.' She waved a hand at his face with attitude. 'That whole "nothing gets to me" façade you got going on bugs me more than anything. Especially now I know it's a big fat lie.' Her eyes widened when a slow smile began to form on his face. '*Really*, you're doing that *now*? When I've just told you I can see right through you?'

'I doubt that.'

If she could see right through him she would know he was thinking how beautiful she was when she was angry. He'd always thought it was a cliché but with Jo it was true. She flashed fire from her eyes; the full force of a passionate nature he'd only got glimpses of in the past made it difficult not to cross the hall. It didn't matter if she unleashed all of her inner fire on him, erupted in an inferno and left him in a pile of sated ashes. If anything it made him want her more.

'Don't do that,' she warned.

His smile grew. 'What am I doing?'

'You know what you're doing.'

'Thinking about coming over there so we can make up?'

'We don't have that kind of relationship.'

'Didn't use to,' he allowed.

'Just because we made an attempt at trying to be friends doesn't mean—'

'That's what you're calling this?' He raised his brows in disbelief. There was no way she could be that naïve.

'I—'

'You're telling me you haven't thought about it.'

She opened her mouth, closed it and then opened it again. 'What are we talking about?'

'I think you know what we're talking about.'

'You mean sex.' She frowned at his chest. 'With you…'

'I was talking about the kiss in the subway station, but if you want go there…'

'I haven't thought about it,' she lied.

Daniel shook his head. 'We've already established you shouldn't do that when you're not any good at it.'

'You're telling me you *have* thought about it?'

'If you mean sex…with you…'

Her eyes narrowed.

'I'm a guy, of course I've thought about it.'

She lifted her chin. *'And?'*

Daniel shrugged in a way he hoped didn't give away the fact just talking about it was turning him on. 'I think two people who spark off each the way we do could have pretty spectacular sex. You don't?'

'I meant the… Yes… *No*… I mean I don't know much about—'

'Spectacular sex?' The fact he had flustered her again brought a knowing smile to his mouth. 'You should try it. There's a lot to recommend it.'

'Wasn't where I was going.' She frowned.

'No?'

'Would you quit that?'

'What am I doing now?'

'Looking at me like a man looks at a woman.'

'Bit difficult to avoid…' His gaze travelled the length of her body, lingering on her breasts.

'That's second-date territory you're in right now.'

'We've had coffee three times.'

She gasped in outrage. 'Those weren't *dates.*'

Unable to resist any longer, Daniel nudged his door frame and stepped forward. 'When it comes to the kiss in the subway station, I think we can do better.'

'Danny, stop.' Her tone was suddenly more of a plea than a warning. She took a step back. 'You and me? *Huge mistake.*'

Reaching out, he took her hand and brought her back to her door frame. 'Who are you trying to convince?'

Before she could reply, he released her hand and framed her face. The tip of her tongue swiped her lips, moistening them in preparation as her gaze lowered to his mouth. When she looked up, doubt flashed across her eyes. He would have used every lesson he'd learnt from the seduction handbook to remove that uncertainty. But as his head lowered her chin lifted and their mouths met before he was ready.

A jolt of electricity zipped through his body. At first he froze, determined to ignore muscles that jerked in response so he could carry out his plan to demonstrate more finesse. He wanted to savour her, spend hours kissing her.

Starting with her mouth…

Capturing her lower lip first, then the upper, he drew from the experience of a lifetime of kisses that paled in comparison. If he'd known kissing her could feel so good, they'd have been doing it a lot sooner. When a breathy sigh escaped her lips, he breathed it in; the first brush of his tongue against hers met with a low hum of approval at the back of her throat. While she simply stood with her spine against the door frame and allowed him to explore, it was easier to control the pace and the demands of his body. The second her hands flattened on his stomach and she started doing a little exploring of her own, his control was tested as it had never been tested before.

The need to thrust against her was excruciating, but he forced himself to settle for pinning her to the door frame with his body. The desire to palm one of her perfect breasts was agonizing, but he forced himself to settle for a hand on her ribcage. Minutes dissolved into nothing but nipping, licking, and the kind of restless hand exploration that skirted them close to the point of no return. In the end it was the woman who was supposed to be lost in the moment *with him* who broke the kiss to point out a different kind of danger.

'Danny…' she mumbled. 'Elevator…'

Listening for long enough to hear someone fighting with the cage door, he leaned back in. Knowing that door they had at least another couple of minutes.

But Jo ducked out of the way, her voice thickened by the drugging effect of desire. 'We're not the only people who live on this floor.'

'They live at the opposite end of the hall,' he replied in a rough voice, which said just as much about the effect desire was having on him. 'But if it's doing it for you go ahead and think about getting caught...'

'You're *bad*,' she whispered.

'I haven't even got started yet,' he whispered back.

To prove his point he allowed his hand to slide up her ribcage so the tip of his thumb could brush the underside of her breast. Her kiss-swollen lips immediately parted on an inward, stuttered breath, head turning as she attempted to look down the hall.

'They can't see what I'm doing,' he reassured her.

She looked into his eyes again. 'Didn't I say where you're headed right now is second-date territory?'

Leaning forward, Daniel nudged his nose against the hair at her temple, breathing in lavender-scented shampoo. 'So when do you want to go out?'

There was a heavy sigh as her hands smoothed across his chest. 'We can't go on a date. We can barely manage a civil cup of coffee.'

'We just need to learn how to communicate better.'

Seemed to Daniel they were making some real headway in that department. He moved his nose to the other side of her temple and took another breath. The lavender wasn't having a calming effect on his body but the fact she was finding him hard to resist certainly seemed to be doing something to his sense of well-being.

She shook her head. 'We can't.'

'Making an effort not to bite each other's heads off might be a good place to start.'

'I meant *this*.'

'You don't mean that,' he said with conviction.

'Yes, I do.'

'No, you don't.'

'Yes, I do.' As he lifted his head she looked up at him from underneath her fringe. 'Could you stop acting like you know me better than I know myself?'

Considering she was no more able to keep her hands off him than he was to keep his off her, Daniel refused to back down. 'Would you have crossed the hall and kissed me?'

'No.'

'Do you regret that I crossed the hall to kiss you?' When she avoided his gaze and focused a small frown on his chest, he added, 'Remember, you suck at lying.'

'No,' she confessed reluctantly. 'I don't regret it.'

A step in the right direction…

She sighed again. 'But I should.'

And a step back…

Lifting the hand at her waist, he smoothed a strand of hair off her cheek. 'Tell me why.'

'There are at least a dozen reasons why we shouldn't be doing this.'

'I had ten on my list.'

She shot him a brief look of frustration. 'The very fact you even *have a list* should tell you I'm right.'

'I've been narrowing it down some.'

When she frowned, he brushed his thumb against her breast and felt her body respond to his touch.

'Danny, stop.'

He leaned in to nuzzle his nose into the hair above her ear. 'Do I need to remind you what I said about making things difficult for me when I want something?'

'There's no room in my life for involvement.'

'You forget you're talking to the guy who never stays in one place long enough for it to get complicated.' He brushed her hair off her shoulder to access her neck.

'I can't think when you're doing that.'

The breathless honesty made his mouth curve into a smile against her skin. *'Good.'*

'But we need to be sensible for a minute.' Her hands flattened against his chest and pushed.

Lifting his head so he could look into her eyes, Daniel discovered the kind of steely determination that suggested he wasn't the only one she was resisting.

'Give me some space, Daniel. I mean it.'

The use of his full name made him frown.

'Please.'

A flash of vulnerability combined with the word she had never used around him before made him step back, but only as far as the opposite side of the door frame. Dropping his arms, he pushed his hands into the pockets of his jeans.

'I'm listening.'

'Don't do that,' she warned with a brief glare. 'If you want us to communicate better it has to start somewhere.'

'We were communicating fine until you started overthinking it.'

'We can't just jump into bed,' she protested.

'No?'

'No. Because to categorize it as friends with benefits we'd need to be friends in the first place and we're *not.'* When he opened his mouth she shook her head. 'I'm not done. Even if we were friends, we both know this is complicated.'

Number nine on his list, as it happened. Or was it eight? If it was eight, what was nine? While he tried to remember Jo continued listing the reasons they shouldn't get involved.

'Your sister is my best friend and your family—'

'What happens between us is no one's business but ours,' he replied in a tone that wouldn't accept any argument on the subject. 'We're consenting adults.'

'You're saying we sneak around and have secret sex?'

'There's a lot to recommend that one too.'

'I can't *lie* to your sister.'

'I didn't ask you to,' he said. 'I'm saying we see where this takes us before we complicate it with outside opinions.'

'We both know exactly where it will take us.'

'Sometimes these things are just a flash in the pan—burn hot, fizzle out fast.' But as the words left his mouth Daniel knew he didn't believe them. Once wouldn't be enough with her, just as one kiss hadn't been enough. After a second kiss he was ready for a third, a fourth and a fifth; preferably within the next few minutes. He wasn't looking for a commitment any more than she was. It wasn't something he could even begin to contemplate until he kicked his subconscious into line. But spending what was left of his short lease with Jo suddenly felt like pretty good therapy to him.

Ignoring the warning in her eyes, he took a step forward. 'Can't hurt if we manage to communicate better, can it? If we follow this through to its natural conclusion, it'll be our decision. I'm not about to send out a mass email so people who know us can add their two cents. If you choose to tell Liv, that's up to you. Won't be you my family will come down on when we're done. It'll be me and I can handle that.'

'I won't be made out to be the victim of seduction.' She frowned. 'I'm a big girl. If something happens, it'll be on equal terms.'

'Wouldn't have it any other way.' He flashed a smile. 'All I'm doing is laying it out for you.'

She wavered. 'So we just try to communicate better and see what happens…'

'Exactly.'

'Knowing neither of us want to get involved…'

'You want no strings, I'm your man.' That she was getting closer to seeing things his way brought his hands out of his pockets. But as he lifted his arms she glanced down.

'What happened to your hand?' Frowning, she took it in one of hers to study the damage more closely.

Daniel looked at the red scratches across the joints of his fingers and knuckles as if he'd forgotten they were there. He forgot a lot of things when he was kissing her.

'Scraped it on a wall,' he replied.

'Does it hurt?'

'No.' Not in the way she meant.

'Looks like it hurts,' she said in a low voice. 'Don't you wear gloves when you're working?'

'They got in the way.' It was as much as he was prepared to say on the subject. Turning his wrist, he threaded their fingers together, his free hand sliding under the hem of her blouse to touch the baby soft skin on her flank.

She trembled in response, long lashes growing heavy and another stuttered inward breath hauled through parted lips.

'I don't know what changed between us or why, but—'

'It's changed,' she finished. 'I know.'

'May as well explore it now it's here…'

Jo searched his eyes in the same way she had when she woke him up. It made him feel equally exposed, like standing in open ground without cover. Remaining still, he forced himself to endure the onslaught with more courage than last time. Her decision might ultimately rest on whether she found what she was looking for but he couldn't do much about that.

It was either there or it wasn't.

'You know I'm going to ask at some point.' She lowered her gaze to watch her palm flatten on his chest. She nodded. 'Just so you're ready for it next time…'

Daniel doubted he would ever be ready and was about to tell her it was a no-go area when she took a breath and confessed, 'I can't believe I'm even contemplating this…'

'It's not going anywhere,' he replied roughly.

'Hmm…' She pushed out her lower lip. 'Not till your lease is up.'

'Not till my lease is up.'

'Well, then,' she said softly as her fingers flexed against his sweater. 'If you're going to convince me to go against my better judgment you best get started.' The hand on his chest

slid up around his neck, her gaze focused on his mouth. 'For
the record, it could take a *lot* of persuasion.'

Daniel's head lowered. 'I can do persuasion.'

'We'll see…'

CHAPTER SEVEN

'I always thought creamy vanilla was the ice cream for me, but recently someone persuaded me to try some wild cherry. Oh, my, what have I been missing all these years?'

'CHEESE slice and a diet soda, please,' Jo said with a smile before she turned towards Daniel. 'Stubborn. Now you think of one word to describe me. And *be nice.*'

He reached a long arm across the heated glass cabinets to pay for their order. 'Because calling me stubborn was supposed to be a compliment?'

'You're saying you aren't?'

'I prefer to call it determination.'

'Admit when you're wrong a little more often, it *could* be called determination,' she allowed, adding an innocent flutter of her lashes when he glanced at her.

'I can admit when I'm wrong.'

'Can you do it out loud?'

When he took a long breath, Jo bit her lip to stifle a chuckle. While the back-and-forth between them hadn't changed all that much, it was less sharp than it had been before. Both of them putting more effort into it helped, as did Daniel's newfound ability to know when she was teasing him instead of taunting him. But there were times she still wondered how long it could last.

'Your turn,' she prompted. It was met with a long enough moment of consideration to merit a sigh. 'Can't think of a word that isn't an insult, can you?'

'I can think of several words that aren't insults after the last few days.' A smile hovered at the corners of his mouth. 'Move closer and I'll whisper them to you.'

'Do I have to remind you why we're in a public place?' She waved an encouraging hand between them. 'Work with me here.'

If all it took to remove any remaining doubts from her mind were the constant reminders of why they were trying to communicate better, they'd have been eating in. Knowing what she did of his wicked streak, quite possibly off each other's bodies. But since the night they had their elevator argument, Jo had been ignoring the small voice inside her head: the one that still thought where they were headed was a huge mistake. When he wasn't there it was louder. Then she would lie in the darkness, hear him on the other side of the wall, and the only thing she could think about when she saw him again was making him feel better. Granted, it made *her* feel better too, but it still hadn't silenced the voice.

'Fearless.'

She blinked. 'What?'

'You wanted a word I'd use to describe you.' Taking their order with a nod of thanks, he turned towards the door. 'There you go.'

'That's how you see me?'

'What's wrong with it?'

Apart from the fact he couldn't be more wrong? 'It's a compliment,' she replied.

'Underestimating me again?' Holding the door open, Daniel lowered his voice as she walked past him. 'Being bad isn't the only thing I'm good at.'

Jo ignored the hum of delight whispering over her body when she thought about how very good he was at being bad.

She could hold a conversation with him without thinking about sex every five minutes. She darn well could!

'No one's fearless,' she announced. 'Everyone's afraid of something; by overcoming it they earn the word *brave*.'

He adjusted his longer stride to hers when they hit the sidewalk. 'What are you afraid of?'

'Oh, no,' she laughed. 'I'm not falling for that one. I say spiders, you'll start a collection.'

'Might consider one of those big hairy guys you keep in a glass case. I heard they're a low-maintenance pet.' He smiled when she shuddered. 'One word wasn't enough to begin with. If I had two I'd have said *fearless* and *wary*.'

'Isn't that an oxymoron?'

'You think I don't know what that means.'

'Word-of-the-day calendars can be very educational.'

'I have another one: manicured and mischievous.'

'Careful, Danny.' She smiled. 'It's starting to sound like you've put some thought into this before today.'

'Tornado in high heels, that's another one…'

Despite the fact she liked everything he'd come up with so far, Jo tutted. 'Little too far over the word-count now.'

'Your turn again. And after you laid stubborn on me, try harder. I might bruise easier than you think.'

When they stopped at a crossing she took her time picking another word. Had to be careful his ego didn't engulf Texas and try to take over the world, didn't she? Mentally crossing out everything pre-communicate-better-days too— *which might take a while*—she gently swayed the skirt that lent itself to the motion. Theme of the day was vintage and the black and white striped fifties dress was the most 'her' she had felt since she started the challenge. It was a much-needed reminder of what her life had been like before everything changed so fast it felt as if her feet had barely touched the ground.

'Can't stop doing that, can you?' he asked.

'Doing what?'

'The thing you're doing with your skirt.'

Rocking her hips a little more, she brightened. 'Is it bothering you?'

'No. Just wondered if you knew you were doing it.'

She shrugged. 'It's a fun dress.'

'And now I'm wondering if you still leave out cookies and a glass of milk for the jolly fat guy in red.'

Despite the obvious amusement in his eyes, Jo felt the need to defend what for her was an ethos for life. 'If you don't make time for fun every now and again the big, bad things can be harder to take.'

'Are you saying I don't know how to have fun?'

From the well of memories she had chosen to forget she sought one that associated Daniel with the kind of fun things she attached to his three brothers. She had dozens of memories of them tossing a football and joshing around but Daniel, not so much. What did he do with his time apart from work, a daily run and utilizing every tool in the seduction toolbox to turn her into a boneless heap of wanton woman?

'Define your idea of "fun" for me,' she demanded as they entered Washington Square Park and she looked up at the iconic arch modelled after the Arc de Triomphe in Paris.

If he asked she would tell him eating lunch close to its shadow was one of her favorite fun things to do, especially on a day like the one they were experiencing. Spiffed up to its former glory, with a backdrop of clear blue sky. She'd stare up at it and imagine she was sitting by the original.

She made the same vow every time she saw it: *Soon*.

Since she was moving up the magazine's shortlist each year, she felt closer than ever to fulfilling the promise.

When she looked at Daniel and found innuendo glinting in his eyes, she felt the usual response skim through her veins and tighten her abdomen. But that wasn't what she'd meant.

'I mean outside of adult fun. What do you do to relax when you're not working?'

'Run, train, gym time; long hours dedicated to maintaining the level of fitness you finally got round to noticing...'

He cut loose his infamous smile, *on her.*

Wow. That thing really did pack a punch up close.

She had forgotten that. But since the memory of the last time he unleashed it on her was buried so deep there must have been a very good reason for forgetting it, Jo decided not to go digging. 'Toss a football in the park, play practical jokes on the guys in your unit or meet up with friends for a beer...' She lifted her brows. 'When's the last time you did anything like that?'

'We tossed a football in camp when I was overseas. Not much else to do when we weren't being shot at.'

She didn't get how he could be so blasé about his time there when it was obvious whatever happened still tortured him. The subject of his nightmares was one they'd avoided but maybe...in the bright light of day...while they were getting along better...

'Not like my inbox was overflowing with emails, was it?' he asked before she could find a place to start.

Jo shook her head. 'You didn't want to hear from me.'

'You'd be surprised the difference an email can make to a Marine in a war zone. I saw guys go for days on the smile they got hearing from folks they barely knew in high school.' His gaze swept the surrounding area for a place to sit before he laid a large palm against the small of her back to guide her. 'It's a reminder of home. Some guys needed that.'

'Did you?'

'My problem was never remembering.' He frowned.

The unspoken *'it's trying to forget'* made Jo's voice soften in response. 'You're not a machine, Danny.'

'There are times it would be a lot easier if I was.'

'You say the stupidest things sometimes.' But as they approached an available bench she wondered what she'd have done if she'd thought an email made a difference to him back then. Even if it was from someone he hadn't liked. 'If I'd known I'd have written.' She smiled up at him. 'You'd have got *War & Peace* on everyday life in Manhattan.'

'With daily tips for the fashion-conscious Marine...?'

'I heard it's all about the camouflage this season.'

'I'll think about letting you write next time I go.'

'You're going again?'

'Not likely to happen soon,' he said in a tone that suggested he was disappointed. 'There's three months left on my papers before I decide whether to re-up.'

'You've already decided, haven't you?'

'Once a Marine, always a Marine.'

Jo frowned at how little she liked the idea of him being overseas again. She might not have lost sleep over it last time, but she knew she would now. 'You're a cop too. Doesn't that mean anything?'

'I've been both for a long time.'

'I know, but it's like you're married to the Marines and fooling around with the NYPD on the side.'

'I don't fool around,' he said seriously.

If he thought it was something she needed to hear, it wasn't necessary. Any relationship she'd heard he had might not have lasted long, but she couldn't remember there ever being a suggestion he was fooling around. He wasn't the kind of guy who cheated on a woman. It was part of the Brannigan loyalty and honour code.

'Kinda feels like you're more faithful to one than the other,' she pointed out in relation to his work. 'Semper Fi, that's the motto, right?'

'*Ooh-rah,*' he replied in a low rumble, smiling when she rolled her eyes. 'The Marines are my first love. You never forget that. Being a cop is different. It's a marriage that was arranged for me before I was born.'

'You didn't want to be a cop?'

'Let's just say it took a while to find my niche.'

Since she'd always assumed all of the Brannigans had the same calling, Jo was surprised. But if he'd loved it so much, 'Why did you leave the Marines?'

'I didn't.'

'You switched to the Reserves and came home.'

'Things change.'

'Do you regret it?' she asked as she sat down.

'Not on the good days,' he replied.

It seemed a tad ironic to Jo she had accused him of not knowing her when she was discovering so many things she hadn't known about him. Usually she liked to think she swayed towards giving people the benefit of the doubt. But with Daniel there had always been a wall of distrust; one they built higher and wider every time their paths crossed. She was still wary of him but that was understandable. Trust wasn't built overnight.

As he turned to hand over the pizza box, she looked into his eyes and saw a hint of shadow. Experiencing an immediate pang of regret, she tried to lighten the mood. 'I've decided I'm giving you a relaxation make-over.'

'If it involves bubble baths and scented candles you can forget it.'

Curling her fingers, she punched him in the upper arm to even up the score for the sucker punch of his infamous smile. 'Don't mock what you haven't tried.'

Daniel glanced at his arm as she shook her hand. 'Been wanting to do that for years, haven't you?'

'You have *no idea*.' Unfortunately, now she knew who would come out of it worse, it wasn't an option any more.

Reaching out, he captured her hand and ran his thumb over the rise and fall of her knuckles. As he repeated the caress heat rushed up her arm in waves. That part she'd almost gotten used to. What she found harder to handle was the message she could read in his eyes as he did it. At first she'd thought it was her imagination. Then, as it was with everything between them of late, she chalked it up to one of the numerous sexual messages he silently transmitted to her. It had been easier to think of it that way. But in the sunlight—the vivid blue of his eyes bright enough to put the sky to shame—it felt like something more.

I'll take care of you, it said.

Jo didn't like it. She didn't need him to take care of her. She could take care of herself.

Holding her gaze hostage, he did something unexpected and bowed his head to place a kiss on the skin he'd caressed. Jo watched, mesmerized, as his chin lifted and he smiled.

Seriously, where had *this* Danny been hiding for the last five and a half years?

'Let me know if you need anywhere else kissed better…'

'Well, that's a shame.' She sighed and reached into the box for her slice of pizza. 'Opportunities to be gallant are rare in this day and age. And you just blew yours.'

When there was a chuckle of deep laughter, she turned her head to study the effect it had on his face. Mocking amusement she was used to; the glint in his eyes that hinted he knew something she didn't and his enjoyment was at her expense, she knew all too well. But the way it relaxed some of the tension around his eyes, suggesting he'd experienced a moment of the kind of fun he obviously needed thanks to *her*?

Well, as it happened, it felt pretty darn good.

She was smiling back at him when her phone rang. Digging in one of the pockets of her skirt to retrieve it, she checked the number and frowned. *Darn it.* Not now.

'Hi, Stu… No, I appreciate it.' She glanced at Daniel from the corner of her eye. 'Can you try and keep him there for me? Thanks.' Pushing the phone back in her pocket, she dropped the pizza into the box and wiped her hand with the napkin. 'I have to go.'

'I'm coming with you.'

Yes, she'd thought he might say that. While he could catch her off guard with some things, in others he was as predictable as queues for the Empire State Building. She shook her head, 'It's your day off. You're going to do something fun.'

'It took two days and a late night for you to free up time in your schedule,' he pointed out. 'Your idea of what we did with it may have differed from mine, but the general idea was to spend it together.'

'I know,' Jo replied with another pang of regret.

He had been remarkably patient in regard to her schedule versus his shift pattern. Discussing it made her realize the number of times he would have to sacrifice much-needed sleep to see her. For a second it made her resent the intrusion of the present by the past a little more than usual. But he had been right about what he could see in her eyes the night he surprised her in the hall. For one month out of every twelve, she was resigned to doing what she had to do.

Leaning forward, she placed a quick kiss on a clean-shaven cheek before standing up. 'I promise to make it up to you when I get back.'

'Nice try.' He stood up with her. 'I'll drive you there. It'll be quicker.'

Not in Manhattan traffic, it wouldn't. 'I know what you're doing and it's not that I—'

Taking a step forward, he laid a hand on the wide red belt at her waist, his voice low. 'Are we headed for an argument?'

'I don't want us to be,' Jo confessed.

Avoiding his gaze, she brushed an invisible piece of lint off his jersey with the backs of her fingers. No matter how addictive it had become, she liked being able to touch him. She liked the heat she could feel through his clothes, the solidness of his presence. But since she couldn't get used to him being there, she lowered her arm.

'Sooner we go, sooner we can be back,' he said firmly.

When he took her hand and turned them around, Jo tried to find a way to get out of it. The idea of him taking a deeper step into her old world than he already had sent a chill down her spine. Jack was the key to a door she didn't want to open.

Behind it was the old Jo, the invisible girl who had been lonely and lost. Despite the need she had for it, Jo knew the risk associated with accepting help. She had watched the effect it had on some of her peers; how well-meaning people with good intentions could begin to make decisions for them until they didn't have control over their lives any more. With hindsight the new Jo supposed it wasn't *that* dissimilar to the battle for independence teenagers fought everywhere. But in the present it felt like a much-needed reminder not to lean on a man like Daniel, even for a moment.

Huge mistake, the little voice repeated.

Something dangerously close to panic crossed her chest as his truck came into sight. Glancing down the street, she saw the sign for the subway station. Looking at his truck again, she frowned at the idea of an argument. The phrase 'rock and a hard place' jumped into her head.

'Danny...' When they stopped to cross the street, she tried to reclaim her hand. 'I—'

'I know you don't want me to go with you.' Tightening his fingers, he turned to face her. 'But if you want me to bend a little from time to time, you have to do a little bending of your own. You know that, don't you?'

Oh, he was *good*. Negotiation 101 obviously hadn't been lost on him during the NYPD training. He knew exactly the tone of deep, rough rumble to use on her, had enough sincerity in his eyes to make her feel she was letting him down if she didn't make an effort. She frowned at his chest again. If it was something other than Jack she could try to bend, but—

'Look at me, Jo.'

With a blink, she obeyed.

'We're good right now, aren't we?'

She nodded. They were. It was another part of the reason she didn't want to take him with her.

'So we go in, you do whatever you need to do, and then we get to enjoy the rest of our day.'

It sounded so simple when he put it like that.

Nudging the tip of his nose against hers, he angled his head and placed a kiss on the corner of her mouth. 'I can think of at least a half-dozen fun things we can do when we get back...'

Eyelids growing heavy, Jo smiled as he placed another kiss on the other corner of her mouth. She knew what he was doing but while the rest of the world disappeared around them she could feel her resistance melting away.

'You have a one-track mind,' she mumbled as he changed the angle of his head.

'There's a reason for that.'

Slanting his mouth over hers, he spent several minutes persuading her to go against her better judgment. She might have issued the challenge after their elevator argument but if she knew how well he could do it...

He lifted his head, long fingers flexed around hers, his alert gaze sweeping over the traffic while she stared at him.

If she could just figure out what it was that hadn't been there before. What made her see him differently and want him so much the memories of all the times they argued faded into the distance...

'Let's go, babe.'

CHAPTER EIGHT

'The jacket you never wore? The jeans you swore you'd get back into one day? Sometimes you have to be firm about the things you keep and the things you let go.'

JO LEANED across the wooden bar to greet the man in front of the optics with a kiss above his greying beard.

'Well, aren't you a picture?' he said with a smile.

Taking a step back, she placed her hands on either side of her waist and struck a pose. 'You like?'

'I do.'

The sound of laughter pulled her gaze to the other side of the room as her hands dropped. 'How far are we in?'

Daniel noticed the change in her voice; as if it was a question she had asked a hundred times but already knew the answer. He stored the information away with her reaction to the phone call. The change in her then had been immediate too. One minute he was sitting next to bright, full-of-life, sassy, sexy Jo and the next it was like sitting next to a shell. At the time it had felt as if something were stolen from him.

Daniel had resented the hell out of that.

'Coming up on three hours,' the man replied.

Jo glanced to her side. 'Sorry.' She waved a hand, 'Daniel, meet Stu. Stu, meet Daniel.'

They shook hands across the bar.

'First time she's brought anyone with her in ten years,' Stu said with a smile. 'Can I get you anything?'

Daniel shook his head. 'Designated driver.'

'Better order something if you're staying.' Jo looked across the room again. 'This could take a while.'

As she walked away, Stu explained, 'It's in the timing. She takes him home too early, he finds his way back. If not here, it's somewhere else.'

Nodding as if he'd already known, he watched her father greet her with an arm around tight, narrow shoulders before making introductions. Immediately Daniel wanted to scoop her up and take her back to where they were before the call came. But he had to treat it as a recon mission. With that in mind he'd let her handle Jack her way, *for now*.

'You could try barring him,' he said dryly.

When he looked at Stu again, he discovered he was being studied with caution. 'Jo said she'd prefer to get a phone call than spend time searching for him.'

'It's good to know she has people who will do that,' he replied with sincerity.

The older man visibly relaxed. 'Used to be more of us, but bars change hands over the years.'

When Jo returned, she lifted her chin a very visible inch before looking Daniel in the eye. 'Is there any point telling you to go home?'

'No,' he replied.

'Figures.' She flashed another smile at Stu. 'I'll take one of your famous coffees if there's a pot on the go.'

'Is the designated driver sure he doesn't want one?'

'He takes his black.'

'I'll bring them over.'

They were sitting in a corner booth when Daniel broached the subject with, 'How many bar owners have your phone number?'

'Danny—'

'It's just a question.'

'No, it's not.' She sighed heavily. 'It's an opening to an argument. Don't make me regret bringing you here.'

Stu arrived with their coffees. As he watched him return to the bar Daniel lowered his voice. 'I'm not going to argue with you.'

'I'm glad to hear it.'

'But I'm not going to stay silent.'

'If what you have to say involves a lecture on how to handle Jack you can forget it. I've been doing this for a long time. I don't need your help.' She reached for her coffee and took a sip.

When she glanced across the bar as she set her cup down, Daniel lifted his hand. Sliding it beneath a curtain of silky hair, he wrapped his fingers around her neck, soothing tense muscles with a firm, circular movement. It took a minute, but eventually her head became heavy against his forefinger.

'*Mmm*, that feels good.'

Ignoring the reaction from his body to the low moan, he smiled. 'Magic fingers…'

'And I didn't even have to put coins in the slot.'

'You can pay me later.'

The brief smile his comment earned faded as she glanced across the bar again. 'It's not that there aren't some things I'm fine talking about…'

'So start there.'

'…but before I do I want your word you won't interfere.' With a blink of long lashes, her gaze tangled with his. 'I mean it, Danny. No advice, no leaflets for places I can get help and when we leave here we don't talk about it again.'

'I'm not the first person you've said that to.'

'You're not the first *Brannigan* I've said it to.' She shrugged a shoulder. 'Liv tried to get involved once.'

If she hadn't, they would have had words. Considering she only tried *once*, it was still tempting. But if he opened his mouth in Jo's defence his sister would know something was up. She could be intuitive that way.

He took a short breath. 'I can't give you my word—'

'Then we're not talking about it.'

'I'm not done.' He moved his fingers to ease the returning tension in her neck. 'Learning to communicate better after so many years of arguing was never going to be easy. If blunt is what it takes from time to time then—'

She arched a brow. 'You know I'm going to remind you of this when it's your turn, don't you?'

The fingers on her neck stilled. She didn't know he had no intention of talking to her about his nightmares. If he hadn't been likely to talk about them before, spending time with her had made him twice as determined. He didn't want the darkness of his subconscious to intrude on what was rapidly becoming a haven. He dropped his arm to his side.

'I shouldn't have said that,' she said with regret. 'I knew this would happen. I should have listened to the voice that told me—'

'What we're doing is still a huge mistake?'

A hint of astonishment mixed with a sparkle of anger in her eyes. 'Not what I was going to say.'

'Tell me I'm wrong.'

'What's happening between us has nothing to do with this,' she argued.

Putting together what she said with his thoughts on the subject of discussing his nightmares, Daniel realized, 'You don't let your old life cross over into the new one and vice versa, right?'

'Not if I can help it,' she admitted.

'How's that working out for you?'

'Was going pretty well...'

'Until me...'

Her expression softened. 'Until you...'

Reaching out, his fingers sought the knots of tension at

the base of her neck again. 'Start with something simple. Tell me how you met Stu.'

Louder laughter pulled her gaze across the room while she considered what to tell him. Judging by the brief frown on her face, it wasn't that simple.

'I was fourteen,' she said in a low voice. 'Figured if I couldn't stop him drinking, I'd make it more difficult. I went to all the bars within an eight-block radius to see where he'd run up tabs. Deal was, they'd stop giving him credit and I'd pay them off a few dollars a week. The ones who gave me most trouble, I paid first. The patient ones—guys like Stu—would take less on weeks I found it tough.' She took a breath. 'Took two part-time jobs and a few years, but I got there. Even made a few friends along the way…'

Earning their respect as she did it, Daniel surmised. He would have liked to have met her back then. But while fourteen-year-old Jo had been surviving the Urban Jungle, a twenty-year-old Daniel was in theatre with the Marines. He could imagine what she would have thought of him if she'd met him before he'd signed up at eighteen. He was a loose gun then; the kind of guy who was more trouble than he was worth. Looking back, he knew he would have had more respect for her than he had for himself.

'Did it slow him down?' he asked.

'No.' She shook her head. 'It forced him outside the eight-block radius. That's when he started disappearing.'

Daniel's fingers stilled again. 'He's the reason you were homeless when Liv met you.'

She shrugged as if it didn't matter. 'I couldn't make the rent. He disappeared when we were already on shaky ground with the landlord. When I knew I couldn't hold out I scouted around for some place dry close to school, packed what I could carry and left. The rest you know.'

Anger flared inside him. 'Why didn't you ask for help? There are people out there who—'

'I was eighteen,' she said with a glare of warning. 'I could take care of myself. All I needed was a few weeks to finish high school and get my diploma.'

Fingers moving, his gaze slid across the bar to acquire a new target. What kind of man did that to his kid? Why was she still taking care of him?

'Where was your mother?' he asked.

Her neck stiffened. 'She died.'

'When?'

'Accident when I was eight.'

'What happened?'

'Hit and run on her way back from the local store.'

He remembered her saying something about Jack being worse one month out of twelve. 'The anniversary of her death is this month, isn't it?'

'Yes.' Leaning forward to reach for her cup, Jo dislodged his hand with a subtle shrug of her shoulders. 'And we're done talking about this now.'

Daniel's gaze slid back to his target. He knew exactly who he was talking to next. Five minutes should do it. But before he went looking for a window of opportunity he had to ask the question he didn't want to ask.

'Was he ever violent with you?'

'Don't—'

'I need to know.'

The rough tone of his voice turned her head, her gaze searching his eyes before her expression softened. 'He's not that kind of drunk. Jack gets happy. That's half the problem. People buy him drinks 'cos he's such a fun guy to be around.' When laughter sounded she smiled ruefully. 'See what I mean?'

'You were lucky,' Daniel replied, when what he really meant was *Jack* was lucky.

'Yes,' Jo said dryly. 'I spent every waking moment of my

adolescence being eternally grateful for the fact my father is an alcoholic.'

Despite thinking it was the most honest thing she'd said on the subject, Daniel shook his head. 'Not what I meant.'

The unexpected touch of a fine-boned hand on his thigh drew a sharp hiss of breath through his lips. His thoughts stuttered to a standstill. As always every muscle in his body jerked in response, searing heat seeping into his veins and thickening his blood.

'I know what you meant,' she said in an intimate voice. 'But you don't have to worry about me.'

Daniel disagreed. Way he saw it, while they were together she was *his* to take care of and *his* to protect.

'He would never hurt me,' she reassured him.

'Would he know if he knocked you over or if you injured yourself carrying him upstairs?' He clamped her hand to his thigh when she tried to remove it. 'How about when you have to clean up after him or when you're losing sleep worrying where he is? Not every bruise is visible.'

'If you don't stop that I'm going to make you leave.'

She could *try*.

'I'm not going to pretend I don't care.'

'Did I ask you to?' She frowned. 'But what you have to remember is this isn't because it's me, Danny. You're *that guy*: the one who feels he has to make a difference.'

'Don't make me out to be a hero.' If she knew him better she would know how woefully short he fell of the definition.

'Then stop trying to be one.' When a second attempt at freeing her hand didn't get her anywhere, she shook her head. 'I don't need you to rescue me. I need you to trust I know what I'm doing and believe I have my reasons for doing it.'

'Tell me what they are.'

As she tore her gaze from his a pained expression crossed her face. 'I don't want to have a fight with you. But if you keep doing this I won't be able to stop it happening.'

'You give me one good reason why you keep doing this and I'll back off.'

'Why do you need to know?' She jerked her brows. 'And don't say it's part of the whole communicating-better thing because this has nothing to do with us.'

'This is a prime example of you not making it easy for people to get to know you,' Daniel replied flatly.

'Getting to know me better isn't high on your list of priorities when you're trying to get me into bed.'

'If it wasn't we'd already have shared a bed.'

'You say that like I don't have a choice.'

'Tell me you don't want me.' When something close to a growl sounded in the back of her throat, he leaned closer. 'I can tell you how much I want you. You're never out of my head. I've spent dozens of hours thinking about the places I want to kiss you and the things I want to do to you. I want to explore every inch of your body, discover all the hidden places you never even knew you had. I want to drive you so crazy that if I don't take you, we'll both go insane. I want—'

'Stop,' she breathed.

'Tell me you don't want me.'

Her eyes darkened. 'You know I do.'

'If I get to know you better, the experience will be better for both of us. You have my word on that.'

She blinked. 'You're very good at this.'

The statement lifted the corners of his mouth. 'Only when I think it's worth the effort.'

'I won't fall for you,' she said firmly.

Daniel shook his head. 'I don't want you to.'

With another blink, she lifted her chin. 'No falling for me either.'

His smile grew. 'Okay.'

'One reason I keep doing this…'

'Just one.' He nodded, silently adding another *for now.*

'Coney Island.'

Daniel wondered if there would ever be a time she didn't surprise him. 'Am I supposed to know what that means?'

'No,' she replied. 'But I can explain it.' She stared into the air beside his head and took a short breath. 'I was ten or eleven. Jack quit drinking for long enough to remember he had a kid and we went to Coney Island for a day.' Her mouth curled into a wistful smile. 'We went on every ride, ate cotton candy and corn dogs until I felt sick and it was one of the best days of my life.'

When her gaze met his, he caught a glimpse of sweet and vulnerable woman at odds with her usual sass and confidence. Something he didn't recognize expanded in his chest, filling the cavity and making it difficult to breathe.

'That's one of the reasons I keep doing this,' she said with a shrug of a shoulder. 'Because I still remember Coney Island and the day I got my dad back.'

As she avoided his gaze Daniel wrapped his arms around her and pulled her close. She nestled her head in the curve between his neck and shoulder. When he felt the warmth of her breath against his skin a wave of protectiveness washed over him, tightening his hold. In response she relaxed with a sigh, which gave him the impression what he had done held more value than anything he could have said. But when she looked up at him and smiled tremulously, the something he hadn't recognized shifted inside his chest again and Daniel sensed trouble. He brushed her hair back from her cheek, focusing on the movement as he bought time to seek out the source of the danger.

Trouble was, she might think she liked living on the edge, but she didn't know how sharp it could be if a person stood on it for long enough. The question had never been *when* he would fall, it was always *where*: one side heaven, the other hell. He had visited the latter too often over the years. It shouldn't have been a surprise he wanted to reach out and grab a taste of the alternative, even if it was just for a while.

But hold on to it for too long and there was a chance he might haul her into the abyss with him, clinging desperately to whatever light he could find in the darkness. It was why he could never ask for something from her that he couldn't return. Risking his life was easier than emotional involvement. When the stakes were at their highest he felt more alive, stronger; free of the things that weighed him down. It was how he felt when he kissed her.

Oh, yeah, he was in trouble all right.

To make matters worse, she angled her chin, her expression suggesting she knew something was wrong.

Daniel took a short breath, 'How much longer do you think we'll be here?'

She glanced across the bar. 'An hour, maybe two…' She looked at him again. 'If you want to go—'

'No,' he said firmly. 'I was just thinking we skipped lunch and you should eat. If Stu can't rustle up a sandwich, I'll go get us something.'

Releasing her, he slid around the booth and walked away. While there were certain things he couldn't give her, he liked to think he could make up for it in other ways. He wanted to take care of her. Not out of a sense of duty attached to his job or the responsibility that stemmed from her connection to his family. Strangely enough it wasn't entirely because she meant something to him, though there was no denying she did. When he thought it over, it kept coming back to one thing. The same thing that had made him retreat when he thought he might hurt her and try to make amends when it felt as if he had.

She was *Jo*.

It was as simple and as complicated as that.

CHAPTER NINE

*'There's a lot of truth in the sayings on a fridge magnet.
For example: How many roads must a man walk down before he'll admit he's lost?'*

HE WAS driving her just the tiniest bit crazy.

'Could you quit doing that?' She slapped his hand.

'Isn't clearing up after dinner usually one of the things a
guy gets brownie points for doing?'

'I could be a closet neat freak for all you know.'

Glancing around her apartment, he had the gall to look
amused. 'Can't be easy in Aladdin's cave...'

Considering every eclectic knick-knack, photo frame and
somewhat haphazard arrangement of soft furnishings was a
much-loved memento of the life he had turned upside down,
Jo took offence. 'People who live in an apartment for longer
than a handful of months have been known to make it look
like home.'

Daniel leaned back against the counter. 'Apparently they
also make friends with everyone inside two blocks. You
should be more careful when you live alone. Think about
varying your routine. The guy in the Chinese place knew
your name and where you lived from your order.'

'Traditionally that's how food gets delivered,' Jo said dryly
as she folded down the edges of the cartons.

'Not when an order is being collected.'

'Do you see potential serial killers everywhere you look?' She frowned at how snippy she sounded. 'I trust in my initial impression of people. There tends to be truth in it until our heads get in the way. You should try it some time.'

'You know I'm going to ask the obvious now, right?'

'Not going there.'

'I can take it.'

'Not my main concern.'

'It's because it opens us up to my initial impression of you, isn't it?' He opened the refrigerator door. 'You telling me you're not curious?'

Placing the cartons on a shelf, she turned to take their glasses to the sink. 'It's got nothing to do with curiosity. I doubt you even remember when it was.'

'I have a long memory.'

She sighed. 'Revisiting the things that started us arguing in the first place probably isn't wise at this point.'

'Can't be any worse than the mood you've been in since I got here. When you're ready to tell me what the problem is let me know.' Closing the door, he pushed his large hands into the pockets of his jeans and continued the conversation as if he hadn't made her feel like a petulant three-year-old. 'We met the fourth of July weekend Liv brought you home.'

No, they didn't. If she was in a better mood than the one she'd been in since *before* he got there, she could have told him exactly when they met. It was—

Lifting her chin, she blinked as the memory made its way up from the deepest recesses of the well where she stored the things she'd chosen to forget. Suddenly she could remember the first time he sucker-punched her with his infamous smile. She could see what he was wearing, how gorgeous he looked, most of all she remembered how she'd *felt*. It didn't take a genius to work out the events between their first and second meeting had an effect too. But it certainly shed a dif-

ferent light on her reaction to him when he foolishly opened
his mouth that fourth of July weekend.

'You were quieter then,' he said.

'Bit difficult to get a word in edgeways when your family
is gathered en masse.' Setting the glass on the drainer with
a shaking hand, she took several calming breaths.

'Roomful of cops is normally enough for most people.'

She nodded. 'There was that too.'

'Shouldn't be a problem unless you feel guilty...'

Grimacing, Jo reminded herself he couldn't possibly know
what she currently felt guilty about. Instead she thought back
to her feelings that day. 'Bit hard to avoid guilt when you're
somewhere you know you don't belong.'

'That's how you felt?'

'I didn't belong anywhere back then.'

'What about now?'

'I like to think I've claimed my own little corner of the
world. You should try that some time too.'

'You think I haven't?' he asked as she turned to face him.

Jo avoided his too-blue gaze when it felt as if he could see
right through her mask of calm. 'The big pile of unpacked
boxes in your apartment would suggest otherwise.'

'Short lease, remember?'

That big ticking clock she could hear? The one telling her
how little time she had to repair the damage inflicted by the
war *she'd* started? Oh, yes, she remembered. Since it sped
up the countdown, it added to the regret she felt for taking
the assignment she was offered that afternoon.

Daniel had started texting her when she was in the office
preparing for an editorial meeting. Initially a continuation
of the word game they'd played—one she didn't intend to
play while they were *working*—she ended up grinning like
an idiot by the time they were swapping comments chock-a-
block with sexual innuendo. He really was *bad*. An hour later
the girls sitting at the desks next to her demanded to know

who 'he' was because it had to be a man to put a smile like *that* on her face. They asked for details and it was tempting to share them, if for no other reason than she hadn't been able to with anyone else.

She was dangerously close to blushing—and she had *never* blushed—when her editor appeared, sent everyone scurrying back to work and asked if she could have a moment. To make matters worse the epitome of unabashedly single, career-driven woman felt the need to enquire about her 'availability' for a big assignment before offering it to her. As a result the words 'yes' and 'absolutely' left Jo's lips before she had time to consider exactly what it meant.

When looking around her apartment led to thoughts of how much she would miss it when she was gone, she frowned. 'Don't you want a place you can call home?'

'New York is home, doesn't matter where I live in it.'

Jo disagreed. She had lived in the city her entire life, but since four weeks of that time had involved sleeping beneath an underpass she knew the difference between living somewhere and having a place to call home. She looked into his eyes again. 'What is it about here you like best?'

He thought about it for a moment. 'You work in New York, you see people face to face. It's not like California where you spend half your life in a car or overseas when you fight an enemy without ever looking into their eyes.'

It was the kind of insight that would have made her like him a lot earlier if she'd given him half a chance. 'When were you in California?'

'I was stationed in San Diego with the Marines.'

Another thing she hadn't known. 'You said work in New York. What is it you like about living here?'

'Same answer.'

'Nothing else?'

'You could try telling me what you're looking for,' he replied with a hint of a smile.

A lump appeared in her throat, forcing her to take a moment and swallow it so she could control her voice. She didn't deserve a smile. Not when she'd been the way she was with him since he landed at her door. It wasn't his fault her head was a mess. Not *entirely*. 'I don't get how you can see here as home without looking for a few hundred square feet to call your own. Aren't you sick of living out of boxes?'

'You forget up until not so long ago those boxes were in storage. Everything I needed I carried on my back.'

'Everything a *Marine* needed,' she clarified. 'You're home now, so why not make one? You can't tell me after the number of times you've moved apartments there haven't been places you liked enough to stay.'

'There were.'

'Then why do you…?' Her voice trailed off as some of the pieces slotted together. 'You move because of the nightmares, don't you? The minute someone hears you or you *think* they've heard you…' She knew instinctively she was right but it didn't make sense. He'd been moving from place to place for as long as she'd known him. She took a short breath. 'I'm just gonna jump right in here…'

'Do you have another speed?'

'Did something happen when you were overseas?'

'It's not the first time you've asked that question.' His eyes narrowed. 'What makes you so sure something happened?'

'If it didn't where do the nightmares come from?'

'How about we try to forget I have them?'

'Go back to pretending I don't know?' Her eyes widened in disbelief. 'Can you even *do* that?'

'Works better if you don't bring it up.'

'How long have you had them?'

The desire she felt to give him what he'd been searching for returned with the shadows in his eyes. There was no point denying it. Since the first night she heard him yelling beyond the wall, it had felt as if he were calling out to her.

Now, if she could take his pain and give him even one night of peace, she would do it for him. Any secrets he wanted to stay hidden she would keep safe, tucked away with one she already carried for him. But when it came to anything more, she couldn't see past a sudden crippling fear of falling for him.

Using every trick she had learnt in the past to hide how she really felt, she lifted her chin. 'What happened to trying to communicate better?'

'The theory behind that was we wouldn't argue as much.' He smirked. 'In case you hadn't got it by now, pushing me on this will have the opposite effect.'

'If having an argument is what it takes to get you to talk to me then we're about to have one.'

'We both know you've been itching to pick a fight with me since I got here.'

The sensation he was backing off again wasn't helping. She *hated* when he did that. Frustration bubbled inside her. 'How long, Daniel?'

'And now I'm Daniel again.' Taking his hands out of his pockets, he pushed off the counter and headed for the chair where he'd tossed his jacket. 'How about I go back into the hall and we try starting tonight over again?'

Jo followed him. 'Whether you like it or not we've been in these nightmares together since you moved in.'

'Now you're using guilt to get me to talk to you?' His fingers closed around his jacket. 'Keep this up and we'll go from communicating better to name, rank and serial number.'

'Do you have any idea how difficult it is to hear you in that much pain?' She frowned as the truth left her lips. 'I spend half the night waiting for it to start and when it does it's *hell*.'

When he clammed up in a way that suggested he had never intended to talk about it, Jo wanted to slap him. Knowing she would have equal difficulty discussing certain things didn't seem to make a difference. She just wanted to help or offer comfort or simply listen while he talked it through. Not to feel so cut off from him when they suddenly had so little time left.

'Yesterday you wanted one reason why I still help Jack. Now I'm asking you for an answer.' Taking a breath, Jo vowed it was the last time she would bend unless he bent a little in return. It was uncomfortable, not to mention a little scary, being out on a limb alone. *'How long?'*

She didn't think she could get into an argument without other things spilling out in the heat of the moment. Things she wasn't ready to talk about yet, if ever. Avoiding his icy gaze, she pointed across the room. 'I'll be over there on the sofa while you decide whether to stay or go.'

It was as much leeway as she could give him. His refusal to talk to her about the nightmares after she'd talked to him about her past felt like a rejection. What was worse, it *hurt*. She should have kept her mouth shut, had no idea why she had confided in him in the first place, and if the first time she shared things with someone ended with her feeling like a fool…

Suffice to say she wouldn't be in a hurry to do it again.

Daniel wavered in a manner that would get him killed on the front line of a battlefield. As she sat down, switched on the television and started jumping between channels he ground his teeth together. But what difference did it make how long he had nightmares? Wasn't as if she could figure out the rest without help, even if she'd worked out why he moved apartments a tad too quick for his liking. Drawing a breath, he decided he could give her the one thing she wanted to know. But it was a case of give a little to get a little. Once he had answered, she was telling him what had been bothering her.

Tossing his jacket back on the chair as she settled on a channel, he walked around the sofa and sat down beside her.

'Eight years.' He eased the remote from her hand. 'And we're not watching a chick-flick.'

'We're not watching something with explosions and a high body count either,' she retorted.

'Car chases.'

'No.'

He continued scrolling through the options at the bottom of the screen. 'Alien invasion: that one's good.'

'Nerd.'

'Bank robbery it is, then.'

She sighed heavily. 'You're going to criticize the police procedure the whole way through this, aren't you?'

'Yup.' Tossing the remote out of her reach, he leaned back and stretched his arms over his head, casually dropping one of them on her shoulders on the way back down.

Her head turned, brows lifted as she looked into his eyes. 'Seriously?'

'What?'

'That move went out with drive-ins.'

'I heard they were making a comeback.' Setting his feet on the chest she used as a coffee table, he pulled her closer to his side.

It took another five minutes for her to take her shoes off. Tossing cushions out of the way, she leaned into him and curled her legs beside her body. Finally she took a breath and looked up at him, her voice low and soft. 'You can't have gone that long without sleep. You wouldn't be upright.'

'Eventually your body says enough's enough. I'm due an eight-hour coma soon.' He reached out and tucked a strand of hair behind her ear. 'With any luck it'll get here at night so I don't wake you up.'

She grimaced. 'Despite what you think I didn't say that to make you feel guilty.'

'I know.' But since he'd already given her more than he planned, it was his turn. 'Tell me what's been bothering you since I got here.'

Turning her head, she dropped it back against his arm, closed her eyes and scrunched up her face. There was a low, strangled sound from the base of her throat before her eyes popped open. Then she turned towards him, tucking her legs underneath her. 'Can we talk about the whole thoughtful and protective combo you've been using on me first?'

'Okay,' he replied with suspicion.

'Could you stop doing it?'

He stifled a smile. 'Taking the independence thing a tad too far, don't you think?'

'See?' She scowled. 'You're doing it again. It's the tone you use.'

'I only have the one voice.'

'No, you don't. It changes.' Lifting a hand, she counted them off on her unfurling fingers. 'There's your considerate voice, your seductive voice, your "I'm in trouble if I don't shut up soon" voice—'

He captured her hand. 'Let's go back to the problem you have with thoughtful and protective.'

'I don't like it.'

Yes, he got that from the number of times she'd resisted it. 'Protect is what I do,' he reasoned. 'Along with the word serve it's written in big letters along the sides of vehicles with big flashing lights on top. You may have noticed them in the city.' A corner of his mouth tugged wryly as he admitted, 'Thoughtful I have to work on from time to time.'

'No,' she said with a small pout. 'You're pretty good at that one too.'

He took a breath. 'Let me get this straight. You want me to not care what happens to you and be more inconsiderate.'

Jo opened her mouth, closed it and rolled her eyes. 'It sounds stupid when you put it like that.'

'Little bit.' He nodded.

She jumped from one subject to another. 'You can't text me when I'm in work.'

'If you were busy you wouldn't have answered.'

'That's not the point. Some of those messages were…' She rocked her head from side to side while seeking a word in the air beside his head.

'I could point out it takes two people to have text sex.'

'We weren't having text sex.'

'Text foreplay,' he corrected. 'Still takes two people.'

She changed subject again. 'What happened yesterday?'

'Might need you to narrow that one down…'

'You backed off,' she said with a note of accusation.

'Said I would, didn't I?'

'Not to the point where finding food was as urgent as someone lying across the bar with a gunshot wound.'

The second he realized he'd stepped into an ambush Daniel swore viciously inside his head. He'd been right to think she knew there was something wrong. On the way home he'd put her uncharacteristic silence down to exhaustion. But she'd been thinking about it the whole time, hadn't she?

'And there's that look again.' She aimed a brief glare at him. 'I swear you're turning me into a harridan.'

'A what?'

'Never mind.'

Without warning she changed position, freeing her fingers so she could brace her hands on his shoulders as she straddled his lap. When she wriggled her hips Daniel clamped his hands on her waist to hold her still before their bodies aligned. It was difficult enough to stay one step ahead of her without the kind of moves he'd pictured them doing naked.

'Talk to me,' she demanded.

'You know I can move you off me if I want to end this conversation.' He set his feet on the floor in preparation.

'Still sitting here, aren't you?' She arched a brow. 'Did you feel bad about trying to play me?'

What the—? Daniel frowned. 'When did I do *that*?'

'All those thoughtful things you claim you have to work at—they're part of your campaign to get me into bed.'

'Considering my many skills in the art of seduction, I'm a little insulted by that.' He shook his head. 'Guy can't make the effort to be nice to you, can he?'

'Being nice isn't supposed to take effort.'

'That's the thing with resistance. It makes everything more difficult.'

'So stop resisting and tell me what happened yesterday.'

Daniel sought a safe route through the minefield they were entering and—since it seemed pointless trying—dumped pretence in favour of a little dose of honesty. 'Think you'll find it any easier to talk to me about why you still have doubts than I'm finding this?'

'No,' she admitted in a thicker voice. 'But while we're on the subject, why don't you have doubts?'

'When it comes to sleeping with you, I thought I'd made it clear where I stand.' One of his hands slipped from her waist to her hip. 'I can run through it again if you like...'

Her eyes darkened. 'Not necessary.'

'Well, then...' Sliding his hand further down her leg, he edged his fingertips beneath the hem of her skirt. Gaze fixed on her face, he watched her reaction as he touched the soft skin on the outside of her thigh.

Full lips parted as she sucked in a low breath. Her long lashes lowered as she focused on his mouth. Distracting them from the topic of conversation wouldn't take much, but while Daniel knew he could get lost in her, he sensed a small corner of her mind wouldn't be there. Selfishly he wanted it to be; for her to share with him the moments when everything became sharper, clearer, there was one common goal and nothing else mattered. No yesterday, no tomorrow, no half an hour ago or two hours from then. He wanted her to see the side of him few people did outside his working environment—before the mistakes were made or the self-recrimination could set in.

'Do you think about when this is over?' she asked in a smaller voice as if she stepped inside his thoughts. 'About the mess we could leave behind?'

'Yes,' he said roughly.

'Me too,' she whispered before distracting him with a swipe of her tongue across her lips. 'Best-case scenario, we end up in a better place than we were before. Worst case—'

'We end up saying things to each other we can never take back,' he finished.

'Yes.'

When Daniel looked into her eyes again he found enough vulnerability to punch a hole in his chest. She didn't just have doubts, she was genuinely terrified...of *him*? What had he done to frighten fearless Jo? When the thought entered his mind, he dismissed it as swiftly as it arrived. A woman didn't kiss as she did, move as she did or look at a man the way she did when she wanted him if she didn't have an intimate knowledge of sex. So what else could it be?

He thought out loud. 'Maybe the problem we have right now is trust...'

Her gaze lowered to the hands that had moved from his shoulders to his chest. 'You're saying you don't trust me.'

'No, babe, that's not what I'm saying.' He took a long breath and chose his words carefully. 'I can't promise you this won't be a mess when it's over...'

'I know.' She smiled the same tremulous smile that had sent up a warning flare for him in the first place.

'Do you know I would never willingly do anything to hurt you?' It floored him how much he needed her to know that. But even as he said the words he knew he had to amend them. 'If anything I said or did in the past—'

'*Don't.*' She pressed a forefinger to his mouth for a second. 'I get it. You think *I* don't trust *you.*'

'Why would you? I haven't done anything to earn it.'

She thought it over for a second. 'It's not that I *don't* trust you. I'm just—'

'Wary,' he supplied, feeling the something he still didn't recognize expand inside his chest when her eyes warmed at the understanding.

'Yes.'

'I'm not sure you should trust me, Jo,' he heard his voice say. 'When I'm around you, *I* don't trust me.'

'Why not?' She used the hand on his jaw to turn his head when he broke eye contact. 'No, I need to look into your eyes when you tell me so I can see if they're there.'

'See if what's there?'

'The blue goes cloudy. You have shadows.' Her fingertips whispered over his jaw. 'They're how I know there's something you're not telling me.'

Daniel felt as if something heavy were pressing down on his chest, each breath requiring considerably more effort.

As if she could sense it, Jo angled her head and looked deeper into his eyes, her hand turning so the backs of lightly bent fingers could skim the side of his neck. 'Tell me why you don't trust yourself around me.'

'I carry a lot of baggage. I'm not willing to offload it on you.' He frowned, both at the confession and the roughness of his voice. So much for the techniques the Marines taught in the event of capture and interrogation. She might as well hand him a pen and paper so he could save them both time by mapping out the weaknesses in his lines of defence.

'You think you're the only one with baggage?'

'No.'

Hand turning, she ran her fingertips under the curved neckline of his sweater, her gaze lowering to watch what she was doing. 'Shall I tell you a secret?' she whispered as her gaze tangled with his again.

Daniel nodded, mesmerized by her eyes and hypnotized by her touch.

'I want you more than I've ever wanted anyone.' When she smiled, it was steeped in sensuality. 'I fantasize about you, what we'll be like together and how it will feel. Right now, when we're like this, I doubt my doubts.'

If she was saying what he thought she was saying...

Leaning in, she pressed her lips to the throbbing pulse on his neck. A jolt of heat seared through his body, settling hot and heavy in his groin. Moving his hands to the curve of her spine, he slid her forward on his lap, aligning their bodies the way nature intended. She took a shuddering breath when she discovered what she was doing to him, moved her hips in a way that made him stifle a groan. He wanted her with a desperation he'd never experienced before. It suddenly felt as if she were a lifeline and if he didn't grab hold of it and hold on tight—

When she whispered in his ear, her warm breath caressed his skin. 'What scares me is how I feel when I can hear you on the other side of the wall and I can't get to you. The times when you're so far away from me it feels like I can't reach out and touch you...'

Daniel had experienced similar scenarios, so he knew how it felt from her point of view. But he had never been on the other side.

She took another shuddering breath. 'I need to know that you're with me and we're in this together...'

For the first time in his life he knew what it felt like to be trapped and helpless. The kind of faith it took to hand over control. He didn't consider himself a hero when he went to work. He was just a guy doing his job, failing more often than he would prefer. The real heroes were people who trusted completely and laid their lives in another person's hands.

'I'm right here, Danny. Let go...'

The words were so low they were almost lost in the storm he could feel raging inside him. It was possible she might not have said them, the need coming more from him than from her. But even if he hadn't imagined them he couldn't let go. If he did a mountain of torn and bleeding emotions would collapse and he would be crushed under their weight. He was too worn down, too exhausted from fighting the demons who took him to hell night after night. If she knew how inadequate he was, the number of times he'd failed someone who reached out to him...

'Jo—' He choked on her name.

'Shh...' Pressing soft lips to his mouth, she fed him kiss after desperately needed kiss.

At first there was only the taste of her, her heat and a sense of glory he had never known could be found in surrender. Then she rocked her hips, grinding her heat against the tight fit of his jeans and lust exploded inside his body with the force of a percussive blast.

With the equivalent of a dying breath, Daniel dragged his mouth from hers to rasp, 'Tell me to go.'

'No.' Full lips curved into a decadent smile against his mouth. 'Make love to me, Danny. *Take me to bed.*'

It was the sweetest command he'd ever been given.

CHAPTER TEN

'Mix and match can have a disastrous outcome if you get it wrong. But step outside your comfort zone and you might discover something unique.'

DENSE lashes fluttered as he started to wake up, the movement absurdly delicate against the masculinity of his face.

Jo smiled when she was looking into vivid blue eyes. 'Good morning, sleepyhead.'

''Morning,' his deep voice replied, the mattress dipping as he rolled towards her. 'What time is it?'

'Saturday o'clock and I believe your shift doesn't start until midnight.' Moving closer to the edge of the pillow, she rested her cheek on her palm. 'I've been thinking…'

'Uh-oh…'

'You know what I've never done?'

'Spent the night waking someone up so you can sleep?'

It was the kind of opening she could have used to get him to talk to her. But considering the major step forward they'd taken in intimacy she found herself wary of taking an equally giant step back. 'I've never spent the day in bed with a sexy naked guy,' she confessed with a dramatic sigh. 'Don't suppose you know where I could find one?'

'I prefer not to start my day with hitting someone.'

'Guess I'll have to settle for you, then.'

He smiled lazily. 'How come?'

'Because you're the only naked guy here?'

'I meant how come you've never spent a day in bed with a sexy naked guy before?'

'Workaholic.' She rolled her eyes. 'Sad, I know.'

'No,' he said in a lower voice. 'Just surprising…'

'There's a little more to my job than sitting in a coffee shop three times a week.'

'After seeing your work schedule I don't doubt that.' He stretched his large body, claiming even more of the bed. 'What I find tough to believe is some other guy hasn't *tried.*'

Jo stifled another smile. 'Correct me if I'm wrong, but until recently weren't you convinced men were throwing me out of their apartments in the middle of the night?'

'That was before I knew you better.'

'And you think you know me better now?'

'I'd like to hope so.' He took a long breath. 'But it's more a case of show than tell.'

Heat flared through her body when he slanted his mouth over hers. Her skin was hyper-sensitive, as if everywhere he'd kissed and caressed while he undressed her had been branded by his touch. If there had been any question her body was tuned into his there was no doubt now. His need magnified hers. His desire for her made her want him more. For years they had been unable to hold a conversation but in one night it felt as if they'd learnt to communicate without words. He dragged his mouth from her lips to blaze a heated trail down her neck, his magic fingers skimming her body from hip to waist. A purr of sinful pleasure ran through her body in response; the combination of strong male and gentle touch unbelievably carnal. But when he moved his hand higher and got to her ribs, she squirmed.

'Mmm,' he hummed in a low, vibrating rumble into her ear. 'That I didn't know.'

'Don't,' she warned unconvincingly.

He did it again.

Amid squeaks of protest and bursts of laughter, naked limbs tangled with sheets. Deeper chuckles of laughter joined hers, filling her with a sudden burst of undiluted joy. When they rolled off the edge of the bed and she landed on top of him, Jo leaned back and blew a strand of hair out of her eyes. She still didn't know why their relationship had changed, but as she smiled down at his grinning face it didn't matter.

All that mattered was he looked as happy as she felt.

Beyond happiness she could feel an irresistible, heart-warming tenderness. Whether it came from him or from her, she didn't know. She ran her fingertips over early morning shadow and warm skin, her gaze studying the different shades of blue in his amazing eyes. How he had looked at her as their bodies joined together was something she would never forget. It felt as if he had given her something she never had to give back. To deny she had given him something in return was pointless.

For the first time, instead of allowing someone to occupy a tiny corner of her heart, she'd given part of it away.

Without warning emotion clogged her throat. Leaving him would be one of the most difficult things she'd ever had to do. How was she supposed to tell him she was leaving when she couldn't cushion it with the confession she didn't want to go? She would miss him. But she'd been alone before. She could do it again. She didn't have a choice. Not if giving up the dream within her grasp meant replacing it with one she could never—

'What is it?' he asked in a deeper, rougher voice.

Unwilling to take a chance he would know she was lying—even if it was just with a shake of her head—she leaned down and pressed her mouth to his. The one more minute she'd once wanted had become one more day. She didn't want what they had to be over yet. She wasn't ready to let go.

In the absence of honesty, she sought the lightness she'd been aiming for when he awoke.

'Know what else I figured out when I was thinking?' she mumbled against his lips. 'A woman must have taught you some of those moves you used on me last night.'

'Not going there,' he mumbled back.

'I'm thinking older woman, younger Danny…'

His mouth curled into a smile. 'Jealous?'

'Since I'm reaping the benefits I was thinking more along the lines of a thank-you card…'

'What makes you think I'm not a natural or inspired?'

'Inspired is good. I'd roll with that if I were you.'

He did, reaching a hand above them for a pillow when Jo was pinned beneath him. Tucking it beneath her head, he smiled a predatory smile. 'This whole day in bed—does it have to be *in* the bed to count?'

She batted her lashes. 'What did you have in mind?'

'Again,' he said in a rumble so soft it was more like a vibration in his chest. 'More a case of show than tell…'

The 'interrupt the interrupted sleep' ploy was clever; he had to give her that. He was feeling better than he had in…

Yeah, it had been a while.

The first real test of how well they were doing appeared on their third night together. When he jolted into reality she was staring at him with wide, fear-filled eyes. But it hadn't been fear for herself, it was fear for *him*. Daniel felt the whispered caress of her touch soothing him. But when he looked at his hands and saw how tight he was holding her upper arms, he was filled with horror. What the hell was he doing? A wave of nausea rolled over him at the thought of leaving a bruise on her skin and he knew he had to get away from her. *Fast*.

She hadn't tried to stop him when he said he was going to run it out of his system. But before he left, her soft voice asked, 'What did it mean?'

He froze in the doorway. 'What did what mean?'

'You kept saying you needed two more; two of what?'

He walked away without answering. But despite the vow he made to place some distance between them, after a quiet shift filled with thoughts of her he was back at her door. Seeing her robbed him of his ability to speak. Determined to show her how much he needed her when unable to say it aloud, he kissed her welcoming smile and took her straight back to bed. One eight hour coma later and he was able to demonstrate what a damn fine specimen of manhood he could be when firing on all six cylinders. Unfortunately, it also meant something else.

But if he was being forced to leave her bed again he was determined to give her an afternoon to remember.

Leaning against a tree at the edge of the photo-shoot in Central Park, his gaze took in the details of a world he knew next to nothing about. Judging from what he had observed he wouldn't have the patience, whereas Jo seemed to thrive on it. She was animated, lively and enthusiastic; sparkling as if she inhabited some kind of secret magical kingdom. She obviously loved what she did. It glowed from her eyes.

For a second he found himself curious what it would feel like to have her look at *him* that way. But since it made the something he didn't want to identify ache in his chest…

'And that's a wrap, boys and girls!'

While models and assistants breathed a visible sigh of relief, the photographer held out a hand to Jo and waggled his fingers. 'Hand it over, my sweet. Have to be careful what awful images of me you place in the public domain…'

'With someone as photogenic as you?' Jo scoffed as she gave him a small digital camera.

Head bowed, he scrolled through the images. 'Not that one. *Definitely* not that one, and when I've deleted everything which doesn't meet my approval we can discuss your new friend.'

'What new friend?'

'The guy who has been watching your every move for the last fifteen minutes.' Waving a hand at a security guard with a silent *let him through* as Jo's gaze found Daniel, he made the comment, 'Obviously doesn't work in fashion...'

'No,' she replied. 'He's a—'

'Don't tell me. It's much more fun to fantasize.'

Daniel stepped over the line to claim his place beside her. 'Hey, babe.'

'Hello, handsome.' The photographer grinned.

Jo bit her lip and stifled a chuckle. *'Behave.* Christophe Devereaux, Daniel Brannigan. Danny, this is Chris.'

'Explains a lot about the smile you've been wearing this morning,' the man remarked as he looked Daniel over. 'How long have you been dating? Because seriously, honey, those clothes?'

'Kinda work for him, don't you think?'

'I suppose, in a blue collar kind of way. But picture him in Armani or Gucci or maybe a little—'

'Not gonna happen,' Daniel said dryly when he got tired of being talked about as if he weren't there. Being objectified was both uncomfortable and unfamiliar and since he'd been dressing himself from the age of two, he didn't need any help.

'Not a fan of labels,' Jo felt the need to explain.

It wasn't necessary in Daniel's opinion. He didn't have to answer to anyone, least of all a guy who obviously spent too much time in front of a mirror.

Christophe blinked. 'Well, *that* must be refreshing...'

Judging by the soft, almost affectionate smile she gave him, Daniel assumed it was a good thing. Somewhat pathetically it forced him to resist the urge to smirk at her friend. Five minutes in her magical kingdom and he suspected he wouldn't be viewed as much of a prince.

'You done for the day?' he asked.

'Yes. But you already knew that or you wouldn't be here. *Someone* obviously sneaked a look at my planner this morning…' Leaning forward, she placed the air kisses Daniel had always hated above each of her friend's cheeks. 'I owe you one for today. Thanks for letting me sit in.'

'We'll call it even for the support you gave me when I was a virtual unknown; nothing quite like a mention on that blog of yours to raise one's profile.' He aimed a haughty, almost territorial look at Daniel. 'Take care of her or you'll have me to deal with.'

Somehow managing to keep a straight face, Daniel gave him a nod in reply. It wasn't much of a threat. What was the guy going to do, fluff him to death? Eager to leave, he took Jo's hand. 'Let's go.'

'Just out of curiosity,' she said as they walked through the park, 'what would you have done if I'd met Liv today the way I was supposed to?'

'Still bugging you, isn't it?'

'That I'm keeping something from my best friend?'

'Even when we come out there will be certain things you can't discuss with her, you know that, right?'

Her eyes widened. '*When* we come out?'

Oh, no, she didn't. 'We're not arguing today. I have plans for what's left of it.'

'Where are we going?'

'Wait and see.'

'Is it a surprise?' She brightened. 'For *me*?'

He smiled when it literally put a skip in her step. 'Do I need to explain the concept of wait and see?'

'Are we there yet?'

'No.'

Several repetitions of the same Q&A later, he stopped in the middle of a path and her brows lifted in anticipation.

'You have two choices. Zoo—' he jerked a thumb over his shoulder '—or that…'

Leaning to the side to look around him, she stilled and for a moment Daniel thought he'd got it wrong. Then her face lit up. 'Are you kidding me?' She threw herself at him. 'I *love* this!' After a tight hug, she stepped back and grasped hold of his hands. 'You're coming on all the rides, right?'

'I'm not sitting on the little wooden horses.'

'Ever kiss a girl on a carousel?'

'Wouldn't that be kissing and telling?'

As they stepped through the gates she turned towards him. 'I refuse to participate in my surprise until you agree to do everything with me.' She focused on his mouth, looked into his eyes and smiled meaningfully. 'But I promise to make it worth your while if you do…'

'Attempting to bribe a police officer?' Daniel assumed a deadpan expression. 'You know I can arrest you for that.'

'*Silly.*' She rolled her eyes. 'If you put me in a cell for the night how will you collect your reward?'

If he was getting to spend the night with her it would be a good point. 'You want pink fluffy stuff on a stick or do you want to eat something sensible?'

'Pink and fluffy.' She tugged on his hand. 'We can take it on the carousel with us.'

Leaning against a ridiculous-looking wooden horse was as much of a compromise as he was prepared to make. While the platform began to move he watched her suck her fingers before peeling off another lump of fluffy candy. She'd been driving him crazy with that move while they stood in line; the glint in her eyes telling him she knew exactly what she was doing. Reaching out, he curled his hand around the back of her neck and pressed his mouth to hers. Intended as punishment for her actions, it instead led to the first sugar rush of his life. When he lifted his head she stayed where she was, eyes closed and a blissful smile on her face.

She sighed. 'Carousels officially rock my world.'

Daniel smiled. Not as much as she rocked his.

Several rides later, he was hooked on her enjoyment and feeling pretty damn proud of himself for satisfying her need for fun. It was another thing he could add to his new list, having scrapped the one he made before they got involved. Now she was his to take care of, his to protect and her needs were his to satisfy; the mantra of *his, his, his* going a long way towards pacifying his inner Neanderthal every time one of the guys running a ride was foolish enough to flirt with her.

They took a break to grab a couple of soft pretzels with mustard. Jo shared her pretzel with a horde of cocky, well-fed pigeons while Daniel managed to share a dollop of mustard with his jeans. Biting down on a corner of her lower lip when he did it, she helpfully tried to remove the stain with a paper napkin until he was forced to remind her they were in a public place. Where there were *children* present. After a leisurely kiss to promise she could do whatever she wanted to him when they got home he watched as she looked over the crowd and smiled. Following her line of vision he discovered one of the children he'd mentioned with what was either a mother or a nanny; lightning-fast fingers fixing a braid in dark hair.

'Do you remember her?' he asked.

'My mom?'

When her smile faded a little, Daniel sought out a hint of regret for asking but couldn't find it. Hypocritical as it was, he wanted to know everything about her while remaining unable to give her the same in return.

He nodded. 'Yeah.'

Jo took a short breath and thought about what to tell him the way she always did when they discussed a subject she found difficult. It was how he knew when she was sharing things with him she hadn't told anyone else, the knowledge both humbling and adding to his guilt for being unable to do the same.

'Little things,' she replied as she fed the last of her pretzel to the pigeons. 'I can remember how she brushed my hair. She used to follow the brush with her hand.' A hint of wistful smile appeared. 'I still do that.'

'I know.' It was part of her morning routine. Watching her dress was almost as fascinating to him as taking her clothes off. When she looked at him in a way that suggested she knew what he was thinking he added another prompt. 'Keep going.'

There was another moment of thought as she selected a gift for him from a cache of precious memories. 'She used to hum when she was doing housework. My dad would say one of the reasons he loved her was because she had a song in her heart. He used to wink at me before he sneaked up behind her to dance with her. It drove her crazy if she was in the middle of doing something but she always laughed.' Jo nodded and smiled again. 'She had a great laugh.'

'What did she look like?'

'On rare occasions Jack will tell me how much I look like her.' She shrugged, the smile disappearing as she hid the hint of pain in her eyes with a blink of long lashes. 'I think it made it difficult for him to look at me when she was gone.'

Despite the matter-of-fact tone to her voice it was the first time he'd felt any empathy for her father. Daniel didn't want to imagine a world without Jo in it but he knew it would be a darker place. 'When did you start calling him Jack?'

'When he stopped being my dad.' She looked into his eyes and angled her chin. 'What was your dad like?'

Swift change of subject noted, Daniel shook his head and avoided her gaze. 'You already know the answer to that.'

'I know what everyone else in your family remembers.'

'You'd be better sticking with their impression. They argued with him less.'

'What did you argue about?'

'His disappointment in me was a favourite topic.'

Disbelief sounded in her voice. 'He *said* that?'

'With due cause.' He glanced at her from the corner of his eye, unwilling to go into detail beyond, 'None of the others ever mention how close I was to being the first Brannigan on the wrong side of the law?'

Her eyes widened. *'Shut up.'*

Pushing to his feet, Daniel turned and held out a hand, drawing her upright when her palm slipped into his. 'What do you want to do next?'

She smiled brightly. 'Finish talking about this comes to mind. I want to know what kind of trouble you got into.'

'And take a chance you might look at me differently?' A frown crossed his face as they walked towards a line of stalls. It was closer to the truth than he cared to admit. But since he wasn't convinced he wanted to know why, he left it alone.

'Well, *that* deserves a suitable punishment,' she retorted. When he glanced at her again, she was looking around. Her eyes lit up. 'Marines can hit targets, right?'

An hour later, he was trying to figure out how he'd ended up being the one carrying a three foot stuffed rabbit through the park. If making him feel like an idiot had been her goal he wasn't the only one who could hit a target. He held it up by long ears and gazed at it in disgust. 'It's cross-eyed.'

'Our imperfections make us unique,' her voice replied from above his head. 'Didn't anyone ever tell you that?'

Daniel looked at the pond. 'I wonder if it floats.'

'You wouldn't.'

'You can go get it when you fall off those rocks.'

'You see…' She turned and cocked a hip. 'I heard from a reliable source it's all about balance…'

He shook his head when she had to hold her arms out to her sides to stay upright. 'I'm not wading in after you.'

'You've got a lot to learn about when a girl wants to be

rescued and when she doesn't.' She turned her back to him and held her arms above her head. *'Catch.'*

Taking an immediate step forward when he realized what she was doing, he caught her in his arms as she fell.

'And you didn't drop the bunny either.' She grinned after checking. *'My hero.'*

Daniel nodded. 'You can use it as a life-preserver.'

Stepping closer to the edge of the water and swinging her back and forth, he smiled when she protested between bouts of lyrical laughter. Stilling, he looked down at her, his gaze roving over her face as he found himself wondering why it had taken so long to open his eyes and see what was right in front of him. Would it have made a difference if they'd got together earlier? Would his life go back to the way it was before when they were done? Maybe he should try to talk to her about—

'That one's new,' she murmured.

'What is?'

'The look in your eyes...'

Before he could scramble his way out of it or distract her with a kiss there was the sound of tinkling music.

She sighed heavily. 'That's my cell phone.'

'Don't answer it.'

'I have to.' She wriggled in his arms until he set her on her feet. Predictably the call resulted in the disappearance of Jo and the reappearance of dull, emotionless Jo.

Before she could say the usual words at the end of the phone call, he took a breath and held out his arm. 'I'm not carrying this thing on the subway.'

'A gentleman would,' she pointed out.

'Pity you're dating me, then, isn't it?'

She didn't try to stop him coming with her. But she would if she knew what he was planning to do. He'd had enough.

First opportunity he got—and he would damn well *make one*—Daniel was having that talk with Jack. Way he saw it, it was overdue.

CHAPTER ELEVEN

'When shopping it's important to keep an open mind. You can't always get what you want but be patient and you might discover exactly what you need.'

'I BETTER make him something to eat,' she said when they got Jack to his apartment a little after dark.

Daniel nodded. 'What else?'

'Check he has groceries.'

'You get what he needs from the store across the street. I'll make him something to eat.' When she wavered he added a firm, '*Go.* I've got this.'

Ignoring the voice in her head, Jo reached for her purse. If she was totally honest, breaking the habit of a lifetime to accept help probably stemmed from the need for a little space. As much as she had loved their afternoon together and felt bad for once again having to interrupt it, the one day she wanted kept turning into another and another. But she couldn't keep stealing memories, threading them together like glowing beads on a precious necklace. She had to tell him, especially when hiding it was slowly killing her. Trouble was she still didn't know why it was so darn difficult to find the words.

Seemed to Jo she'd been spilling her guts on pretty much every other subject, including things she'd never shared with anyone else. He was almost as good at getting her to do that as he was at avoiding sharing anything with her that did more than scratch the surface of his life.

Yes, that was bugging her too.

Halfway to the store she realized she hadn't checked the refrigerator to see what was there. But when she returned to the apartment she heard Daniel's voice say, 'I think it's time we had a talk.'

Jo froze inside the doorway. What was he doing?

'I'm only gonna say this once. You might not care what effect your actions have on your daughter, but I do. Cause her any heartache I'll be in your face 24/7. We clear?'

She was about to take a step forward when Jack replied, 'I love my Jo.'

'Did you love her when she ended up living on the streets because of you?' Daniel asked bluntly. 'She could have died. Someone she knew did—she tell you that?'

'No.'

'Course she didn't. Jo deals with things on her own; kills her to ask for help even with small stuff. If she knew I was talking to you right now she would kick my ass.'

True. Or at least be angry with him for interfering. But instead she remained frozen to the spot, unable to breathe.

'She's like her mom,' Jack said.

'Losing her that way can't have been easy.'

'It wasn't.'

'I'm sorry, Jack,' Daniel said with sincerity. 'I genuinely am. But do you think your wife would be happy Jo lost both her parents that day?'

Jo's eyes widened. How did he know that?

'If you want to honour her memory, this isn't the way to do it.' Daniel's voice took on the rough edge that always got to her. 'One day your beautiful daughter will meet someone, get married and have kids of her own. You want to miss out on your grandkids too? Wouldn't your wife want you to look for a piece of both of you in their eyes?'

Jack cleared his throat and answered, 'She would.'

The pain in his voice made Jo regret all the times they hadn't talked about her mom. They should have. But at eight she had found grief hard to handle and in later years she'd had too many other things to deal with. Then it was too late. Or so she'd thought. Hadn't been when she talked to Daniel, had it? Memories of her mom had flowed off her tongue as if they'd needed to be said. There had to be trust between them for her to have done that. The same trust that allowed her to stand silently by a door and let Daniel handle Jack his way.

She'd never let anyone do that before.

'You're going to have to shape up,' Daniel said. 'If I was the father of those kids I don't think I could trust you with them. But I'd want them to get to know you in the same way I'd want them to know about their grandmother. It would be nice if they could hear it from the man who loved her.'

Jo looked down and realized she had set a palm on her stomach. There was no question of her being pregnant but she had never thought about the kind of man she would want to be the father of her children. Frankly she'd never thought about *having* children. After all, she was twenty-four, wasn't like there was a rush. But with his mile-wide protective streak she knew Daniel would be an amazing dad. The thought of smaller versions of him another woman had given him…

Wow. Jo really didn't like that image *at all*.

'Still love her,' Jack said in a low voice.

'You ever think about getting grief counselling? I know someone who runs a group. It won't stop you drinking— you're the only one who can do that—but it might do you good to talk about her.' There was a brief pause before Daniel said, 'Lock stuff away, it can be harder to deal with. Trust me, I *know*.'

'You're a good man,' Jack said. 'Glad my girl has you in her life.'

So was she. There were dozens of things she would never forget about her time with him. But suddenly it didn't feel like enough any more.

'I'll drop the card by next week,' Daniel's voice said. 'Now let's see what we can get done before Jo comes back.'

As they moved she slipped back through the door, quietly closing it behind her. At the bottom of the stairs she swiped her cheeks and stared at the moisture she found on her hands. Crying was right up there with blushing on the list of things she never did. What was happening to her?

Pushing through the door, she walked across the street in a daze. She felt as if she was in shock. Not the least little bit as she'd thought she would feel if she fell in love. Surely feeling so numb meant she *wasn't* in love? Inside the store she picked up a basket and wandered aimlessly along the aisle. If she hadn't known there was a chance she was *falling* in love then what had she been so afraid of? Why was it so difficult to tell him she was leaving? Would she have reacted the way she did to the image of kids she hadn't given him?

Was she having a teensy little bit of a meltdown?

If it hadn't felt that way she might have reacted quicker when she rounded the corner. But by the time she realized what was happening it was too late.

Where was she?

With everything squared away and Jack sound asleep on the covers of his rack, Daniel drummed his fingers on the kitchen counter. He checked his wristwatch. She should have been back already. Restless, he decided to go look for her.

Jogging down the stairs and across the street, he opened

the door to the convenience store and checked the aisles. No Jo. Walking to where he assumed the checkout was he rounded a corner. There she was. An unwarranted sense of relief washed over him, but when her gaze darted to him and a brief look of agony crossed her face, he knew something was wrong.

Stilling, he looked to his left. *Son of a—*

'Don't move!'

Swiftly identifying the weapon pointed at the man behind the counter, Daniel made eye contact with the perp holding it. 'Take it easy. No one needs to get hurt.'

'Anyone come in with you?'

'No.' He took an instinctive step closer to Jo to shield her body with his. 'But you might want to think about locking the doors.'

'I said *don't move!*'

An unfamiliar buzz of fear swarmed over him, immediately replaced by a gathering rage he had to beat off with a mental stick. Since going Marine on the guy who'd placed his woman in danger wasn't going to help anyone but him, Daniel reined in his emotions and replaced them with rigid control. 'I'm just gonna lock that one.'

Without looking at her, he pointed a finger at the door a couple of feet past Jo. From what he could tell it was one of only two points of entry for a tactical team. While placing her within snatch and grab territory, it also put her directly in the line of fire. Daniel would take a bullet before he let anything happen to her. It was as simple as that.

'Why are you helping me?' The perp's gaze shifted between each of his hostages before he came to the conclusion Daniel was the greater threat.

Good call.

'I'd prefer not to get shot.' When a low gasp came from over his shoulder as the gun swung towards him, Daniel shrugged his shoulders and sent her a hidden message. 'I've got a hot date with a fiery redhead tonight.'

She was smart enough not to mention he was a cop, but he didn't want her to identify him by name. If an association was made between them, she could be used for leverage.

'Give him the money,' he told the man behind the counter.

'I don't want money. I want *my kid*,' yelled gun guy.

Couldn't walk into a simple hold-up, could she?

'I already said she's not here,' said the man behind the counter, drawing the perp's focus.

'Then you call her and get her to bring him down here.' The gun turned sideways, prodding the air. 'Do it *now*!'

Daniel moved his arm back and pointed his finger at the ground to indicate Jo should get behind him. In his peripheral vision he saw the slight shake of her head. She had chosen the wrong time to defy him. If he didn't have a job to do they'd be having the argument of a lifetime.

Sirens sounded in the distance.

'You called the cops?' the guy yelled.

Since he doubted the convenience store had a silent alarm, Daniel assumed a witness called 911. 'Still time to get out…'

The gun shifted direction again. 'Did *you* call them?'

'With my record?'

'What did you do?'

'Dealing.' He patted a pocket of his jacket to gauge the level of interest. 'Get us out of here before the cops arrive, I'll give you a sample.'

'I want my kid.'

So much for that idea. 'You do what you gotta do but I can't be here. They find me carrying, I violate my parole.'

'No one's going anywhere till I get my kid.'

'You've got hostages. They'll send in a SWAT team.' Daniel suppressed a threatening smile in case it fed into his deep-seated need to go feral. 'I heard those guys shoot first, ask questions later.' When his words garnered a glance towards the back of the store, he took a step forward. 'Let's go.'

'They'll catch us.'

Another step. 'Not if we move now.'

'I need time to think.'

Another step. 'I'm not going back inside.'

'Shut up and let me think!'

When there was a low clicking that indicated a round had been chambered, Daniel knew he was out of time.

'Get down!'

Launching forward, he grasped the gun arm, pushing it back and up. Tins scattered as he slammed it against a metal shelf. Once, twice and there was a cry of pain before the gun hit the ground. He kicked it out of reach, stepped forward, hooked an ankle and toppled the guy back onto the floor. Dropping to his knee, he flipped the body over, twisting the arm he held as he reached for the other one. From the moment he moved until the guy was restrained took less than ten seconds.

Once it was done, his gaze immediately sliced through the air to Jo. 'You okay?'

She nodded.

It didn't slow his heart rate. If anything, the fact she was standing on her feet added to the flood of rage he'd been suppressing. Which part of *'get down'* hadn't she got?

'I'm okay,' another voice announced, making Daniel swear viciously inside his head. There had been two hostages, Officer Brannigan, count them; one, *two*.

'Both of you get out of here. *Now*.' As he fought the red haze rapidly forming around the edge of his vision, he turned his head and saw her take a step towards him. 'I mean it, Jo,' he warned. 'You walk out that door, you go straight to the nearest squad car and you damn well stay there.'

It was the first time since his pre-Marine days he'd been

angry enough to yell his damn head off. He'd let her leave the apartment alone. Better still, he'd *sent her* to the store. If he hadn't gone looking for her, if he hadn't been there, if a loose round had gone off…

Grinding his teeth together, he focused on deep, measured breaths. His initial reaction was they'd gone beyond a promise she'd never go to the neighbourhood alone at night. If he had his way she'd be lucky to ever see daylight again. His second thought was every day of a life they shared would be a battle between her independence and his need to protect her. Fact was she didn't belong in his world any more than he did in hers.

'Who *are* you?' asked a muffled voice from the floor.

'You don't stay still, I'll be your ticket to the nearest emergency room.' Adjusting his position, he reached into the back pocket of his jeans. When he heard footsteps, he held his badge over his head.

'Yeah, we know. Still got a bit of a problem with taking time off, don't you?'

He glanced upwards. 'Hey, Dom.'

'Hey, Danny.' Dom grinned.

As the perp was cuffed and taken from him, Daniel got to his feet and headed for the door. He'd known the payback for his eight-hour coma was going to be a bitch, been prepared to pay the price when he knew there was time with Jo as a reward for holding on to his sanity. But to have one of the scenarios associated with his nightmares become *reality*…

As he crossed the street his gaze cut through flashing lights to locate her. Adrenalin still pumping, every tense muscle in his body strained with the need to get to her, haul her into his arms and never let go. But as she started to turn towards him, he stopped dead in his tracks.

For a second everything simply went silent.

Then it hit him.

How could he not have known? How in hell had he not

seen it coming? He'd stood on the edge of bridges, rappelled out of choppers, faced gunfire, crawled into narrow spaces where he could be crushed like a bug and had never once been as fearful as he was in that store. And now he knew why.

Turning away before she looked at him, Daniel dug out his cell phone. The call he made for back-up would most likely add to the fallout but he needed time to regroup and he couldn't do that when she was there.

Unable to tear her gaze from him for long, Jo watched as he paced the street while talking on the phone. She wanted to be strong. As calm and collected as he was. But in comparison to the numbness she felt walking into the store, her emotions were all over the place. If he'd been shot…if she'd *lost* him while he tried to protect her…

'You're Danger Danny's girl?'

Nodding, she dragged her gaze from him to look at the uniformed officer. 'I'm Jo.'

'Dom Molloy—I worked with Danny out of the ninth before he moved to the ESU. It's nice to meet you, Jo.' The dark-haired man smiled in greeting. 'I need to ask some questions and take a statement. You feel up to that?'

She nodded again. 'Yes.'

'We'll go over here where it's quieter.'

'Okay.' Jo looked over her shoulder at Daniel while they left. She didn't want to be somewhere she couldn't see him, but she wasn't going to let him down. She would answer all of the questions clearly and concisely and make sure everyone knew how amazing he had been. The need to step into his arms and stay there until some of his warmth and strength seeped into her shaking body would have to wait.

In comparison to the event itself, which had happened in slow motion, the wrap-up seemed to fly by. Next thing she knew a voice called her name and she was blinking in surprise.

Liv folded her in a brief, tight hug before studying her face with concern. 'Are you okay?'

'I'm fine.' Her gaze moved from Liv to Blake and then back to Liv again. 'What are you doing here?'

'Danny called.'

'She was too wound up to drive,' Blake explained.

'What he means is I was worried sick about you.'

Jo opened her mouth to say there was no need when a deep voice sounded behind her and her breath caught.

'She's given a statement. She can go now.'

Spinning on her heels, she looked up at Daniel and drank in the sight of him. Her gaze lowered briefly to his chest to take inventory while she curled her fingers into fists at her sides. He was okay, she reassured her pounding heart. He was *right there*. She could stand and look at him without feeling the need to cling to him like a drowning woman. She *could*!

'What happened?' Liv asked.

'Suspected EDP; she walked into a 10-52.'

Jo had no idea what that meant but she was too busy trying to keep her head above an unexpected wave of pain to ask. The image was too close to her earliest memory of him—the ache to have him acknowledge her existence as desperate as it had been back then. If Mr Cool-Calm-And-Collected didn't look at her soon she was going to—

'Why are you in street clothes?' Liv inevitably asked.

'I'm off duty,' her brother replied.

'Then why are you here?'

'None of your business,' he said in his don't-mess-with-me voice. 'And if you cross-examine her on the way home there'll be one less monkey-suited brother at your wedding.'

'Like Mom will let that happen.'

Daniel crossed his jaw. 'Get her out of here, Liv.'

'Wait a minute.' When he walked away, Jo followed him. 'I don't even merit a "see you later"?'

He kept walking.

'Come back here.' She scowled at his broad back. *'Danny!'*

He turned and looked her straight in the eye. 'If I come back over there I'm going to yell at you.'

Even hidden behind a mask of restraint, the force of his anger knocked her back on her heels. She was wrong. He wasn't the least little bit cool and calm. Judging by the set of his shoulders he was barely collected. It might not have been the reaction she'd hoped for but it was better than nothing.

'What were you doing in there?' she asked in a far from steady voice.

'My job.'

'Is part of your job to see how many times you can almost get yourself killed before you get it right?'

'If it costs our life to get someone out, that's the price we pay.' He waved an arm at his side. 'Ask any of these guys in a uniform and they'll tell you the same thing.'

She gaped at him. 'You have no idea why I'm upset right now, do you?'

'I *warned you* about the danger in this neighbourhood,' he replied through gritted teeth.

'You're *blaming me* for this?' She could hear her voice rising. 'Do you think I went looking for a speeding bullet so you could jump in front of it and prove me wrong about needing to be rescued? I *know* the risks you take for other people, Danny. I just don't want you to take them *for me.'*

'I'm supposed to stand there and let you get shot?'

The thread she was hanging from snapped. 'Do you think I wanted you in there? I spent every second after I walked into that mess *praying* you wouldn't come find me! I knew what you would do but knowing and seeing it happen are two different things. Danger is *your* addiction, Danny, not mine. I know it doesn't matter to you who it is you're try-ing to save—'

'It doesn't matter who—?' He clamped his mouth shut, then nodded firmly. 'That's it. You're leaving now.'

'I'm not—' When he stepped forward, Jo took a step back. *'Don't you dare!'* He bent at the knee and tossed her over his shoulder, marching forward while she struggled. 'Put me down, Danny! I *hate* when you do this.'

'Where's your car?' he barked at his sister.

'End of the street,' she replied on what sounded like a note of amusement.

'Don't *help* him.' Jo lifted her hands, attempting to get her hair out of her eyes so she could glare at his sister. 'I want you to file for a restraining order. If you don't I'm reporting your unmitigated jackass of a brother for assault.'

He tossed her higher up his shoulder and kept walking.

Not caring if she was dropped on her rear, Jo continued fighting. 'You might have fooled me for a while, you great ape, but now I remember everything that bugged me most about you.'

He stopped and swung her from side to side before asking, 'Jeep on the corner?'

'Yes,' Blake said.

Was no one on *her* side?

'Don't for a single second think we're kissing and making up after this either,' she said without thinking as he started walking again. 'There isn't anything you can say or do that—'

'Did she just say kissing?' Liv asked.

'Yup,' Blake replied.

Daniel dropped her onto her feet by the Jeep and aimed a filthy look her way. *'Well done.'*

'Like they hadn't figured it out already,' Jo bit back before glancing at Liv. 'Thanks for jumping to my defence.'

'After you kept this little secret?'

'Leave her alone,' Daniel warned.

A burst of laughter left his sister's lips. 'Oh, I haven't even got started on you yet. If you think I'm not going to ask what your intentions are towards my best friend—'

'This is where I tend to leave them to it,' Blake told Jo in a low voice.

'Tempting,' she replied. 'But give me a minute.' Placing a thumb and forefinger between her lips, she whistled loudly.

When the siblings looked at her, she drew on her rapidly waning strength and looked at Daniel first. 'You're in enough trouble already. If you weren't such an idiot you would know what I needed to avoid this meltdown when you walked out of the store. In case you hadn't got it already, protecting me from your sister *wasn't it*.' She turned her attention to Liv. 'And if you can think of a way I could have told you I was using one of your brothers to test the chocolate theory, feel free to let me know.' She glared at each of them in turn and lifted her chin. 'Anything else anyone wants to say?'

'I'm good.' Liv nodded before looking at Daniel. 'You?'

He glanced down at her from the corner of his eye. 'I ever thank you for bringing her home with you?'

'You're welcome.'

When he looked at her, Jo could feel some of his anger had dissipated, but not by much. She really didn't think she could take much more. For sixteen years she had stood on her own two feet, faced everything life threw at her and *nothing* had ever got to her the way he did. She should hate him for that, but she didn't. That was the problem. She felt so many things at once she couldn't untangle them to make sense of it all.

'Finished yelling at me now?' he asked in a gruff voice.

Oh, that was *so* unfair. He'd even managed to say it in a way that made it feel as if she weren't the only one struggling. The girl who had always considered herself a fighter had never felt the need to run away more keenly.

'You want me to leave? Congratulations, Danny, *you win*.' The secret she'd kept tripped off the tip of her tongue. 'I'm booked on a flight to Paris in six days.'

Daniel looked stunned. 'What?'

'You heard me. No big deal, right? Just moves our schedule up a little.' Unable to continue looking at him and with her throat closing over, Jo turned away. When she reached for a handle to open the Jeep, her shoulders slumped. 'Can someone open the door, please?' There was a high-pitched blip and a click of locks. 'Thank you.'

The trip home was long and interminably silent, but Jo didn't want to talk. Instead she turned her head and watched the blur of colours and lights and people as the city went by. It wasn't how she'd wanted to tell him, but it was done now and there was nothing she could do to take it back.

'Where are we going?' she asked when something outside the windows didn't seem quite right.

'Our place,' Liv replied.

Jo shook her head. 'No, Liv, I want to go home.'

They conceded without too much fuss, which Jo appreciated in her exhaustive state. But after insisting she would see her all the way into the apartment, Liv turned to her with concern in her eyes. 'You're not okay, are you?'

Jo shook her head.

'Brannigan men can be a little thick-skulled. But Danny—'

'Liv—' Jo grimaced '—please don't.'

'Just this one thing and then I'll stop.' She took a short breath. 'Back when Danny was a kid he could make his body and his hands do whatever he wanted them to do. I heard he could toss a perfect spiral with a football at two—throw a killer curve with a baseball at three. Dad thought it made him cocky; felt he had to bring him down a peg or two by pushing him till he learnt he had limits. All it did in the end was make Danny twice as determined, ten times harder on himself, and half as communicative. Dad never broke him, not on the surface. But it doesn't mean he doesn't have feelings or can't be hurt...'

'I know,' Jo said on a harsh whisper.

'Try telling him what Paris means to you and he might—'

Emotion clogged her throat again. *'Liv—'*

'I'm stopping now.' She folded Jo into another hug. 'You had a rough night. Go get some sleep. I'll check in on you in the morning.'

Jo stood in the centre of the room for a long time after her best friend left, feeling more alone than she'd ever been. Paris had been her dream for a long time. But with it far off in the distance she'd never spared a moment to think about the things she would leave behind. She had worked long and hard, fought for a sense of security and been blessed with more than she dared hope for in the days when it all seemed so far away. But to leave the city she loved, her home, her friends...

To leave the man she loved...

It might have taken a while for her to admit it, but it was there: solid and fixed and unshakable. She loved him.

But there was no point pretending he felt the same way. If he wanted to share his life he would want to share it all: the good and the bad. By holding back he was saying she wasn't the one for him. If he could share everything with her the way she had started to with him... If she knew he loved her as much as she loved him...

She shook her head and held back the tears she desperately wanted to shed. In six days she would go to Paris.

End of story.

CHAPTER TWELVE

'New shoes, desserts, nights out; what do they have in common? When there's more than one option available there's nothing worse than having to make a choice.'

THE scenario of the nightmare was no surprise after the events in the convenience store. But the outcome was different.

A shot rang out.

Daniel looked at her. He knew she could see the agony on his face but fought to hide it from her. She staggered forward as he turned, reached for him as he dropped to his knees. Then she was sobbing, their fingers trying to stem the flow of red.

'It's okay,' he said gruffly.

'Don't leave,' she choked.

The pain flayed her soul. As Jo woke up she curled into a ball, hot tears rolling down her cheeks, soaking the pillow. It was the first nightmare she'd ever experienced. How he had got through so many of them...how strong he had to be not to lose his mind... He was so very brave...

She stilled and held her breath, blinking in the darkness, listening to the sounds coming through the wall. The impetus came as a large chunk was torn off her heart. She had to go to him. She didn't have a choice.

Not when he was calling her name.

* * *

When Daniel opened the door large watery eyes looked up at him. After tossing tangled tresses of hair over her shoulder, her hands tugged on the belt of a dressing gown. She made a quick study of his face, scowled briefly at his naked chest, then caught her soft lower lip in her teeth and took a breath.

'I can't do this any more,' she confessed in a crackly voice as she shouldered past him. 'We need to talk.'

Talking was the last thing he wanted to do, particularly if it involved sitting still. When something happened Daniel couldn't control, his reaction had always been the same. He had to keep busy. Keep moving. Keep pushing his body until his mind had time to work through it. Lying down sure as hell hadn't helped. Not when he'd been subjected to eight years' worth of failings in one session.

It was tough to believe he could love someone enough to deserve them when he was filled with self-loathing. He frowned as he closed the door. 'You're supposed to be with Liv.'

'I wanted to sleep in my own bed.' Realization crossed her eyes. 'What was the plan if we didn't walk into a stick-up? A night in one of the hotels you stayed in after you got back?'

He scrubbed a palm over his face. 'Jo—'

'Make me coffee.'

'I'm not making you coffee.' He glanced briefly at his watch. 'It's four in the morning.'

'We're talking about this.'

'No, we're not.'

'Yes, we are,' she insisted. 'If you don't talk about it then everything stays locked up in your head and no matter what you do it won't go away. I think you know that.'

He did. He'd said something similar to Jack. But pushing him when she already had him on the run wasn't the right move.

Daniel looked anywhere but into her eyes. Way he saw

it, she was right to get as far away from him as possible. It wouldn't take long for a smart woman like her to work out how much more he needed her in his life than she needed him. Since he didn't plan on sticking around for that revelation, he should thank her for beating him to the punch.

'Do you know you were calling my name tonight?' she asked.

He nodded.

'You remember every detail of them when you wake up?'

He nodded again.

After a brief silence, she sighed. 'Go put on a T-shirt. I'll make my own coffee.'

Daniel used it to buy time, splashing water on his face and blinking at the bathroom sink before he dug out a T-shirt. He had to let her say her piece. The break had to be clean. If it wasn't it would take longer to heal. When he returned, she was sitting at the breakfast bar, her gaze fixed on his chest as he walked across the room. He lifted a fist to rub the ache it created, a cavalry charge of sensation thundering across his senses. Coupled with the need to do something physical, his body leapt to attention—cocked, primed and ready for action. But no matter how tempting it was when she looked ruffled and soft and sexy, he couldn't get lost in her any more.

Waiting for him to sit opposite her, she slid a mug across the counter. 'You should drink decaf.'

'Bit pointless drinking coffee if it's not got caffeine.'

She flashed a brief smile. 'I feel the same way. But you should consider it.'

'It won't make a difference.'

'Are the nightmares always worse after your eight-hour coma?'

'Payback.'

Inky lashes swept downward, her gaze studying her mug

as she turned it in her hands. 'Did you have the nightmares when you were overseas?'

'Slept like a baby.'

'Explains why you're happy to go back.'

'It's part of it,' he allowed.

'What happened to me in this one?' she asked.

Daniel pressed his mouth into a thin line. Even while she was sitting in front of him, the images remained sickeningly clear in his mind. He honestly didn't know how he could look at her every day, feel the way he did and resist the urge to smother her in the protectiveness she didn't want from him. She would try to soothe and reassure with a whispering touch and softly spoken words but even that wouldn't help.

A man like him should take care of the people he loved. It wasn't supposed to be the other way round.

'We're not talking about it,' he said firmly. 'I know you want me to but I can't.'

Her gaze lifted, her voice soft. 'Yes, you can.'

'No.' He amended the statement, 'I *won't*.'

'Not to me…'

'Not to you…' Looking into her eyes was costing him, but he forced himself to do it without wavering.

She stiffened. 'You were never going to talk to me about this, were you?'

'No.'

The sense of betrayal was palpable. While she'd trusted him with her body and some of her closely guarded memories, he had let go in the bedroom the way she wanted him to but never with anything else.

When her gaze lowered again, Daniel's roved over her hair, long lashes, lush lips and everything in between as if he felt he had to memorize her before she disappeared. She was so damn beautiful, so fragile in body but so strong in spirit. If she needed him as much as he needed her…if she loved him even half as much as he loved her, then maybe—

She cleared her throat. 'About Paris…'

'What about it?' he said flatly.

'I didn't plan on telling you the way I did.'

'Good to know.'

She shrugged. 'It's been my dream for a long time. I've wanted to go there since I went to work at the magazine and heard about the shortlist they have for the position.' She swiped a strand of tangled hair behind her ear. 'Career-wise it's a golden opportunity.'

Daniel quietly exhaled the breath he hadn't realized he was holding. *Her dream* and he would let her give it up for a *maybe*? He was a selfish son of a—

'I wasn't supposed to go this year,' she continued. 'The girl who was broke her leg and if I'd known—'

'When did you know?' he heard his voice ask.

'Since the day you started texting me.'

'The night you had sex with me for the first time…'

'The night we *made love* for the first time…' Jo corrected. 'And I swear if you try to make me regret a single—'

'That's what was bothering you.' It made sense to him now. By ambushing him and pushing him on things he didn't want to talk about, she found a way to avoid telling him. Did she know then how much he needed her? How desperate he was to have her?

'Among other things.' She nodded as if confirming his thoughts. 'I wanted to tell you…tried…I just couldn't…'

Do that to him? In case he begged her to stay?

'Before you got on a plane would have been nice,' he said dryly before lifting the mug to his mouth. Since drinking the coffee had the same effect as swallowing acid, he set it back down. 'What else didn't you tell me?'

'Don't do that,' she warned as her gaze lifted. 'I could have left you a Dear Danny letter. Instead I'm here trying to do what you won't: *talk*.'

'If you want to leave, leave.'

'You say that like I think I need your permission.'

A corner of his mouth tugged wryly. 'It's just as well you don't. Didn't hesitate when it came to accepting the offer, did you?' He leaned forward, lowering his voice conspiratorially. 'I'd heard when couples get involved in more than spectacular sex they talk over a decision like that.'

Averting her gaze, she blinked with bewilderment into the middle distance. 'Why do I suddenly feel like this is my fault and nothing to do with you? How did that happen?' She arched a brow at him. 'If you're done playing the jilted lover, maybe you should take a look at the facts and be honest with me. We both said we weren't looking for anything serious. We agreed to see where it took us and that we wouldn't fall in love. Did any of that change for you?'

'Did it change for you?'

'I asked first.' When she realized what she'd said she rolled her eyes. A huff of laughter left her lips, but when she spoke there was a crack in her voice. 'You think this is easy for me? You think I found what happened last night easy? I'm going to Paris. That's not going to change. But if there's something you want to say to me before I go—'

Drawing on every second of training he'd ever been given, Daniel looked her straight in the eye and lied. 'There isn't.'

Time stretched like taffy while she decided whether to believe him. Daniel's protesting heart thundered in his chest while he maintained rigid control over the crippling weakness of his emotions. She'd never know how staggeringly unprepared he had been to fall in love or how far out of his weight he'd been punching when he got involved with her.

'That's that, then.' She stared at him for another moment. For a second he thought he could see her eyes glistening but when she spoke again her voice was flat. 'I've got to go.'

He might have had the strength to leave it at that if she hadn't glanced at him as she stood up. She did it as if she couldn't help herself, a brief frown indicating her annoyance.

But that one brief glance into her eyes revealed enough raw vulnerability to tear through Daniel like a knife. It twisted sharply in his chest as he realized what he'd done, or rather *hadn't* done when he should. At the one time she'd needed him anywhere close to as much as he needed her, he'd let her down. With a blinding flash of clarity he realized what she'd wanted from him outside the convenience store. The one simple act it would have taken to avoid what she referred to as a meltdown.

The knowledge broke him so hard and so comprehensively the walls of his resistance collapsed into dust. While he couldn't get down on his knees and beg her to stay or ask her to give up her dream for a maybe, there was one thing he could do.

Across the room in a heartbeat, he flattened his palm on the wood, his voice gravelly. 'I can't leave you like this.'

'You're not the one doing the leaving, remember?' She yanked on the door handle. 'Let me go, Danny.'

'Not till you let it out.' He reached out to draw her to him. 'Come here.'

'No.'

When she took a step back, he took a step forward. She slapped his arms with the backs of her hands, tried to twist free and then pushed him hard in the chest with her palms.

'That's it,' Daniel encouraged. 'Go ahead and hit me if that's what you need to do. I can take it.'

'Why are you doing this?' she choked as she shoved his chest again. 'Why can't you just leave me alone? I *hate* you.'

'I know.'

Her small hands curled into fists against his shoulders. Leaning on them, she lowered her head and pushed her full body weight against him. 'And I *never* cry!'

'Delayed shock,' he reasoned as he circled her body with his arms.

'Let me go,' she pleaded.

'I can't, babe. Not till you let it out.'

Somewhere in the middle of mumbled protests and calling him names, her fists gripped handfuls of his T-shirt. Then she wasn't pushing him away any more. She was holding on tight and leaning on him. It was so close to what he wanted her to do for the rest of their lives Daniel came dangerously close to confessing how he felt, the words forming in his chest instead of his mind.

'I've got you,' he said gruffly.

The first racking sob ripped his heart out. He tightened his arms in response, holding her close as pain reverberated through his body. All she needed was a moment to get it out and then she would be fine. She would rediscover the joy she found in life, light up from inside the way he loved best and at least while she was in France, living her dream, Daniel would know she was happy.

So he held her while an eight-year-old mourned her mother and a fourteen-year-old showed how scared she had been every time a difficult bar owner got in her face. He smoothed silky hair while the eighteen-year-old faced her first night without a roof over her head and watched a boy she knew bleed to death in the arms of a female cop who would become her best friend.

He remained silent and solid; standing guard over her so the world would never know she had a moment of weakness after a lifetime of being strong. It was their secret. One he would keep for her until the day he died.

'Tell me to stay,' she whispered in a voice so low and muffled he had to strain to hear it.

'I can't do that,' he whispered back.

If she wanted to stay he wouldn't have to tell her. Part of the reason he loved her so much was because she was a born fighter. She might not believe it in her weakened state but his Jo was fearless in the face of adversity. She reached out and grabbed what she wanted with both hands. It was the final confirmation Daniel needed that he wasn't it. Not for her.

Gradually she regained control. 'I'm okay now,' she said against his chest. Leaning back, she swiped her cheeks. 'Might need a tissue, but apart from that…'

'You can use my T-shirt,' Daniel volunteered roughly.

She smiled tremulously. 'Shut up.'

When she looked up at him, as hard as it was to take, he knew she was going to be fine without him. A long enough break from him to catch up on her sleep, the first glimpse she got of her dream and she would bounce right back—probably a lot faster than he would. Unable to resist, he lowered his head for a soft, slow kiss; one intended to show her how he felt when he still couldn't say the words.

He loved her—he always would—and if she ever needed a chest to cry on all she had to do was come find him and he'd be there.

As their lips parted her fingertips whispered over his jaw, head leaning into the palm that framed her face.

He looked into her eyes. 'Go grab your dream, babe.'

'You try and get rid of a few,' she replied with a small, wavering smile as she lowered her hand to his chest.

'I will,' he promised.

When she dropped her arm and stepped around him, Daniel stayed where he was, unable to watch her leave.

CHAPTER THIRTEEN

*'The mark of a best friend is someone who will tell you
yes, your ass does look big in those jeans. It may be tough
to admit but sometimes we all need an intervention.'*

ATTENDING Sunday lunch with the Brannigans might not have
been the best idea she ever had. Not when pretending she was
fine and looking forward to Paris was wearing her mask thin.

Surrounded by people who looked like Danny in a house
filled with pictures of him didn't help any more than the
work she'd used to fill the days before she left. But at least
now she knew why he had been so easy to avoid. According
to his siblings he had an EMT cert due for renewal; one that
required he immediately jump on an empty spot in an available course.

Jo knew she should be grateful when there was a very
good chance seeing him again would have resulted in the
same plea she'd made last time. But she ached for another
glimpse of him in the same way her chest ached if she held
her breath for too long. She missed him so much the pain
was debilitating.

She missed the little leap of anticipation her pulse made
when her phone said she had a text or there was a knock on
her door. She missed the kiss that suggested the time he'd
spent away from her was filled with thoughts of getting her

naked again. She missed the calmness on his face when he slept in bed beside her; how it smoothed out the creases at the corners of his eyes. She missed his clean masculine scent, the heat of his touch, the punch of his infamous smile, the rumble of his voice and the sound of his laughter… She even missed arguing with him at the times he bugged her most. She just missed him.

'Who's for cheesecake?' his mother asked.

Since the traditional gathering for Sunday lunch had been turned into a 'Bon Voyage' party, Jo pinned yet another false smile into place. 'Me, please.'

Turning to hand over the pile of dessert plates to Liv in the seat beside her, she saw her friend still. 'You okay?'

'Forgive me,' she whispered as she looked into Jo's eyes and took the plates.

'What for?'

The sound of a door slam was followed by a familiar deep voice. 'I know I'm late. Not my fault. Took half of Ed Marks' shift when his wife went into labour and at the end of it some idiot flipped over a car avoiding a cat.'

Jo's breath caught. Oh, she was *so* not ready for this. She couldn't sit there, *opposite him*, and pretend she was fine.

'Your plate is in the oven,' his mother called. 'It's hot, so use a cloth.'

Frozen in place, gaze glued to the table in front of her, Jo wondered if she looked as shocked as she felt. Her cheeks felt as if they were on fire.

'How do you flip over a car avoiding a cat?' Tyler asked from further down the table.

'Beats me,' Daniel's voice said as he got closer.

By the time Jo saw his waist appear she was pretty sure she was having a panic attack. She checked for the symptoms. Racing pulse, lack of oxygen, light head, shaking hands… She stifled a burst of semi-hysterical laughter.

Just as well there was a fully re-certified EMT in the room, wasn't it?

'Can't blame the driver for a series of freak events.' He dropped the plate into his place and shook his hand.

'I said the plate was hot,' his mother said as he kissed her cheek. 'Boy or girl?'

'Don't know yet.' He pulled out his chair. 'Said I'd be happy with a Danielle or a Daniel... So what's the big family emergency I had to...?'

As his voice trailed off if felt as if the whole room went silent. Jo continued staring at the table, her heart beating so loud she was surprised no one could hear it. This was *not happening* and she was not going to cry even if it felt as if she'd sprung a damn leak over the last few days.

As he sat down opposite her she thought about looking at him and knew she couldn't do it. It had been difficult enough leaving him last time without telling him how she felt. She didn't think she could do it twice.

'Jo?'

Her gaze jumped sharply to the left where a cheesecake was waiting on a serving dish. She couldn't eat that. She'd choke.

'I don't think... I'm not...' Pressing her lips together, she sucked in a breath through her nose and swallowed hard before looking at Daniel's mother. 'Packing still...blog to write...' She flashed a smile as she jerked a thumb over her shoulder. 'I should...' She nodded. Pushing her chair back, she stood up and ducked down to kiss a cheek. 'Thanks for lunch.'

Practically running into the hall, she yanked her coat from the rack and left. It was official: she would have to live in France for the rest of her days.

As she stormed down the path and argued with the latch on the gate, she started to get angry at him for the first time since he'd let her walk away. Why couldn't he have left things the way they were when she hated him? She'd been *comfortable* hating him. He had no business making her fall in love with him, and what the hell was with the whole tenderness thing when her heart had been breaking? She swung open the gate. Of all the inconsiderate, unforgivable, inconceivably hurtful things he could possibly have done—

'Why aren't you in Paris?'

She swung around when she heard the deep rumble of his voice, anger giving her the strength she needed to face him. 'Did you know I'd be here?'

'Did it *look* like I knew?'

'I don't know. I couldn't look at you!'

He frowned at her, looking every bit as angry as she felt. 'Somewhat ironic considering I couldn't keep my eyes off you.'

Jo glanced at the house, realization dawning when she saw a twitching curtain at a window. 'Were we just ambushed?'

'I thought you'd met my family,' he said dryly. 'Didn't I mention how much they love to stage an intervention?'

'Staging an intervention suggests this is a problem which can be fixed,' she snapped at him. 'Since you made it obvious it can't you can go back in there and explain why.'

Daniel's eyes narrowed. 'What happened to equal terms and not being made out to be a victim of seduction?'

'You want to tell them I seduced you, go right ahead, but if you think for a single second I'm going to let them look at me like some poor broken-hearted sap who was foolish enough to fall in—' She slapped a hand over her mouth, her eyes widening with horror.

Angling his head, Daniel looked at her from the corner of his eye and took an ominous step forward, his voice low. 'You want to finish that sentence for me?'

Jo dropped her arm to her side and glared at him. 'How about you hold your breath while you wait? And don't think I haven't figured out another of your lies, Daniel Brannigan.

I *knew* you had a problem with me being here on a Sunday. The second you thought I was gone you were back in that chair.'

He stilled and rocked back on his heels. His gaze searched the air for a moment as he crossed his jaw and then he looked her straight in the eye. 'I got to give it to my family—their timing is excellent. Having carried this around for a week I'm ready to offload and it's not like either of us was going to make the first move this time, was it?' He took a short breath. 'You want to know the problem? For five and a half years you were a giant pain in my ass. There were times I used to wish you would get hit by a cab or a piano would fall on you.'

'That's so sweet.' She smirked.

He took a measured step forward, the predatory gleam in his eyes making her feel as if he were a hunter and she were the prey. 'Then you start dressing like every guy's ideal cross between a librarian and a stripper.'

She gasped. 'I have *never* dressed like a stripper!'

'One word: *boots*. And did it sound like a complaint?' He took another measured step forward. 'You make me crazier than any woman I've ever known. You're so confident and independent you make it virtually impossible for a guy to figure out where he's supposed to fit into your life.'

She popped her fists onto her hips and angled her chin. 'He could try not letting me leave. It's a lot easier to fit into someone's life if they're on the same continent.'

'You said it was your dream.'

'Dreams *change*.'

'I know.'

She faltered. 'Are you telling me they're gone?'

He stilled a couple of feet away from her. 'Oh, I'm sure they'll be back. But it turns out they're less frequent when I have a bigger problem to deal with.'

'Feel free to not talk about that either.'

'I'm over here trying to tell you I'm in love with you and you'd still prefer to fight with me? Okay.' He shook his head and folded his arms. 'What do you want to know? Should I start at the beginning? First nightmare was my dad having his heart attack. I couldn't resuscitate him.'

'You weren't here when he died.' Jo frowned. 'Liv said he was on his own.'

'He was.' Daniel nodded. 'He died a couple of hours after I left. I came home on leave to tell him I was staying in the Marines, he reminded me he'd agreed to give his consent on the proviso I would come back and join the family business. Didn't mention he wanted me here 'cos he was sick, but after an hour of yelling at me about loyalty, duty, responsibility and not reacting particularly well to the fact Uncle Sam had taught me not to flinch under fire, I thanked him for his support over the years and walked out.'

The information made her frown. 'How does that make his death your fault?'

Pressing his mouth into a thin line, his shoulders dropped in a very visible hint of the weight he'd carried for so long. 'You need more, here goes. Next up was Liv—I was standing in the station the night she walked in covered in blood. At the time I thought it was hers—she wouldn't let me near her, said she was evidence. Brannigans watch over each other: my dad did it for Johnnie, Johnnie did it for Reid and so on till it was my turn with Liv. I figured she was tough, she knew what she was getting into—she didn't need my help. I was *wrong.*'

Since Jo knew more about the events of that night than he did, she had to clear her throat before she could speak. 'That wasn't your fault any more than Aiden's death was Liv's.'

He ignored her. 'The two more I was yelling about that night? Inches of space I needed to put pressure on an artery. Guy was trapped under a wall. He died.'

Her gaze immediately lowered to the hand he had scraped

on a wall, the pieces falling into place. 'They're all the people you've lost or came close to losing. You torture yourself even though you know it wasn't your fault.'

'It's my job to save lives—to be there when people need me. No matter how I try I keep messing that up.'

When her gaze lifted, for the first time Jo could see through the shadows in his eyes to the pain; the starkness of it almost breaking her in two. 'You were there for me,' she told him in a voice thick with emotion. 'Doesn't that count?'

'Except I wasn't, was I?' His deep voice was rougher than she'd ever heard it before. 'The one time you needed me to be there I let you down.'

Jo searched his eyes, frowning with confusion. 'You threw yourself in front of a gun for me. I've never been as scared as I was when you did that. I tried to find the words to tell you but I couldn't. If you'd died saving me, if I'd *lost you*…'

When he looked at her with enough yearning to take her breath away, she blinked. 'Wait a minute…what did you say?'

He pushed his hands into the pockets of his jeans. 'The one time you needed—'

'No.' She made a jumping motion with her forefinger. 'Go back further…' A sudden flare of hope made her heart falter and skip a beat. 'Did you say you're in love with me?'

The warmth in his eyes seemed to smooth the grimness from his face, making him look younger and unbelievably vulnerable. 'Was beginning to wonder if you'd noticed…'

Jo's faltering heart leapt, did handsprings and swelled to proportions that made it feel as if it couldn't be contained in her chest. 'If you're in love with me, then why did you let me leave, you idiot?' Realization dawned. 'You were scared…*of me*?' She took a step closer and looked deeper into his eyes, searching for answers, her voice filled with wonder when she found them. 'No, not of me—of how you felt about me… But I asked if you wanted to tell me anything and—'

He shifted his weight from one foot to the other in a move

she found impossibly endearing. 'I'm not the kind of guy who's gonna read you poetry or wear his heart on his sleeve. I think you know that by now. When it comes to how I feel the only way I can show it is by—'

'Protecting the people you love and looking after them.'

'Yes.'

'The things I told you I didn't want from you...'

His mouth tugged wryly. 'Yes.'

'So you were afraid to tell me you needed me because you didn't think I felt the same way?'

He let out a long breath. 'I'm always going to need you more than you need me.'

'You are *so* competitive.' Jo shook her head, the move immediately contradicted by the smile blossoming on her lips. She shrugged a shoulder a little self-consciously. 'I know I may have given the impression I don't need you but I thought you knew me better by now. I don't need you to protect me from every bump in life. But that doesn't mean there aren't times... I've needed you for longer than... I guess I was so focused on other things... Maybe I never knew...but I do now...'

Daniel released a small smile. 'You know you've been doing that a lot this last while.'

'Losing the ability to speak?' She puffed a soft burst of laughter. 'Yeah, I'd noticed that. I blame you.'

'Nothing new there, then.'

'Oh, there's something new,' she whispered.

As if some kind of shutter had been lowered, her feelings showed clearly in her eyes for the first time. Daniel's hunger for her entwined with a depth of tenderness that shook him to the very foundation of who he'd thought he was. The connection he felt to her in response to her need was a visceral tug. It drew him forward and pulled him in. He took his hands out of his pockets as he stepped forward.

She took a stuttered breath when he was close enough to

drag a knuckle along the skin of her cheek, her hand shaking as it flattened on his chest, directly above his pounding heart. Her throat convulsed before she spoke. 'You're wrong to think I don't need you, Danny. I needed you the day we met but I was too scared to admit it. What we have now was a dream too far out of my reach then, so I told myself I didn't want it.'

He threaded his fingers into silky hair as he framed her face. 'Your dream involved a guy who could feed you one of the worst lines you'd ever heard?'

Jo shook her head. 'That's not when we met.'

'What?'

'You think we met that fourth of July weekend. We didn't. We met two months before that.'

Daniel frowned. 'I'd have remembered.'

'Would you?' She lifted her brows and smiled tremulously. 'I was no one then.'

'You've never been no one,' he said firmly.

'I was invisible to most of the world; though in fairness that was partly my fault.' She blinked and took a deep breath. 'Make yourself invisible and you can fall between the cracks in the system. That worked for me for a long time. But you wouldn't believe how badly you want to be seen when you're homeless. The number of people who will walk past you without ever looking you in the eye…' When her voice wavered she took another short breath. 'Liv was the first. Then one day she was there with her partner talking to me when another squad car pulled up across the street and you got out.'

Daniel frantically searched his normally reliable memory as inky lashes lowered and she focused on the hand resting on his chest.

'You started talking to Liv, exchanged a few jokes with her partner—'

'Tell me I looked at you,' he rasped.

Her gaze lifted, shimmering with deeply felt emotion. 'Oh, you did something much worse. You looked straight into my eyes and smiled at me.' She blinked back tears. 'It was like…the sun coming out from behind a cloud or… *stardust*. I'd never seen anything like it before. When you took it away…when you left…' She cleared her throat and shrugged. 'For a second you had turned a graduate of the school of hard knocks into some starry-eyed, weak-at-the-knees daydreamer and I *hated you* for that. Because when you were gone and I wasn't blinded by that infamous smile of yours I had to open my eyes again.'

Daniel hadn't known it was possible to love someone the way he loved her. He wished he had been ready for her back then, that it hadn't taken so long to see what was right in front of him. Most of all he wished he'd been brave enough to take a chance on what he could have missed if the people who loved them hadn't banged their stubborn heads together. But if she'd fallen in love with him, unworthy as he was, he couldn't be too far beyond redemption to turn things around.

'Starry-eyed dreamers didn't survive in the world I lived in then,' she explained in her softest voice. 'So I toughened up, got twice as hard and the next time you saw me you didn't stand a chance.'

When the memory came to him, Daniel closed his eyes for a second. 'Did you have a really dumb hat?'

She blinked at him. 'What?'

The image was still foggy. 'It had ears.'

'Floppy dog ears.' She nodded as if he were insane to think anything else. 'I had three but it was my favourite. They were winter ski-hats a store donated to charity.'

Daniel smiled indulgently as he tucked a strand of hair behind her ear. 'It was *May*.'

'A person loses something like seventy per cent of their body heat through their head so I figured at night…' She bit down on her lower lip. 'You remember.'

'I asked Liv about you.' He wrapped an arm around her waist and drew her to him. 'Thought you were under age… You looked about sixteen with those braids in.'

'Nope, eighteen. I can't believe you remember.'

Lowering his head, he breathed in lavender shampoo, a deep-seated sense of contentment washing over him. 'You didn't look like that next time I saw you…'

'Liv took me for my first girly make-over.'

Nudging the tip of his nose into her fringe, he pressed a light kiss to her temple, his mouth moving against her skin as he confessed, 'You deserved better than that line. You were right to cut me down the way you did.'

'It was a really bad line,' she agreed as she hooked a thumb into one of the belt loops of his jeans. 'But you didn't deserve my response, Danny. I started a five-and-a-half-year war between us when we could have been doing this…'

'No,' he disagreed. 'You were eighteen. I was twenty-four. Six years made a bigger difference then. But even if it hadn't we weren't ready for this. While you were stepping out into the world and claiming a corner of it, I'd already started to retreat.' Leaning back, he used a thumb beneath her chin to lift it and looked into her mesmerizing eyes. 'I'm not gonna find talking about the nightmares easy, babe. But I'm willing to try. You'll have to work with me on that and a couple of other things. Being less protective won't be easy either and I know we'll argue about that. I can be—'

'Oh, I *know*. But so can I…' She silenced him with a soft, all-too-brief kiss. 'Still fell in love, didn't we?'

'You better be sure about that,' he warned. ''Cos once you say you're mine, that's it. We're gonna have to work at this every day but—'

'We will.' Love glowed from her eyes, lighting her up like a beacon. 'I love you, Danny. Even when I wanted to I couldn't make it go away. I don't want it to now. So if you need me to say it—yes, I'm yours.' She sighed, her gaze lowering. 'I can't get out of Paris...'

'I don't want you to, babe.' Daniel shook his head, his palm smoothing over her hair. 'The last few days I've run over dozens of different ways we could have made this work if you loved me the way I love you. How long will you be gone?'

'Three months.' She grimaced.

'Half a tour of duty...' He smiled when she looked at him. 'Way I see it, you going overseas is no different. You'd wait for me, right?'

She nodded. 'Yes.'

'Well, then, look at it this way—we get more opportunities for phone sex and conjugal visits...'

'I do fly home for Liv's wedding next month,' she pouted.

'I reckon I can book some time off either side of that for a couple of long weekends in Paris.' He lowered his head. 'How hot do you think I can make you for me before I get there?'

'Pretty hot.' She smiled as her chin lifted. 'If you pick the right words...'

'I'll buy a dictionary.'

'Did I mention the reason I'm still here is because of an air traffic controller thing? Or ground crew... I forget now...' she mumbled against his mouth.

'Tell them I said thanks.' He angled his head. 'How long have we got?'

'Two days...'

Her lips parted when he kissed her; the sweet taste of her breath caught on his tongue. His fingers slid deeper into her hair, palm cupping the back of her head as he deepened the kiss and the arm around her waist brought her closer. Perfect breasts crushed against his chest, fine-boned hands gripped a shoulder and the back of his neck. They could pack a lot into two days. It was sure as hell a challenge he was willing to accept. But before he did...

He leaned back and looked down at heavy-lidded eyes and kiss-swollen lips. 'They're at the window, aren't they?'

Jo glanced sideways and chuckled. 'Yes.'

'Want to see how fast I can make them move?' He grinned. 'You stay here. I'll be right back. Watch the window.'

As he turned and jogged towards the house, Jo looked at the window and laughed. Biting down on her lip, she gently swung her skirt while she waited for him to come back. She'd never been so happy. Danny loved her. He. Loved. Her. How could she have been so afraid of something so wonderful? Everything was so clear to her now, as if a veil of fear had been removed from her eyes. She should have viewed love the same way she viewed life and the moments of fun she was so addicted to. Grabbing hold of the good things and holding on tight made the tough stuff easier to take. Together they could face anything, even if it was the weaknesses within themselves. Her pulse sang loudly with a mixture of love, lust and joyous laughter when he returned and finally Jo could hear what it was saying. It had been singing to him all along. Two words, repeated over and over again in elated recognition.

It's you: he was her guy.

'Miss me?'

'Yes,' she answered without hesitation.

'Just so you know. If I ever thought I'd be doing this, I didn't picture it with an audience.' He took a deep, satisfied breath and smiled. 'But since one of them brought you into my life and the rest of them kept you here until I was ready for you, it seems kinda appropriate.'

Jo smiled back at him. 'What are you talking about?'

'This.'

She gasped as he lowered to one knee. 'Danny, you don't have to do that.'

His brows lifted. 'You think I'm letting you go to Paris without everyone knowing you're mine?'

'I'm coming back.'

'And when you do we plan on spending the rest of our lives together, right?'

'Yes.'

He waved the small box in his hand. 'That's usually what one of these says to the world.'

'You bought a ring?' Her eyes widened.

'Do you think you could shut up for a minute?'

She pressed her lips together. 'Mmm-hmm.'

When he spoke again his deep rough voice was laced with heartfelt sincerity. 'Jorja Elizabeth Dawson. You've been an adopted member of this family for a long time. I want to make it official by giving you my name. I love you, Jo. Will you...' he smiled his infamous smile '...marry me?'

Jo tried loosening her throat to speak.

'This is traditionally where you give me an answer,' he hinted heavily.

When she nodded frantically in reply, it shook the word loose. 'Yes.' She framed his gorgeous face with her hands and leaned down to kiss him. 'Yes, yes, yes.'

Large hands lifted to her waist, squeezing tight as he pushed to his feet and her arms moved to circle his neck. It felt as if they couldn't hold on to each other tight enough, even when he crushed her to him and lifted her off her feet. After swinging her feet from side to side, he set her down and opened the box. 'For the record, I did look at rings when I was running through ways of making this work. Did it while wearing tactical gear, so didn't take *any* flack from the rest of the team. Then I remembered this.' He took the ring out and reached for her hand. 'You can thank Grandma Brannigan and the fact I was her favourite grandson after I rescued her cat from a tree when I was seven. Might need to get it resized but…' He stared at her finger as it slipped into place. *'Maybe not…'*

Jo smiled at the winking sapphire, the same blue as his eyes when they darkened and she knew he wanted her. 'It fits.'

'Guess you were meant to have it, then, weren't you?'

She beamed when he looked at her.

'You ready to go back in? Sooner we finish lunch, the more time we can spend in bed before you leave.'

'I'm a course ahead of you,' she pointed out smugly as their fingers threaded together. 'Eat fast.'

A suspicious silence met them in the hall as Danny took her coat and hung it on the rack. It was just as quiet in the dining room when they stepped into it hand in hand. When Danny looked down at her from the corner of his eye she grinned. Who did their family think they were kidding? It was only as they approached the table emotion started to get the better of her. When he reached for her chair, his mother broke the silence.

'Everyone move round. Give Jo her place beside Danny.'

Long fingers squeezed hers as everyone moved and he led her around the table. She'd watched it happen with Johnnie's wife and when Liv brought Blake home, but Jo had never thought one day the gesture would be made for her. It was almost too much. Suddenly she belonged in a way she never had anywhere else. Sitting by the man she was going to spend the rest of her life with, she looked at the faces of the people she loved as they acted as if nothing unusual had happened.

She held up pretty well until she got to Liv, but when she did there was no stopping the tears. *Thank you*, she mouthed.

Liv's eyes shimmered, a hand waving in front of her body until Blake placed a napkin in it.

When Jo looked at Danny, he shook his head and glared at his sister. 'Stop making my fiancée cry.'

It was all it took to fill the room with sound.

'Missed your chance, Ty.'

'Not over till the pretty lady says, "I do."'

'I'm not wearing a monkey suit twice in one year.'

'You'll do as you're told, Reid Brannigan.'

Danny leaned in for a quick kiss before fending off his mother's offer to reheat his food, leaving Jo to sigh happily as she was handed a slice of cheesecake. Turned out the ideal guy *had* moved in across the hall from her.

Who knew?

* * * * *

THE GIRL FROM
HONEYSUCKLE FARM

BY
JESSICA STEELE

Jessica Steele lives in the county of Worcestershire, with her super husband, Peter, and their gorgeous Staffordshire bull terrier, Florence. Any spare time is spent enjoying her three main hobbies: reading espionage novels, gardening (she has a great love of flowers) and playing golf. Any time left over is celebrated with her fourth hobby: shopping. Jessica has a sister and two brothers, and they all, with their spouses, often go on golfing holidays together. Having travelled to various places on the globe, researching backgrounds for her stories, there are many countries that she would like to revisit. Her most recent trip abroad was to Portugal, where she stayed in a lovely hotel, close to her all-time favourite golf course. Jessica had no idea of being a writer until one day Peter suggested she write a book. So she did. She has now written over eighty novels.

CHAPTER ONE

PHINN tried hard to look on the bright side—but could not find one. There was not so much as a glimmer of a hint of a silver lining to the dark cloud hanging over her.

She stared absently out of the window of her flat above the stables, barely noticing that Geraldine Walton, the new owner of the riding school, while somehow managing to look elegant even in jeans and a tee shirt, was already busy organising the day's activities.

Phinn had been up early herself, and had already been down to check on her elderly mare Ruby. Phinn swallowed down a hard lump in her throat and came away from the window, recalling the conversation she'd had with Kit Peverill yesterday. Kit was Ruby's vet, and he had been as kind as he could be. But, however kind he had been, he could not minimise the harshness that had to be faced when he told her that fragile Ruby would not see the year out.

Phinn was quite well aware that Ruby had quite a few health problems, but even so she had been very shaken. It was already the end of April. But, however shaken she had been, her response had been sharp when he had suggested that she might want to consider allowing him to put Ruby down.

'No!' she had said straight away, the idea not needing to be considered. Then, as she'd got herself more collected,

'She's not in great pain, is she? I mean, I know you give her a painkilling injection occasionally, but…'

'Her medication is keeping her relatively pain-free,' Kit had informed her. And Phinn had not needed to hear any more. She had thanked him for his visit and had stayed with Ruby for some while, reflecting how Ruby had been her best friend since her father had rescued the mare from being ill treated thirteen years ago, and had brought her home.

But, while they had plenty of space at Honeysuckle Farm in which to keep a horse, there had been no way they could afford to keep one as a pet.

Her mother, already the breadwinner in the family, had hit the roof. But equally there had been no way that Ewart Hawkins was going to let the emaciated mare go back to the people he had rescued her from. And since he had threatened—and had meant it—to have them prosecuted if they tried to get her back, her owners had moved on without her.

'Please, Mummy,' Phinn remembered pleading, and her mother had looked into her pleading blue eyes, so like her own, and had drawn a long sigh.

'You'll have to feed and water her, *and* clean up after her,' she had said severely. 'Daily!'

And Ewart, the battle over, had given his wife a delighted kiss, and Phinn had exchanged happy grins with her father.

She had been ten years old then, and life had been wonderful. She had been born on the farm to the best parents in the world. Her childhood, given the occasional volcanic explosions from her mother when Ewart had been particularly outrageous about something, had been little short of idyllic. Any major rows between her parents, she'd later realised had, in the main, been kept from her.

Her father had adored her from the word go. Because of some sort of complication at her birth, her mother had had to stay in bed, and it had been left to Ewart to look after the newborn. They had lived in one of the farm cottages then, only moving to the big farmhouse when Grandfather and then Grandmother Hawkins had died. Phinn's father had bonded with his baby daughter immediately, and, entirely uninterested in farming, he had spent hour after hour with his little girl. It had been he who, advised by his wife, Hester, that the child had to be registered with the authorities within forty-two days of her birth, had gone along to the register office with strict instructions to name her Elizabeth Maud—Maud after Hester's mother.

He had never liked his mother-in-law, and had returned home to have to explain himself to his wife.

'You've called her—*what*?' Hester had apparently hit a C above top C.

'Calm down, my love,' he had attempted to soothe, and had gone on to explain that with a plain name like Hawkins, he had thought the baby had better have a pretty name to go in front.

'Delphinium!'

'I'm not having my beautiful daughter called plain Lizzie Hawkins,' he'd answered, further explaining, 'To be a bit different I've named her Delphinnium, with an extra "n" in the middle.' And, to charm his still not mollified wife, 'I'm rather hoping little Phinn will have your gorgeous delphinium-blue eyes. Did you know,' he went on, 'that your beautiful eyes go all dark purple, like the Black Knight delphinium, when you're all emotional?'

'Ewart Hawkins,' she had threatened, refusing to be charmed.

'And I brought you a cabbage,' he'd said winningly.

The fact that he had brought it, not bought it, had told her that he had nipped over some farmer's hedge and helped himself.

'Ewart Hawkins!' she'd said again, but he had the smile he had wanted.

Hester Rainsworth, as she had been prior to her marriage,

had been brought up most conventionally in a workaholic family. Impractical dreamer, talented pianist, sometime poet and would-be mechanical engineer Ewart Hawkins could not have been more of an opposite. They had fallen in love—and for some years had been blissfully happy.

Given a few ups and downs, it had been happiness all round in Phinn's childhood. Grandfather Hawkins had been the tenant of the farm, and on his death the tenancy had passed to her father. The farm had then been her father's responsibility, but after one year of appalling freak weather, when they had spent more than they had earned, Hester had declared that, with money tight, Ewart could be farmer and house-husband too, while she went out and found a job and brought some money in.

Unlike his hard-working practical father, Ewart had had little interest in arable farming, and had seen absolutely no point in labouring night and day only to see his crops flattened by storms. Besides, there'd been other things he'd preferred to do. Teach his daughter to sketch, to fish, to play the piano and to swim just for starters. There was a pool down at Broadlands, the estate that owned both Honeysuckle Farm and the neighbouring Yew Tree Farm. They hadn't been supposed to swim in the pool, but in return for her father going up to the Hall occasionally, and playing the grand piano for music-lover Mr Caldicott, old Mr Caldicott had turned a blind eye.

So it was in the shallows there that her father had taught her to dive and to swim. If they hadn't taken swimwear it had been quite all right with him if she swam in her underwear—and should his wife be home when they returned, he'd borne her wrath with fortitude.

There was a trout stream too, belonging to the Broadlands estate, and they hadn't been supposed to fish there either. But her father had called that a load of nonsense, so fish they had. Though, for all Phinn had learned to cast a fine line, she could never kill a fish and her fish had always been put back. Afterwards they might stop at the Cat and Drum, where her father would sit her outside with a lemonade while he went inside to pass time with his friends. Sometimes he would bring his pint outside. He would let her have a sip of his beer and, although she thought it tasted horrible, she had pretended to like it.

Phinn gave a shaky sigh as she thought of her dreamer father. It had been he and not her mother who had decorated her Easter bonnet for the village parade. How proud she had been of that hat—complete with a robin that he had very artistically made.

'A robin!' her mother had exclaimed. 'You do *know* it's Easter?'

'There won't be another bonnet like it,' he had assured her.

'You can say that again!' Hester had retorted.

Phinn had not won the competition. She had not wanted to. Though she had drawn one or two stares, it had not mattered. Her father had decorated her hat, and that had been plenty good enough for her.

Phinn wondered, not for the first time, when it had all started to go so badly wrong. Had it been before old Mr Caldicott had decided to sell the estate? Before Ty Allardyce had come to Bishops Thornby, taken a look around and decided to buy the place—thereby making himself their landlord? Or…?

In all fairness, Phinn knew that it must have been long before then. Though he, more recently, had not helped. Her beautiful blue eyes darkened in sadness as she thought back to a time five, maybe six years ago. Had that been when things had started to go awry? She had come home after having been out for a ride with Ruby, and after attending to Ruby's needs she had gone into the big old farmhouse kitchen to find her parents in the middle of a blazing row.

Knowing that she could not take sides, she had been about to back out again when her mother had taken her eyes from the centre of her wrath—Ewart—to tell her, 'This concerns you too, Phinn.'

'Oh,' she had murmured non-committally.

'We're broke. I'm bringing in as much as I can.' Her mother worked in Gloucester as a legal assistant.

'I'll get a job,' Phinn had offered. 'I'll—'

'You will. But first you'll have some decent training. I've arranged for you to have an interview at secretarial college. You—'

'She won't like it!' Ewart had objected.

'We all of us—or most of us,' she'd inserted, with a sarcastic glance at him, 'have to do things we don't want to do or like to do!'

The argument, with Phinn playing very little part, had raged on until Hester Hawkins had brought out her trump card.

'Either Phinn goes to college or that horse goes to somebody who can afford her feed, her vet and her farrier!'

'I'll sell something,' Ewart had decided, already not liking that his daughter, his pal, would not be around so much. He had a good brain for anything mechanical, and the farmyard was littered with odds and ends that he would sometimes make good and sell on.

But Hester had grown weary of him. 'Grow up, Ewart,' she had snapped bluntly.

But that was the trouble. Her father had never grown up, and had seen no reason why he should attempt it. On thinking about it, Phinn could not see any particular reason why he should have either. Tears stung her eyes. Though it had been the essential Peter Pan in her fifty-four-year-old father that had ultimately been the cause of his death.

But she did not want to dwell on that happening seven months ago. She had shed enough tears since then.

Phinn made herself think back to happier times, though she had not been too happy to be away from the farm for such long hours while she did her training. For her mother's sake she had applied herself to that training, and afterwards, with her eye more on the salary she would earn than with any particular interest in making a career as a PA, she had got herself a job with an accountancy firm, with her mother driving her into Gloucester each day.

Each evening Phinn had got home as soon as she could to see Ruby and her father. Her father had taught her to drive, but when her mother had started working late, putting in extra hours at her office, it was he who had suggested that Phinn should have a car of her own.

Her mother had agreed, but had insisted *she* would look into it. She was not having her daughter driving around in any bone-rattling contraption he'd patched up.

Phinn had an idea that Grandmother Rainsworth had made a contribution to her vehicle, and guessed that her mother's parents might well have helped out financially in her growing years.

But all that had stopped a few months later when her mother, having sat her down and said that she wanted to talk to her, had announced to Phinn's utter amazement that she was moving out. Shocked, open-mouthed, Phinn had barely taken in that her mother intended leaving them when she'd further revealed that she had met someone else.

'You mean—some—other man?' Phinn had gasped, it still not fully sinking in.

'Clive. His name's Clive.'

'But—but what about Dad?'

'I've discussed this fully with your father. Things—er—haven't been right between us for some while. I'll start divorce proceedings as soon as everything settles…'

Divorce! Phinn had been aware that her mother had grown

more impatient and short-tempered with her father just lately. But—*divorce*!

'But what—'

'I'm not going to change my mind, Phinn. I've tried. Lord knows I've tried! But I'm tired of the constant struggle. Your father lives in his own little dream world and…' She halted at the look of protest on her daughter's face. 'No, I'm not going to run him down. I know how devoted you are to him. But just try to understand, Phinn. I'm tired of the struggle. And I've decided I'm not too old to make a fresh start. To make a new life for myself. A better life.'

'Th-this Clive. He's part of your fresh start—this better life?'

'Yes, he is. In due time I'll marry him—though I'm not in any great hurry about that.'

'You—just want your—freedom?'

'Yes, I do. You're working now, Phinn. You have your own money—though no doubt your father will want some of it. But…' Hester looked at her daughter, wanting understanding. 'I've found myself a small flat in Gloucester. I'll write down the address. I'm leaving your father, darling, not you. You're welcome to come and live with me whenever you want.'

To leave her father had been something Phinn had not even thought about. Her home had been there, with him and Ruby.

It was around then, Phinn suddenly saw, that everything had started to go wrong.

First Ruby had had a cough, and when that cleared she'd picked up a viral infection. Her father had been marvelous, in that he'd spent all of his days looking after Ruby for her until Phinn was able to speed home from the office to take over.

The vet's bill had started to mount, but old Mr Duke had obligingly told them to pay what they could when they could.

Phinn's days had become full. She'd had no idea of the amount of work her mother had done when she was home. Phinn had always helped out when requested, but once she was sole carer she'd seemed to spend a lot of her time picking up and clearing up after her father.

And time had gone by. Phinn had met Clive Gillam and, contrary to her belief, had liked him. And a couple of years later, with her father's approval, she had attended their wedding.

'You want to go and live with them?' her father had asked somewhat tentatively when she had returned.

'No way,' she'd answered.

And he had grinned. 'Fancy a pint?'

'You go. I want to check on Rubes.'

It seemed as though her mother's new marriage had been a signal for everything to change. Mr Caldicott, the owner of the Broadlands estate, had decided to sell up and to take himself and his money off to sunnier climes.

And, all before they knew it, the bachelor Allardyce brothers had been in the village, taking a look around. And, all before they could blink, Honeysuckle Farm and neighbouring Yew Tree Farm, plus a scattering of other properties, had all had a new landlord—and an army of architects and builders had started at work on Broadlands Hall, bringing its antiquated plumbing and heating up to date and generally modernising the interior.

She had spotted the brothers one day when she was resting Ruby, hidden in the spinney—property of Broadlands. Two men deep in conversation had walked by. The slightly taller of the two, a dark-haired man, just had to be the Tyrell Allardyce she had heard about. There was such a self-confident air about the man that he could have been none other than the new owner.

Phinn had seemed to know that before she'd overheard his deep, cultured tones saying, 'Don't you see, Ash...?' as they had passed within yards of her.

Ash was tall too, but without that positive, self-assured air that simply exuded from the other man. Listening intently, he must have been the younger brother.

Tyrell Allardyce, with his brother Ashley, had called at Honeysuckle Farm one day while she was out at work. But from what her father had told her, and from what she had gleaned from the hotbed of local gossip, Ty Allardyce was some big-shot financier who worked and spent most of his time either in London or overseas. He, so gossip had said, would live at Broadlands Hall when his London commitments allowed, while Ashley would stay at the Hall to supervise the alterations and generally manage the estate.

'Looks like we're going to be managed, kiddo,' her father had commented jocularly.

Highly unlikely!

Further village gossip some while later had suggested that Mrs Starkey, housekeeper to the previous owner of Broadlands, was staying on to look after Ashley Allardyce. It seemed—though Phinn knew that, village gossip being what it was, a lot of it could be discounted—that Ashley had endured some sort of a breakdown, and that Ty had bought Broadlands mainly for his brother's benefit.

Phinn thought she could safely rule that out—the cost of Broadlands, with all its other properties, must go into millions. Surely, if it were true that Ashley had been ill, there were cheaper ways of finding somewhere less fraught than London to live? Though it did appear that the younger Allardyce brother *was* living at the Hall. So perhaps Mrs Starkey, whom Phinn had known all her life, was looking after him after all.

Everything within this last year seemed to be changing. To start with, old Mr Duke had decided to give up his veterinary practice. It was a relief that she had just about settled with him the money she'd owed for Ruby's last course of treatment. Though it had worried Phinn how she would fare with the new man who had taken over. Mr Duke had never been in any hurry for his money, and Ruby, who they calculated had been about ten years old when they had claimed her, was now geriatric in the horse world, and rarely went six weeks without requiring some treatment or other.

Kit Peverill, however, a tall mousy-haired man in his early thirties, had turned out to be every bit as kind and caring as his predecessor. Thankfully, she had only had to call him out twice.

But more trouble had seemed to be heading their way when, again clearing up after her father, she'd found a letter he had left lying around. It had come from the Broadlands estate, and was less of a letter but more of a formal notice that some effort must be made to pay the rent arrears and that the farm must be 'tidied up'—otherwise legal proceedings would have to be initiated.

Feeling staggered—she'd had no idea that her father had not been paying the rent—Phinn had gone in search of him.

'Ignore it,' he had advised.

'Ignore it?' she'd gasped.

'Not worth the paper it's written on,' he had assured her, and had gone back to tinkering with an old, un-roadworthy, un-fieldworthy quad bike he had found somewhere.

Knowing that she would get no sense out of him until his mind-set was ready to think of other things, Phinn had waited until he came into supper that night.

'I was thinking of going down to the Cat for a pint—' he began.

'I was thinking we might discuss that letter,' Phinn interrupted.

He looked at her, smiled because he adored her, and said, 'You know, little flower, you've more than a touch of your mother about you.'

She couldn't ignore it. One of them had to be practical. 'What will we do if—er—things get nasty—if we have to leave here? Ruby…'

'It won't come to that,' he'd assured her, undaunted. 'It's just the new owner flexing a bit of muscle, that's all.'

'The letter's from Ashley Allardyce…'

'He may have written it, but he will have been instructed by his big brother.'

'Tyrell Allardyce.' She remembered him very clearly. Oddly, while Ashley Allardyce was only a vague figure in her mind, his elder brother Ty seemed to be etched in her head. She was starting to dislike the man.

'It's the way they do things in London,' Ewart had replied confidently. 'They just need all the paperwork neatly documented in case there's a court case. But—' as she went a shade pale '—it won't come to that,' he repeated. 'Honeysuckle Farm has been in Hawkins care for generations. Nobody's going to throw us off this land, I promise you.'

Sadly, it had not been the first letter of that sort. The next one she had seen had come from a London firm of lawyers, giving them formal notice to quit by September. And Phinn, who had already started to dislike Tyrell Allardyce, and although she had never hated anyone in her life, had known that she hated Ty that he could do this to them. Old Mr Caldicott would never, ever have instructed such a letter.

But again her father had been unconcerned, and told her to ignore the notice to quit. And while Phinn had spent a worrying time—expecting the bailiffs to turn up at any moment to turf then out—her father had appeared to not have a care in the world.

And then it had been September, and Phinn had had something else to worry about that had pushed her fear of the bailiffs into second place. Ruby had become quite ill.

Kit Peverill had come out to her in the middle of the night, and it had been touch and go if Ruby would make it. Phinn, forgetting she had a job to go to, had stayed with her and nursed her, watched her like a hawk—and the geriatric mare had pulled through.

When Phinn had gone back to work and, unable to lie, told

her boss that her mare had been ill, she had been told in return that they were experiencing a business downturn and were looking to make redundancies. Was it likely, should her horse again be ill, that she would again take time off?

Again she had not been able to lie. 'I'll go and clear my desk,' she'd offered.

'You don't have to go straight way,' her employer had told her kindly. 'Let's say in a month's time.'

Because she'd known she would need the money, Phinn had not argued. But she never did work that full month. Because a couple of weeks later her world had fallen apart when her father, haring around the fields, showing a couple of his pals what a reconstructed quad bike could do, had upended it, gone over and under it—and come off worst.

He had died before Phinn could get to the hospital. Her mother had come to her straight away, and it had been Hester who, practical to the last, had made all the arrangements.

Devastated, having to look after Ruby had been the only thing that kept Phinn on anything resembling an even keel. And Ruby, as if she understood, would gently nuzzle into her neck and cuddle up close.

Her father had been popular but, when the day of his funeral had arrived, Phinn had never known he had so many friends. Or relatives, either. Aunts and uncles she had heard of but had seen only on the rarest of occasions had come to pay their respects. Even her cousin Leanne, a Hawkins several times removed, had arrived with her parents.

Leanne was tall, dark, pretty—and with eyes that seemed to instantly put a price on everything. But since the family antiques had been sold one by one after Hester had left, there had been very little at Honeysuckle Farm that was worth the ink on a price ticket. Thereafter Leanne had behaved as decorously as her parents would wish.

That was she'd behaved very nicely until—to his credit—

Ashley Allardyce had come to the funeral to pay his respects too. Phinn had not been feeling too friendly to him, but because she did not wish to mar the solemnity of the occasion with any undignified outburst—and in any case it was not him but his elder brother Ty who was the villain who went around instigating notices to quit—she'd greeted Ashley calmly, and politely thanked him for coming.

Leanne, noticing the expensive cut of the clothes the tall, fair-haired man was wearing, had immediately been attracted.

'Who's he?' she'd asked, sidling up when Ashley Allardyce had gone over to have a word with Nesta and Noel Jarvis, the tenants of Yew Tree Farm.

'Ashley Allardyce,' Phinn had answered, and, as she'd suspected, it had not ended there.

'He lives around here?'

'At Broadlands Hall.'

'That massive house in acres of grounds we passed on the way here?'

The next thing Phinn knew was that Leanne, on her behalf, had invited Ash Allardyce back to the farmhouse for refreshments.

Any notion Phinn might have had that he would refuse the invitation had disappeared when she'd seen the look on his face. He was clearly captivated by her cousin!

The days that had followed had gone by in a numbed kind of shock for Phinn as she'd tried to come to terms with her father's death. Her mother had wanted her to go back to Gloucester and live with her and Clive. Phinn had found the idea unthinkable. Besides, there was Ruby.

Phinn had been glad to have Ruby to care for. Glad too that her cousin Leanne frequently drove the forty or so miles from her own home to see her.

In fact, by the time Christmas had come, Phinn had seen more of her cousin than she had during the whole of her life.

Leanne had come, she would say, to spend time with her, so she would not be too lonely. But most of Leanne's time, from what Phinn had seen, was being spent with Ash Allardyce.

He had driven Leanne back to the farmhouse several times, and it had been as clear as day to Phinn that he was totally besotted with her cousin. Phinn, aware, if village talk were true, of his recent recovery from a breakdown, had only hoped that, vulnerable as he might still be, he would not end up getting hurt.

Because of a prior arrangement Leanne had spent Christmas skiing in Switzerland. Ash had gone too. For all Phinn knew his notice-to-quit-ordering brother might have made one of his rare visits to Broadlands and spent his Christmas there, but she hadn't seen him, and she'd been glad about that. The notice to quit had never been executed. It had not needed to be.

Since Phinn had no longer had a job, she'd no longer needed a car. Pride as much as anything had said she had to clear the rent arrears. She had formed a good opinion of Ash Allardyce, and did not think he would discuss their business with Leanne, but with him becoming closer and closer to her cousin, she had not wanted to risk it. She did not want any one member of her family to know that her father had died owing money. She'd sold her car and sent a cheque off to the lawyers.

Though by the time all accounts had been settled—and that included the vet's last bill—there had been little money remaining, and Phinn had known that she needed to get a job. A job that paid well. Yet Ruby had not been well enough to be left alone all day while she went off to work.

Then Leanne, on another visit, having voiced her opinion that Ash was close to 'popping the question' marriage-wise, had telephoned from Broadlands Hall to tell her not to wait up for her, that she was spending the night there.

It had been the middle of the following morning when Leanne, driving fast and furiously, had screeched to a halt in the middle of the farmyard. Phinn, leaving Ruby to go and find out what the rush was about, had been confronted by a furious Leanne, who'd demanded to know why she had not told her that Broadlands Hall did *not* belong to Ash Allardyce.

'I—didn't think about it,' Phinn had answered defensively. Coming to terms with her beloved father's death and settling his affairs had taken precedence. Who owned Broadlands Hall had not figured very much, if at all, in her thinking at that particular time. 'I told you Ash had a brother. I'm sure I did.'

'Yes, you did!' Leanne snapped. 'And so did Ash. But neither of you told me that Ash was the *younger* brother—and that he doesn't own a *thing*!'

'Ah, you've met Ty Allardyce,' Phinn realised. And discovered she was in the wrong about that too.

'No—more's the pity! He's always away somewhere—away abroad somewhere, and likely to be away some time!' Leanne spat. 'It took that po-faced housekeeper to delight in telling me that Ash was merely the estate *manager*! Can you imagine it? There was I, happily believing that any time soon I was going to be mistress of Broadlands Hall, only to be informed by some jumped-up housekeeper that some poky farm cottage was more likely to be the place for me. I don't think so!'

Phinn doubted that Mrs Starkey would have said anything of the sort, but as Leanne raged on she knew that once her cousin had realised that Ash was not the owner of Broadlands, it wouldn't have taken her very long to realise the ins and outs of it all.

'Come in and I'll make some coffee,' Phinn offered, aware that her cousin had suffered something of a shock.

'I'll come in. But only to collect what belongings of mine I've left here.'

'You—er—that sounds a bit—final?' Phinn suggested at last.

'You bet it is. Ten minutes and the village of Bishop Thornby has seen the last of me.'

'What about Ash?'

'What about him?' Leanne was already on her way into the house. 'I've told him—nicely—that I'm not cut out for country life. But if that hasn't given him something of a clue—tell him I said goodbye.'

Ash did not come looking for her cousin, and Honeysuckle Farm had settled into an unwanted quietness. With the exception of her mother, who frequently rang to check that she was all right, Phinn spoke with no one other than Ruby. Gradually Phinn came to see that she could do nothing about Leanne having dropped Ash like a hot brick once she had known that he was not the one with the money. Phinn knew that she could not stay on at the farm for very much longer. She had no interest in trying to make the farm a paying concern. If her father had not been able to do it with all his expertise, she did not see how she could. And, while she had grown to quite like the man whom Leanne had so unceremoniously dumped, the twenty-nine-year-old male might well be glad to see the back of anyone who bore the Hawkins name.

She had no idea if she was entitled to claim the tenancy, but if not, Ash would be quite within his rights to instigate having her thrown out.

Not wanting the indignity of that, Phinn wondered where on earth she could go. For herself she did not care very much where she went, but it was Ruby she had to think about.

To that end, Phinn took a walk down to the local riding school, run by Peggy Edmonds. And it turned out that going to see Peggy was the best thing she could have done. Because not only was Peggy able to house Ruby, she was even—unbelievably—able to offer Phinn a job. True, it wasn't much of a job, but with a place for Ruby assured, Phinn would have accepted anything.

Apparently Peggy was having a hard time battling with arthritis, and for over a year had been trying to find a buyer for what was now more of a stables than a riding school. But it seemed no one was remotely interested in making her an offer. With her arthritis so bad some days that it was all she could do to get out of bed, if Phinn would like to work as a stable hand, although Peggy could not pay very much, there was a small stall Ruby could have, and she could spend her days in the field with the other horses. As a bonus, there was a tiny flat above one of the stables doing nothing.

It was a furnished flat, with no room for farmhouse furniture, and having been advised by the house clearers that she would have to pay *them* to empty the farmhouse, Phinn got her father's old friend Mickie Yates—an educated, eccentric but loveable jack-of-all-trades—to take everything away for her. It grieved her to see her father's piano go, but there was no space in the tiny flat for it.

So it was as January drew to a close that Phinn walked Ruby down to her new home and then, cutting through the spinney on Broadlands that she knew so well, Phinn took the key to the farmhouse up to the Hall.

Ash Allardyce was not in. Phinn was quite glad about that. After the way her cousin had treated him, dropping him cold like that, it might have been a touch embarrassing.

'I was very sorry to hear about your father, Phinn,' Mrs Starkey said, taking the keys from her.

'Thank you, Mrs Starkey,' Phinn replied quietly, and returned to the stables.

But almost immediately, barely having congratulated herself on how well everything was turning out—she had a job and Ruby was housed and fed—the sky started to fall in.

By late March it crash-landed.

Ruby—probably because of her previous ill-treatment— had always been timid, and needed peace and quiet, but was being bullied by the other much younger horses. Phinn took her on walks away from them as often as she could, but with her own work to do that was not as often as she would have liked.

Then, against all odds, Peggy found a buyer. A buyer who wanted to take possession as soon as it could possibly be achieved.

'I'll talk to her and see if there's any chance of her keeping you on,' Peggy said quickly, on seeing the look of concern on Phinn's face.

Phinn had met Geraldine Walton, a dark-haired woman of around thirty, who was not dissimilar to her cousin in appearance. She had met her on one of Geraldine's 'look around' visits, and had thought she seemed to have a bit of a hard edge to her—which made Phinn not too hopeful.

She was right not to be too hopeful, she soon discovered, for not only was there no job for her, neither was there a place for Ruby. And, not only that, Geraldine Walton was bringing her own staff and requested that Phinn kindly vacate the flat over the stable. As quickly as possible, please.

Now, Phinn, with the late-April sun streaming through the window, looked round the stable flat and knew she had better think about packing up her belongings. Not that she had so very much to pack, but... Her eyes came to rest on the camera her mother, who had visited her last Sunday, had given her to return to Ash on Leanne's behalf.

Feeling a touch guilty that her mother's visit had been a couple of days ago now and she had done nothing about it, Phinn went and picked up the piece of photographic equipment. No time like the present—and she could get Ruby away from the other horses for a short while.

Collecting Ruby, Phinn walked her across the road and took the shortcut through the spinney. In no time she was approaching the impressive building that was Broadlands Hall.

Leanne Hawkins was not her favourite cousin just then.

She had been unkind to Ash Allardyce, and, while Phinn considered that had little to do with her, she would much prefer that her cousin did her own dirty work. It seemed that her mother, who had no illusions about Leanne, had doubted that Ash would have got his expensive camera back at all were it not for the fact that he, still very much smitten, used it as an excuse to constantly telephone Leanne. Apparently Leanne could not be bothered to talk to him, and had asked Phinn to make sure he had his rotten camera back.

Phinn neared the Hall, hoping that it would again be Mrs Starkey who answered her ring at the door. Cowardly it might be, but she had no idea what she could say to Ash Allardyce. While she might be annoyed with Leanne, Leanne was still family, and family loyalty said that she could not say how shabbily she personally felt Leanne had treated him.

Phinn pulled the bell-tug, half realising that if Ash was still as smitten with Leanne as he had been, he was unlikely to say anything against her cousin that might provoke her having to stand up for her. She...

Phinn's thoughts evaporated as she heard the sound of someone approaching the stout oak door from within. Camera in one hand, Ruby's rein in the other, Phinn prepared to smile.

Then the front door opened and was pulled back—and her smile never made it. For it was not Mrs Starkey who stood there, and neither was it Ash Allardyce. Ash was fair-haired, but this man had ink-black hair—and an expression that was far from welcoming! He was tall, somewhere in his mid-thirties—and clearly not pleased to see her. She knew very well who he was—strangely, she had never forgotten his face. His good-looking face.

But his grim expression didn't let up when in one dark glance he took in the slender, delphinium-blue-eyed woman with a thick strawberry-blonde plait hanging over one shoulder, a camera in one hand and a rein in the other.

All too obviously he had recognised the camera, because his grim expression became grimmer if anything.

'And you are?' he demanded without preamble.

Yes, she, although having never been introduced to him, knew very well this was the man who was ultimately responsible for her father receiving that notice to quit. To quit the land that his family had farmed for generations. It passed her by just then that her father had done very little to keep the farm anything like the farm it had been for those generations.

'I'm Phinn Hawkins,' she replied—a touch belligerently it had to be admitted. 'I've—'

His eyes narrowed at her tone, though his tone was none too sweet either as he challenged shortly, 'What do you want on my land, Hawkins?'

And that made her mad. 'And you are?' she demanded, equally as sharp as he.

She was then forced to bear his tough scrutiny for several uncompromising seconds as he studied her. But, just when she was beginning to think she would have to run for his name, 'Tyrell Allardyce,' he supplied at last. And, plainly unused to repeating himself, 'What do you want?' he barked.

'Nothing you can supply, Allardyce!' she tossed back at him, refusing to be intimidated. Stretching out a hand, she offered the camera. 'Give this to your brother,' she ordered loftily. But at her mention of his brother, she was made to endure a look that should have turned her to stone.

'Get off my land!' he gritted between clenched teeth. 'And—' his tone was threatening '—don't *ever* set foot on it again!'

His look was so malevolent it took everything she had to keep from flinching. 'Huh!' she scorned, and, badly wanting to run as fast as she could away from this man and his menacing look, she turned Ruby about and ambled away from the Hall.

By the time she and Ruby had entered the spinney, some

of Phinn's equilibrium had started to return. And a short while later she was starting to be thoroughly cross with herself that she had just walked away without acquainting him with a few of the do's and don'ts of living in the country.

Who did he think he was, for goodness' sake? She had *always* roamed the estate lands freely. True, there were certain areas she knew she was not supposed to trespass over. But she had been brought up using the Broadlands fields and acres as her right of way! She was darn sure she wasn't going to alter that now!

The best thing Ty Allardyce could do, she fumed, would be to take himself and his big city ways back to London. And stay there! And good riddance to him too! She had now met him, but she hoped she never had the misfortune of seeing his forbidding, disagreeable face ever again!

CHAPTER TWO

SOMEHOW, in between worrying about finding a new home for herself and Ruby, Phinn could not stop thoughts of Ty Allardyce from intruding. Though, as the days went by and the weekend passed and another week began, Phinn considered that to have the man so much in and out of her mind was not so surprising. How *dared* he order her off his land?

Well, tough on him! It was a lovely early May day—what could be nicer than to take Ruby and go for a walk? Leaving the flat, Phinn went down to collect her. But, before she could do more than put a halter on the mare, Geraldine Walton appeared from nowhere to waylay her. Phinn knew what was coming before Geraldine so much as opened her mouth. She was not mistaken.

'I'm sorry to have to be blunt, Phinn,' Geraldine began, 'but I really do need the stable flat by the end of the week.'

'I'm working on it,' Phinn replied, at her wits' end. She had phoned round everywhere she could think of, but nobody wanted her *and* Ruby. And Ruby fretted if she was away from her for very long, so no way was Ruby going anywhere without her. Phinn had wondered about them both finding some kind of animal sanctuary, willing to take them both, but then again, having recently discovered that Ruby was unhappy with other horses around, she did not want to give her ailing mare more stress. 'Leave it with me,' she requested, and a few minutes later crossed the road on to Broadlands property and walked Ruby through the spinney, feeling all churned up at how it would break her heart—and Ruby's—to have to leave her anywhere.

The majestic Broadlands Hall was occasionally visible through gaps in the trees in the small wood, but Phinn was certain that Ty Allardyce would by now be back in London, beavering away at whatever it was financiers beavered away at. Though just in case, as they walked through fields that bordered the adjacent grounds and gardens they had always walked through—or in earlier days ridden through—she made sure that she and Ruby were well out of sight, should anyone at the Hall be looking out.

Hoping not to meet him, if London's loss was Bishops Thornby's gain and he *was* still around, Phinn moved on, and was taking a stroll near the pool where she and her father had so often swum when she did bump into an Allardyce. It was Ash.

It would have been quite natural for Phinn to pause, say hello, make some sort of polite conversation. But she was so shaken by the change in the man from the last time she had seen him that she barely recognised him, and all words went from her. Ash looked terrible!

'Hello, Ash,' she did manage, but was unwilling to move on. He looked positively ill, and she searched for something else to say. 'Did you get your camera all right?' she asked, and could have bitten out her tongue. Was her cousin responsible in any way for this dreadful change in him? Surely not? Ash looked grey, sunken-eyed, and at least twenty pounds lighter!

'Yes, thanks,' he replied, no smile, his eyes dull and lifeless. But, brightening up a trifle, 'Have you seen Leanne recently?' he asked.

Fleetingly she wondered if Ash, so much in love with Leanne, might have found cause to suspect she was money-minded and, not wanting to lose her, not told her that it was his brother who owned Broadlands. But she had not seen her cousin since the day Leanne had learned that Ash was not the one with the money and had so callously dropped him.

'Leanne—er—doesn't come this way—er—now,' Phinn answered, feeling awkward, her heart aching for this man who seemed bereft that his love wanted nothing more to do with him.

'I don't suppose she has anywhere to stay now that you're no longer at Honeysuckle Farm,' he commented, and as he began to stroll along with her, Phinn did not feel able to tell him that the only time Leanne had ever shown an interest in staying any length of time at the farm had been when she'd had her sights set on being mistress of Broadlands Hall. 'I'm sorry that you had to leave, by the way,' Ash stated.

And her heart went out to this gaunt man whose clothes were just about hanging on him. 'I couldn't have stayed,' she replied, and, hoping to lighten his mood, 'I don't think I'd make a very good farmer.' Not sure which was best for him— to talk of Leanne or not to talk of Leanne—she opted to enquire, 'Have you found a new tenant for Honeysuckle yet?'

'I'm—undecided what to do,' Ash answered, and suddenly the brilliant idea came to Phinn that, if he had not yet got a tenant for the farm, maybe she and Ruby could go back and squat there for a while; the weather was so improved and it was quite warm for early summer. Ruby would be all right there. But Ash was going on. 'I did think I might take it over myself, but I don't seem able to—er—make decisions on anything just at the moment.'

Ash's confession took the squatting idea from Phinn momentarily. Leanne again! How *could* she have been so careless of this sensitive man's fine feelings?

'I'm sure you and Honeysuckle would be good for each other—if that's what you decide to do,' Phinn replied gently.

And Ash gave a shaky sigh, as if he had wandered off for

a moment. 'I think I'd like to work outdoors. Better than an indoor job anyway.' And, with a self-deprecating look, 'I tried a career in the big business world.'

'You didn't like it?'

He shook his head. 'I don't think I'm the academic type. That's more Ty's forte. He's the genius in the family when it comes to the cut and thrust of anything like that.' Ash seemed to wander off again for a moment or two, and then, like the caring kind of person he was, he collected himself to enquire, 'You're settled in your new accommodation, Phinn?'

'Well—er…' Phinn hesitated. It was unthinkable that she should burden him with her problems, but the idea of squatting back at Honeysuckle was picking at her again.

'You're not settled?' Ash took up.

'Geraldine—she's the new owner of the stables—wants to do more on the riding school front, and needs my flat for a member of her staff,' Phinn began.

'But you work there too?'

'Well, no, actually. Er…'

'You're out of a job *and* a home?' Ash caught on.

'Ruby and I have until the end of this week,' Phinn said lightly, and might well have put in a pitch for his permission to use Honeysuckle as a stop-gap measure—only she chanced to look across to him, and once more into his dull eyes, and she simply did not have the heart. He appeared to have the weight of the world on his shoulders, and she just could not add to his burden.

'Ruby?' he asked. 'I didn't know you had a child?'

He looked so concerned that Phinn rushed in to reassure him. 'I don't.' She patted Ruby's shoulder. 'This lovely girl is Ruby.'

His look of concern changed to one of relief. 'I don't know much about horses, but…'

Phinn smiled. There wasn't a better-groomed horse anywhere, but there was no mistaking Ruby's years. 'She's getting on a bit now, and her health isn't so good, but—' She broke off when, turning to glance at Ruby, she saw a male figure in the distance, coming their way at a fast pace. Uh-oh! Ash hadn't seen him, but she didn't fancy a row with Ty Allardyce in front of him. 'That reminds me—we'd better be off. It's time for Ruby's medication,' she said. 'Nice to see you again, Ash. Bye.'

And with that, unfortunately having to go towards the man she was starting to think of as 'that dastardly Ty Allardyce', she led Ruby away.

'Bye, Phinn,' Ash bade her, seeing nothing wrong with her abrupt departure as he went walking on in the opposite direction.

With Ruby not inclined to hurry, there was no way Phinn could avoid the owner of the Hall, who also happened to be the owner of the land she was trespassing on. They were on a collision course!

Several remarks entered her head before Ty Allardyce was within speaking distance. Though when he was but a few yards from her—and looking tough with it—her voice nearly failed her. But in her view she had done nothing wrong.

'Not back in London yet, I see!' she remarked, more coolly than she felt.

'Why, you—' Ty Allardyce began angrily, but checked his anger, to demand, 'What have you been saying to my brother?'

While part of Phinn recognised that his question had come from concern for Ash, she did not like Ty Allardyce and never would. 'What's it got to do with you?' she challenged loftily.

His dark grey eyes glinted, and she would not have been all that surprised had she felt his hands around her throat—he looked quite prepared to attempt to throttle her! 'It has everything to do with me,' he controlled his ire to inform her shortly. 'You Hawkins women don't give a damn who you hurt...'

'Hawkins women!' she exclaimed, starting to get angry herself. 'What the devil do you mean by that?'

'Your reputation precedes you!'

'Reputation?'

'Your father was devastated when your mother dumped him. My—'

Mother *dumped* him! Phinn was on the instant furious, but somehow managed to control her feeling of wanting to throttle *him* to butt in with mock sarcasm. 'Oh, really, Allardyce. You truly must try to stop listening to village gossip…'

'You're saying he *wasn't* devastated? That his reason for not paying the rent had nothing at all to do with the fact that your mother took up with some other man and left your father a total wreck?'

Oh, Lord. That quickly squashed her anger. She did not doubt that her father *had* been capable of conveying his marriage break-up as his reason without exactly saying so. But his marriage break-up had had nothing to do with him not paying the rent—the fact the rent had not been paid had been more to do with her mother's hands no longer being on the purse strings. It was true, Phinn had discovered, that the rent had only ceased to be paid when her mother had left.

'What went on between my father and mother is nothing at all to do with you!' Phinn stated coldly, wanting her anger back. 'It's none of your business…'

'When it comes to my brother I'll make it my business. You've seen him! You've seen how gutted he is that your cousin ditched him the same way your mother ditched your father. I'm not having another Hawkins anywhere near him. Get off my land and stay off it! And,' he went on icily when she opened her mouth, 'don't give me "Huh!" This is your last warning. If I catch you trespassing again I'll have you in court before you can blink!'

'Have you quite finished?'

'I hope never to have to speak to you again,' he confirmed. 'You just leave my brother alone.'

'Be glad to!' she snapped, her eyes darkening. 'I don't know what Bishops Thornby ever did to deserve the likes of you, but for my money it was the worst day's work he ever did when old Mr Caldicott sold this estate to you!' Thereafter ignoring him, she addressed the mare. 'Come on, Rubes. You're much too sweet to have to stand and listen to this loathsome man!'

With that, she put her nose in the air and sauntered off. Unfortunately, because of Ruby's slow gait, she was prevented from marching off as she would have wished. She hoped the dastardly Allardyce got the idea anyway.

Her adrenalin was still pumping when she took Ruby back to her stall. Honestly, that man!

Phinn wasted no time the next day. Once she had attended to all Ruby's needs, she made the long walk up to Honeysuckle Farm. She walked into the familiar farmyard, but, having been away from the farm for around three months, as she stood and stared about she was able to see it for the first time from a different perspective. She had to admit to feeling a little shaken.

Rusting pieces of machinery littered the yard, and there was a general air of neglect everywhere. Which there would be, she defended her father. Had he lived he would have repaired and sold on the rusting and clapped out pieces. Had he lived...

Avoiding thoughts that some of the machinery had lain there rusting for years, and not just since last October when her father had died, and the fact that the place had become to be more and more run-down over the years but that until today she had never noticed it, Phinn went to take a look at the old barn that had used to be Ruby's home.

The secure door latch had broken years ago, but, as her father had so laughingly said, they had nothing worth stealing so why bother repairing it? That his logic was a touch different from most people's had all been part of the man she had adored. It hadn't been that he was idle, he'd just thought on a different and more pleasurable level.

The barn smelt musty, and not too pleasant. But it was a sunny day, so Phinn propped the doors open wide and went in. Everything about the place screamed, *no!* But what alternative did she have? Ruby, her timid darling Ruby, would by far prefer to be up here in the old barn than where she was. Had Phinn had any idea of Ruby's fear of the other horses she would never have taken her there in the first place. Too late now to be wise after the event!

Looking for plus points, Phinn knew that Ruby would be better on her own, away from the younger horses. As well as being timid, Ruby was a highly sensitive mare, and with their mutual attachment to each other, Honeysuckle was the best place for them. Another plus: it was dry—mainly. And there was a field. Several, in fact. Overgrown with weeds and clutter, but in Phinn's view it wouldn't take her long to clear it and put up some sort of temporary fencing.

With matters pertaining to Ruby sorted out in her head, Phinn crossed the yard, found a ladder, and was able to gain entry into the farmhouse by climbing up to a bedroom window. Forcing the window did not take a great deal of effort, and once in she went through to what had once been her own bedroom.

It smelt musty, but then it hadn't been used in months. There was no electricity, so she would have to do without heat or light, but looking on the brighter side she felt sure that Mickie Yates would cart her few belongings up for her. Mickie had been a good friend of her father's, and she knew she could rely on him not to tell anyone that she was squatting—trespassing, Allardyce would call it if he knew—at Honeysuckle.

Phinn left Honeysuckle Farm endeavouring not to think what her mother's reaction to her plan would be. Appalled would not cover it.

By Thursday of that week Phinn was trying to tell herself that she felt quite enthusiastic about her proposed move. She had been to see Mickie Yates and found him in his workshop, up to his elbows in muck and grease, but with the loveliest smile of welcome on his face for her.

Whatever he thought when she asked for use of him and one of his vehicles to transport her cases and horse equipment on Friday she did not know. All he'd said was, 'After three suit you, Phinn?'

She knew he would be having his 'lunch' in the Cat and Drum until two fifty-five. 'Lovely thank you, Mickie,' she had replied.

It was a surprisingly hot afternoon, and Phinn, not certain when she would be in the village again, decided to walk Ruby to the village farrier. It would be even hotter at the forge, so she changed out of her more usual jeans and top, exchanging them for a thin, loose-fitting sleeveless cotton dress. Donning some sandals, she felt certain that by now grumpy Allardyce *must* be back in London, where he surely more particularly belonged.

Perhaps after their visit to Idris Owen, the farrier and blacksmith, a man who could turn his hand to anything and who had been another friend of her father's, Phinn and Ruby might take another stroll in the shady spinney.

Knowing that she should be packing her belongings prior to tomorrow's move, she left her flat—and on the way out bumped into Geraldine Walton. Geraldine seemed difficult to miss these days. But for once Phinn was not anxious about meeting her.

'You do know I shall want the flat on Saturday?' Geraldine began a touch stiffly, before Phinn could say a word.

'You shall have it,' she replied. 'Ruby and I are moving tomorrow.'

Geraldine's severe look lightened. 'You are? Oh, good! Er…I hope you've found somewhere—suitable?'

Phinn ignored the question in her voice. Villages being villages, she knew she could not hope to keep her new address secret for very long. But, her new address being part of the Broadlands Estate, the longer it was kept from Ty Allardyce the better. Not that she was aware if Geraldine even knew him, but there was no point in inviting more of his wrath—and a *definite* court summons—if they were acquainted.

'Most suitable,' she replied with a smile, and, aiming to make the best of what life was currently throwing at her, she went to collect Ruby.

Idris greeted Phinn with the same warm smile she had received from Mickie Yates. Idris was somewhere around fifty, a huge mountain of a man, with a heart as big. 'How's my best girl?' he asked, as he always did. No matter what time of day she visited, he always seemed to have a pint of beer on the go. 'Help yourself,' he offered, as he checked Ruby's hooves and shoes.

Phinn still did not like beer any better than she had when she had first tasted it. But it was blisteringly hot in there, and to take a healthy swig of his beer—as encouraged so to do in the past by her father—was now traditional. She picked up the pot and drank to her father's memory.

When he was done, Idris told her that she owed him nothing, and she knew he would be upset if she insisted on paying him. So, thanking him, she and Ruby left the smithy and headed for the small wood.

Keeping a watchful eye out for the elder Allardyce, Phinn chatted quietly to Ruby all the way through the spinney, and Ruby, having a good day for once, talked back, nodded and generally kept close.

Once out of the shaded spinney, they strolled towards the pool with the heat starting to beat down on them. Ruby loved the warmth, and Phinn, catching a glimpse of the pool, had started to think in terms of what a wonderful day for a swim.

No, I shouldn't. She attempted to ignore that part of her that was seeing no earthly reason why she shouldn't take a quick dip. She glanced about—no one in sight. They ambled on, reaching the pool and some more trees, and all the while Phinn fought down the demon temptation.

She would never know whether or not she would have given in to that demon had not something happened just then that drove all other thoughts from her head. Suddenly in the stillness she heard a yell of alarm. It came from the dark side of the pool. It was the cry of someone in trouble!

In moments she had run down the bank and did not have to search very far to see who was in trouble—and what the trouble was! Oh, God! Her blood ran cold. Across from the shallow end was a dark area called the Dark Pool—because that was precisely what it was: dark. Dark because it was overhung with trees and the sun never got to it. Not only was it dark, it was deep, and it was icy. And everyone knew that you must *never* attempt to swim there. Only someone *was* in there! Ash Allardyce! He was flailing about and quite clearly close to drowning!

All Phinn knew then was that she had to get to him quickly. There was a small bridge spanning the narrow part of the pool, but that was much farther down. And time was of the essence. There was no time to think, only time to act. Her father had taught her lifesaving, and had taught her well. Up until then it was a skill she had never needed to use.

Even as these thoughts were flashing thought her mind Phinn was kicking off her sandals and pulling her dress over her head. Knowing she had to get to Ash, and fast, and all before she could query the wisdom of what she was doing, Phinn was running for the water and taking a racing dive straight in.

After having been so hot, the water felt icy, but there was no time to think about that now. Only time to get to Ash. Executing a sprinting crawl, Phinn reached him in no time flat, gasped a warning, 'Stay still or you'll kill us both,' turned him onto his back and, glad for the moment that he was twenty pounds lighter than he had been, towed him to the nearest bank, which was now on the opposite side from where she had first seen him.

How long he had been struggling she had no idea. 'Cramp!' he managed to gasp, and managed to sit up, head down, his arms on his knees, exhausted, totally drained of energy.

It had all happened so quickly, but now that it was over Phinn felt pretty drained herself, and had an idea she knew pretty much how a mother must feel when she had just found her lost child. 'You should have had more sense,' she berated him with what breath she could find. 'Everybody *knows* you don't swim in *that* part of the pool.' Suddenly she was feeling inexplicably weepy. Shock, she supposed. Then she remembered Ruby, and looked to the other bank. She could not see her. 'I'll be back,' she said, and took off.

Not to swim this time—she didn't feel like going back in there in a hurry—but to run down to the small bridge. It fleetingly crossed her mind as she ran to wonder if Ash had perhaps been a touch suicidal to have chosen to swim where he had. Then she recalled he had said he'd had a cramp, and she began to feel better about leaving him. She had been brought up *knowing* that a deep shelf had been excavated on that side of the pool for some reason that was now lost in the mists of time. The water was deep there—nobody knew how deep, but so deep as to never heat up, and was regarded locally with the greatest respect. Ash, who hadn't been brought up in the area, could not possibly have known unless someone had told him. Well, he knew now!

Phinn ran across the bridge, and as she did so she saw with

relief that Ruby had not wandered off and that she was quite safe. Phinn's relief was short-lived, however, because in that same glance she saw none other than Ty Allardyce. Phinn came to an abrupt halt.

Oh, help! He was facing away from her and had not yet spotted her. He was looking about—perhaps searching for his brother? He was close to Ruby. Then Phinn saw that he was not only close to Ruby, he had hold of her rein. Phinn knew then that it was not his brother he was searching for but Ruby's owner—and that Ruby's owner was in deep trouble!

As if aware of someone behind him, Ty Allardyce turned round. Turned and, as if he could not believe his eyes, stared at her.

And that was when Phinn became aware of how she was dressed—or rather *undressed*. A quick glance down proved that she was as good as naked! Standing there in her wet underwear she was conscious that her waterlogged bra and briefs were now transparent, the pink tips of her breasts hardened and clearly visible to the man staring at her.

Her face glowed a fiery red. 'A gentleman would turn his back,' she hissed, with what voice she could find.

Ty Allardyce favoured her with a hard stare, but was in no hurry to turn around. 'So he would—for a lady,' he drawled.

Phinn wanted to hit him, but she wasn't going any closer. And he, surveying her from her soggy braided hair down to the tip of her bare toes, took his time, his insolent gaze moving back up her long, long shapely legs, thighs and belly. By this time her arms were crossed in front of her body. Strangely, it was only when his glance rested on her fiercely blushing face that he gave her the benefit of the term 'lady' and, while still holding Ruby's rein, turned his back on her.

In next to no time Phinn had retrieved her dress and sandals and, having been careless how her dress had landed, found that her hands were shaking when she went to turn it right side out.

But once she had her dress over her shoulders, she felt her former spirit returning. She had to go close up to him to take Ruby's rein, and, as embarrassed as she felt, she somehow managed to find an impudent, 'Lovely day for a dip!'

His reply was to turn and favour her with one of his hard stares. It seemed to her as if he was deciding whether or not to pick her up and throw her in for another dip.

Attempting to appear casual, she moved to the other side of Ruby. Not a moment too soon, she realised, as, not caring for her insolence, 'That's it!' he rapped, his eyes angry on her by now much paler face. 'I've warned you twice. You'll receive notice from my lawyers in the morning.'

'You have my address?' she enquired nicely—and felt inclined to offer him her new address; but at his hard-eyed expression she thought better of it.

Ty Allardyce drew one very harsh, long-suffering breath. 'Enough!' he snarled. 'If you're not on your way inside the next ten seconds, I shall personally be escorting you and that flea-bitten old nag off my land!'

'Flea-bitten!' she gasped. How *dared* he?

'Now!' he threatened, making a move to take Ruby's rein from her.

'Leave her alone!' Phinn threatened back, her tone murderous as she knocked his hand away. She was not sure yet that she wasn't going to hit him—he was well and truly asking for it! Emotional tears sprang to her eyes.

Tears he spotted, regardless that she'd managed to hold them back and prevent them from falling. 'Of for G—' he began impatiently. And, as if more impatient with himself than with her, because her shining eyes had had more effect on him than her murderous threat, 'Clear off, stay off—and leave my brother alone!'

Only then did Phinn remember Ash. A quick glance to the other side of the pool showed he had recovered and was getting to his feet, which told her she could safely leave him. 'Wouldn't touch either of you with a bargepole,' she told Ty loftily, and turned Ruby about and headed in the direction of the spinney.

With everything that had taken place playing back in her mind, Phinn walked on with Ruby. She had no idea how long it was since she had seen Ash in trouble—ten perhaps fifteen minutes? A glance to her watch showed that it did not care much for underwater activity and would never be the same again.

She felt ashamed that she had very nearly cried in front of that brute. *Flea-bitten old nag!* But she started to accept—now that she was away from him, away from the pool—that perhaps she had started to feel a bit of reaction after first seeing Ash in difficulties, taking a header in to get him out, and then, to top it all, being confronted by Ty Allardyce.

Yes, it must be shock, she realised. There was no other explanation for her thinking, as she had at the time, that Ty Allardyce had been sensitive to a woman's tears.

Sensitive! She must be in shock still! That insensitive brute didn't have a sensitive bone in his body! How could he have? He had actually called her darling Rubes a flea-bitten old nag! Oh, how she wished she had hit him.

Well, one thing was for sure. She would take great delight in marking any lawyer's letter that arrived for her tomorrow 'address unknown', before she happily popped it in the post box to be sent speedily straight back whence it came!

CHAPTER THREE

AS SOON as she had settled Ruby, Phinn went to the stable flat, stripped off, showered and washed the pool out of her hair. Donning fresh underwear, a pair of shorts and a tee shirt, she wrapped a towel around her hair and made herself a cup of tea. She admitted that she was still feeling a little shaken up by the afternoon's events.

Although, on reflection, she wasn't sure which had disturbed her the most: the unexpectedness of coming upon Ash Allardyce without warning and her efforts to get the drowning man to the bank, or the fact that his hard-nosed brother had so insolently stood there surveying her when she had stood as near to naked as if it made no difference.

He quite obviously thought she had taken advantage of the hot weather to strip off to her underwear and have a swim in waters that belonged to his lands. And he hadn't liked that, had he? He with his, 'Clear off, stay off—and leave my brother alone!'

She cared not whether Ash ever told him the true facts of her swim. She had always swum there—weather permitting. Though she did recall one marvellously hysterical time when it had come on to rain while she and her father had been swimming, and he had declared that since they couldn't get any wetter they might as well carry on swimming.

Barefooted, she padded to get another towel and, because her long hair took for ever to dry naturally, she towelled it as dry as she could, brushed it out, and left her hair hanging down over her shoulders to dry when it would.

Meantime, she packed her clothes and placed a couple of suitcases near the door, ready for when Mickie Yates would come round at three tomorrow afternoon. Now she had better start packing away her china, and the few ornaments and mementoes she had been unable to part with from her old home.

The mantelpiece was bare, and she had just finished clearing the shelves, when someone came knocking at her door. Geraldine coming to check that she was truly leaving tomorrow, Phinn supposed, padding to the door. She pulled it open—only to receive another shock!

Finding herself staring up into the cool grey eyes of Ty Allardyce, Phinn was for the moment struck dumb. And as he stared into her darkening blue eyes, he seemed in no hurry to start a conversation either.

The fact that she was now dry, and clad in shorts and top, as opposed to dripping and in her underwear as the last time he had studied her, made Phinn feel no better. She saw his glance flick to her long strawberry-blonde hair, free from its plait, and pulled herself sharply together.

'As I live and breathe—the lesser-spotted superior Allardyce,' she waded in. 'Now who's trespassing?'

To his credit, he took her remark equably. 'I should like to talk to you,' he said for openers.

'Tough! Get off my—er...' *damn* '...doorstep.'

His answer to her command was to ignore it. And, much to her annoyance, he did no more than push his way into what had been her sitting room-cum-kitchen.

'You're leaving tomorrow?' he suggested, his eyes moving from her suitcases to the boxes of packed teacups, plates and ornaments.

Phinn fought to find some sharp comeback, but couldn't find one. 'Yes,' she replied, belligerent because she saw no reason to be any other way with this man who wanted to curtail her right to use and respect his grounds as her own.

'Where are you going?' he enquired, and she hated it that, when she could never remember any man making her blush before, this man seemed to be able to do so without the smallest effort.

'I—er…' she mumbled, and turned away from him, walking towards the window in a vain hope that he had not noticed she had gone red.

'You're looking guilty about something,' he commented, closing the door and coming further into the room, adding, as she turned to face him, 'I do hope, Miss Hawkins, that I'm not going to wake up on Saturday morning and find you camping out on my front lawn?'

The idea amused her, and despite herself her lips twitched. And she supposed that 'Miss Hawkins' was one better than the plain 'Hawkins' he had used before. But she quickly stamped down on what she considered must be a quirk in her sense of humour. 'To be honest, that was something I hadn't thought of doing,' she replied.

'But?'

This man was as sharp as a tack! He knew full well that there was a 'but'. 'But nothing,' she replied stiffly. She didn't want a spanner thrown into the works of her arrangements at this late stage. But Ty Allardyce continued to look back at her, his mind fully at work, she didn't doubt. 'Well, I've things to do. Thank you for popping by,' she said coolly, moving towards the door, knowing full well that this wasn't a social call, but at a loss to know what else one would call it.

'What you would need,' he stated thoughtfully, his glance lighting briefly on her long length of leg in the short shorts, 'is somewhere you can lay your head, and somewhere where at the same time you can stable that—'

'Her name is Ruby,' Phinn cut in, starting to bridle. 'The flea-bitten old nag, as you so delightfully called her, is Ruby.'

'I apologise,' he replied, and that surprised her so much she could only stand there and blink. And blink again when he went on. 'Do you know, I really don't think I can allow you to go back to Honeysuckle Farm? It—'

'How did you know I intended to go there?' she gasped in amazement. Surely Mickie hadn't…?

He hadn't. 'I didn't know. That is I wasn't sure until you just this minute confirmed it.'

'Clever devil!' she sniffed. Then quickly realised that she was in a hole that looked like getting bigger and bigger—if she couldn't do something about it. 'Look,' she said, taking a deep breath, 'I know you're cross with me—full-time, permanently. But I wouldn't harm the place. I'd—'

'Out of the question,' he cut in forthrightly.

'Why?' she demanded, when common sense told her she was going about this in totally the wrong way.

'There aren't any services up there for a start.'

'I won't need any. I've got a supply of candles. And it's too warm for me to need heating. And…'

'And what if it rains and the roof leaks?'

'It doesn't. I was up there the other…' Oh, grief—just think before you speak!

'You've been inside?' he demanded. 'You still have a key?'

'Yes and no.' He looked impatient. She hated him. 'Yes, I've been inside. And, no, I haven't got a key.'

'You got in—how?'

It wouldn't have taken much for her to tell him to get lost, but she was still hopeful of moving back to Honeysuckle Farm tomorrow. 'I—um—got in through one of the bedroom windows,' she confessed.

'You climbed in…' He shook his head slightly, as if hardly believing this female. 'You include breaking and entering in your list of skills?'

'I'm desperate!' she exclaimed shortly. 'Ruby's not well, and—' She broke off. Damn the man. It must still be shock— she was feeling weepy again. She turned her back on him, wanting to order him out, but ready to swallow her pride and plead with him if she had to.

But then, to her astonishment and to her disbelieving ears, she discovered that she did not have to plead with him at all. Because, staggeringly, Ty Allardyce was stating, 'I think we can find you somewhere a bit better than the present condition of Honeysuckle Farm to live.'

Things like that just did not happen for people like Delphinnium Hawkins—well, not lately anyhow. She stared at him open-mouthed. He didn't like her. She definitely didn't like him. So why? 'For Ruby too?' she asked slowly.

'For Ruby too,' he confirmed.

'Where?' she asked, not believing it but desperately wanting to.

'Up at the Hall. You could come and live with—'

'Now, wait a minute!' she cut in bluntly. 'I don't know what you think I am, but let me tell—'

'Oh, for heaven's sake!' He cut her off irritably. Then, taking a steadying breath, let her know that she could not be more wrong. 'While I'll acknowledge you may have the best pair of legs I've seen in a while—and the rest of you isn't so bad either…' She refused to visibly blench, because he must be referring to the sight he'd had of her well-proportioned breasts, pink tips protruding. 'I have better things to do with my free time than want to bed one of the village locals!'

Village locals! Well, that put her in her place. 'You should be so lucky!' she sniffed. But, with Ruby in mind, she could not afford to be offended for very long. 'Why would you want me living up at the Hall?'

'Shall we sit down?' he suggested.

Perhaps her legs would be less on display if she sat down. Phinn moved to one chair and he went and occupied the other one. Then, waiting until she looked ready to listen, he began, 'You did me a service today that will render me forever in your debt.'

'Oh, I wouldn't say that.' She shrugged off his comment, but realised then that he now knew all about his brother's attack of cramp. 'See where trespassing will get you!'

'Had you not trespassed...had you not been there—' He broke off. 'It doesn't bear thinking about,' he said, his jaw clenching as if he was getting on top of some emotion.

'Ash wasn't to know that that part of the pool is treacherous. That you have to stick strictly to the shallows if you want to swim,' she attempted lightly.

But Ty was not making light of it, and seemed to know precisely how tragic the consequences could have been. 'But you knew it. And even so—according to Ash when he was able to reflect back—you did the finest and fastest running racing dive he'd ever seen. He said that you dived straight in, not a moment's hesitation, to get him out.'

'Had you arrived a little earlier than you did, I'd have happily let *you* go in,' she murmured, starting to feel a touch embarrassed. With relief she saw, unexpectedly, the way Ty's mouth had picked up at the corners and knew her attempt at humour—her intimation that she would quite happily have let him take his chances on drowning—had reached his own sense of humour.

Though he was not to be drawn away from the seriousness of their discussion it seemed, because he continued. 'You saved my brother's life with not a thought for your own, when you knew full well about that treacherous side of the pool. You went straight in.'

'I did stop to kick my sandals off and yank my dress over my head,' she reminded him, again attempting to make light of it.

But then wished that she hadn't, when grey eyes looked straight into hers and he commented, 'I have not forgotten,' adding in a low murmur, 'I doubt I ever shall. I thought you'd been skinny-dipping at first.' He brought himself up short. 'Anyhow, Ash—for all he's lost a lot of weight—is still quite heavy. Had he struggled, you could both have drowned. Dear God—' He broke off again, swallowing down his anguish.

Seeing his mental torment, and even if she didn't like him, Phinn just had to tell him, 'Ash didn't struggle. It wasn't an attempt at suicide, if that's what you think. It was cramp, pure and simple. The water's icy there. There's a deep shelf… He…'

Ty Allardyce smiled then. It was the first smile he had ever directed at her and her heart went thump. He was *so* handsome! 'I know he wasn't attempting to take his own life,' he agreed. 'But from that remark it's obvious that you've observed that my brother is…extremely vulnerable at the moment.'

Phinn nodded. Yes, she knew that. 'I know you blame me in part, but truthfully there was nothing I could have done to stop it. I mean, I didn't know that Leanne would—er—break it off with him the way she did.'

'Perhaps I was unfair to blame you,' Ty conceded. 'But to get to other matters—Ash tells me you have a problem, with no job and no home for you and your—Ruby. I,' he stated, 'am in a position to offer you both.'

A home *and* a job? Things like this just did *not* happen. 'I don't want your charity!' she erupted.

'My God, you're touchy!' Ty bit back. But then, looking keenly at her, 'You're not…? Are you in shock? Starting to suffer after-effects from what happened today?'

Phinn rather thought she might be. And—oh, grief—she was feeling weepy again. 'Look, can you go back to being nasty again? I can cope with you better when you're being a brute!'

He wasn't offended, but nor was he reverting to being the brute that always put her on her mettle. 'Have you any family near?' he asked, quite kindly.

This—his niceness—was unnerving. So unnerving that she found she was actually telling him. 'My mother lives in Gloucester, but…'

'I'll drive you there,' he decided. 'Get—'

'I'm not—' she started to protest.

'Stop being argumentative,' he ordered. 'You're in no condition to drive.' And, when she would have protested further, 'You'll probably get the shakes any minute now,' he went on. 'It will be safer all round if I'm at the wheel.'

Honestly—this man! 'Will you stop trying to bulldoze me along?' she flared crossly. 'Yes, I feel a bit shaken,' she admitted. 'But nothing I can't cope with. And I'm not going anywhere.'

'If I can't take you to your mother, I'll take you back to the Hall with me.' He ignored what she had just said.

'No, you won't!' she exploded, going on quickly. 'Apart from anything else, I'm not leaving Ruby. She's—'

'She'll be all right until you pick her up tomorrow,' he countered. 'You can—'

'You can stop right there. Just *stop* it!' she ordered. 'I'm not going anywhere today. And when I do go, Ruby goes with me.'

Ty Allardyce observed the determined look of her. And, plainly a man who did not take defeat lightly, he gave her a stern expression of his own. 'I'll make you some tea,' he said, quite out of nowhere—and she just had to burst out laughing. That just made him stare at her.

'I'm sorry,' she apologized, and, quickly sobering, 'I know tea is said to be good for shock, but I've had some tea and I don't want more. And please,' she went on before he could argue, 'can we just accept that I know you truly appreciate my towing Ash back onto terra firma this afternoon and then forget all about it?'

Steady grey eyes bored into her darkened blue ones. 'You want to go back to me being the brute up at the Hall who keeps trying to turf you off his land?'

Phinn nodded, starting to feel better suddenly. 'And I'll go back to being the—er—village local…' Her lips twitched, and she saw his do the same before they both sobered, and she went on. 'The village local who thinks you've one heck of a nerve daring to stop me from doing things I've always done on Broadlands land.'

He nodded, but informed her, 'You're still not going back to Honeysuckle Farm to live.'

'Oh, come on!' she exclaimed. 'I have to leave here tomorrow. Geraldine wants the flat for a member of her staff, and I've promised I'll move out.'

'That, as I've mentioned, is not a problem. There's a home and a job waiting for you at the Hall.'

'And a home for Ruby too?'

'At the moment the stable is being used for storage, but you can clear it out tomorrow. It's dry in there and—'

'It has water?'

'It has water,' he confirmed.

'You have other horses?' she asked quickly, and, at his questioning look, 'Ruby's a kind of rescue mare. She was badly treated and has a timid nature. Other horses tend to gang up on her.'

'You've no need to worry on that score. Ruby will have an idyllic life. There's a completely fenced-off paddock too that she can use.'

Phinn knew the paddock, if it was the one she was thinking of. As well as being shaded in part by trees, it also had a large open-ended shed a horse could wander into if it became too hot.

All of a sudden Phinn felt weepy again. She would be glad when this shock was over and done with! Oh, it did sound idyllic.

Oh, Ruby, my darling. 'This is a—a permanent job?' she questioned. 'I mean, you're not going to turf me out after a week?'

'It wouldn't be a permanent position,' he replied. Though he added before she could feel too deflated, 'Let's say six months definite, with a review when the six months are up.'

'I'll take it,' she accepted at once, not needing to think about it. She would have six months in which to sort something else out. Trying not to sound too eager, though unable to hold back, she said, 'I'll do it—whatever the job is. I can cook, clean, garden—catalogue your library…'

'With a couple of part-time helpers, Mrs Starkey runs the house and kitchen admirably, and Jimmie Starkey has all the help he needs in the grounds.'

'And you don't need your library catalogued?' she guessed, ready to offer her secretarial skills but suspecting he had a PA in London far more competent than she would be to take care of those matters.

'The job I have for you is very specialised,' Ty Allardyce stated, and before she could tell him that she was a little short in the specialised skills department, he was going on. 'My work in London and overseas has been such that until recently I've been unable to spend very much time down here.'

At any other time she might have thrown in a sarcastic *We've missed you*, but Ty Allardyce was being deadly serious, so she settled for, 'I expect you keep in touch by phone.'

He nodded. 'Which in no way prepared me for the shock I received when I made what was meant to be a snatched visit here a couple of weeks ago.'

'Ah—you're talking…Ash?'

'You've noticed the change in him?'

Who could fail to? 'He's—not ill?'

'Not in the accepted sense.'

'Did Leanne do this to him?' She voiced her thoughts, and saw his mouth tighten.

'I couldn't believe that some money-grabbing female could so wreck a man, but—' He broke off, then resumed, 'Anyhow, I felt there was no way I could return to London. Not then. Not now—without your help.'

'I'll do anything I can, naturally.'

'Good,' he said. 'The job is yours.'

She stared at this man who she had to admit she was starting to like—though she was fully prepared to believe that shock did funny things to people, but still felt no further forward. 'Er—and the job is what, exactly?'

'I thought I'd just said,' Ty replied, 'I want you to be Ash's companion.'

Her mouth fell open. 'You want me to be your brother's *companion*?' she echoed.

'I'll pay you, of course,' Ty answered, seeing absolutely nothing untoward in what he was proposing.

'You want me to be his paid companion?' she questioned again, as it started to sink in. 'His—his minder?'

'No, not minder!' Ty answered shortly. 'I've explained how things are.'

'Not really you haven't,' Phinn stated, and was on the receiving end of an impatient look.

'The situation is,' he explained heavily, 'that while I can do certain parts of my job in my study, via computer and telephone, other matters require my presence in London or some other capital. I've been down here for two weeks more than I originally intended already. And, while I have a pressing need to get back to town, I still don't feel ready to leave Ash on his own.'

Phinn thought about it. 'You think I might be the person to take over from you for a while?'

'Can you think of anyone better than someone who has actually risked their own life for him, as you did today?'

'I don't know about that,' she mumbled.

'Ash likes you. He enjoyed talking to you the other day.'

'Um—that was the day you told me to leave him alone, to—'

'I was angry,' Ty admitted. 'I didn't want another Hawkins finishing off what your cousin had done to him. But that was before I was able to reason that he was still so ensnared by her that other women just don't exist for him. Frankly, Ash wouldn't fancy you even if you *did* use your beauty to try to hook him.'

Beauty? Hook him? Charming! At that point Phinn was in two minds about whether or not she wanted the job. She felt sorry for Ash—of course she did. As for her cousin...she was feeling quite angry with Leanne. But...then Phinn thought of Ruby, and at the thought of a stable *and* a paddock there was no question but that she wanted the job.

'I haven't the first idea what a paid companion is supposed to do... I mean, what would I have to do? You wouldn't expect me to take him down to the pub and get drunk with him every night, I hope?'

'You like beer?' he asked sharply.

'No!' she shot straight back.

'You'd been drinking this afternoon,' he retorted, obviously not caring to be lied to. 'There was a smell of beer on your breath.'

'Honestly!' she exclaimed. And she was thinking of *working* for this man who could sniff out beer at a hundred paces! But what choice did she have? 'If you must know, I hate the stuff. But I've been having a courtesy swig out of Idris Owens' beer tankard ever since I was ten years old—it's a sort of tradition, each time I go to the farrier. It would have been churlish to refuse his offer when I took Ruby to have her hooves checked over by him this afternoon.'

For a moment Ty Allardyce said nothing, just sat there looking at her. Then he said quietly, 'Rather than hurt his feelings, you quaffed ale that you've no particular liking for?'

'So what does that make me?' she challenged, expecting something pretty pithy in reply.

But, to her surprise, he replied in that same quiet tone. 'I think it makes you a rather nice kind of person.' And she was struck again by the change in him from the man she had thought he was.

'Yes, well…' she said abruptly—grief, she'd be going soft in the head about him in a minute. Buck up, she instructed herself. This man could be iron-hard and unyielding without any trouble. Hadn't she witnessed that for herself? 'So I'm—er—to take over the sort of guardianship of Ash from you while you—um—go about your business?'

'Not quite,' Ty replied. 'What I believe Ash needs just now is to be with someone who will be a sensitive ear for him when he needs to talk. Someone to take him out of himself when he looks like becoming a little melancholy.'

'You think I've got a sensitive ear?'

Again he looked steadily at her. 'You'll do,' he said. And he would have left it at that, but there were questions queuing up in Phinn's mind.

'You think it will take as long as six months for Ash to—um—get back to being his old self?'

'Hopefully nowhere near as long. Who knows? Whatever—I'm prepared to guarantee stabling and a place for you to rest your head for the whole six months.'

'Fine,' she said.

'You'll start tomorrow?'

And how! 'You'd better let me have your phone number,' she requested, overjoyed, now it had had time to sink in, that by the look of it Ruby was going to have a proper stable and a paddock all to herself.

'Why would you want my phone number?' Ty asked shortly.

'Oh, for goodness' sake!' she erupted at her new boss. 'So I can ring Ash and ask him to come and pick me up with my belongings. I can bring Ruby over later.'

'You want to inspect her accommodation first?'

'I'd—er—have put it a little more tactfully,' she mumbled. 'But, yes, that's the general idea. I could still ask Mickie if you don't want Ash to do it.'

'Who's Mickie?'

'He lives in the village. He's a bit eccentric, but he has a heart of gold. He—er—' She broke off—that was more than he needed to know.

She quickly realised that she should have known better. '"He—er—" what?'

Phinn gave a resigned sigh. 'Well, if you must know, I'd already arranged for Mickie to take my cases and bits and pieces up to Honeysuckle Farm for me tomorrow.'

Ty Allardyce shook his head, as though she was a new kind of species to him. 'Presumably he would have kept quiet about your whereabouts?'

'Well, there you are,' she said briskly, about nothing, and then fell headlong when, in the same bracing tone, she said, 'Had I not sold my car, I...' Her voice trailed away. 'Well, I did,' she added quickly. And then, hurriedly attempting to close the interview—or whatever it was, 'So I'll get Mickie to—'

'You sold your car?' Ty Allardyce took up.

'Yep.' He didn't need to hear more.

And nor did he, she discovered. Because what this clever man did not know he was astute enough to decipher and guess at. 'According to my lawyers, you paid a whole whack of back rent before you handed in the keys to the farm,' he commented slowly. Adding, 'Had I thought about it at all, I'd have assumed that the money came from your father's estate. But—' he looked at her sharply '—it didn't, did it?'

She shrugged. 'What did I need a car for? I thought I'd got a steady job here—no need to look for work further afield. Besides, I couldn't leave Ruby on her own all day.' Phinn halted, she'd had enough of talking about herself. 'Have you told Ash that you were going to offer me a job?'

Ty looked at her unspeaking for some moments, and then replied, 'No.'

She saw it might be a little awkward if Ash objected strongly. 'How do you think he'll take my moving in to be his companion?' No point in ducking the question. If Ash did not want her there, then the next six months could be pretty miserable all round.

'My brother feels things very deeply,' Ty began. 'He has been hurt—badly hurt. In my view it would be easier for him if he didn't know the true reason for your being at the Hall.'

'I wouldn't be able to lie to him,' Phinn said quickly. 'I'm not very good at telling lies.'

'You wouldn't have to lie.'

Phinn looked into steady grey eyes and felt somewhat perplexed. 'What, then?' she asked. 'I can't just ring him out of the blue and ask him to come and get me.'

'It won't be a problem,' Ty assured her. 'Ash knows that you and Ruby have to leave here. I'll tell him that, apropos of you having nowhere to go, I called to thank you for what you did today and offered you a temporary home.'

Phinn's eyes widened. 'You think he'll believe such philanthropy?' she queried—and discovered that her hint of sarcasm was not lost on him.

'My stars, I pity the poor man who ends up with *you*!' he muttered under his breath, but then agreed, 'Normally I doubt he'd believe it for a moment. But, apart from him not being too concerned about anything very much just now, he's as grateful to you as I am that you were where you were today.' The matter settled as far as he was concerned, he took out his wallet, extracted his business card, wrote several numbers on it and, standing up, handed it to her.

Phinn glanced at the card in her hand and read that he had

given her his office number, his mobile number, the phone number of his London home and the one she had asked for—the number of the Hall.

'No need to have gone raving mad,' she commented. She had only wanted one telephone number, for goodness' sake!

'Just in case,' he said, and she realised he meant her to ring him if she felt things were going badly for Ash. 'Feel free to ring me at any time,' he added.

'Right,' she agreed, and stood up too. She found he was too close and, feeling a mite odd for no reason, took a step away.

'How are you feeling now?' he thought to ask before he turned to the door.

'Feeling?' For a moment she wasn't with him.

Without more ado he caught hold of both of her hands. When, his touch making her tingle, she would have snatched her hands back, he held on to them. 'You're not shaking,' he observed—and then she *was* with him.

'Oh, I think the shock has passed now,' she informed him, only then starting to wonder if this man—this complex kind of man—had stayed talking with her as long as he had so as to be on hand if she looked like going into full-blown shock. 'You're kinder than I thought,' she blurted out, quite without thinking—and abruptly had her hands dropped like hot coals.

'Spread that around and I'll have to kill you,' he said shortly. And that was it. He was gone.

Starting to only half-believe that Ty Allardyce had been in the flat and made that staggering, not to say wonderful job and accommodation offer for her and Ruby, Phinn went quickly to the window that overlooked the stableyard.

He was there. She had not dreamt it. Ty Allardyce was in the stableyard talking to Geraldine Walton. What was more, Geraldine was smiling her head off. Never had Phinn seen her look more animated or more pleasant.

Phinn added 'charm' to Ty Allardyce's list of accomplishments, and wondered what he was talking to Geraldine about. Keeping out of sight, she watched for a minute or so more, and then the two of them disappeared.

While they were gone she observed that there was a pick-up vehicle in the yard that did not belong to the stables. She assumed that Ty Allardyce had driven over in it.

She soon saw that her assumption was correct. When he and Geraldine Walton appeared again, he was hauling a bale of straw and Geraldine was wheeling a bale of hay. Phinn watched as the two bales were loaded onto the pick-up. She kept out of sight as the two disappeared again, and then reappeared with the special feed Phinn herself had bought for Ruby, who needed it on account of her teeth not being what they once had been.

Feeling little short of amazed, Phinn watched as the two chatted a little while longer, before Ty got into the pick-up and drove away.

Was he a mover or was he a mover? My heavens, it had all been cut and dried as far as he was concerned before he had even left Broadlands! Ty Allardyce needed someone trustworthy to keep his brother company while he returned to the business he had already neglected for far too long, and he had it all planned out before he had come to see her!

While he might not have cared for her standing up to him over her right to trespass, it was plain that in his view, when it came to being trustworthy with his brother, there was no higher recommendation than that she had that day taken a header into the pool to get his brother out when Ash had got into difficulties. Plan made, all that he'd needed to do was come and see her and—as it were—make her an offer she couldn't refuse.

That he had known in advance that she would not refuse his offer was evidenced by the fact he had driven over in the pick-up. Efficient or what? Since he would be at the stables, he might as well collect a few things and save an extra journey later.

Feeling a little bit stunned by the man's efficiency, Phinn went out to check on Ruby. Inevitably, it seemed, she bumped into Geraldine Walton.

'You didn't say you were starting work up at the Hall?' Geraldine commented, and seemed more relaxed than she had before.

Phinn felt a little stumped as to how to reply. There was no way she was going to reveal to anyone the true nature of her job at the Hall. On the other hand, given that Geraldine could be tough when she had to be, she did not want to part with bad feelings.

'I'm just hoping my secretarial skills aren't too rusty,' she answered lightly. It was the best she could do at a moment's notice, and she hoped it would suffice as a white lie. 'Must go and check on Ruby,' she added with a smile, and went quickly on.

Ruby came over to her as soon as she saw her, and Phinn told her all about the move tomorrow, and about the nice new paddock all to herself. Ruby nuzzled into her neck appreciatively—and Phinn came near to feeling relaxed for the first time in an age.

She stayed talking to Ruby for quite some while, and was in fact still with her when she thought that perhaps she had given Ty plenty of time in which to tell his brother that from tomorrow on they were to have a house guest.

Realising she had left her mobile phone and the phone numbers Ty had given her back in the flat, she parted from Ruby briefly while she nipped back to the accommodation she would be vacating in the morning.

Finding the card, she dialled the number of the Hall and, for no known reason expecting that Ash would be the one to answer her call, was a little nonplussed to hear Ty's voice. 'Allardyce,' he said, and she knew straight away that it was him.

'Oh, hello, Ty—er—Mr Allardyce,' she stumbled, feeling a fool.

'Ty,' he invited, and asked, 'Did you want to speak with Ash?'

'If I may,' she replied primly. And that was it. A few minutes later Ash was on the line.

'I wanted to ring you,' he said, before she could say a word. 'We hadn't got your number, but I wanted to thank you so much, Phinn, for what you did today. I didn't get a chance before. When I think—'

'That's all right, Ash,' she butted in. 'Er—actually, Ty stopped by to thank me. Um—I think you must have told him about my need to move from here?'

'I'm glad I did. Ty says he knows we can never repay you, but that he's offered you and your horse temporary accommodation here until you can sort something out.'

'You don't mind?'

'Good Lord, no! Ty's suggested I get busy sorting out the old stable in the morning.'

'I'll come and help!' Phinn volunteered promptly. 'Actually, I'm without wheels, so if you could come and collect me and some of my stuff, it…?'

'I owe you—big-time. Nine o'clock suit?'

Phinn went to bed that night with her head buzzing. She barely knew where to start when she thought of all that had happened that day. Drinking beer in the forge! That ghastly picture of Ash in trouble! His complex brother! His amazing offer! All in all, today had been one almighty day for huge surprises.

Strangely, though, as she lay in the dark going over everything in her head, it was Ty Allardyce who figured most largely in her thoughts. He could be hard, he could be bossy—overbearing, even—but he could be kind too. Complex did she say? Ty Allardyce was something else again.

She remembered the way he had taken her hands in his, and

recalled the way she had tingled all over. Don't be ridiculous, she instructed herself. Just look forward to going to Broadlands Hall to be a companion to Ash so that Ty can get back to the work he so obviously loves.

From her point of view, things couldn't be better. When she thought about it, a return to Honeysuckle Farm had been a far from ideal solution. Both she and Ruby would fare much better at Broadlands. They were truly most fortunate.

But—Phinn fidgeted in her bed—why was she feeling just a little disturbed? As if there was something not quite right somewhere?

CHAPTER FOUR

PHINN was up and about long before Ash called for her the next day. She had tended to Ruby's requirements earlier, and spent her time waiting for Ash in folding Ruby's blankets and in getting the mare's belongings together.

Turning Ruby out into the field for the last time, Phinn cleaned out her stall so that Geraldine would have nothing to complain over. But even though she felt sure Ruby's new accommodation would be adequate, she still wanted to look it over before she moved her.

A little after nine Ash drove into the yard and found her waiting for him. He looked dreadfully tired, Phinn thought, as though his nights were long and tortuous.

'Ready?' he asked, pushing out a smile.

'There's rather a lot to cart over,' she mentioned apologetically.

They had almost finished loading the pick-up when Geraldine Walton appeared, and Phinn introduced the two. 'You manage the estate, I believe?' Geraldine commented pleasantly, clearly having been in the area long enough to have picked up village gossip.

'Something like that,' Ash muttered, and hefted the last of Phinn's cases into the back of the pick-up. 'That it?' he asked Phinn.

She smiled at him and, feeling that he had perhaps been a little off with Geraldine, smiled at her too. 'I'll be over for Ruby later,' she confirmed.

'She'll be fine until then. No need to rush back. I'll keep an eye on her,' Geraldine promised.

A minute or so later and Ash was driving the pick-up out of the stableyard. Her job, Phinn realised, had begun. 'Er—Ty gone back to London?' she enquired—more to get Ash to start talking than because she had any particular interest in his brother.

But Ash took his glance from the road briefly to give her what she could only describe as a knowing look as he enquired, 'Didn't he phone you before he left?'

There was no reason why he should phone, as far as Phinn was aware, and she almost said as much—but that was before, on thinking about that knowing look, the most astonishing thought hit her! It couldn't be—could it?

She tried to look at the situation from Ash's angle. Given that she was unable to tell Ash that the real reason she was coming to live at the Hall was in order to keep an eye on him and, unbeknown to him, be his companion, did Ash think that there was more in his brother's invitation for her to stay at the Hall than his gratitude after yesterday's events?

She opened her mouth to tell Ash bluntly that there was nothing going on between her and his brother Ty, nor likely to be, but the moment had passed. Then she was glad she had said nothing; she had obviously got it wrong. In actual fact, when she thought of the glamorous females that Ty probably dated, she was doubly glad she had said nothing. Far better to keep her mouth shut than to make a fool of herself.

Ash drove straight to the stable. There were bits and pieces of packing cases outside, she noticed as they drove up. 'I was supposed to have the stable empty before you got here, but I—er—got kind of sidetracked,' Ash excused.

'Well, with two of us I don't suppose it will take us very

long,' Phinn said brightly, more concerned with having a look inside than anything else just then.

Taking into account that there were more packing cases inside, plus an old scrubbed kitchen table and other items which she guessed had come out of the Hall when it had been modernised, the stable was more than adequate—even to the water tap on one wall. Indeed, once she had got it all spruced up, brushed out, and with fresh straw put down, it would be little short of luxury for Ruby.

'Roll your sleeves up time!' she announced.

'You don't want to go into the house and check on your room first?'

Where she laid her head that night was immaterial to Phinn just then. Her first priority was to get Ruby settled. 'I'm sure it will be fine,' she answered. 'Will you help?'

Reluctantly at first, Ash started bundling boxes out of the way. And then gradually he began to take over. 'Leave that one,' he ordered at one stage, when she tried to manhandle what had been some part of a kitchen cabinet. 'I'll move that.' And later, 'What we're going to have to do is to take this lot down to the tip.'

Sacrilege! Phinn took out her phone and pressed out Mickie Yates's number. With luck she'd get him before he went for lunch, and she needed to talk to him anyway.

She was in luck. He was home. 'Mickie? Phinn Hawkins.'

'I haven't forgotten,' he replied, a smile in his voice. 'Three o'clock.'

'Change of plan,' she stated. 'I'm—er—working and staying at the Hall for a while.' She could feel Ash's eyes on her, and felt awkward. 'The thing is, we're clearing out the stable for Ruby. Can you find homes for some kitchen units and the like that still have some life in them, do you think?'

'Today?'

'That would be good.'

'An hour?'

'That would be brilliant.'

'See you, lovely girl.'

Putting her phone away after making the call, Phinn looked up to find that Ash was staring at her. 'You're working here?' he enquired.

She went red. Grief—what *was* it about these Allardyce brothers? 'Shut up—and help me move this,' she ordered—and to her great delight, after a stunned moment she saw a half-grin break on Ash's features. It seemed an age since she had last seen him smile.

She was delighted, but a moment or two later she distinctly heard him comment, 'She blushes, and Ty says he'll try and get back tonight...' And then she heard him deliberately sing a snatch of 'Love Is in the Air'.

'Ash,' she warned.

'What?' he asked.

What could she say? 'Nothing,' she replied.

'Sorry,' he apologized. 'Am I treading all over your tender feelings?'

There was no answer to that either. 'Now, where did I put that yard broom?' she said instead, but knew then she had to believe that Ash thought that there might be something going on between her and his elder brother.

What? After only seeing her once? Though on second thought, how did she know that since Ty did not want Ash to know the real reason she was there, Ty had *not* instigated or at least allowed Ash to nurture such thoughts? He could quite truthfully have told Ash that, apart from the time she had called at the house with his camera, they had bumped into each other on a couple of other occasions and stopped for a chat.

That, 'Get off my land!' and a threat to summons her for trespass hardly constituted 'a chat' was neither here nor there.

But it was plain Ash thought that there was more to Ty inviting her to live under his roof and offering to stable her horse than appeared on the surface. Hadn't she herself asked Ty, 'You think he'll believe such philanthropy?' Clearly Ash did not. What Ash had chosen to believe was that she was some kind of would-be girlfriend to his brother. And, bearing in mind that she could not tell Ash the truth, there was nothing she could do to disabuse him of the idea.

Having reached the conclusion that Ash was not so down as she had at first thought, she saw the more cheerful mood he had been in while they had been busy start to fall away once the stable was empty of impedimenta and Mickie Yates had called and carted everything away.

'I think I'll take a shortcut through the spinney and collect Ruby,' Phinn said lightly. Straw was down; water was in the trough they had unearthed and scrubbed.

'I'll drive you there if you like?' he offered, but she knew that his heart was not in it.

For a moment she wondered if the fact that Geraldine had the look of her cousin and it would upset him had anything to do with it. If so, perhaps it would be kinder not to trigger memories of Leanne should Geraldine be about.

'No need,' she answered gently. But, bearing in mind that he had seemed happier when working, she went on. 'Though if you're strolling down anywhere near the paddock you might check if it's Ruby-friendly for me.'

Ash nodded and went on his way. By then Phinn was learning to trust Ty enough that if he thought the paddock was suitable for Ruby, there would be no stray barbed wire or plant-life dangerous to horses.

She was feeling sorely in need of a shower and a change of clothes, but Ruby still had to be Phinn's first priority. She wanted her away from the other horses, and so went as quickly as she could to get her.

First she was met by Geraldine—a smiling Geraldine—who offered to supply her with hay and straw from her own supplies. 'You can have it for the price I pay for it,' she offered pleasantly.

Thanking her, feeling cheered, Phinn went looking for Ruby, and was instantly rewarded when Ruby spotted her straight away and came over to her as fast as she could. 'Come on, darling,' Phinn murmured to her softly. 'Have I got a lovely surprise for you.'

Ruby did not have much of an appetite, and after staying with her for a while as she got used to her new surroundings, Phinn left her and went over to the house.

She went in though the kitchen door and at once saw Mrs Starkey, who was at the sink scrubbing new potatoes. She smiled when she saw her. 'Come in, Phinn, come in. Your room's all ready for you.'

'I hope I haven't put you to a lot of trouble?' Phinn apologised.

'None at all! It will be nice having you in the house,' Mrs Starkey answered cheerfully, more than happy, it seemed, in her now streamlined kitchen. 'Dinner's usually about seven-thirty, but I've made you a sandwich to tide you over. Or you could have some soup, or a salad, or…'

'A sandwich will do fine, Mrs Starkey. What I need most is a shower and a change of clothes.'

Mrs Starkey washed and dried her hands. 'Come on, then. I'll show you your room. Ashley came in earlier with your belongings and took them up for you. I hope it's all right? I've had your cardboard boxes put in the storeroom, but…'

'That's lovely.' Phinn thanked her, and as they climbed the winding staircase asked, 'Where is Ash? Do you know?'

For a brief second or two the housekeeper lost her smile. 'I think he's taken himself off for a walk. He didn't want anything to eat, and he barely touched his breakfast.' She shook her head. 'I don't know,' she said, more to herself than anything as they went along the landing.

Phinn was unsure what, if anything, to answer. But she was saved having to make a reply when Mrs Starkey halted at one of the bedroom doors.

'Here we are,' she said, opening the door and standing back for Phinn to go in. 'I hope it's to your liking.'

Liking! 'Oh, Mrs Starkey, it's lovely!' she cried. And it was.

'I'll leave you to get settled in and have your shower.' Mrs Starkey seemed as pleased as Phinn herself.

Phinn stood in the centre of the recently refurbished room and turned very slowly around. The huge, high-ceilinged, light and airy room, with its own modernised bathroom, was more of a bedsitting room than anything. One wall had been given over to built-in wardrobes, with a dressing table in between—far more wardrobe space than she would ever need, Phinn mused. And there was a padded stool in delicate cream and antique gold in front of the dressing table area that had a light above it.

The bed was a double bed, with a cream and antique gold bedcover. At the foot of the bed was a padded cream ottoman, and further in front of that a padded antique gold-coloured chaise longue. A small round table reposed to the side of it, and to the side of that stood a small matching padded chair.

Remembering her cold and draughty bedroom at Honeysuckle Farm, where she would have been returning today but for the turn of events, Phinn could only stare in wonder. She took another slow turn around again—and she had thought Ruby's accommodation luxurious!

Feeling a little stunned, and thinking that she would not want to leave when her six months at Broadlands Hall were over, Phinn went to inspect the bathroom. She was not disappointed. There must be a snag, she pondered. And, stripping off, stepped into the shower—certain that the plumbing or some such would prove faulty.

It proved not faulty. The water was fine, as hot or not as she would have wished.

Refreshed from her shower, Phinn quickly dressed in some clean clothes and, with her thoughts on introducing Ruby to the paddock, swiftly left her room—she could unpack later. She went to the kitchen.

'Tea or coffee?' Mrs Starkey asked as soon as she saw her. And only then did Phinn realise that she felt quite parched.

'Actually, I'd better go and see to Ruby. But I'll have a glass of water,' she answered. No time to wait for tea or coffee.

'Juice?' Mrs Starkey offered, and as Phinn glanced at the motherly woman she suddenly felt as if she had come home.

'Juice would be lovely,' she replied gratefully. And while she drank her juice she saw Mrs Starkey fold her sandwich up in a paper napkin.

'Our John never used to have a moment to breathe either,' she remarked, handing over the sandwich with a smile.

'Thank you, Mrs Starkey,' Phinn said, and had her empty glass taken out of her hand when she would have taken it over to the sink and washed it, and the sandwich pressed in its place.

Life was suddenly good. Phinn all at once realised that she was feeling the best she had felt since her father had died. Now, who did she thank for that? Ty, Ash, Mrs Starkey—or just the passage of time?

Whatever—just enjoy.

Another plus was that Ruby appeared a little hungry. Some of her special feed had gone anyway. Phinn took her down to the fenced-off paddock, checked she had water, and sat on the fence eating her sandwich while Ruby found her way around.

After a while Phinn got down from the fence. Ruby was not her only concern, but this was her first day, and apart from having to clear out the stables and make everything ready, Phinn had not got into any sort of pattern as yet. But she was mindful that she should be looking out for Ash.

Leaving Ruby, Phinn went looking for him. He had gone for a walk, Mrs Starkey had said. But that had been hours ago.

Phinn had gone some way, and was near to the pool when through the trees she caught a glimpse of something blue. If memory served, Ash had been wearing a blue shirt that morning. Should she leave him or keep him company?

The matter was solved when she recalled that she was being *employed* to keep Ash company. She went forward, making sufficient noise so as not to suddenly startle him. She found him sitting on the bank, his expression bleak, and her heart went out to him. How long had he been sitting there, staring at the water without really seeing anything but her cousin?

'Can you believe this glorious weather?' she asked, for something to say.

'Get Ruby over okay?' Ash roused himself to ask.

'The paddock's a dream!'

'Good,' he replied politely, and made no objection when she decided to sit down beside him.

Sitting down beside him was one thing. Now she had to think of something to talk about! 'Are you really the estate manager?' she asked, playing the companion role by ear.

'It doesn't need much managing,' he replied.

'You reckon?'

'You know differently?' he countered, and she sensed an interest—slight, but a spark of interest nevertheless.

'No. Not really,' she answered hurriedly. 'Only...'

'Only?'

'Well, I couldn't help noticing the other day when I was walking through Pixie End Wood that there are one or two trees that need taking out and new ones planting in their place.'

'Where's Pixie End Wood?'

Phinn worked on that spark of interest. 'If I'm not too busy with Ruby tomorrow I'll take you there, if you like?'

He nodded, but she knew his interest was waning. 'How's Leanne?' he asked, totally unexpectedly.

Oh, Ash. Phinn knew, just as she knew that there was nothing she could do to help, that Ash was bleeding a little inside. 'We're not in contact,' she replied. 'It's like that with relatives sometimes. You rarely ever see each other except for weddings and—' She broke off, spears of sad memory still able to dart in unexpectedly and stop her in her tracks.

'I'm sorry.' Ash, like the normally thoughtful person he was, sensed what she had not been able to say. The last time Leanne had surfaced had been to attend Phinn's father's funeral. 'Come on,' he said, shaking off his apathy in the face of Phinn having a weak moment. 'Let's go and see how Ruby likes her new digs.'

By early evening Phinn was in her room again, wondering at her stroke of luck at being at Broadlands. Because her watch had stopped working she was having to guess at the time, but she thought it had been around six that evening when she and Ash had returned to the house. She had come straight to her room and begun finding homes for her belongings.

She had been surprised, however, when opening a drawer in her bedside table, to find an envelope with her name on it. When she had opened it, it had been to extract a cheque written and signed in Ty's firm hand, for what she presumed was her first month's wages.

She felt a little hot about the ears when, never having been paid in advance before, she wondered if Ty had guessed at the parlous state of her finances. The fact that the cheque was for more than she would have thought too made her realise the importance he gave to his brother's welfare. In his view Ash needed a companion when Ty could not be there himself— and he was prepared to pay up-front for that cover.

Knowing that she was going to do her best to fulfil that role, Phinn, surmising that 'companions' probably ate with the family, went to assess her wardrobe. She had several decent dresses, but she had no wish to be 'over the top'. Jeans were out, she guessed, so she settled for a smart pair of white trousers and topped them with a loose-fitting short blue kaftan.

It seemed an age since she had last used anything but moisturiser on her face, but she thought a dab of powder and a smear of lipstick might not be a bad idea. Why, as she was studying her finished appearance, she should think of Ty Allardyce she had no idea.

She hadn't seen him since yesterday. Nor had she heard him come home. Would he be there at dinner? Did she want him there at dinner? Oh, for goodness' sake—what the blazes did it matter where he was? He—

Someone tapping on her door caused her to break off her thoughts.

And, on her answering the door, who should be standing there but none other than the subject of her thoughts? She felt suddenly shy.

'Hungry?' Ty enquired easily.

She at once discounted that she was in any way shy of him. 'Mrs Starkey said dinner was around seven-thirty,' Phinn responded. Shy or not, she glanced away from those steady grey eyes and raised her left hand to check the time on her wrist. No watch!

'It's seven forty-five,' Ty informed her.

'It isn't!' she exclaimed. Where had the day gone?

'You look ready to me,' he observed. And, stepping back, he clearly expected her to join him.

A smile lit the inside of her. Ty must have come up the stairs purposely to collect her. 'Busy day?' she enquired, leaving her room and going along the landing with him.

'Not as physically busy as you, from what I hear. Ash tells me you put him to shame.'

She shook her head. 'Once Ash got into his stride it was

he who did the lion's share of lumping and bumping,' she stated, and saw that Ty looked pleased.

'And your friend Mickie Yates came and took everything away?'

'You don't mind?'

'Good Lord, why would I?' Ty replied, and startled her completely when, totally away from what they had been talking about, he shot a question at her. 'Where's your watch?'

Taken by surprise, she answered, 'It got wet,' quite without thinking. And was halfway down the stairs when Ty stepped in front of her, turned and halted—causing her to have to halt too.

'You mean you forgot to take it off when you did your Olympian dive yesterday?'

'I can't think of everything!' she exclaimed. 'It will be all right when it dries out,' she added off-handedly, knowing that it would never work again, but not wanting to make an issue of it. It hadn't been an expensive watch, after all.

'As you remarked—you're no good at telling lies.' He neatly tripped her up.

What could she do? Say? She gave him a cheeky grin. 'The paddock is lovely,' she informed him.

He shook his head slightly, the way she noticed he did when he was a little unsure of what to make of her.

Dinner was a pleasant meal, though Phinn observed that Ash ate very little. For all that the ham salad with buttered potatoes and a rather fine onion tart was very palatable, he seemed to be eating it for form's sake rather than because he was enjoying it.

'Did you find time to get into the estate office today?' Ty, having included her in all the conversation so far, put a question to his brother.

'Who wants to be indoors on a day like today?' Ash replied. 'I'll see what I can do tomorrow,' he added. Ty did not press him, or look in any way put out. And then Ash was confessing, 'Actually, I think Phinn would make a better estate manager than me.'

Phinn opened her mouth, ready with a disclaimer, and then noticed Ty's glance had switched to her. He was plainly interested in his brother's comment.

'I'm beginning to think that nothing Phinn does will surprise me,' he said. 'But—' he glanced back to Ash '—why, particularly?'

'Apparently I'm being taken on a tour of Pixie End Wood tomorrow. Phinn tells me there are a couple of trees there that need felling, and new ones planting.'

Ty's glance was back on her, and she was sure she looked guilty. She knew that he was now aware that her trespassing had not been limited to the few places where he had witnessed it.

When, after dinner, a move was made to the drawing room, Phinn would by far have preferred to have gone to the stable. But, even though she felt that Ty would not expect her to be on 'companion duty' when he was home to keep his brother company, she was aware that there were certain courtesies to be observed when living in someone else's home.

And so, thinking that to spend another ten minutes with the Allardyce brothers wouldn't hurt, she went along to the drawing room with them. But she was hardly through the door when she stopped dead in her tracks.

'Grandmother Hawkins' table!' she exclaimed, all the other plush furnishings and antique furniture fading from her sight as she recognised the much-loved, much-polished, small round table that had been theirs up until 'needs must', as her father had called their impecunious moments, and the table had been sold.

'Grandmother Hawkins?' Ash enquired. 'You mean you once owned that table?'

Grandmother Hawkins had handed it down to Phinn's parents early in their marriage, when they'd had little furniture of their own. They had later inherited the rest of her antiques. 'It's—er—lovely, isn't it?' she replied, feeling awkward and wishing that she hadn't said anything.

'You're sure it's yours? Ty bought it in London.'

'I'm sure. We sold it—it wasn't stolen. We—er...' She had been about to say how it had been about the last one of their antiques to go, but there was no need for anyone to know of their hard-up moments. 'It was probably sold to a dealer who sold it on.'

'And you recognise it?'

'I should do—it was my Saturday morning job to polish it. I've been polishing it since I was about three years old.' A gentle smile of happy remembering lifted her mouth. 'My father's initials are lightly carved underneath. We both got into trouble when he showed me how to carve mine in too. My mother could never erase them—no matter how much she tried.'

'The table obviously holds very happy memories for you,' Ty put in quietly.

'I had the happiest of childhoods,' she replied, and suddenly felt embarrassed at talking of things they could not possibly be interested in.

'You were upset when your father sold it?' Ty enquired, his eyes watching her.

She looked at him in surprise, the blue top she wore reflecting the deepening blue of her eyes. How had he known it was her father who had sold the table and not her mother? 'He was my father!' she protested.

'And as such could do no wrong?' Ty suggested quietly.

She looked away from him. It was true. In her eyes her father had never been able to do anything wrong. 'Would you mind very much if I went and took a look at Ruby?'

She flicked a quick glance back to Ty, but his expression was inscrutable. She took that to mean that he would not mind, and was on her way.

Ruby had had the best of days, and seemed truly happy and

content in her new abode. Phinn stayed with her, talking softly to her as she did every evening. And as she chatted to her Phinn started once more to come near to being content herself.

She was still with Ruby when the mare's ears pricked up and Phinn knew that they were about to have company.

'How's she settled in?' Ty asked, coming into the large stable and joining them.

'I think we can safely say that she loves her new home.'

Ty nodded. Then asked, 'How about you?'

'Who could fail to love it here? My room's a dream!'

He looked pleased. 'Any problems I should know about?' he asked. 'Don't be afraid to say—no matter how small,' he added.

'It's only my first day. Nothing untoward, but—' She broke off, caught out by the memory of Ash giving her that knowing look that morning.

'What?' Ty asked.

My heavens, was he sharp! 'Nothing,' she answered. But then she thought that perhaps she *should* mention it. 'Well, the thing is, I think Ash seems to have got hold of the idea that—um—you and I—are—er—starting some sort of...' Grief, she knew she was going red again.

'Some sort of...?' Ty questioned, not sparing her blushes.

And that annoyed her. 'Well, if you must know, I think he thinks we're starting some sort of romantic attachment.' There—it was out. She waited for him to look totally astounded at the idea. But to her astonishment he actually started to grin. She stared at him, her heart going all fluttery for no good reason.

Then Ty was sobering, and to her amazement he was confessing, 'My fault entirely, I'm afraid.'

'Your fault?'

'Forgive me, Phinn?' he requested, not for a moment looking sorry about anything. 'I could tell the way his mind was working when I told him I'd asked you to stay with us for a while.'

Phinn stared at him. 'But you didn't tell him—?' she gasped.

'I thought it better not to disabuse him of the notion,' Ty cut in.

'Why on earth not?' she bridled.

'Now, don't get cross,' Ty admonished. 'You know quite well the real reason why you're here.'

'To be Ash's companion.'

'Right,' Ty agreed. 'You're here to keep him company—but he's not to know about it. From where I'm viewing it, Ash has got enough to handle without having the added weight of feeling under too much of an obligation for what you did for him yesterday. He's indebted to you—of course he is. We both are,' Ty went on. 'The alternative—what could have happened had you not been around and had the guts to do what you did—just doesn't bear thinking about. But he's under enough emotional pressure. I just thought it might take some of the pressure from him if he could more cheerfully think that, while things might be going wrong for him in his personal life, I—his big brother—was having a better time of it and had invited you here more because I was smitten than because of what we both owe you.'

Despite herself, Phinn could see the logic of what Ty had just said. She remembered how down Ash had seemed when she had come across him on the bank today. She recalled that bleak expression on his face and had to agree. Ty's brother did not need any extra burden just now.

'As long as you don't expect me to give you a cuddle every now and then,' she retorted sniffily at last.

She saw his lips twitch and turned away, and, feeling funny inside, showed an interest in Ruby.

'As pleasant as one of your cuddles would surely be, I'll try to hold down my expectations,' Ty replied smoothly, and for a minute she did not like him again, because again he was making her feel a fool. All too plainly the sky would fall in before he would want to be anywhere near cuddling distance with *her*.

'Are you home tomorrow?' she turned to enquire, thinking that as it was Saturday he might well be.

'Want to take me to Pixie End Wood too?'

She gave him a hostile look, bit down on a reply of *Yes, and leave you there*, and settled for, 'You intimated you'd neglected your work in London. I merely wondered if you'd be going back to catch up.'

'You don't like me, do you?'

At this moment, no. She shrugged her shoulders. 'I can take you or leave you,' she replied, to let him know that she was not bothered about him one way or the other. But flicking a glance to him, she saw she had amused him. Not in the least offended, he looked more likely to laugh than to be heartbroken.

'How's the...Ruby?' He made one of his lightning switches of conversation.

Ah, that was different. Taking the talk away from herself and on to Ruby was far preferable. 'She's happy—really settled in well. She's eaten more today than she has in a while. And this stable, the paddock—they're a dream for her.'

'Good,' Ty commented, and then, dipping his hand into his trouser pocket, he pulled out a wristwatch and handed it to her. 'You'll need one of these until your own dries out,' he remarked.

Having taken it from him, Phinn stared at the handsome gentleman's watch in her hand. 'I can't...' she began, trying to give it back to him.

'It's a spare.' He refused to take it. 'And only a loan.'

She looked at him, feeling stumped. The phrase 'hoist with her own petard' came to mind. She had told him her watch would be all right again once it had dried out—but he knew that, no matter how dry it was, it would never be serviceable again.

'I'll let you have it back in due time.' She accepted it with what dignity she could muster, and was glad when, with a kind pat to Ruby's flank, Ty Allardyce bade her, *'Adieu,'* and went.

Phinn stayed with Ruby, wondering what it was about the man that disturbed her so. In truth, she had never met any man who could make her so annoyed with him one second and yet on the point of laughter the next.

Eventually she said goodnight to Ruby and returned to the house, musing that it had been thoughtful of Ty to loan her a watch. How many times that day had she automatically checked her left wrist in vain?

The evidence of just how thoughtful he was was again there when, having gone up the stairs and into her room, Phinn discovered that someone had been in there.

She stood stock still and just stared. The small round table that had been by the antique gold chaise longue had been removed. In its place, and looking every bit as if it belonged there, was the small round table that had been in the drawing room when last she had seen it.

'Grandmother Hawkins' table,' she said softly, and felt a warm glow wash over her. Welcome home, it seemed to be saying. She did not have to guess who had so thoughtfully made the exchange. She knew that it had been Ty Allardyce.

Phinn went to bed liking him again.

CHAPTER FIVE

PHINN sat on the paddock rail around six weeks later, keeping an eye on Ruby, who'd had a bout of being unwell, and reflecting on how Broadlands Hall now seemed to be quite like home. She knew more of the layout now. Knew where Ty's study was—the place where he always spent some time when he was there.

Most of the rooms had been smartened up, some replastered and redecorated. The room next for redecoration was the music room—the room in which she had often sat listening with Mr Caldicott while her father played on his grand piano. The music room door was occasionally left open, when either Wendy or Valerie, who came up from the village to clean, were in there, giving the room a dusting and an airing. Apparently the piano had been left behind when all Mr Caldicott's other furniture had been removed. Presumably Ty had come to some arrangement with him about it.

Phinn patted Ruby's neck and talked nothings to her while at the same time she reminded herself that she must not allow herself to become too comfortable here. In another four or so months, probably sooner if she were to get anything established for Ruby, she would have to begin looking for a new home for the two of them.

But meantime how good it was to not have that worry

hanging over her head as being immediate. What was immediate, however, was the vet's bill that was mounting up. Last month's pay cheque had already gone, and the cheque Ty had left on Grandmother Hawkins' table for her to find a couple of weeks ago was mostly owed to Kit Peverill.

'Don't worry about it,' Kit had told her when she had settled his last veterinary bill. 'There's no rush. Pay me as you can.'

He was kind, was Kit, and, having assumed she had come to the Hall to work in the estate office, he had called to see Ruby as soon as he could when Phinn had phoned. She could not bear to think of Ruby in pain, but Kit had assured her that, though Ruby suffered some discomfort, she was not in actual pain, and that hopefully her sudden loss of appetite would pick up again.

Kit had been kind enough to organise some special food for Ruby, and to Phinn's surprise Geraldine Walton had arrived one day with a load of straw. Ash had been off on one of his 'walkabouts' that day. But soon after that Geraldine had—again to Phinn's surprise—telephoned to say she had a surfeit of hay, and that if Ash was available perhaps he would drive over in the pick-up and collect it.

Having discovered that Ash was at his best when occupied, Phinn had asked him if he would mind. 'Can't you manage without it?' he had enquired, clearly reluctant.

'Yes, of course I can,' she'd replied with a smile. 'I shouldn't have asked you.'

He had been immediately contrite. 'Yes, you should. Sorry, Phinn, I'm not fit company these days. Of course I'll go.' Muttering, 'With luck I shall miss seeing the wretched woman,' he went on his way.

From that Phinn gleaned that it was not so much the errand he was objecting to, but the fact that he did not want any contact with the owner of the riding school and stables. Which gave her cause to wonder if it was just that he had taken an aversion to Geraldine. Or was he, despite himself, attracted to her and a little afraid of her because of what another woman with her colouring had done to him?

Phinn had kept him company as much as she could, though very often she knew that he wanted to be on his own. At other times she had walked miles with him all over the estate lands.

She had talked with him, stayed silent when need be, and when he had mentioned that he quite liked drawing she had several times taken him sketching down by the trout stream. Which had been a little painful to her, because it was there that her father had taught her to sketch.

She had overcome her sadness of spirit when it had seemed to her that Ash appeared to be less stressful and a shade more content when he lost himself as he concentrated on the sketch he was creating.

But Ash was very often quite down, so that sometimes she would wonder if her being there made any difference to him at all. A point she had put to Ty only a week ago. Cutting her nose off it might have been, had he agreed with her and suggested that he would not hold her to their six-month agreement. But it was nothing of the sort!

'Of course you've made a difference,' Ty assured her. 'Apart from the fact I feel I can get back to my work without being too concerned over him, there is a definite improvement from the way he was.'

'You're sure?'

'I'm sure,' he replied, and had meant it. 'Surely you've noticed that he's taking more of an interest in the estate these days? He was telling me on the phone only the other day how you had both met with some forester—Sam...?'

'Sam Turner,' she filled in. 'I was at school with his son Sammy. Sammy's followed in his father's footsteps.' And then, getting carried away, 'Ash and I walked the whole of

Pixie End Wood with Sam and Sammy...' She halted. 'But you probably know that from Ash.'

Ty hadn't answered that, but asked, 'Is there anybody you don't know?'

For the weirdest moment she felt like saying, *I don't know you.* Weird or what? Anybody would think that she *wanted* to know him—better. 'I was brung up around here,' she replied impishly—and felt Ty's steady grey glance on her.

'And a more fully rounded "brung-up" female I've never met,' he commented quietly.

'If I could decide whether that was a compliment or not, I might thank you for it,' she replied.

'It's a compliment,' he informed her, and she had gone about her business wondering about the other women of his acquaintance.

By 'fully rounded' she knew he had not been talking about her figure—which if anything, save for a bosom to be proud of, she had always thought a little on the lean side. So were his London and 'other capitals' women not so generally 'fully rounded'? And was being 'fully rounded' a good thing, or a bad thing? Phinn had given it up when she'd recalled that he had said that it was a compliment.

But now, sitting on the rail mulling over the events of these past weeks, she reflected that Ty, having employed her so that he could go about his business, seemed to come home to Broadlands far more frequently than she had thought he would. Though it was true that here it was Friday, and he had not been home at all this week.

Phinn felt the most peculiar sensation in her insides as she wondered, today being Friday, if Ty would come home tonight? Perhaps he might stay the whole weekend? He didn't always. *Some filly up in London*, her father would have said.

But she did not want to think about Ty and his London fillies. Phinn titled her head a fraction and looked to Ruby, who was watching her. 'Hello, my darling Rubes,' she said softly, and asked, 'What do you say to an apple if I ask Mrs Starkey for one?'

Mrs Starkey was continuing to mother her, and Phinn had to admit she did not object to it. Occasionally she would sit and share a pot of tea with the housekeeper, and Phinn would enquire after Mrs Starkey's son, John, and hear of his latest doings, and then go on to talk of the various other people Phinn had grown up knowing.

Bearing in mind her own mother had taken up golf, and was more often out than in, Phinn *had* made contact with her to let her know of her move. After her mother's third-degree questioning Phinn had ended the call with her mother's blessing.

About to leave her perch and go in search of an apple for Ruby, Phinn just then heard the sound of a car coming up the drive and recognised Kit Peverill's vehicle. She had asked him to come and look Ruby over.

Ruby wasn't too sure about him, but was too timid by nature to raise any strong objections. Instead she sidled up to Phinn and stayed close when he had finished with her.

'She'll do,' he pronounced.

'She's better!' Phinn exclaimed in relief.

'She's never going to be better, Phinn,' Kit replied gently. 'You know that. But she's over this last little upset.'

Phinn looked down at her feet to hide the pain in her eyes. 'Thank you for being so attentive,' she murmured, and, leaving Ruby, walked to his vehicle with him to collect some medication he had mentioned.

'It's always a pleasure to see you, Phinn,' he commented, which took her out of her stride a little, because he had never said anything like it before. Indeed, she had always supposed him to be a tiny bit shy, more of an animal person than a people person. But she was to discover that, while shy, he was not so shy as she had imagined. And that he quite liked people too as well as animals, when he coughed, and followed up with, 'Er—in fact, I've been meaning to ask you—er—how do you feel about coming out with me one night—say, tomorrow night?'

Phinn kept her eyes on the path in front while she considered what he had said. 'Um…' She just hadn't thought of him in a 'date' situation, only a 'vet' situation. 'We—I'm…' Her thoughts were a bit muddled up, but she was thinking more about how long she would want to leave Ruby than of any enjoyment she might find if she dated this rather pleasant man.

'Look, why not give me a ring? I know you won't want to be away from Ruby for too long, but we could have a quick bite over at the Kings Arms in Little Thornby.'

Phinn was on the point of agreeing to go out with him, but something held her back. Perhaps she would go if Ty came home this weekend. Surely she was not expected to stay home being a companion to Ash if Ty was there to keep him company?

'*Can* I give you a ring?' she asked.

After Kit had gone, Phinn thought it time she attended to her duties, and went looking for Ash. The sound of someone busy with a hammer attracted her towards the pool, and she headed in that direction where, to her amazement, she found Ash on the far side, hammering a large signpost into the ground. In bold red the sign proclaimed 'DANGER. KEEP OUT. TREACHEROUS WATER'. Close by was another post, from which hung a lifebelt.

Ash raised his head and saw her. 'Thought I was useless, didn't you?' he called, but seemed the happiest she had seen him since her cousin had done a brilliant job of flattening him.

What Phinn thought was that he was an extremely bruised man, who loved well, but not too wisely, and was paying for it.

'I think you're gorgeous,' she called back with a laugh, and felt a true affection for him. Had she had a brother, she would have liked one just like Ash.

Ash grinned, and for the first time Phinn saw that perhaps her being there *was* making a bit of a difference. Perhaps Ash was starting to heal. Phinn went to get Ruby an apple.

It started to rain after lunch, and although Ruby did not mind the rain, it was heavy enough for Phinn to not want to risk it for her. After stabling her she went indoors, and was coming down the stairs after changing out of damp clothes when the phone in the hall rang.

Phinn had spotted Mrs Starkey driving off in her car about fifteen minutes ago, and, with Ash nowhere to be seen, she picked up the phone with a peculiar sort of hope in her heart that the caller would not be Ty, ringing to say that he wouldn't be home this weekend.

An odd sort of relief entered her soul when the caller was not Ty but Geraldine Walton again, with an offer of more straw. 'I'm running out of space under cover here, so if Ash could pop over he'd be doing me something of a favour,' Geraldine added.

'It's very good of you think of me,' Phinn replied, feeling for certain now that Ash was more the cause for the call than the fact that Geraldine had more straw than she knew what to do with. Geraldine had said not one word about having surplus stocks when she had wandered over yesterday to settle what she owed her! 'Ash isn't around just now. But I'd be glad of the straw,' she accepted.

Phinn was about to go looking for Ash, and found she did not have to when he came crashing in through the front door. 'It's bucketing down out there!' he exclaimed, shaking rain from his arms.

'You don't fancy going out again?'

'Need something?' he enquired, at once willing to go on an errand. He hadn't heard what the errand was yet!

'Geraldine Walton has more straw…' Phinn did not have to say more. Though this time Ash did not seem quite as reluctant as he had before.

'I'll wait for this to give over first,' he said, and, as she herself had done, he went up to change.

The house seemed so quiet when, a half-hour later, keys to the pick-up in hand, Ash left for Geraldine Walton's stables.

Feeling restless suddenly—even Mrs Starkey was out—Phinn was about to go and have a chat to Ruby when, as she was walking past, she saw that the music room door was again open. Either Wendy or Valerie must have left it ajar.

About to close the door and walk on by, Phinn, with her hand on the door handle, found she was hesitating. She had nowhere near the natural talent her father had had for the piano, but he had instructed her well.

It was an age since she had last played. An age since she had last wanted to play. Phinn pushed the door open wider and took a few steps into the room.

She took a few more steps, and a few more, and was then looking down at the piano keys—the lid having been left open because that was best for the piano.

The keys invited. She stretched out a hand and played one note—and then another. And as she stood there she could almost hear her father say, 'Come on, kiddo, let's murder a little Mozart.'

A sob caught the back of her throat. She coughed away the weakness, but felt drawn to sit down on the piano stool. And that was all it took.

She was rusty from lack of practice, but the notes were there—remembered. Her father had loved Mozart. She played Mozart in his memory, remembering the good times they had shared, remembering his laughter. Oh, how he'd loved to laugh…

How long she sat there, 'murdering' Mozart's Concerto Number Twenty-Three, Phinn had no idea. Nor did she have any idea quite when memories of her father started to merge with thoughts of Ty Allardyce.

Nor, when she had just come to the end of the adagio, did she know how long Ty Allardyce had been standing there, watching her. For she felt rather than saw him, and looked up, startled. And then she was startled *and* totally confused. She took her hands from the keys immediately.

'How long have you been standing there?' she gasped, feeling choked suddenly.

'Long enough to know you're a sensitive soul with a splendid touch. And a talent you have been keeping very well hidden.'

She abruptly stood up and, feeling highly emotional just then, moved away from the piano. 'It needs tuning!' she said, purely because she was otherwise bereft of words. She made for the door, but had to halt when Ty blocked her way. 'I'm sorry,' she apologized, for using the instrument. 'You don't mind…?' Her all at once husky voice trailed away, words still defeating her.

'Don't be sorry. I didn't know you could play.' He seemed slightly staggered by his discovery. But he collected himself to tell her, 'Out of tune or not—that was quite beautiful.'

Tall and dark, he looked down at her, still blocking her way. 'I—thought everyone was out…' she began, but he was stretching out a hand to her cheek.

'What's this?' he asked gently, looking down into the deep blue of her eyes. Then, so tenderly she could scarcely believe it, Ty touched her skin and wiped away a stray tear that had rolled down the side of her face uninvited by her. And Phinn at that moment felt too utterly mesmerised to move. Who would have suspected him of such tenderness? 'Sad memories?' he asked softly.

'I—haven't played since my father died,' she replied, her voice still holding that husky note.

'You're still mourning him,' Ty stated.

'We were close. But it's getting better,' she said, and for the first time she felt that it really was.

'Oh, come here,' Ty murmured and, taking a hold of her, he pulled her into his arms. 'I think it's high time someone gave you a hug,' he voiced from above her head.

And, most peculiarly, Phinn found that she was snuggling into his hold and truly liking the feel of his broad manly chest against her face. But she stirred against him. She did not want to move, but this could not be right.

'You've come home for some peace and tranquillity,' she began. 'Not to...' She pulled back from him. 'I'm all right now,' she said.

Ty let her go and stepped back, his grey eyes searching her face. She smiled up at him, to prove that she was indeed all right, and he smiled back. 'If I promise to get the piano tuned, will you promise to come in here and play whenever you want to—regardless of who's in and who's out?' Phinn stared at him numbly, and he smiled and made her feel weepy again, when he assured her, 'This is your home now.'

Too full suddenly to say a word, Phinn quickly went by him—out from the music room, along the hall, and straight up the stairs to her room. She had acknowledged that Ty did strange things to her long before she got there.

Collapsing onto the bedroom chair, she found her thoughts were not of her father, as they so often had been, but of Ty Allardyce and the complex man he was.

After having been ready at one time to throw her off his lands, he was now telling her that this, Broadlands Hall, was her home! Obviously he was only referring to it being her temporary home, but still the same, Ty just saying what he had had the effect of making her feel less rootless—albeit only temporarily.

She remembered that oh, so tender touch to her cheek, remembered the gentle way he had held her in his arms, and, most oddly, felt that she wanted to be back in his arms, back being held by him again.

But if he was a complex man, what about her? Only then did she realise how overwhelmingly pleased she was that he was home!

Which—the fact that it pleased her to know he was there—made it seem somewhat illogical to her that she felt reluctant to go down and see him again. Shy? Her? Never! She glanced at her watch. His watch. And felt decidedly not herself. What on earth was the man doing to her, for goodness' sake?

Nothing! Nothing at all, she told herself stoutly. Grief, it was just that, having been around men pretty much all her life—her father's friends, mainly—she had never met any man quite like Tyrell Allardyce.

Still the same, since he was home to keep his brother company—if Ash was back—Phinn saw no good reason to go down.

She did, however, leave her room briefly to go and check on Ruby. But she returned to her room and, when clothes had never particularly bothered her before—what she wore being immaterial so long as it was clean and respectable—she spent some time wondering if she should perhaps put on a dress for a change.

Ten minutes later, having dithered on the yes or no question for more than long enough, Phinn decided she must be going mental! Smart trousers and a top had been good enough all this week. Why on earth would she want to wear a dress just because Ty was home?

At seven twenty-five, wearing the smart trousers and a top, Phinn went down the stairs to the drawing room, where the two brothers were in idle conversation.

Her glance went straight to Ty, who looked across the moment she came in. He made no mention of her piano-playing activities, and she was grateful for his sensitivity there.

'Would you like something to drink, Phinn?' he enquired

courteously. She shook her head. She wasn't shy; she knew that she wasn't. She just felt not herself somehow. 'Then perhaps we'd better go and see what Mrs Starkey has in store for us,' he said with a smile.

What Mrs Starkey had in store, after a superb cheese soufflé starter, was trout with almonds as a main course—which gave Ash cause to remark to his brother, 'Phinn took me fly-fishing yesterday.' Lack of space had dictated that her father's piano had to go, but Phinn had been unable to part with his fishing equipment. 'You know—the trout stream I sketched? It's hidden behind Long Meadow,' Ash continued.

'Long Meadow?' Ty queried, with a glance to Phinn.

'Been there years,' she obliged.

'You should see Phinn cast a line!' Ash went on. And then reported, 'She's promised to teach me to tie a fly.'

Ty's gaze was on her again, with that expression on his face that she was getting to know. 'Is there nothing you cannot do?' he asked lightly.

'Heaps of things,' she replied, and felt obliged to mention, since this clever man must know full well that her casting skills had been learned while trespassing in waters that belonged to the estate, 'Old Mr Caldicott used to appreciate the odd trout.'

Ty looked from her to the trout on his plate. 'You caught these yesterday?'

But even while she was shaking her head, Ash was chipping in. 'Not Phinn. Me. Phinn went all girly on me and put her catch back. Though…' Ash looked down at his own plate '…I don't remember mine being this big.'

'You'll never make a fisherman, Ash,' Phinn butted in, aware that all the fishermen *she* knew exaggerated sublimely. She guessed that Mrs Starkey's errand that afternoon had included a visit to the fishmonger's in town.

And while Ash was grinning, Ty asked him what else he

had been up to that week. 'Walked a lot. Fished a lot,' Ash answered. 'Ran an errand for Phinn. Oh, and prior to the specialists you arranged getting here to survey and check out the Dark Pool, I took delivery of that danger notice we talked about and hammered it in. Looks all right too—even though apart from us it's only trespassers that are likely to see it.'

Ty looked to Phinn, and as her lips twitched on recalling the way he had threatened to have her summonsed for trespassing, his rather pleasant-shaped mouth picked up too, and there seemed to be only the two of them there, in a kind of small, intimate moment between them.

And then Ash was going on. 'Phinn thinks I'm gorgeous, by the way.'

Phinn shared a grin with Ash, feeling just then that they had become firm friends. But, happening to glance back at Ty, she saw that he was suddenly looking more hostile, if anything. Certain then that she had imagined any kind of an intimate moment with him, she could only wonder what she had done wrong now.

For courtesy's sake, in front of Ash, she pretended that she was unaffected whichever way Ty looked at her, or however hostile he was. What had happened to the tender, understanding man of that afternoon?

Phinn ate her way through the rest of her meal, but could not wait to be able to leave the dining room. The moment the meal was at an end, she was getting to her feet.

'If you'll excuse me?' she said politely to no one in particular. 'I'll go along and check on Ruby.' Both men were on their feet too. Phinn did not wait to find out whether they objected or not.

Having been stewed up inside for the last half-hour, Phinn calmed down as she tended to Ruby. And the calmer she became, gradually she began to see what Ty's hostile look had been all about. Ash, because of her cousin, had got himself

into quite a state. Ty, seeing her and Ash getting on so well—
and for all his previous opinion that his brother was so
ensnared by her cousin that other women did not exist—must
now be afraid that another of the Hawkins clan was getting
to him. There was no other explanation for that hostile look.

Well, he need not worry. She and Ash were friends and
nothing more. And, conscious of how concerned Ty had been,
and probably still was, about Ash, she had one very good way
of putting him straight.

Though before she could go and see him she spotted
Ruby's ears pricking up, and had a fair idea then that she
wouldn't have to wait that long.

Nor did she. And as Ty stepped into the stable, before she
could say anything, he got in first. 'I wanted a word with you.'

For one dreadful moment Phinn thought he was going to
ask her to leave. But even with that sinking feeling in the pit
of her stomach, pride stormed in to make her aggressive. 'I
didn't do it—whatever it was!' she stated, showing a fair
degree of hostility of her own.

Ty stared at her in some surprise. 'Heaven help us!' he
grunted. 'Do you always meet trouble halfway?'

'I'm in trouble?' she questioned belligerently.

'You will be if you don't shut up and let me get a word in!'

She opened her mouth, and then closed it. Then opened it
again to tell him, 'Whatever it is, don't raise your voice and
frighten my horse!'

'Oh, God, you're priceless,' Ty muttered, and, putting his
hand into his trouser pocket, he pulled out something and
handed it to her. 'Here,' he said, 'I got you this.'

Having taken it from him, Phinn looked and was stunned
at what he had given her. 'A watch!' she gasped. And not just
any old watch, but a most beautiful watch!

'The one you have on is much too big for your delicate
wrist,' he commented.

But just then Phinn suddenly noticed the maker's name, and warm colour rushed to her face. 'You got this especially for me?' she questioned—it must have cost a mint! Hurriedly she thrust it back at him. 'No, thank you,' she told him primly.

'No?' He seemed quite taken out of his stride—as if it had never occurred to him that she would not accept it. 'What do you mean, no?' he questioned shortly.

'It's too expensive!'

'Don't be ridiculous!' he rapped.

And that infuriated her. 'Don't you call me ridiculous!' she hissed, even in her fury mindful of Ruby. 'My watch—if that's meant to be a replacement—cost only about forty pounds. I wouldn't even hazard a guess at the price you paid for that one.' And, as Ty continued to stare at her, 'If you want this one back—' she began, starting to undo the clasp.

Ty's hand coming to hers to stay her action caused a tingle to shoot through her body. 'Keep it on,' he ordered. Then all at once his tough expression changed. 'Have I offended you, Phinn?' he asked softly.

And just then, right at that very moment, Phinn knew— quite absurdly—that she was in love with him. Just like that she knew.

Again, from the pure emotion of the moment, she went red. Though she somehow managed to keep her head to tell him, 'Right is right and wrong is wrong. And that—' indicating the watch in his hand '—is wrong.'

Ty studied her for long silent moments. Then, slipping the watch back into his pocket, 'I don't think I've ever met anyone with quite such high morals as you,' he stated.

'Then you've been mixing with totally the wrong company,' she replied with an impish grin, though was uncertain that she wanted to be considered too much of a goody-goody. Although, on thinking about it, to have trespassed quite happily all over his land without the smallest compunction did, she felt, rather tarnish her goody-goody halo a little bit. 'Anyhow, I rather wanted to have a word with you too.' She looked from him, scared for a moment that this new love she felt for him might somehow be visible to him.

'What's wrong?' he asked sharply.

'Nothing's wrong!' she snapped back, moving away from Ruby—if they were going to have a row, she would prefer that her Rubes, so sensitive to atmosphere, did not know about it. 'The thing is,' she went on more calmly—time now to let him know that *this* Hawkins wasn't after his brother, or him either for that matter, time to let him know that she had other fish to fry. 'Er...' How to get started? 'Will you be here tomorrow night?' She said it the only way she could: bluntly.

Ty eyed her for a couple of solid seconds. 'You're asking me for a date?' he enquired, his expression completely serious.

Phinn rolled her eyes heavenward. 'It's not your birthday!' she answered snappily but then, probably because a date with Ty sounded like just so much bliss, 'I have other irons in the fire,' she informed him snootily. 'Kit, the vet, has asked me out tomorrow night.'

'The vet? He's been here?'

'Several times, actually. Ruby has been unwell.'

'She's better now?' he asked tersely.

Phinn declined to go into details of the anxiety of it all, but agreed that Ruby was well again. 'So, given that I wouldn't want to leave her for too long, I presume I'm allowed some time off—if you're at home?'

Ty studied her as though he did not care very much for this conversation. But then suddenly he smiled. It was a silky kind of smile; one she had no belief in!

And she knew that she was right not to have belief in it when, his voice as silky as his smile, he said, 'My dear Miss Hawkins, how could you have forgotten?'

She quickly racked her brains, but could think of nothing she had forgotten. 'Forgotten what?'

'That you can't possibly go out with him.'

'Why can't I?' she demanded belligerently.

He smiled again. Love him she might, but she still wanted to swipe that smile off his face. 'How can you go out with another man,' he enquired pleasantly, 'when you know full well that you're supposed to be my girlfriend?'

For a stunned couple of seconds, Phinn stared at him, speechless. And then it was that she remembered that Ty did not want Ash to know that the real reason she was there was to keep him company, and that she had gone along with that. She had also agreed that Ash had enough of a burden weighing on him, and had agreed too, she supposed, to let Ash believe what he obviously believed—that she was there more as Ty's friend than his. In fact his girlfriend—would-be—sort of.

In actual fact, now she came to think of it, she did not feel too put out that her dating facility had been curtailed. But she gave Ty a look of disgust for his trouble anyway, and, muttering an old family saying, 'Well, give me a kiss and lend me tuppence!' which was meant to convey her disgust, she turned sharply away from him.

Then nearly died of fright when, spinning her back round to him, Ty replied, 'Anything to oblige,' with a wicked kind of gleam in his eyes. And the next thing Phinn knew Ty had hauled her into his arms and his head was coming down.

Desperately she tried to avoid his lips, but with one hand moving up to the back of her head he held her still. Then his mouth settled over hers and she was lost.

Unhurriedly, he eased her lips apart, and while her heart hammered frantically away inside her, he held her close up against him. And Phinn never wanted it to end.

A discreet kind of cough from the doorway made her jerk

away from Ty. But he still had an arm about her waist as they both turned to see a grinning Ash standing there.

'Sorry to interrupt,' he said, not looking sorry at all, but looking very much like the Ash she had known before her cousin had so unceremoniously dumped him. 'But the vet's been on the phone. I didn't know if it would be important or not, now that Ruby seems better, but I said you would call him back.'

'Oh, thanks, Ash,' Phinn replied, trying to gather her scattered wits. And, needing to be on her own, 'I'll go and call him now,' she added.

But so much for being on her own to sort her feelings out. 'I'll come with you,' Ty offered, and while Ash went on his way, actually whistling 'Love Is in the Air', Phinn left the stable hoping that Ty had no idea of what the tune was.

She was still feeling all of a fluster from Ty's kiss—which she had to admit, reluctantly, that she might have inadvertently invited—when, with Ty still by her side, they reached the house.

They were in the hall and within a yard of the phone when, with Phinn making no attempt to slow her speed, Ty caught a hold of her arm. 'Make the call from here,' he ordered. 'Tell him you're spoken for.'

And bang went her feeling of being all mixed up inside. 'Like blazes, I will!' she erupted, not taking kindly to being so bossed about—after he had kissed her so wonderfully too! If she rang Kit Peverill at all, it would be in the privacy of her room and on her mobile.

But, with Ty still holding her arm, the matter was settled when the phone just then rang. Ty stretched forward and picked it up. 'Allardyce,' he said, and while he listened Phinn was thinking it might be some business call and she could make her escape. 'Phinn's here now,' she heard him say. And then he was handing the phone to her and insisting, 'Tell him.'

Phinn sent him a malevolent look, which bounced straight off him, and took hold of the phone. She guessed the call must be from Kit, and wished Ty Allardyce would clear off because, although he had let go of her arm, he was still standing there, clearly bent on listening to her every word.

'Hello,' she managed pleasantly, after taking a calming breath.

'I hope you don't mind me ringing again, Phinn,' Kit replied, a touch diffidently. 'Only I'm on call, and I thought I'd leave you my on-call number so I wouldn't miss you when you rang. Er—have you thought any more about tomorrow night?'

She felt uncomfortable, and that feeling was not helped when Ty Allardyce seemed immune to her killing looks. 'The thing is, Kit…' she began. 'I—um—I'm sorry.'

'You can't make it?' He sounded disappointed. 'Perhaps some other time? If…'

'Well, to be honest—' since the deed had to be done, she now wanted it done and out of the way '—your invitation—er—sort of caught me on the wrong foot. That is—I've just—er—started seeing someone.' There—it was done.

'Oh,' Kit mumbled. 'Oh, all right.' And, 'Er—if it doesn't work out…'

'Of course,' she replied, but could not help but feel awful, even if she now knew that she did not want to date Kit. But, as she put the phone down, it did not make her any less cross with Ty Allardyce. 'Satisfied?' she asked him waspishly.

And he smiled, a more genuine smile this time. 'Don't be mad at me, Phinnie,' he said charmingly. 'You know he doesn't mean anything to you.'

'How do I know?' Smile or no smile she was at her belligerent best. 'We—Kit and I—we might have been—er—made for each other.'

But Ty was shaking his head. 'I kissed you, Phinn. But you kissed me back.' And, as warm colour stained her cheeks, 'You wouldn't have done that had the vet been in there with so much as half a chance.'

Phinn stared at him open-mouthed. 'How did you get to know so much about women?' she exclaimed in disgust. But then, as jealousy nipped for the first time ever in her life, 'Don't tell me!' she ordered. 'I don't want to know!' And with that she turned about and stormed angrily away.

But the truth of the matter was, he was right. He thought she had high morals, and while she did not know about that, what she *did* know was that he was right in that she would not have returned his kiss had she felt anything at all for Kit Peverill. More, having fallen in love with Ty Allardyce, she knew without doubt that the idea of being in any man's arms other than his was absolutely abhorrent to her.

Now, why had she gone and fallen in love with him? Of all the idiotic things to do, wasn't that the cruncher? Kiss her he might—if invited. And she could not deny her inviting words were probably enough for any red-blooded male—be she his pretend girlfriend or no. But when it came to the love stakes idiotic was what it truly was. Because worldly, sophisticated men like Tyrell Allardyce just did not fall in love with lippy, trespassing 'village locals' like her.

Phinn returned to the stable to chat to Ruby. She had only just discovered her feelings for Ty, but one way and another she was finding it all very disheartening.

Though, whatever else happened during the remainder of her time at Broadlands, all Phinn knew—with Ty Allardyce knowing so very much about women—was that she was going to have to keep her feelings for him extremely well hidden!

CHAPTER SIX

SATURDAY began with a miserable wet dawn, but Phinn could not be down. She'd had a restless night, and awoke to know that her love for Ty was no figment of her imagination. It was still there this morning and, while she would take great care that he would never know of it, it gave her a feeling of joy to know that he was here, at home.

She did not want to think of how it would be when he went back to London, but decided that for the moment she would just enjoy knowing that he was sleeping under the same roof.

. Phinn showered and dressed early and, with her hair pulled back in a band, slipped quietly out of the house.

It was while she was talking to Ruby that Phinn realised she must have begun to fall in love with Ty as far back as when he had offered them a home. Incredible as it seemed, it must have been then. She clearly recalled thinking then that there was something not right about it somewhere. Now she knew what it was—some sixth sense had been trying to warn her that before too long she was going to get hurt.

Too late now to do anything about it. She was in love with him, and that love was here to stay. She knew that.

When Phinn went back to the house, both Ty and Ash were at breakfast. All at once feeling a sudden eagerness to see Ty again, she hastened up the stairs to wash and tidy signs of the stable from her before going quickly down again.

'Ty wants to take a walk around the estate. Coming with us?' Ash asked.

Normally she would have liked nothing better. But, sensitive to the two brothers, she thought that perhaps they might need some brotherly time together, and they would probably talk more easily if she were not there.

'I've a date with…' Pure wickedness made her look at Ty— there was a glint in his eyes that said he was listening, and was daring her to have a date with the vet. 'With a pitchfork, a wheelbarrow and, by special request, Jimmie Starkey's compost heap.'

'Whatever turns you on,' Ash replied, and, with a smile, 'If you prefer mucking out the stable to a morning spent in fascinating company…'

Phinn grinned at him, affection for him in her look, and real pleasure in her heart as she noticed how his appetite had started to pick up. With luck that twenty or so pounds he had lost would soon be put back on again.

'Did you sleep well?' Ty butted in sharply.

Taken by surprise, Phinn turned to him, startled. 'Do I look haggard?' she queried.

One sleepless night and she looked a wreck!

His answer was to study her for all of one full minute. And, just when she was thinking that she was going to go red at any second, 'You look quite beautiful,' he answered, so entirely unexpectedly and sounding so much as if he meant it, that she did blush.

She recovered quickly, however, and, having realised that his remark had to be because Ash was there, and that Ty was merely playing his role of being interested in her, she told him lightly, 'I'm still not coming with you.'

Up in her room after breakfast, she went and stared at her face in the mirror. She wanted to be beautiful. She wanted Ty to think she was beautiful. But did a straight nose, wide and quite nice delphinium-blue eyes, eyebrows that were a shade darker than her strawberry-blonde hair, a dainty chin and a fairly nice forehead—oh, and a complexion that, yes, had been remarked on in the past as 'quite something'—constitute beauty? Her phone rang and put an end to her daydreaming.

It was her mother, her morning's golf having been cancelled because Clive had a heavy cold. 'How are things, darling? And how's Ruby?' It was good to chat to her mother, and they talked for some while, with her mother ending, 'When are we going to see you?'

Promising to try and pay them a visit soon, Phinn rang off, reflecting that her mother had a very different life now from the one she had had with her father. But this wasn't getting Ruby's stable sorted.

The early-morning rain had cleared when, changed into old jeans and a tee shirt, Phinn turned Ruby out into the paddock and went back to the stable. Before she could start work, though, Ty Allardyce appeared. How she loved him! Her heart raced. How he must never know.

'The weather's cleared for your walk,' she offered, friendly, polite—that was the way. But, forget it. Ty, it seemed, had come looking for a fight.

'Have you been in touch with Peverill?' he questioned bluntly, coming to stand but a yard from her. What happened to *You look quite beautiful*? Phinn thought.

'Since my telephone conversation with him last night, you mean?'

Ty gave her an impatient look. 'I passed your room—you were on the phone with someone.'

What big ears you have! For one delicious moment, Phinn had the weird notion that Ty had sounded jealous. See where falling in love got you—it made you weird in the head! All he was bothered about was the thought that she might blow their cover by going out with the vet after all.

Despite her inner turmoil, Phinn smiled at him sweetly. 'You don't really mind if I chat on the phone to my mother occasionally? It's ages since I last saw her.'

Ty's annoyed look instantly fell away. 'I've been a brute again, haven't I?' He did not expect an answer.

He got one anyway. 'You can't help it. It's your nature,' Phinn replied—and just had to laugh. She didn't believe it for a moment. What *was* his nature was a big brother's need to look out for his younger brother—and if that included taking her to task if he thought she was going to put a spoke in the wheel of the progress he had made so far, he would.

But Ty was unoffended by her remark, and actually seemed amused by it. Then, taking on board what she had just said about not having seen her mother for ages, and remembering she had sold her car, he was serious as he suggested, 'There are several vehicles here if you'd like to go and visit your mother.' And, as an afterthought, 'I'll take you to see her myself, if you prefer.'

'Wouldn't dream of it,' Phinn replied, thinking again what a complex man he was. He had come to see her ready to sort her out, and here he was offering to spend some of his precious weekend taking her family visiting!

'Or why not invite her and her husband here for a meal? Your mother could see where—'

Phinn stopped him right there. 'Do you know, Ty,' she butted in, 'when you forget to be a brute, you sometimes surprise me by being really, really nice?'

He looked taken aback. But then, as if noting from her solemn-eyed expression that she was being sincere, his tone changed when he quietly stated, 'You do realise that if you carry on in that vein, you're in serious danger of being kissed again.'

Oh, my, how he could make her heart race! Phinn teetered on the brink of saying, *Promises, promises*—but instinctively knew that such a remark was bound to guarantee that Ty *would* kiss her. And, while heart and soul she would welcome his kisses, she knew that that way lay danger: danger of Ty, with his experience.

Which was why she forced herself to take a step away from him. 'One kiss in twenty-four hours is more than enough for us village locals,' she told him primly.

His lips twitched. 'You're never going to let me forget that "village locals" comment, are you?'

'Not if I still know you when you're a hundred,' she replied cheerfully. And offered nicely, 'If you want to help I'm sure I can rustle up another pitchfork from somewhere.'

He looked amused. 'You certainly know how to say good-bye to a man,' he said, declining her offer, and went.

After that, the day seemed to fly by. Ty and Ash came back from their inspection of the estate, with Ty approving of Sam Turner's suggestions for keeping Pixie End Wood healthy.

After a quick lunch he said he had arranged to call in at Yew Tree Farm. 'Anyone like to come?' he asked.

'You and Phinn go,' Ash suggested. 'If Phinn will loan me her rods, I fancy having another go at casting.'

'Oh, I don't—' Phinn began. Ash was welcome to borrow her fishing equipment, but Ty wouldn't want her with him when he went to call on his tenants at Yew Tree Farm.

'That's fine,' Ty cut in. 'See you in half an hour then, Phinn.'

She opened her mouth to protest, saw Ty was looking at her with something of a stern expression, and, probably because deep down she wanted to spend some time with him, 'Off-hand, I can't think of anything I'd rather do,' she remarked.

Of course Ty thought she was being saucy, but she did not care. Did not care either that he would probably just as soon go on his own. But if he wanted Ash to think that they were more friendly than they were, who was she to argue?

'Ruby all right?' Ty queried when, thirty-five minutes later, with Ash in possession of her father's fishing equipment, Phinn sat beside Ty in his car and they set off.

Ruby, in Phinn's view, was a nice safe topic. 'She's feeling great today,' she replied happily.

'But doesn't always?'

'Poor love, she's getting on a bit. Sometimes she's fine for weeks on end, but just lately—well, she's had more bad days than good.'

'And that's where the vet comes in?'

Not so safe a topic. 'Kit has been brilliant.' She gave the vet his due. 'Most attentive.'

'I'll bet,' Ty muttered. Then, plainly not interested in the vet, 'Tell me about Phinn Hawkins,' he requested.

'You know everything.'

'I very much doubt that,' he replied.

'What do you want to know?'

'You could start by telling me your first name?' he suggested.

And have him laugh his socks off? Not likely! 'You know my first name.'

'Phinn doesn't begin with a "D",' he countered. She wondered how on earth he knew that her first name began with a "D". 'Your father's initials were "E.H." The only other initials carved into the underside of Grandmother Hawkins' table are "D.H".'

'You checked?' she asked, startled.

'I spotted the initials when I purchased the table, obviously. Since I was the one who upended it to take it to your room, I couldn't very well miss seeing them again.'

'I never did thank you for that lovely gesture. I did—do— appreciate it.'

'So, what does the "D" stand for?' Stubbornly, she refused to answer. 'You're not going to deny the "D" is yours, I hope?'

'So, about me. I was born at Honeysuckle Farm and was adored by my parents and grandparents. Because my mother was quite poorly after having me—some complication or other—my father looked after me, and he never stopped even when she was well again.'

'As he adored you, you in turn adored him?' Ty put in.

'Absolutely! He was wonderful. A gifted pianist. A…'

'It was he who taught you to play?'

'Yes.' She nodded, remembering those hours at the piano. 'Just as he taught me so many other things.'

'Go on,' Ty urged, when she drifted off with her thoughts for a second or two.

'You can't possibly be interested.'

'I wouldn't have asked had I not been interested,' he replied—a touch sharply, she felt. She mustn't go reading into it that he might be interested in any personal way in Phinn Hawkins. 'What "many other things" did he teach you?'

'Apart from how to trespass all over Broadlands?'

'He taught that one well,' Ty commented—but she sensed amusement rather than censure in his tone.

'He also taught me to respect the property I was trespassing on. Not to fish out of season, where to swim and where not to swim.'

'How to perform a flat-out racing dive?'

'We owe that one to him,' she murmured.

'That alone forgives him anything he ever did wrong,' Ty said quietly, and they both knew they were talking of her rescue dive. 'The courage it took to do it, though, was all your own,' he added.

But Phinn loved him, and did not want him to relive a time when he might have lost his beloved brother in what was a very heart-tearing memory for him. 'Anyhow,' she said brightly, 'having bought me many books he thought I should be reading, and having many times taken me out of school when he thought they were neglecting areas they should be teaching me, he would take me round museums and art galleries. We went everywhere—concerts, opera... And when town got too much we would come home and walk through the woods, and he would teach me about trees and animals. Teach me how to sketch, how to fish, tie a fly and appreciate Mozart.' She smiled as she confessed, 'I learned by myself how to take a swig of my father's beer down at the pub without pulling a face at the foul taste.' Her smile became a light laugh as she added, 'I supposed I learned by myself too, how to cuss and swear. I was less than four years old, it seems when I apparently came out with a mouthful that nearly sent my grandmother into heart failure and saw my mother banning my father from taking me anywhere near the Cat and Drum.'

There *was* a smile in Ty's voice when he suggested, 'You grew out of cussing very quickly, I take it?'

'In record time, I think you could say—and the ban was lifted,' she answered with a grin. 'And that is more than enough about me. Your turn.'

'Turn?' he queried, as if he had no idea what she meant.

'Oh, don't be mean! I've just talked my head off about me!'

'You can't...'

'Possibly be interested? That's my line! And I am.'

'Interested in me?'

'In a purely reciprocal way,' she replied—she who was avid to know every last little thing about him. 'According to Ash, you're a genius when it comes to business.'

'Business is quite good at the moment,' he replied—rather modestly, Phinn thought.

'You mean it's thriving?'

'It occupies a lot of my time.'

'But you love it?'

'It adds that bit of adrenalin to my day,' he admitted, adding, 'I'm out of the country all of next week.'

Her heart sank. It was being greedy, she knew, but if Ty was going to be out of the country all next week, then there was absolutely no chance whatsoever that he would come down to Broadlands any weekday evening.

'Ash will miss you,' she said, but could easily have substituted her own name.

'He'll be all right,' Ty answered. 'With you here I can safely go away, knowing that he could never have a better guardian.'

Feeling that they were getting away from the subject of him, Phinn was just about to ask him which university he had attended when she suddenly became aware that they were driving through the land farmed by Nesta and Noel Jarvis, the tenants of Yew Tree Farm. And the further they drove on, with flourishing fields on either side of the road, the more the contrast between Yew Tree Farm and Honeysuckle Farm hit her full square. Yew Tree Farm was thriving! The Jarvises must have had the same hard times that Honeysuckle had experienced. But where Honeysuckle had gone under, Yew Tree had somehow survived—had borne the fall in wheat prices, the rising cost of fuel, and had continued to make the farm the success it was today.

Neighbours of Honeysuckle, they had suffered the same vagaries of weather, all the wet summers, and must have endured the same machinery breakdowns, yet—they were thriving!

Phinn was reduced to silence as Ty steered his vehicle into the farmyard. No air of neglect here. No heaps of rusting machinery. Remembering Honeysuckle and its neglected air the last time she had seen it, she did not want to get out of the car. Perhaps she could stay where she was. Ty had said he was merely going to call in—perhaps his business would not take that long.

But, no, he was coming round to the passenger side and opening the door. Already he had a hand on her arm. 'If your business is private…' she suggested.

Ty looked at her, and seemed to guess from her expression that something was amiss, because, 'What is it?' he asked. But before she could tell him both Nesta and Noel Jarvis, having heard their vehicle, had come out to greet them.

Not wanting to cause a fuss, Phinn shook her head at Ty and, with his hand on her arm, stepped from the car. She pinned a smile on her face as Mr and Mrs Jarvis recognised her.

'You know Phinn, of course,' Ty commented as he shook hands with the couple.

'Phinn, my dear, how are you?' Nesta Jarvis asked. They had known Phinn all her life, and had both been at her father's funeral. 'We heard you were working at Broadlands now. How are you getting along?'

'We would be lost without her, Mrs Jarvis,' Ty commented, and enquired of Noel Jarvis, 'Busy time of year for you, I expect?'

They did not overstay their welcome, but while Ty politely refused an offer of refreshments and went into the study with Noel, Phinn stayed and had a cup of tea with Nesta. They passed the time with Nesta enquiring after her mother, and Phinn enquiring after the Jarvises' son and two daughters. The girls had married and moved away, while the son, Gregory, had married and now lived in a farm cottage, working with his father.

Phinn was still in a quiet frame of mind when, having said farewell to the Jarvises, she sat beside Ty on the journey back to the Hall.

Then suddenly Ty was steering the vehicle into a lay-by and pulling up. Phinn turned in her seat to look at him. 'Are you going to share it with me, Phinn?' he asked quietly, seriously.

She could have told him that there was nothing to share, but at the very least she owed him an apology. She swallowed on a knot of emotion, then with a shaky sigh began. 'I hated you when you gave us notice to quit. But you were right. We weren't paying the rent—and the place was a tip.'

'That wasn't your fault,' Ty put in quietly.

But she wasn't having that. 'You asked if there was nothing I couldn't do—well, I well and truly messed up there! I should have made more of an effort, but I didn't. And it's taken going to Yew Tree Farm today and seeing what a well-run farm should look like for me to see it.'

'Don't beat yourself up about it, Phinn,' Ty instructed her seriously. 'You had a home to run. Nobody would have expected you to be out riding a tractor all day.' She still felt she should have done more. Though it was a fact that Ty certainly made her feel better when he asked, 'Would your father have been happy for you to take on *his* work?'

Put like that, no, he would not. Her father might not have shown much interest in running the farm, but she knew he would have taken great exception had she attempted to take over. Her mother had often called her her father's playmate, and Phinn knew she would have taken the fun out of what had been his last days had she said that she had work to do each time he asked her to go somewhere with him. He had disliked it intensely when she had left the farm each day to go to her job at the accountants.

'How do you always know how to say just the right thing?' she asked Ty, and he smiled a gentle smile.

But, as her heart seemed to skip a beat, his smile deepened and he murmured conspiratorially, 'I'll bet Noel Jarvis can't play the piano like your father could.'

Oh, Ty. She loved him so. 'I bet he couldn't have trimmed my Easter bonnet like my dad did either,' she said, and was able to laugh. She loved Ty the more that he did not think her odd, but seemed to *know* that her dad trimming her Easter bonnet had been something rather special.

'All right now?' he asked.

She nodded. 'Yes,' she said. 'And—thank you.' And she felt the world was a wonderful place when, leaning across to her, Ty placed a brief kiss on her cheek.

'Let's go home—and see if Ash has caught any more trout.'

What they did find when they reached the house was that

there was a beat-up old car on the drive. And as they went in Phinn clearly heard what to her was the unmistakable sound of a piano tuner at work.

She stopped dead in her tracks. 'Mr Timmins?' she queried of Ty, who had halted with her.

'Mr Timmins,' he agreed with a grin.

Phinn sailed up to her room. Mr Timmins never worked on Saturday afternoons for *anyone*! But, remembering Ty's wonderful grin, she felt just then that *she* would do anything for Ty too.

All too soon Saturday gave way to Sunday. It was a joy to her that Ty had decided not to leave for London until very early on Monday morning, but to Phinn the hours on Sunday went by in a flash.

That evening after dinner, while she *wanted* to stay in the drawing room, where Ty was, she made herself get to her feet.

'I'm for bed,' she said, to no one in particular. And, because she just had to look at him, 'Have a good trip next week,' she bade Ty.

He stood up and walked to the door with her—purely for Ash's benefit, she knew. 'See you hopefully on Friday,' he murmured when they halted at the door, out of earshot of Ash.

Phinn nodded. 'Bye, you,' she said, and looked up into a pair of steady grey eyes.

'Bye yourself,' he said softly, and, to make her heart go positively wild, he bent down and, otherwise not touching her, gently kissed her on the mouth.

Phinn wheeled away from him without a word. Only when she got to her room and closed the door did she put her fingertips to the lips he had kissed. Oh, my!

It was not the same Broadlands without Ty there. The summer had temporarily disappeared, and it did nothing but rain on Monday. Bearing in mind that Ash still had a tendency to be a bit down occasionally, mainly in the afternoon,

Phinn sought him out and offered to give him a fly-tying lesson.

But on Tuesday *she* was the one who was down. Ruby was ill again. Kit Peverill was as good as ever, and recommended a new medicine for Ruby. New and expensive.

'I'd like her to have it,' Phinn told him, wanting the best for her Rubes, even if she had no idea how she was going to pay for it.

'Don't worry about settling your account straight away,' Kit said kindly, just as if he knew she was near to broke.

But she did worry about it. Before Kit had asked her out, the fact she sometimes owed him money had not unduly bothered her. She'd always known that she would pay him some time. But now that he had asked her out it seemed to make it more of a personal debt to him, somehow. And she did not like it.

By Thursday, however, Ruby was starting to pick up again, her new medication obviously suiting her. Phinn knew then that, whatever the cost, there was no way Ruby was going to stop taking it.

It was raining again at lunchtime, and while on the one hand Phinn was delighted with Ruby's progress, she could not lose that niggle of worry about owing the vet money.

Ash came and found her in the stables, and he did not seem very bright either. Phinn had an idea. It was too wet to take Ash off for a good long walk, but there was somewhere else she could take him.

'If you were very good, Ashley Allardyce, I might think of taking you down to the pub for a pint,' she told him, managing to sound more bright than she felt.

Ash looked at her, considered the proposition and, with not much else happening in his life just then, accepted. 'If you promise to behave yourself, I might come,' he said. And, since they would both be soaked if they walked anywhere very far in the present downpour, 'The pick-up okay?'

The Cat and Drum was full of its usual lunchtime regulars. 'Take a seat over there,' Phinn instructed him. 'I'll get the drinks.'

'No, I'll get them,' Ash insisted.

'Actually, Ash, I rather wanted to have a private word with the landlord.'

'Devious maid,' Ash accused, though he didn't seem to mind that there had been a motive behind her invite to the pub. 'Make mine a pint.'

Telling Bob Quigley that she would like a quick word with him, Phinn delivered Ash his pint and returned to have a discussion with the landlord.

Phinn had finished her discussion with him when, as she half turned, she saw that Ash was deep in conversation with none other than Geraldine Walton!

Far from being the grumpy kind of man he had been with Geraldine when she had first introduced the two, Phinn observed that Ash seemed in no particular hurry to cut short the conversation they were having. In fact, to Phinn's mind, Ash seemed suddenly to be very much lifted from his earlier mood.

In no hurry either to interrupt them, and wondering if Geraldine usually stopped by the Cat at lunchtime or if she had been passing and had recognised the pick-up parked outside, Phinn was glad just then to be accosted by Mickie Yates.

'What are you doing in this iniquitous place, young lady?' he greeted her warmly.

'Mickie!' she exclaimed, and kissed his whiskery cheek.

Chatting with Mickie took up a good five minutes—but Ash and Geraldine were still finding things to talk about. Don't hurt him! Phinn thought, finding protective feelings for Ash rushing to the surface. But then she reminded herself that, while Geraldine could not afford to be a softie and run a successful business, the owner of the riding school and stables was nowhere as hard-hearted and avaricious as her cousin Leanne.

Rather than have Ash look over and think he might be

obliged to come back to her, Phinn stayed turned away from him. Jack Philips, an old friend of her father, came up to her, and then Idris Owen joined in, in to collect fresh supplies to take back to his forge. She could have chatted with them all day.

Eventually a much more cheerful Ash came over to them. When they at last left the pub, he asked if she had seen Geraldine Walton there, and Phinn replied, 'I did, actually. I hope you don't think me rude, but I didn't want to be impolite to my father's old friends and come over.'

'If you'd accepted all the drinks they offered you'd be staggering,' was all he replied.

Ruby continued to make progress, and Kit Peverill visited early on Friday morning to check her over and give her an injection. And still it rained. But with Ruby settled, a long day was stretching out in front of Phinn. Ty might be home tonight—but how to fill in those yawning hours between now and then? Then she had another idea.

One of the outbuildings had come in for modernisation when Ty had purchased Broadlands, and now served as the estate office. But so far Phinn had not seen the inside of it, and doubted that Ash had spent very much time in there either.

Bearing in mind, if village gossip had been correct, that Ash might have endured some kind of breakdown when working in an office environment, Phinn was wary of suggesting anything that might set him back in any way, but after she had spent some quality time with Ruby, Phinn went looking for him. She found him in the drawing room, staring out of the window at the rain.

'It's a lovely spot here,' she commented when, having heard her come in, Ash looked round.

'It is,' he agreed.

'I've just walked past the estate office. It struck me—I've never seen the inside of it.'

'I wish I didn't have to,' Ash muttered, explaining, 'I've been very neglectful. The paperwork is piling up in there.'

'Hmm...' Phinn murmured, and then offered lightly, 'Do you know, Ash? Today just might be your lucky day.' And, at his querying look, 'It just so happens that I'm a qualified secretary, with a certificate that says I'm good in office administration.'

Ash looked at her in surprise. 'No?'

'Yes,' she replied. And then offered, 'I bet together we could lick your paperwork into shape in no time.'

'You're on!' He grabbed at the offer.

Before she could think further they were out of the house, had the office door unlocked and the lights switched on against the dull day. In no time they were hard at it, tackling the paperwork.

They worked steadily through the rest of the morning, with Phinn keeping an eye on Ash in case the work they were doing was having any ill effect. It wasn't. In fact the more of the backlog they cleared, the brighter Ash seemed to become.

'Oh, Ty's already dealt with that,' he said at one point, having unearthed a letter from Noel Jarvis, enquiring about the possibility of Noel and his son purchasing Yew Tree Farm. 'It seems he phoned Ty in London when his letter here went unanswered.'

'That's probably why we went there last Saturday,' Phinn commented.

'It was,' Ash confirmed. 'Apparently the previous owner of Broadlands always refused to split up the estate. But with Ty saying I can have Honeysuckle Farm if I want it, he's quite happy to sell Yew Tree to the Jarvises. Ty said they have kept it in splendid shape all these years, and ought to have it—' He broke off. 'Oh, Phinn, I'm sorry. I wasn't meaning that Honeysuckle...'

'Don't apologise, Ash,' Phinn said quickly, feeling that she had grown up quite a lot recently. As short a while ago as last week she would have been upset to hear anyone compare Honeysuckle with Yew Tree unfavourably. But last Saturday, when she had felt so awful about the very same thing, Ty had made her feel better.

True, Honeysuckle was a mess. But she could have done little about that—not if she hadn't wanted to make her father's life less fun than it had been. Ty—darling Ty—had put that into perspective for her.

Oh, she did so hope he would come home tonight. It had been an unbearably long week without him. She didn't know if she would be able to take it if he did not come back tonight. She just could not face thinking of the emptiness if he did not come home the entire weekend either!

After a break, while she went and spent some time with Ruby, Phinn returned to the office feeling quite pleased with how much she and Ash had cleared between them. Only some pieces of filing and a few letters to type now, and the office would be more or less as up to date as it was ever going to be.

Phinn was in actual fact tearing away, typing the last of the letters, when—Ash having wandered off to 'get some oxygen to my brain'—the door opened. Her eyes on the page to the left of her, while her fingers raced over the keyboard, she assumed it was Ash returning.

She finished the letter and, as Ash had not made any kind of comment, looked up—and held in a gasp of breath. It was not Ash who had come in but Ty!

Warmth and joy filled her heart. She could not think of a thing to say, and just hoped she had not gone red.

Grey eyes held blue eyes, and then Ty was shaking his head slowly. 'Phinnie Hawkins,' he murmured, 'you never cease to amaze me.'

'Good,' she said impishly, but for no reason felt a touch embarrassed suddenly. 'I used to work as a secretary.'

Again he shook his head slightly. 'You worked as well as kept house?'

Like millions of other women, she didn't doubt. 'You thought all my day consisted of was a little light dusting?' she derided.

'The inside of that farmhouse was shining when I went there,' Ty documented. He paused, and then added, 'But, in addition to keeping the place immaculate, it was *you* who earned to put food on the table.'

Instantly her derision fell from her. She wasn't having that. 'Actually, my father was very clever. He could make, mend, repair and sell things. He was a good provider!' she said stoutly. She wished she hadn't mentioned that her father had sold things as soon as she'd said it. Ty already knew where one of their antiques had gone.

But, as if not wanting to fall out with her, Ty replied seriously, 'You don't have to defend him to me, Phinn. How could he be anything *but* a fine man to have produced such a lovely daughter?'

Phinn looked at him wide-eyed. Oh, my—did he know how to make a girl feel all flustered inside! And yet he had sounded as if he meant it—that 'lovely daughter' bit. 'Okay, so now that we all know you graduated from charm school with honours, what can we do for you?'

'I saw the light on. I thought it was Ash in here,' Ty remarked, and then asked, 'How's he been this week?'

'He's all right,' Phinn assured him. 'He's occasionally a bit down, but generally I think he's picked up quite a bit. Anyhow, I've been watching him today, and he seems fine with the office work.'

'You've been in here most of the day?'

'A lot of it. We've cleared most of the backlog—' Phinn broke off as just at that moment Ash came back.

'What do you think of my new PA?' he asked Ty. And, not waiting for him to answer, 'She's great,' he complimented her. With a smile to her, he looked at his brother to tell him cheerfully, 'In fact, were she not spoken for, I would seriously ask her to consider *me*!'

Phinn smiled happily. She knew that Ash was only teasing, but it was good to see him so uplifted. But when, smiling still, she glanced at Ty, she caught a glimpse of something in his expression that suggested he was not best pleased with his brother's comment.

A second later, however, and she knew that she was mistaken. Because Ty was telling his brother good-humouredly, 'Keep your hands off, Ash,' and then seemed about to depart.

Just to show how little she cared where he went, she said, 'This is the last letter, Ash.' Pretending to be more interested in the job in hand than in either of the Allardyce brothers. 'If you'd like to sign them, I'll take a walk down to the postbox.'

Getting ready to go down to dinner that night, Phinn was again beset by an urge to wear a dress. Crackers—absolutely! She'd lived in trousers for so long now—apart from that one very memorable occasion down at the pool—that she was bound to evoke some sort of comment if she went down wearing something Ash would call 'girly'.

As usual both Ty and Ash were down before her, and, taking her place at the dining table, Phinn felt a flicker of anxiety. She wanted to have a word with Ty later, but was unsure how he would react.

'Did Phinn tell you she frogmarched me down to the pub for a pint yesterday lunchtime?' Ash asked Ty.

Ty turned to her, his grey eyes taking in her wide blue eyes and superb complexion. 'Nothing Phinn does surprises me any more,' he answered lightly. But, with his glance still on her, he asked, 'Are you leading my brother into bad ways?' his mouth curving upward good-humouredly.

'It's my opinion that Ash is perfectly capable of getting into mischief without my help,' she replied, and loved Ty so when he smiled at her. She looked away, got herself under control, and then asked, 'How was your trip?'

The meal passed with Ash asking questions about business and Ty saying that they didn't want to bore Phinn to death—when in truth she wanted to know everything about him. When pressed, he gave a light account of what he had been doing that week.

Phinn started to feel nervous when the meal came to an end and the three of them ambled from the dining room. She felt comfortable enough now not to have to pay a courtesy ten-minute visit to the drawing room with them before she went to see Ruby.

As the two men turned towards the drawing room, and she made to go the other way, she called out, 'Ty!' He halted, and while Ash halted too at first, he must have realised that this was a private moment, because with a hint of a smile on his face he carried on walking.

'Phinn?' Ty encouraged, his eyes on her suddenly anxious face.

'The thing is. Well, I need to see to Ruby now. But—er—can I have a word with you later?'

Ty's expression became grim on the instant. 'If you're thinking of leaving, forget it!' he rapped sharply.

And that rattled her. She was uptight enough without that. 'Forget what I said about charm school!' she erupted, and stormed angrily away from him.

His voice followed her. 'I'll be in my study.'

'Huh!' she snorted in disgust.

As usual, being with Ruby for any length of time calmed her. And really, now that she was calm enough to think about it, Ty sounding so well and truly against her leaving Broadlands was rather flattering.

'So we'll stay, Rubes, my darling,' she told the old mare. 'Not that we've anywhere else to go. I know you like it here—

and between you and me, but don't tell him, it would break my heart to leave.'

All of which put Phinn in a mellow frame of mind when she was ready to go back to the house. Nipping into the downstairs cloakroom to wash her hands, brush any stray bits of straw from her and push tendrils of strawberry-blonde hair from her forehead, Phinn rehearsed what she was going to ask. She didn't know why she felt so nervous. There was no way Ty could refuse.

She left the cloakroom hoping that Ty, aware by now of the length of time she spent with Ruby each evening, would be in his study as he'd said, and that she would not have to go looking for him.

As she went along the hall, she saw that the study door, which was usually closed, now stood open. *Oh, Ty!* She saw it as a sign of welcome, and again felt all squishy inside about him at his thoughtfulness.

Reaching the door, she tapped lightly on it, and her heart did a now familiar flutter as Ty came to the door and invited her in.

'Take a seat,' he offered, indicating a dark brown leather button-back chair and closing the door.

'It won't take that long,' she replied, as he turned to his computer and closed down the work he had been doing.

'You've changed your mind about leaving?' he questioned sternly.

'That was in your head—never in mine!' she replied, wishing she felt better.

'You're certainly looking guilty about something,' he answered shortly.

'No, I'm not!' she exclaimed. Needing some breathing space suddenly, she decided to take the seat he had offered a few seconds ago.

'Has the vet been here?' Ty demanded, taking the office chair and turning it to face her. When Phinn went red—purely because this interview was about money and the vet's bill she couldn't pay, he accused, 'What have you been up to?'—and she could have hit him!

'I haven't been up to anything! And of *course* the vet's been here! Ruby hasn't been well! And if I'm flushed it's not because I'm guilty of anything, but because I'm embarrassed! Honestly!' she fumed.

'Embarrassed? You?'

'Oh, shut up and listen,' she flared, doubting that any of his other employees had ever told him to shut up. But Ty did just that, for he said not another word, and she began floundering to find the right way to say what she had to. Then she realised that after the way this interview had started it just could not get any worse, and so she plunged. 'Is it all right with you if I take a part-time job?'

'You've got a job!' Ty shot back at her forthrightly, before she could blink.

'I know that!' she erupted. 'But this would only be part-time—in the evenings.'

'With the vet?' he charged, before she could draw another breath.

'*No!*' she protested, exasperated. He seemed to have the vet on the brain! 'I just thought that—well, Ruby will be all right on her own for a few hours, and Ash is looking so much better now... His appetite's picked up and he's generally not so—er—bruised as he was, say a month ago. And what with you coming home some evenings to keep him com—'

'If it's not Peverill, who else have you been in contact with?' Ty cut in.

She didn't want to tell him! All this in answer to what to her mind had been a perfectly simple question! Stubbornly she refused to answer. But Ty, at his most unfriendly, was waiting—and not yielding an inch.

'Oh—if you must know—' she exploded, nettled. 'Er...'

Oh, damn the man! 'As Ash mentioned, we went down to the pub yesterday,' she said shortly.

Ty's expression did not lighten any. 'I'm all ears,' he invited.

She sent him a cross look, but had to go on. 'Well, the thing is, I was talking to Bob Quigley…'

'Bob Quigley? Another of your chums?'

'He's the landlord of the Cat and Drum,' she supplied impatiently. Now that she had got started, she wanted it all said and done quickly. Heavens above, it was only a tiddly request, after all!

'So you were talking to Bob Quigley down at the pub…?'

Phinn was about to mention how Ash had seemed to be getting on very well with the new owner of the riding school and stables, but she checked and decided not to—all the quicker to get her request over and done with. 'Well, the upshot of it is, that—well…' She was as impatient with herself as Ty obviously was. 'He—the landlord Bob—offered me a job.'

Ty looked at her with raised brows. 'Behind the bar?' He seemed more amused than anything.

'Yes,' she muttered.

Ty took that on board. 'Know anything about being a pub barmaid?' he enquired coolly, his amused look fading.

'Not the first thing,' she admitted. 'But when I asked Bob if he was fully staffed, he said he would give me a job any time.'

'I'll bet he did!' Ty barked bluntly.

'I wish you'd stop blowing hot and cold!'

'How do you expect me to react? Presumably it's not the company you're after, so what it boils down to is that I'm not paying you enough!'

Feeling contrite suddenly, she said, 'It's not that…' She was embarrassed again, and looked away from him. 'The thing is…'

She glanced back to Ty, and was totally undone when, as if seeing her embarrassment, he changed tack and asked gently, 'What, Phinn? Tell me.'

Phinn took a couple of shaky breaths. 'Well, the thing is, I'm starting to owe the vet big-time. And he's okay about that,' she added quickly. 'He knows that I'll pay him as soon as I can. But…'

'But?' Ty encouraged when she ran out of steam.

'Well, I've owed Kit before. And I didn't mind owing him before. But—well, now that he's asked me out, it—er—makes my debt to him sort of personal, and—well, I'd rather work a couple of hours each evening down at the Cat than leave my account unpaid.'

Ty leaned back in his chair, his expression softening. 'Oh, Phinn Hawkins, what am I going to do with you?' he asked. And then, not really wanting an answer, 'You'd desert us in the evenings, all because Peverill has taken a shine to you?'

She guessed Ty was making light of it because he could see how uncomfortable she was feeling. 'That's about it,' she mumbled. 'Kit's told me there's no hurry, that he knows I'll pay him when I can. But I feel kind of—awkward about it, and…'

'Oh, we can't have that,' Ty said, shaking his head, but finding a smile for her. 'Quite obviously I shall give you a raise.'

'No!' she protested, feeling hot all over. 'I consider I'm overpaid by you as it is.'

'And *I* consider, dear Phinn,' Ty said to make her bones melt, 'that Ash and I would be totally lost without you.'

'Rubbish!'

'Not so. You've no idea how just by being here you brighten the atmosphere. You're so good with Ash—sensing his mood…'

'Tosh!'

'Not to mention that the office has never been straighter than it is today,' he went on, as if she hadn't spoken. 'And, given that I didn't take you on to do secretarial work, that makes me in *your* debt.'

'No!' she denied woodenly.

'You deserve a bonus at least.'

'No!' she maintained.

'Look here, Phinnie.' Ty changed tack again. 'See it from my point of view. You must know that I truly cannot have my girlfriend out working when I come home especially to see her.'

How that made her heart pump overtime! He had so truly sounded as if he really meant it. Thank goodness for common sense. But taking anything personal out of the equation, she could see that Ash might think it a touch peculiar if when Ty came home, *she* went out.

'I...' she said helplessly, and started to feel more anxious than ever.

'Don't worry at it, Phinn,' he instructed. 'I can see exactly why you don't want to owe Peverill—and I think you're quite right. But from my point of view you're doing more than enough here without taking on extra work. So I'll ring the vet and tell him to send Ruby's accounts to me.'

'What for?' she asked, feeling more than a shade bewildered.

'I'll settle them.'

'No, you won't!' she bristled hotly.

'Yes, I will,' he replied firmly—no argument. And, to show that the interview was over, he turned from her and reactivated his computer.

Phinn stared at him. He was not looking at her, and she guessed that since he had been abroad and out of his office all week he wanted her to go so that he could catch up on the week's business events.

With the utmost reluctance, feeling that she could argue with him until she was blue in the face and it would do no good, Phinn, with a heavy sigh but not another word, left his study.

She was on her way upstairs when the unpalatable truth hit her. Ty had appreciated her reason for not wanting to owe the vet because, as he had said, the vet had taken a shine to her. But by that same token Ty had just as good as told her that it was all right for her to owe the vet's bill to Tyrell Allardyce because—quite clearly—he, Ty, had *not* taken a shine to her.

She went to bed mourning that he had not—nor ever would. And spent a sleepless night aware that she was far too unsophisticated to appeal to the sophisticated tastes of Ty Allardyce.

CHAPTER SEVEN

THE weather improved over the weekend and, having been in touch with Bob Quigley to thank him but to tell him she would not be needing a job after all, Phinn was sitting on the paddock rail on Sunday morning watching Ruby. Joy filled Phinn's heart at how well her mare was doing. Then she heard male voices as Ty and Ash came from the house.

A short while later, however, and Ty had left his brother and had come looking for her. He reached her, but for a moment or two said nothing—just observed her in her jeans and tee shirt, with her hair bunched back from her face in a rubber band.

This man she loved so much had the most uncanny knack of making her feel shy! She flicked her glance from him, paying particular attention to climbing down from the fence.

'What have I done wrong now?' she asked, once she was standing beside him.

'Who said you'd done anything wrong?' Ty countered lightly.

'Well, you haven't come over just for a bit of a chat,' she replied, feeling that there must be a reason for Ty coming to seek her out.

He shrugged. 'Could be I thought that—purely to give some authenticity to our relationship—perhaps I should take you out to dinner one evening.'

Her heart spurted again; there was nothing she would like better. But their 'date' wouldn't be for her benefit, but for Ash's. So she stayed outwardly cool to reply, 'We haven't got a relationship.'

'Stop being difficult!' Ty admonished. 'You know how sensitive Ash is. He'll start to wonder soon why you and I—'

'There is no you and I. And anyway, Mrs Starkey is the best cook in these parts. I'd sooner eat her dinners than anyone else's.'

'Difficult, did I say!' Ty grunted. 'Does any man *ever* get to date you?'

'The vet nearly did—once,' she retorted. And oddly, at that shared memory, they both seemed to find it funny—and both grinned.

'Oh, Miss Hawkins,' Ty murmured—which meant nothing, but she thought that perhaps he did quite like her. Then he sobered, and said, 'Actually, Phinn, Ash and I are on our way up to Honeysuckle Farm. Would it be too painful for you to join us?'

After seeing the way Yew Tree Farm had been run last Saturday—the way a farm should be run—Phinn rather thought that to see dilapidated Honeysuckle again would be extremely painful.

'I'd rather not,' she replied quietly, realising that Ash was not the only Allardyce who was sensitive. Ty was sensitive too—in this case to her feelings.

As was proved when he accepted without fuss that she would not visit the farm with them. 'There's every chance that Ash will take over the farm,' he commented.

'I'm sure he'll make a very good job of it,' she replied.

'You don't mind?'

'I'd rather Ash was there than anyone else,' she answered. Ty just stood and looked at her for long, long moments. 'What?' she asked, wondering if she had a smut on her nose.

'D'you know, Phinn Hawkins, you're beautiful inside as well as out?'

Oh, Ty! She wasn't sure that she wasn't going to buckle at the knees, so she turned from him and propped her arms on the fence, looking to where Ruby was happily looking back at her.

'I'm still not going out with you!' she threw over her shoulder—and had to hang firmly on to the rail when Ty did no more than move her bunched hair to one side and planted a warm kiss to the back of her neck—and then departed.

The hours dragged by while Ty was away with Ash, but positively galloped when they came back. And again that Sunday Ty decided to leave it until Monday morning before, extremely early, he left Bishops Thornby for London.

Phinn ached with all she had for him to come back on Monday evening, but it was Wednesday before she saw him again. Ash had gone on his own to spend some more time up at Honeysuckle, and she and Ruby had spent a superb day, with Ruby so much better and the weather perfect.

In fact it was late afternoon when, leaving Ruby in the paddock, Phinn decided to check in the office to see if anything there needed to be attended to. She had her back to the main house and was walking towards the office when she first heard a footfall and then—incredibly—someone behind her calling her name. But not the name she was used to!

'Delphinnium!' The call was soft, the voice male.

She froze. On the instant stood rooted. Then, shocked, she spun swiftly around. There stood Ty, with a grin cracking his face from ear to ear. 'How did you know?' she gasped in amazement. Where had he sprung from? She hadn't heard him arrive!

Ty, enjoying her utter stupefaction, continued to grin. 'I was driving near the church when I saw the vicar,' he answered. 'Very obligingly, he let me look at the baptismal register.'

Starting to recover, she came out fighting. 'If you breathe a word to anyone…' she threatened.

'What's it worth to stay quiet?' Ty asked, not a bit abashed.

But, interested, he enquired, 'Where did you get a name like that anyhow?'

'Blame my father,' she sighed. 'I was supposed to be Elizabeth Maud, only he disobeyed his instructions when he went to register my birth—and thereby guaranteed that his only daughter would remain a spinster throughout the whole of her life.'

'How so?' Ty enquired, looking intrigued.

'With a name like mine, there is absolutely no way,' Phinn began to explain, 'that I'm going to stand up in a white frock in front of any vicar and have my intended roll in the aisle laughing to hear me declare that "I, Delphinnium Hawkins, take you, Joe Bloggs…"'

Ty looked amused, seemed happy to be home, and that gave her joy. 'Your name will be our secret,' he said conspiratorially. And then, while Phinn had drifted off on another front to wonder at the goings-on in this man's clever brain that, when he must have other much more high-powered matters going on in his head, he had paused to check out her name, he was asking, 'Talking of frocks—not necessarily a white one—have you got one?'

'You want to borrow it?' she asked, covering the fact that she was feeling a touch awkward. Was what he was actually saying that he was fed up with seeing her so continually in trousers?

His lips twitched at her retort, but he replied seriously enough. 'Apart from the fact that it's more than high time those fabulous legs had an airing, I've some people coming to dinner on Saturday—a couple of them will be staying overnight.'

'I can have my dinner with Mrs Starkey if—' she began, and saw a sharp look of hostility enter his expression.

'What the blazes are you talking about?' he cut in shortly.

'You won't want me around if you're entertaining,' Phinn tried to explain.

'Give me strength!' Ty muttered. 'If you haven't got it yet, *you*, *Delphinnium* Hawkins, are part of my family now!' he informed her angrily.

'Not the hired help?' Being short-tempered wasn't his prerogative. 'And don't call me Delphinnium!'

'You're asking for trouble!'

'Trouble is my middle name—and nobody asked you to adopt me!'

Ty gave an exasperated sigh. 'Sometimes I don't know whether I should wallop your backside or kiss you until you beg for mercy!' he snarled.

And, having made him so angry, when he had previously looked so happy, Phinn was immediately contrite. 'Don't be cross with me, Ty,' she requested nicely. 'I'm sorry,' she apologised, and, because he did not look ready to easily forgive her, she went closer and stretched up—and kissed him.

She felt his arms come about her. But he held her only loosely, but his anger was nullified. 'Now who's been to charm school?' he asked.

And she grinned. 'For you, I'll come to your table on Saturday. And for you—I'll wear a dress.'

His grey eyes stared down into her blue ones. 'You'd better clear off before I start some kissing of my own,' he growled. But he let her go, and Phinn, her heart drumming, cleared off quickly to the paddock gate.

Ty came home again on Thursday evening, and again on Friday, and by Saturday Phinn knew the names of the two people who would be staying with them overnight. They were brother and sister, Will and Cheryl Wyatt. Cheryl had apparently just sold her apartment and was between accommodation. She was staying with her brother until she found the right property to purchase.

Ruby was off-colour again on Saturday, so Phinn was out of the house with her when the brother and sister arrived, and missed seeing them.

Having gone to her room to clean up, Phinn decided she was in no hurry to go down again—which gave her plenty of time to stand under the shower. She shampooed her hair too, and later, robe-clad and with a towel around her hair, she surveyed her wardrobe. Her dresses were not too plentiful, and were mainly Christmas or birthday presents from her mother. But, again thanks to her mother, what dresses she had were of good quality.

Having surveyed them for long enough, the one that stood out from all the others was a plain heavy silk classic dress in a deep shade of red. She did not own any inexpensive fun jewellery, but felt the low neckline called for something. The dress definitely called for her hair to be other than pulled back in a band or plaited into a braid. And suddenly Phinn started to feel nervous. Which was odd, because she had never felt nervous about meeting new people before!

All the other people expected at dinner, as well as being his friends, were people Ty did business with, and nerves were still attacking as the time neared when she knew she must go downstairs. Standing before the full-length mirror, she surveyed the finished product. Good heavens—was that her?

She felt like herself, but gone was the lean and lanky, perpetually trouser-clad female she was used to. In her place was a tall, slender woman who curved in all the right places.

Her dress was shorter than she remembered—just above the knee. It seemed strange, ages since she had even last seen her knees. Was the neckline too low? Not by today's standards, she knew, but she wasn't used to revealing a bit of cleavage. Perhaps Grandmother Hawkins' pearls—rescued by her mother before her father could sell them—would bring the eye away from her bosom?

Phinn had used only a discreet amount of make-up, but somehow her wide eyes seemed to be much wider. Because there was no way the watch Ty had loaned her went with her outfit, the pearls were her only jewellery.

Her eyes travelled up to her hair, now confined by pins into an elegant twist on the top of her head.

All in all, she did not think she had dressed 'over the top'. She guessed that Ty's friends would be on the sophisticated side, and did not want to let him down. He had more or less asked her to wear a dress, hadn't he? Or—a dreadful thought struck her—had he? Had he just been teasing? They had been talking about 'a frock', hadn't they, when he had asked her if she possessed one?

Had he been joking? He hadn't actually *asked* her to wear a dress, she recalled. Would he be amazed to see her in anything but trousers?

Phinn was just about to make a rapid change into her more usual dinnertime garb when all at once she heard someone tap on her door.

For all of five seconds she was in a fluster. She had no clue who was on the other side of the door, but, glancing at the watch on her bedside table, Phinn saw that it was not yet seven.

She went to the door and opened it the merest trifle. She looked out. Ty stood there. Ty, magnificent in dinner jacket and bow tie. She opened the door wider, feeling better suddenly, with no need to hide what she was wearing. She was glad that Ty had hinted that she might feel more comfortable in a dress. By the look of it, even though it was with friends, tonight's dinner was a semi-formal affair—she would have felt very under-dressed had she stuck to her usual trousers and top.

'Oh, my…!' Ty breathed, his eyes travelling over her as she stood framed in the doorway. 'You look sensational!'

The compliment pleased her, warmed her. 'You're not looking so bad yourself,' she responded, and laughed. She was wearing higher heels than normal, but he still stood above her.

'I feel I should lock you away in a glass case somewhere,' he answered, and—*ooh*, she loved him so.

'That good, eh?' she queried impishly. And in that moment,

for her, there did not seem to be any other people in the world except the two of them.

'Stunning,' he replied. 'I'd like to—' Just then the sound of someone at the door came, and Ty broke off. 'Saved by the bell,' he said humorously. 'Ash will see to it. Actually, Phinn, I notice you aren't wearing a watch. If you feel lost without one, I thought you might agree to borrow this.' And, putting his hand into his dinner jacket pocket, he withdrew the watch he had tried to give her before.

'You were supposed to have taken that back to the jewellers!' she exclaimed.

'I tried. They wouldn't have it,' he lied—quite blatantly.

'Tyrell Allardyce!' she admonished.

'Yes, sweet Delphinnium?' he replied—and she just had to laugh.

She took the watch from him. 'I'll return it to you tomorrow,' she said.

'Agreed,' he answered, without argument.

And she smiled. 'If I wasn't wearing lipstick, I'd kiss you,' she commented.

'Don't let that stop you,' he encouraged.

'I hear voices. I believe your guests are waiting for you.'

'Damn,' he said—and so started the most wonderful evening of her life.

Ty's friends-cum-business associates ranged in age from late twenties to late forties. There were seven of them in all, and Phinn tried to remember their names as the introductions were made—with not one of them questioning who she was and why she was there.

There were ten seated at the large round dinner table. Phinn was seated opposite Ty, which suited her well, because it gave her the opportunity of glancing at him every so often. Funnily enough, it seemed to her that every time she looked across to him that Ty was looking back at her.

She realised then that her imagination must be working overtime, so concentrated on chatting to Will Wyatt, who was around the same age as Ty, and who was seated on her right. She chatted equally to the man on her left, an older man named Kenneth.

In talking to the two men, and feeling quite at ease with them, Phinn discovered that she had more general knowledge than she had realised. She knew that she had her father to thank for that because, aside from taking her to museums and art galleries, it had been her father who had encouraged her to ask questions and form her own opinions. It had been her father with whom she had discussed the merits and de-merits of painters and writers. And it was all there in her head—just waiting to be tapped.

'What do you think of Leonardo?' Kenneth asked at one point.

'A true genius,' Phinn answered, always having much admired Leonardo da Vinci—and then she and Kenneth were in deep discussion for the next ten minutes, until Will Wyatt accused Kenneth of monopolising her.

'I have the advantage of being married—to my good lady here,' Kenneth replied, looking to his wife, who was deep in conversation with the man to the left of her. 'Therefore Phinn is quite safe with me. You, on the other hand, young Will…'

In no time the three of them were laughing. It was then that Phinn happened to glance across to Ty. He was not laughing. He wasn't scowling either. He was just—looking. Feeling all mixed-up inside, Phinn stayed looking at him, her brain seeming to have seized up. Then Cheryl Wyatt, seated to the left of Ty, placed a possessive hand on his arm to draw his attention—and all of a sudden, as Ty glanced to Cheryl and smiled, Phinn was visited by another emotion. An emotion that had visited her briefly once before and was one she did not like. Jealousy.

It was the only small blip of the evening.

Wendy and Valerie, Mrs Starkey's usual helpers in the house, had been roped in to help serve the meal. But when everyone adjourned to the drawing room afterwards, Phinn took off kitchenwards.

She was in the throes of telling Mrs Starkey how well everything had gone when Ty appeared, on the very same errand.

'Thank you, Mrs Starkey. Everything was perfect,' he said, and Mrs Starkey beamed with pride. Phinn guessed she and her staff would be well rewarded for their efforts, and moved towards the kitchen door.

She went out into the hall feeling a touch awkward suddenly. A moment later Ty was joining her, and they were strolling back along the hall.

'I don't want you to think—' she began in a rush, but was stopped when Ty placed a hand on her arm and halted her. 'I—er...' She faltered. He waited, saying nothing, just standing there looking down at her as if he liked looking at her. 'I know—er—I mean I know I'm not the hostess here...'

'A very lovely hostess you would make,' he put in lightly. Which did little to ease her feeling of awkwardness. 'I wanted to thank Mrs Starkey—' She broke off. 'I didn't know if...'

'If I would think to do so?' Ty looked kindly down at her. 'Who else would I expect to do the honours for me, little Phinn, but an adopted member of my family?'

'Oh, Ty,' she said softly, and didn't know just then quite how she felt.

If Ty included her as his family because he felt under some kind of obligation, because through her he still had a brother, then she did not want to be part of his family. If, on the other hand, he regarded her as family because he enjoyed having her under his roof—albeit temporarily—then there was nothing she would like better than to be considered part of his family. But she could never explain that to him—not without the risk of showing him how very much she loved him.

She opted to change tack. 'By the way, I meant to thank *you*. Kit Peverill says you rang him and asked him to forward all the accounts for Ruby's care to you.'

'You've seen Peverill?' Ty asked sharply. 'Has he been here?'

Phinn looked at him, exasperated. 'You're never the same two minutes together!' she erupted. 'Of *course* he's been here. I've an elderly horse. I want a vet who's local—a vet who knows me, who knows Ruby, who I can trust to drop everything but emergencies when I call!' She gave a heated sigh, and, having got that off her chest, an impish look came into her eyes. 'Hmm…Kit said, incidentally, that he hadn't known that *you* were the man I had just started seeing until your call about the account. He rather put two and two together and assumed… Anyhow, at just that point his phone rang with an emergency, and he'd gone before I could tell him differently. Er…'

'There's more?'

'It's just that this is a small village, and while I'm sure Kit won't gossip, he'll only have to say some small thing in passing about me having a boyfriend and it will be all over the place before you can blink.'

Phinn half supposed she'd expected Ty to be cross—for all it was more his doing than hers. But he wasn't cross—not at all. He merely replied equably, 'I reckon my shoulders are broad enough to take it.'

'Fine,' Phinn murmured, and moved on. But when they came to the part of the hall where he would turn into the drawing room to join his guests, she halted briefly to ask, 'Would you mind if I went along to see Ruby?'

'You'll be missed,' Ty replied.

Her heart gave a giddy flip at the ridiculous idea that Ty, personally, would miss her. 'There goes that charm again!' she scorned humorously, and headed for the outside door.

She was not the only one outside, Phinn soon discovered, because she was on her way to the stable when Will Wyatt called out, 'Where are you off to?'

She turned, startled. 'What are you doing out here?' she asked lightly.

'When you disappeared I thought I might as well ease my sorrows with a cigar,' Will replied. 'Wherever you were dashing off to, can I come too?' he asked.

Charm, she rather thought, was catching. 'Do you like horses?'

'Love them!' he said promptly, and as promptly stamped out his cigar.

Ruby had picked up again, but Phinn knew from experience that it did not mean that she would stay up. Phinn introduced her to Will Wyatt, who was lovely and gentle with her, and she warmed to him.

They were still with Ruby when her ears twitched, and a few seconds later Ty appeared, with Cheryl Wyatt in tow. 'Ty thought we'd find you here!' Cheryl exclaimed. But, as if she understood that Ruby had health problems, she was gentle with her too, and Phinn found she liked the other woman—if not the possessive way she was hanging on to Ty's arm.

'We'll leave you to say goodnight to Ruby,' Ty commented, edging Cheryl towards the door, and turning as though waiting for Will to join them.

Will didn't look as if he was likely to take the hint, so it was left to Phinn to look at him and say, as though making a general comment, 'I won't be long.'

They were a good group, Ty's friends, and time flew by until all but Will and Cheryl Wyatt made to depart. Apparently the departing guests all had properties out of London, either in Gloucestershire or one of the neighbouring counties.

Shortly after they had gone, Phinn took a glance to the lovely watch she had on and was amazed to see that it had gone midnight! 'If no one minds, I think I'll go up,' she said, to no one in particular.

'Do you have to?' Will asked.

'I shall be up early in the morning,' she replied, because he was so nice.

'Then so shall I,' he answered.

'Er—good,' she said politely. She would be getting up early to go and check on Ruby; she had no idea what Will intended to do.

By morning she discovered that he did, as he had said, love horses. He came into the stable at six o'clock to see Ruby anyhow. That morning Phinn was dressed in her usual jeans and a tee shirt, with her hair pulled back in a rubber band. It did not seem to put him off.

'Ever get up to London?' he enquired as she got busy with a pitchfork.

'Not usually,' she replied.

'If you fancy it, I'd like to take you to a show. You needn't worry about getting back. You could stay the night.'

Phinn gave him a startled look.

'Cheryl will be there too!' he hurriedly assured her, correctly interpreting Phinn's look. 'I didn't mean…'

Phinn forgave him. She was in the middle of thanking him for his invitation, but refusing, when Ty came in and joined them.

'Couldn't sleep?' he asked his friend Will.

'The bed was bliss,' Will replied. 'I was just asking Phinn to come to a show with me—Phinn could stay overnight with Cheryl and me, and…'

'Phinn wouldn't want to leave Ruby overnight.' Ty refused for her.

'You or Ash could look after her for one night, surely?' Will turned to Ty to protest.

Phinn shook her head. 'Thank you all the same, Will, but no way.'

'Mrs Starkey is making an early breakfast,' Ty cut in, and as Phinn got on with her chores, Will, so not to offend his host or his host's cook, went with him.

Will did not ask her out again, but came to find her when they all decided to go for a long walk—exercise needed after the previous evening's dinner and this morning's full breakfast. 'Do come with us,' he urged. 'Ash tells me there's not a thing about this area that you don't know.'

Perhaps because she fancied a walk, Phinn went with them—though was not too enamoured that more often than not Cheryl appeared to be walking with Ty, as though his partner.

Brother and sister left shortly after lunch, with Will kissing Phinn's cheek and saying he would be in touch. But as soon as Broadlands returned to normal, Phinn went to chat with Ruby.

Nobody wanted very much in the way of food at dinnertime. And with Ty spending time in his study catching up, and Ash in one of the other rooms watching one of his favourite programmes on television, Phinn went first to see Ruby, and then decided to turn in.

She was in her pyjamas, face scrubbed, body showered, hair brushed out of the band it had been in all day, when she remembered the watch. Ty was staying tonight, but would be leaving very early in the morning for London. She was tempted to take it along to his room, but…

But why not? Ty was not averse to popping into her room when he wanted to leave her salary cheque. And anyway, he was in his study downstairs. It would only take but a moment, and she would by far prefer that the expensive watch was in his possession before he went off tomorrow. He was off on his travels again, so heaven only knew when he would be home again.

Not giving herself time to think further, and just in case anyone was about, Phinn threw on a light robe. She was by then aware of which room was Ty's and, picking up the dainty watch, she quickly left her room. At his door, for form's sake, she tapped lightly on the wood paneling, but not waiting for an answer quickly went straight in.

Only to stop dead in her tracks! The light was on, and Ty was not downstairs in his study as she had been so sure he was. Barefooted, his shirt unbuttoned prior to his taking a shower—or whatever was his normal night-time procedure— there he stood.

'I'm sorry—sorry!' Phinn exclaimed, flustered, realising she must have been in her bathroom cleaning her teeth and so had not heard him passing her door. She held out the watch while at the same time wanting to back to the door. 'I thought you were downstairs. Only I—um—wanted this watch in your safekeeping before you left.'

Ty didn't move, and made no attempt to take the watch from her but, as if women entering his bedroom was an everyday event—and she did not want to think about *that*— he invited, 'Come in and talk to me,' doing up a couple of shirt buttons as he spoke. 'I don't bite.' And when she looked at him, a touch startled by his invitation, 'Well, not usually anyway,' he said, the corners of his wonderful mouth picking up.

But Phinn, while she would have liked nothing better than to talk to him, looked down at her thin pyjamas and lightly robed self. 'What do you want to talk about?' she asked. It might be normal for him to chat the night away with women in their night clothes, but it was a first for her.

'Well, you might want to tell me how you enjoyed the weekend, for one thing?' Ty suggested.

'I did,' she replied. Ruby had picked up again, so all was right with her world.

'You liked my friends?'

He asked as if it mattered to him that she should like his friends. That thought warmed her, and Phinn for the moment forgot she was feeling awkward. Since Ty wasn't attempting to take the watch from her, she stepped further into his room and placed it down on top of a mahogany chest of drawers.

'Very much,' she answered. 'Kenneth made me laugh, and I thought his wife, Rosemary, was sweet.'

'You know you were a big hit with them,' he commented, moving casually to close the door.

Phinn looked at him, again startled, as the door closed. 'Er—you're not going to attempt to seduce me, are you?' she asked warily.

Ty burst out laughing, his superb mouth widening. 'What a delight you are!' he remarked, but replied, 'That wasn't my intention, but if you…?' He left the rest of it unsaid, but his mouth was still terrifically curved in a grin. 'I just thought we could have a private moment or two while you let me know what you're going to tell Will Wyatt when he rings.'

'What makes you think he's going to ring?'

'You know he is. He's totally captivated by you.'

She would not have put it as strongly as that. 'He's nice,' she commented.

'You're not going out with him,' Ty stated more than asked.

'As Your Lordship pleases,' she responded, and just had to laugh.

'Are you making fun of me?' Ty asked, coming a dangerous couple of steps nearer.

'Would I dare?' she asked demurely.

'I wouldn't put it past you to dare anything, Phinn Hawkins,' Ty answered. And, when she looked as though she would turn about and go, 'Do you want to go out with him?' he demanded, with no sign of a grin about him now.

It did not take any thinking about. The only man she wanted to go out with was the one standing straight in front of her. 'I'm not going up to London to go out with him, and since I wouldn't want to leave Ruby for more than a couple of hours, I can't see any point in him coming down here to take me out.'

'Which doesn't answer my question.'

'I know,' she replied impishly.

'You *do* know you're likely to drive some man insane?'

'You say the sweetest things.'

Ty looked at her mischievous expression, his glance going down to her uptilted mouth. 'You'd better go!' he said abruptly, and brushed past her as though to go and open the door.

But he did not make it because, her pride rearing at being thrown out—dammit, it was *he* who had asked her to stay!— Phinn at the same time moved smartly to the door. And somehow they managed to collide slap-bang into each other.

Angrily, Phinn put out her arms to save herself, but somehow found that she was holding on to Ty. And Ty, in his efforts for stability, somehow had his hands on her waist. And then, as they looked into each other's eyes, it was as if neither could resist the other.

Ty let out a groan, his words seeming to be dragged from him. 'I want to kiss you.'

Phinn shook her head to say no, but found that the person in charge of her was saying, quite huskily, 'If memory serves, you kiss quite nicely, Tyrell Allardyce…' The rest didn't get said. It was swallowed up as Ty's head came down and his lips met hers.

It was one very satisfying kiss, but at last he raised his head from hers. 'You don't kiss too badly yourself,' he commented softly, looking deeply into her eyes.

'I do my best,' she answered, mock-demurely.

'Want to go for seconds?' he questioned lightly, and, while she was unsure what Ty meant by that, what she did know was that to be in his arms was pure and utter bliss and she never wanted it to stop.

Unsure what to answer, Phinn followed her instincts and

stretched up and kissed him. And that was all the answer he needed because, lightly at first, Ty was returning that kiss, and bliss just did not begin to cover it. Her heart rejoiced to be this close to him, to be held in those firm arms.

Her arms went around him and as he held her so she held him. She could feel his body through her thin clothing and loved the closeness with him. Yet even as Ty ignited a fire in her, she found she wanted to get yet closer.

She felt his hand at the back of her head, his lips leaving hers as he buried his face in her long, luxurious strawberry-blonde hair. And then his lips were finding hers again—and she knew that as she wanted him, so Ty wanted her.

With his arms around her, he pulled her to him. 'Sweet darling,' he murmured, and she was in a mindless world where she *was* his sweet darling.

For how long they stood, delighting in each other's kisses, Phinn had no idea, but only knew that she was with him wherever he led.

A small spasm of nervousness attacked her, nevertheless, when, compliant in his arms, she let Ty move with her to the inviting king-size bed. But, incredibly, he seemed to notice her hesitation, for, with his arms still around her, he paused and looked down into her slightly flushed face.

'Everything right with you?' he asked tenderly—and she was utterly enchanted.

She looked tenderly back and found her husky voice to say, 'Oh, yes,' and to add, 'But I do believe you *are* seducing me.'

Ty smiled into her eyes. 'Believe?' he echoed. 'Don't you know?'

She smiled back. She loved him. What else mattered? She wondered if she should tell him that she had never been this way with a man before, but did not want him to think her a fool, so instead she kissed him. And Ty needed no further encouragement.

Phinn was enraptured when he undid her robe and slid it from her shoulders. And she loved, adored him when, once she was clad only in her pyjama shorts and a thin-strapped pyjama top, his eyes travelled down over her.

Ty took her in his arms once more, and then she realised that they had been merely skating around the preliminaries, because with a gradually increasing passion Ty was teaching her what lovemaking was all about.

She felt his warm hands come beneath her thin top, felt those hands warm on the skin of her spine, and was drowning at his every spine-tingling touch.

When those same hands moved to the front of her and, seeking ever upwards, he at last captured her breasts, her cry of sweet rapture mingled with his groan of wanting.

He kissed her, moulding and caressing her breasts as his kiss deepened. But, as if tormented beyond reason at the sight of her, as if tormented to uncover the splendour in his hold, Ty pulled back. 'I want to see you,' he breathed.

Phinn swallowed hard to hide her shyness. 'I want to see you too,' she murmured huskily, and got her wish when, unhurriedly, Ty removed his shirt.

His chest was magnificent and she stared in wonder before leaning forward and placing a kiss there. And she was delighted when, as she leaned forward, Ty pulled her top over her head. Then, as she stood before him, her top half uncovered, he pulled back to study her. 'Oh, my sweet one,' he said softly, as he surveyed her creamy swelling full breasts with their hardened pink tips. 'You are totally exquisite.' And he took first one hardened pink peak into his mouth, then released it to taste the sweetness of the other.

Phinn swallowed hard when his hands went to the waistband of his trousers, and buried her face in his shoulders. Then she knew more bliss—utter bliss—when they stood thigh to thigh. His hands at her back, he caressed unhurriedly downwards.

His body was a delight to her, 'Oh, Ty,' she cried. 'I want you so much.'

'And I you, sweet darling,' he murmured, and moved with her as though to take her to lie down on the bed with him.

But while Phinn was unaware that she had made any slight movement of hesitation, Ty seemed to sense one. Because he paused, his glance gentle on her. Just that—no movement. Just waiting. If she had any objection to make, now—even at this late stage—was the time to state it.

And, looking at him, Phinn almost told him that she loved him, but somehow felt that that was not what he would want to hear. So instead, foolish or not, she realised that in all fairness she ought to say something.

'Er...' she began hesitantly. 'I'm, er—a bit...'

The words seemed to stick in her throat, but Ty wasn't going anywhere. With his warm hands still holding her, he said gently, 'You want to make love with me, but you're a bit...?' And, as if he simply could not resist her gorgeous breasts, he bent to kiss them.

'Well...' She took a steadying breath as he pulled back to look at her. 'Have you any idea what you're doing to me?' she asked, side-tracked, the feel of his mouth at her breast still with her.

'If it's anything similar to what you're doing to me, I'd say it's pretty dynamic,' he answered, and smiled, and kissed her—but made no move to lie down with her. 'You're a bit—what?' he prompted gently again.

'Well, the thing is—I'm not at all sure how these things go...but I—er...'

'Tell me, sweet love,' he invited, when she got stuck again.

And suddenly she wanted it all said and done quickly. 'The thing is...' she began in a rush, then halted, got her second wind, and rushed on again. 'Well, I feel a bit of a fool because I've no idea whether you need to know to not but...' Oh, heavens, so intimate, half undressed, nearly completely undressed, and still those private words would not come! That was until, totally impatient with herself, she burst out, 'I've no idea if you need to know that I've never—um—been this f-far before.'

On the instant Ty stilled, his expression changing from that of a tender ardent lover to disbelief at what it sounded as if she was saying. Then his look changed to one of utter astonishment as it started to quickly sink in, and from astonishment to a look of being completely shaken.

Ty was stern faced as he gripped hard on to her naked shoulders. 'Just what, exactly,' he urged—a little hoarsely, she thought, 'are you saying?'

'Well, I wasn't sure... That is, I don't know if I'm supposed to say, or if it's all right for you to just—er—find out, but...'

'Oh, my God!' He was incredulous. 'You're a virgin!' He seemed stunned.

'Does it matter?' she asked, feeling more than a touch bewildered—and heard Ty take what she assumed to be a long-drawn steadying breath.

'Right at this moment,' he commented tautly, 'I want you more than you can know.' His glance moved down to her breasts and he gave a groan as he ordered, 'For sanity's sake, cover yourself up!' And when Phinn, more than a little confused at what he was saying, was not quick enough, he swiftly picked up her thin robe from the carpet and as quickly wrapped it around her. Then, running a fevered hand across his forehead, he said, 'I want you, Phinn. Don't mistake that. But I need space to try and think straight.'

Phinn stared at him. She felt even more unsure, which made her feel nervous—and a fool. And a split second later she knew, while the rest of her brain was just so much of a mish-mash, that the moment was lost! Knew with crystal clarity that she was never ever going to know the full joy of sharing her body with Ty, the man she loved.

And in the next split second, while everything in her still cried out for her to be his, her pride began to stir. And as her pride started to surge upwards because Ty needed to *think* whether to reject her *or not*—so her pride took off and rocketed into orbit. *Reject her!* 'Take all the time and space you need,' she exploded furiously—damn it, her voice was still husky. 'I'm leaving.'

'Phinn, don't—' Ty tried to get in.

'I won't!' she hurled at him, and was already on her way. 'Trust me—I won't.'

CHAPTER EIGHT

THE hours until dawn were long and painful. Ty might have said that he wanted her and not to make any mistake about that. But that he'd had to *think* about it showed that he could not have wanted her as much as he had said he did.

Her watch—his watch—showed it was just before four when Phinn heard the faint sound of Ty leaving the house. She wanted to leave too, and never to come back.

She had told him she had wanted him. For heaven's sake, what more proof did he need that she was his for the taking? She had stood—she blushed—semi-naked in front of him. And he—he had rejected her!

In fear and mortification that Ty might have seen that she loved him, that she had given away her feelings for him, Phinn wanted to run and hide. To run and hide and never to have to see him again. But she could not leave—there was Ruby.

Phinn spent many countless, useless minutes in wondering what, if anything, Ty thought about her. But in the end, with more scorched cheeks, she realised that from his point of view making love with her did not have to mean that he cared anything about her at all. Given that once the kissing had started they had soon established there was a certain chemistry between them, from Ty's point of view it did not have to mean a thing.

Nursing sore wounds, Phinn showered and dressed early and went to see Ruby. Phinn had sometimes wondered through Ruby's various bouts of illness if, for Ruby's sake, she was wrong not to have her put down. But as she spoke gently to her that morning, and Ruby nuzzled into her, Phinn knew that she could never do that.

That Monday was a busy day for phone calls. Her mother rang, and Phinn again promised to try to go and see her soon. And Will Wyatt rang, asking her not to forget him and telling her that he was working on a plan to get Ty to invite him for a long weekend soon.

In a weak moment Phinn wondered if Ty would ring. But that was fantasy, for he never did. And why would he, for goodness' sake? He lived in a fast-paced sophisticated environment, where sophisticated women abounded. He hadn't the time nor the inclination—obviously—to bring a 'village local' virgin up to speed.

Realising she was in danger of letting what was now firmly fixed in her head as Ty's rejection of her sour her outlook, Phinn turned her back on the memory of Ty's unbelievable tenderness and his heady passion with her, and concentrated on why she was there.

'Where are you off to, Ash?' she asked him, when she saw him setting off across the fields. He was so much better now than he had been, so much brighter all round, that she had begun to feel that her role in watching him was now more or less redundant. But Ty was paying her to be Ash's companion, and whatever feelings went on in her head about Ty, a job was a job.

'I thought I'd stretch my legs and think about farming matters.'

'Shall I come with you?'

That was Monday.

On Tuesday, with Ruby once more in fine fettle, Phinn again latched on to Ash when he said he was going up to

Honeysuckle Farm with a view to checking out some improvements he wanted to make. By then, with Ty so constantly in her head, her aversion to going to the neglected farm where she had been brought up seemed to be secondary.

Bearing in mind she was being well paid to keep Ash company, when she saw him making for the pick-up on Wednesday, she went over to him. But before she could open her mouth to invite herself to go along too, wherever he was going, Ash beat her to it.

'Phinn—dear Phinn,' he began sensitively, 'as my honorary sister, I love you dearly. But would you mind if just this once I went out on my own?'

Phinn looked at him. He had put on weight, the dark shadows had gone from beneath his eyes, and he was a world away from the wretched, heartsore man she had known a couple of months ago.

She was not in the least offended, and grinned at him as she replied, 'Depends where you're going.'

For a moment or two he looked as though he wasn't going to tell her. But then—just a touch sheepishly, Phinn thought—he answered, 'If you must know, I thought I'd meander over to Geraldine Walton's place and see how she feels about having dinner with me on Saturday night.'

Phinn just beamed at him. 'Oh, Ash. I couldn't be more pleased!' she exclaimed.

'She hasn't said yes yet!'

She would, Phinn knew it. 'Best of luck,' she bade him, and went to chat to Ruby.

By the look of it, her work at Broadlands was done—and that was worrying. Matters financial were crowding in on her, but Phinn could not see how she could continue to take a salary from Ty when she wasn't doing anything.

By afternoon, however, Phinn had something more to worry about. Ruby had stopped eating. Trying not to panic, Phinn rang Kit Peverill, who was out at one of the neighbouring farms but said he would call in on his way back. Which he did.

'Doesn't look too good, Phinn,' he said, after examining Ruby.

Phinn's low spirits dropped to zero. She clenched her jaw as tears threatened. 'Is she in pain?'

'I'll give her an injection to make her comfortable,' he replied. 'It should last her a couple of days, but call me sooner if you need to.'

Phinn thanked him, and as he went down the drive she saw Ash returning in the pick-up. 'How did it go?' she asked Ash, but had no need to. The smile on his face said it all.

'As you yourself have discovered—who could resist the Allardyce charm?' He grinned.

Who, indeed? But she had other matters on her mind just then. 'Was that the vet's Land Rover I passed in the drive?'

'Ruby's not so good.'

Sympathetically, Ash went back with her to see Ruby, who seemed to Phinn to be losing ground by the hour. Phinn had no appetite either, and spent the rest of the day with Ruby, only leaving when Ash came and said that Mrs Starkey was preparing a tray for her.

'I'll come in,' Phinn told him. No way could she eat in front of the sick mare.

Ash, Phinn discovered, had turned into her minder. He took turns with her in staying with Ruby. And, because Ruby had taken to Ash, with his gentle way of talking to her, Phinn left Ruby with him when she needed to shower, or to try to get down the sandwich Mrs Starkey had provided for her.

Phinn called in Kit Peverill again on Thursday—his expression told her what Phinn would not ask.

Phinn stayed with Ruby the whole of Thursday night. Ruby died on Friday morning. Phinn did not know how she would bear it—but Ash was marvellous.

Ash might not have been at his best in an office environment, but when Ruby died he more than showed his worth. As Ruby went down, Ash took charge. And Phinn was never more grateful.

'I'll go and phone the vet and make all the other necessary phone calls while you say goodbye to her, darling,' he said gently. 'Leave everything to me.' With that, he left the stable.

An hour later Phinn left Ruby. She saw Ash without actually seeing him, and, her face drained of colour, went walking.

For how long she walked over land that she had once ridden over with Ruby, she had no idea. She was miles from the house when she came to a spot where she and Ruby had unexpectedly come across a recently fallen tree trunk. She could feel Ruby's joy as they had sailed right over it even now. Ruby was not a jumper, and they had both been exhilarated. Ruby had given her a look that Phinn would have sworn said, *Hey—did you see me do that?*

When Phinn returned to the stable, hours later, the vet had been and gone—and so too was Ruby gone. The stable doors were open, the stable cleaned and hosed down by Ash, and Ash was coming over to her.

'They took her as gently as they could,' he promised. 'I've arranged to collect her ashes—I thought you might want to scatter them over her favourite places.' And, looking into her face, 'You look tired,' he observed. 'Come on, Mrs Starkey's got some of your favourite soup waiting for you.'

More or less on automatic pilot, Phinn went and had some soup, was fussed over by Mrs Starkey, and told to go and rest by Ash. Phinn felt too numbed to argue, and went and lay on her bed.

She thought she might have slept for a while, but she felt lifeless when she awakened. She took a shower and changed into fresh trousers and a shirt. She felt a need to do something, but had no idea what.

Brushing her hair, she pulled it back in a band and went outside. She did not want to go into the stable, but found her feet taking her there. It was where Ash found her some ten minutes later.

Leaving the stable together, they walked out into the late-afternoon sun. 'I don't know of anything that's going to make you feel any better, Phinn, but if you want me to come walking with you, want me to drive you anywhere, or if you'd like me to take you out somewhere for a meal, you've only to say.'

Phinn had held back tears all day, but as she turned to him her bottom lip trembled and she knew that she was close to breaking. 'Oh, Ash,' she mumbled, and liked him so much, felt true affection for him, when, placing a gentle arm around her, he gave her a hug. Needing his strength for just a brief moment, Phinn held on to him.

It *was* only a brief moment, however, because suddenly she became aware that there was a car parked in front of the house—a car she had not heard pull up.

It was Ty's car, and he was standing next to it, looking their way. Ash had not seen him, but Phinn could not miss the fact that Ty was positively glaring at her! Even from that distance there was no chance of missing that he was furious about something. Something so blisteringly anger-making that a moment later, as if he did not trust himself, Ty had swung abruptly to his right and gone striding indoors.

So much for her wondering, as she had so often since last Sunday, how she was ever going to face him again. Forget tenderness, forget gentleness—Ty had looked as though he could cheerfully throttle her!

With a shaky sigh, Phinn stepped out of Ash's hold. 'You've been a gem today, Ash,' she said softly. 'I'll never forget it.'

'I'm here for you, love,' he said, but let her go when she pulled out of his hold. 'I'm going to the office. Want to come?'

Phinn shook her head. She felt lost, and didn't know where she wanted to go. But the sanctuary of her room was as good a place as any.

Before she could get there, however, she had to run the gauntlet of one very thunderous-looking Tyrell Allardyce. She had hoped he might be in the drawing room, his own room or his study, and that she might be able to reach her room without seeing him.

So much for hope! Phinn had barely stepped into the hall when Ty, as if waiting for her, appeared from his study. His demeanour had not sweetened any, she noted. As was proved when, looking more hostile than she had ever seen him, 'In my study—*now*!' he snarled.

Go to blazes and take your orders with you, sprang to her mind. But, since he was obviously stewed up about something— forget 'sweet darling'—she'd better go and get it over with.

Phinn walked towards him, past him and into his study. But she had hardly turned before he had slammed the door shut and was demanding explosively, 'Just what the hell sort of game do you think you're playing?'

Phinn sighed. She really did not need this. Yet how dear he was to her. She wanted to hate him. But, furious with her or tender with her, she loved him in all his moods.

'I'm—not with you,' she replied quietly.

'Like hell you're not! How long's it been going on?'

She still wasn't with him. 'How long has what been going on?'

Ty gave her a murderous impatient look. 'Naïve you might be, but you're not *that* naïve,' he roared, and Phinn, having been spent all day, started to get angry.

'Don't throw that back at me!' she erupted, warm colour rushing to her face at his reference to her having disclosed to him, in a very private moment, that she was inexperienced.

'I'll do whatever I like!' Ty fired back. 'You're here to

look after my brother, not to try and send him down the same downward spiralling road your cousin did!'

'That's most unfair!' Phinn charged hotly.

'Is it?' he challenged, with no let up in his fury. 'What's your plan? To trot into his bedroom one night when he's half undressed and have a crack at losing your virginity with him too?'

Crack was the operative word. Without being aware of what she was doing, but incensed and in sudden fury that Ty could so carelessly demean something that had been so very special to her, infuriated beyond bearing that he could say such a thing, Phinn hit him! She had never hit anybody in her life. But all her strength went into that blow.

The sound of her hand across Ty's cheek was still in the air when Phinn came to her senses. She did not know then who was the more appalled—her or Ty. He by what, in his fury, he had just said—she by what, in her fury, she had just done. Either way, it was clear, as he stared dumbfounded at her, that no female had ever hit him before.

Phinn felt absolutely thunderstruck herself as she stared at the red mark she had created on the side of his face. 'Oh, Ty,' she mourned, tears spurting to her eyes, a tender, remorseful hand going up to that red mark. 'I'm so sorry.' Still Ty looked at her, as if speechless. 'I'm—a bit upset,' she understated.

'*You're* upset!' he exclaimed.

'Ruby...' she managed, and knew then that the floodgates she had kept determinedly closed all day were about to break open.

'Ruby?' Ty questioned, his senses alert, his tone softening.

Had he stayed furious with her, nasty with her, Phinn reckoned she might have been able to hang on until she reached her room. But when Ty, who obviously didn't know about Ruby but had sensed all was not well with her, started to show a hint of sympathy, Phinn lost it. She made a dive for the door, but before she could escape Ty had caught a hold of her.

'Ruby?' he repeated.

'Ruby…' The words would not come. Tears were already falling when she at last managed, 'Ruby—she died today.'

'Oh, sweetheart!' In the next instant Ty had taken her in his arms and was holding her close up to him—and Phinn's heart broke.

Sobs racked her as Ty held her close. He held her and stroked her hair, doing his best to comfort her as tears and sobs she could not control shook her. Having held her emotions in check all day, it seemed that now she had given way she was unable to stop.

Ty was still holding her firm when she at last managed to gain some semblance of control. 'I'm—s-sorry,' she apologised, and attempted to pull away from him. His answer was to hold her more tightly to him. 'I'm sorry,' she repeated. 'I—haven't cried all day.'

'I'm sorry too,' he murmured soothingly. 'And I'm glad I was here when you finally let go the grip on your emotions.'

Phinn took a shaky breath that still had a touch of a sob to it. 'Ash has been marvelous,' she felt she should tell him. 'He saw to everything for me.'

'When he's on form he's good in a crisis,' Ty agreed.

'I'm all right now,' Phinn said, trying to shrug out of his comforting hold.

'You're sure?'

She nodded, wanting to stay exactly where she was. 'I look a mess,' she mumbled.

'You look lovely,' he answered, taking out a handkerchief and gently mopping her eyes, now red from weeping.

'You're a shocking liar,' Phinn attempted, and took a small step backwards.

Ty, still holding her, looked down into her unhappy face. And, oddly, it seemed the most natural thing in the world that they should gently kiss. Phinn took another step back and Ty, as if reluctantly, let her go. Phinn left his study to go up to her room.

It was not the end of her tears. Tears came when she least expected them.

Not wanting to break down again, should tears appear unexpectedly at the dinner table, Phinn went to tell Mrs Starkey not to make dinner for her and say that if anyone asked she had gone to bed.

'Can I make you an omelette, or something light like that, Phinn?' Mrs Starkey asked.

But Phinn shook her head. 'That's very kind of you, Mrs Starkey, but I'm not hungry. I'll just go and catch up on some sleep.'

In actual fact Phinn slept better than she had anticipated. Though she was awake for a long while, and heard first Ash come to bed and then, later, Ty. She didn't know how she knew the difference in the two footfalls, she just did.

She tensed when Ty seemed to halt outside her bedroom door, but she knew that he would not come in. After last Sunday bedrooms were sacrosanct. That was to say she knew she would never again trespass into his bedroom. By the same token—remembering that chemistry between them—Ty was giving *her* bedroom a wide berth.

Having awakened early, at her usual time, Phinn felt tears again spring to her eyes when, throwing back the covers, she realised that there was nothing—no darling Ruby—to dash out of bed for.

Phinn dried her eyes and pulled the covers back over her, and thought back to yesterday. Not Ruby dying—that would live with her for ever. And, while she would always remember her gentle, timid Ruby, Phinn did not want to dwell on her dying. Instead she thought of happier times. Times when she and Ruby had galloped all over Broadlands, the wind in her hair, Ruby as delighted as Phinn.

Fleabitten old nag indeed! But now Phinn was able to smile at the memory. Ty had been pretty wonderful in finding a stable to make Ruby's last days comfortable.

He had been pretty wonderful to her too, when he had come home yesterday, Phinn considered, remembering how he had cradled her to him as she had wept all over him. He had mopped her up and…

And she had hit him, Phinn recalled. Not a tap, but a full-on whack! Oh, how could she? But she wasn't going to think about unpleasant things. She had been down in the pits yesterday and, while she knew she would not get over Ruby in a hurry, Phinn also knew, remembering the dark pit she had descended into when her father had died, that it would get better.

Meantime…Phinn was just thinking that she might as well get up after all when someone knocked lightly on her door and Ash, bearing a tray, came in.

'Mrs Starkey thought you might like breakfast in bed. I told her I'd bring it up and see how you were.'

'Oh, Ash,' Phinn protested, sitting up and bringing the bedclothes over her chest. 'Everybody's being so kind.'

'You deserve it,' he replied, and asked, 'Here or on the table?'

'Table,' she answered, thinking, as Ash placed the breakfast tray down on Grandmother Hawkins' table, that she would sit out as soon as he had gone and eat what she could.

'How are you this morning?' Ash asked as he turned back to her.

'Better,' she said.

'Good. I'll leave you to your scrambled egg before it gets cold,' he added, and on impulse bent down and kissed her cheek.

He meant nothing by it other than empathy with the circumstances of her losing her best friend. But the man who had suddenly appeared in the doorway to the side of him did not appear to share the same empathy.

'*Ash!*' he said sharply to his brother.

Phinn looked from one to the other. Never had she known Ty to speak so sharply to him. But, while she was wondering if the two brothers—whom she knew thought the world of each other—were on the point of having a row, Ash did no more than grin at her and say pleasantly, 'Ty,' to his brother.

As Ty stepped into the room, Ash stepped out and closed the door.

'Does Ash usually bring you breakfast in bed?' Ty demanded.

'*Now* what have I done?'

'Apart from showing too much cleavage?' Ty snarled.

Phinn glanced down to where the covers had just a second ago slipped down. Her barely pyjama-top-covered breasts were now on view. 'Had I known I was receiving visitors I'd have worn an overcoat!' she flared, quickly covering herself.

Ty did not care for her sarcasm. That much was plain. 'You're quite obviously feeling better this morning!' he rapped.

Phinn was fed up with him. 'You're never the same two minutes together!' she accused hotly, remembering the way he had tenderly dried her eyes in his study yesterday. 'Is there a purpose to your visit?' she demanded hostilely.

'Not the same as my brother's, clearly!'

'As you once mentioned, Ash has a sensitive side. He brought me breakfast for Mrs Starkey and stayed to ask how I was feeling.'

Ty was unimpressed. 'You just leave him alone!' he ordered.

'Leave him alone?' she echoed.

'I don't want to pick up the pieces when another Hawkins does the dirty on him!'

Phinn stared at Ty in disbelief. Was that what he thought of her? She took a hard pull of breath—that or weep that Ty could say such a thing to her. 'Close the door on your way out!' she ordered imperiously—and, oh, heavens, that was it!

She knew she had angered him when his expression

darkened—and that was before he strode over to the bed. 'I'll go when I'm ready!' he barked, standing threateningly over her.

But in Phinn's view she did not have to sit there and take any more. In a flash she was out of bed and snatching up her robe from the end of it as she went.

'Stay as long as you like!' she snapped. 'I'm off to take a shower.'

Wrong! 'You don't care who you hurt, do you?' Ty snarled, whipping the robe away from her and spinning her round to face him.

Hurt? Him? Hardly likely. He must be referring to Ash. 'You've got a short memory!' she erupted. What had happened to *you're so good with him*?

'Not as short as yours!' Ty grated, and with that he caught a hold of her and pulled her into his arms. 'Less than a week ago you were mine for the taking!' he hurled at her vitriolically. 'Let me remind you!' And, without waiting for permission, he hauled her pyjama-clad body up against him. The next Phinn knew, his mouth was over hers. Not tenderly, not gently, but punishingly, angrily, furiously—and she hated him.

'Let me go!' she hissed, when briefly his mouth left her.

'Like hell,' he scorned, and clamped his lips over hers again. And while holding her in one arm, his other hand pushed the thin straps of her pyjamas vest to one side.

Then his lips were seeking her throat; his hands were in her long flowing hair as he held her still. 'No,' she protested—he took no notice. She pushed at him—that did no good either and in fact only seemed to provoke him further, because his hand left her hair, but only to capture her left breast. 'Don't!' she cried. She ached for his kisses, but not like this.

Ty ignored her 'Don't' but as if enflamed by the feel of her lovely breast in his hold, the next she knew her vest pyjamas top was pulled down about her waist and her pink-tipped breasts were uncovered and Ty was staring at her full creamy breasts as though mesmerised.

He stretched out a hand as though to touch one of those pink peaks and Phinn could not take any more.

'No, Ty,' she cried brokenly. 'Not like this.'

She thought he was going to ignore her, but then it was as though something in her tone had got through to him. Got through to this man who liked to keep his sensitivity well hidden. Because Ty pulled his hand back and stared at her, at the shine of unshed tears in her eyes. And some of his colour seemed to ebb away.

'Oh, God!' was wrenched from him on a strangled kind of sound, and in the next moment he had stepped away from her. A split second later, as if the very hounds of hell were after him, Ty abruptly spun away from her and went striding from the room.

It was the end, and Phinn knew that it was. She had no idea what had driven the civilised man she knew him to be to act in the way he had, and, while she might forgive him, she had an idea—with that agonised *Oh, God!* still ringing in her ears—that it would be a long while before he would be able to forgive himself.

And all, she knew, because of Ash. Ty had been rough on her when he had first known her on account of his protectiveness of Ash. But she had thought Ty had learned that she would never hurt his brother. But, no. Despite what had taken place between her and Ty previously, he had twice witnessed what he had thought to be a tender scene between her and Ash—yesterday, when he had arrived home and had seen Ash with an arm around her, and just now, when he had been passing her open door and had spotted Ash kissing her cheek on an impulse of the moment. As he had said, he feared that another Hawkins would 'do the dirty' on Ash again.

Feeling defeated suddenly, Phinn knew that she was leaving. What was there to stay for? By the look of it, Ty would clap his hands when she went. As he had said himself, when Ash was on form he was good in a crisis. Which meant that since Ash had taken over yesterday, when Ruby had died—tears sprang to her eyes again—Ash was back to his old self and was no longer in need of a companion.

With her appetite gone, Phinn ignored the breakfast tray that Mrs Starkey had so kindly prepared and went and took a shower.

She had almost completed her packing when she heard the sound of a car engine. She went to the window and was in time to see Ty's car being driven out of the gates at the bottom of the drive.

Pain seared her that she would never see Ty again. Not that she had anything that she particularly wanted to say to him, but... Perhaps it was just as well that she left before he got back.

Ten minutes later, acknowledging that she could not take all her luggage with her—not without transport—Phinn remembered how yesterday Ash had offered to drive her anywhere she wanted to go.

Phinn cancelled that thought when she realised that with Ty being so anti he would just love it when he got back to learn that she had made use of Ash to take her and her belongings to Gloucester.

She had no idea how her mother would take her arriving on her doorstep and asking to stay until she had found other accommodation, but, since her mother had stated more than once that she would like her to live with her and Clive, Phinn didn't think she would have any major objection.

Knowing that her mother would most likely cancel her golfing arrangements if she rang her and asked her to come and pick her up, Phinn opted to ring Mickie Yates.

Disappointingly, he was not answering his phone. She

gathered he must be off somewhere on one of his various pursuits. She did think of asking Jimmie Starkey to take her, but that did not seem fair somehow. He was a hard worker, like his wife, and had earned a weekend to himself.

In the end she knew that she would have to try and make it to Gloucester by bus—if buses in Bishops Thornby still ran on a Saturday. Phinn would contact Mickie at some other time to collect the remainder of her belongings for her.

She left the watch Ty had loaned her on her grandmother's table. She gave a shaky sigh as she recalled Ty's kindness in bringing that familiar table up to her room so she should feel more at home. Then, with a last look around her room, she determinedly picked up one suitcase and left her room.

It was with a very heavy heart that she descended the stairs, but she tried to cheer herself up by reminding herself that her stay had only been going to be temporary anyway.

She had just reached the bottom stair, however, and hefted her case down into the hall, when a sound to her left made her jerk her head that way.

Ty! Colour—hot colour—seared her skin. She had thought he had gone out, and that she would never see him again! But her high colour came from remembering that awful scene in her bedroom earlier. 'I thought I saw you driving your car down the drive!' she said witlessly.

He ignored her comment, his eyes glinting when he could not avoid seeing she had luggage. 'Where do you think you're going with that case?' he demanded shortly.

'I'm leaving,' Phinn replied—and waited for his applause.

It did not come. What came was Ty striding forward and hefting her case up and away from her. 'We'll see about that!' he grated, and, leaving her to follow, her suitcase in his grip, he strode from her in the direction of the drawing room.

Phinn hesitated for a second or two, torn between a need to go and—oh—such a hungry yearning need to stay. Her need to stay—if only for a minute or two longer, while Ty presumably sorted her out about something—won.

'As long as you intend to keep your hands to yourself!' she called after him spiritedly, that lippy part of her refusing to die, no matter what.

A moment later she followed. She was unsure what Ty intended to have a go at her about now. All she hoped was that she would be able to get out of there without hitting him again or with her pride intact—preferably both.

CHAPTER NINE

TY HAD not cooled down at all, Phinn observed when she entered the drawing room. Her case was on the floor a yard from him, and he had his back to her, but his expression when he turned to survey her standing there was most definitely hostile.

'You want me to apologise?' he queried, his tone quiet. But hostility was still there lurking, Phinn felt sure.

She shrugged her shoulders. 'Suit yourself,' she replied, and saw that her remark had not sweetened him any.

He walked by her to firmly close the drawing room door, then came back to stand in front of her. And off on some other tack, he demanded, 'Where do you think you're going?'

'Not that it's any business of yours, but—'

'Not my business?' he echoed. 'You waltz in here, disrupt the whole household, and—'

'Now, just a minute!' Love him she might, but she didn't have to take his false accusations. 'For a start, *you* invited me here. Yes, I know I've had an easy ride of it…' Oh, damn. Those tears again, as a fleeting memory of her riding Ruby got to her. She looked down at the carpet while she gathered herself together.

But suddenly Ty had come closer, hostility forgotten. 'Oh, Phinn,' he murmured softly. 'My timing is, as ever, all to pieces where you're concerned. You are grieving for Ruby, and all I'm doing if giving you more grief.'

'Don't be nice to me!' Phinn cried agitatedly. 'When you're wearing your hard-as-blazes hat I can cope, but…'

'But not when I go soft on you?' he queried. 'I shall have to remember that,' he commented—a touch obscurely, Phinn felt, since after today she would not be seeing him again.

'Look, I have to go. I've—er—got a bus to catch.'

'Bus!' He looked scandalised, and let her know how he felt about that in no uncertain tone. 'You can forget that, Phinn Hawkins!' he told her bluntly.

'Ty, please. Look…'

'No, *you* look. I know this isn't the best of times for you. And I know you've had almost a year of one upset after another. And I so admire the way you have battled on. But, at the risk of upsetting you further, I'm afraid I cannot let you leave until we've talked our—problem through. And, whatever happens, you are certainly not going anywhere with that case by bus.'

'I'm—not?' What was there to talk about? Oh, heavens—had he seen her love for him and considered that a 'problem' to be talked through? No way was she talking *that* problem through!

'If you're still set on leaving after—' He broke off, then resumed steadily, 'I'll take you anywhere you want to go. But first come and sit down. I'll get Mrs Starkey to bring us some coffee.'

'I don't want coffee—er—thank you,' Phinn refused primly.

She wasn't sure that she wanted to sit down either. But, taking the chair furthest away from the one she thought he would use, she went and sat. Only to find that Ty, as if wanting to be able to read her expression, had pulled up a chair close by.

'I'm aware I'm in your debt,' she said in a rush. She did not want him reading any unwary, unguarded look in her eyes or face, no matter how fleeting. He was as sharp as a tack was

Ty Allardyce. 'But I intend to get a job. Obviously I'll settle my debt with you as soon as—'

'For God's sake!' Ty burst in. 'Don't you know, after what you did for Ash, that I shall be forever in *your* debt?'

'This is about money. I don't like owing money,' Phinn retaliated, shrugging his comment away. 'Circumstances have caused me to accept you paying the vet...' She bit her lip. Darling Ruby again. 'Look, Ty,' she said abruptly, 'I know that you don't approve of my—er—friendship with Ash. That you fear I might hurt him. But I never would. Trust me, I never would. Apart from Ash not being interested in me in that sort of way—romantically, I mean—I'm not like my cousin...'

'Ash isn't interested in you that way?' Ty immediately took up. And was at his belligerent best, when he barked, 'You could have fooled me!'

'Why? Because you saw him with a sympathetic arm around me yesterday? He's sensitive. You know he is. He guessed I'd got Ruby on my mind this morning—and kissed my cheek in the empathy of the moment.'

'He doesn't normally go around kissing you?'

For heaven's sake! 'He leaves that to you!' Phinn snapped, then realised she did not want to remind him of how he had kissed her before—apart from earlier—and her willingness in that department. 'Look,' she rushed on, starting to feel exasperated, 'I know all this fuss is solely about your protection of Ash, and your fear I'm another avaricious Hawkins ready to hurt him, but I promise you the only way I can hurt him is in the way a sister might unthinkingly hurt her brother.'

Ty's eyebrows shot up. 'You see Ash in a *sisterly* light?' he challenged sceptically, everything about him saying that he did not believe a word of it. And that annoyed her.

'Of course I do! The same way that Ash thinks of me as his honorary sister!'

'He thinks of you as his *sister*?' Ty's disbelief was rife.

'Don't you two ever talk to each other?' Phinn exclaimed.

'Apparently not. Not about our deepest emotions, obviously.'

Phinn guessed it was a 'man thing', because never had she known two brothers so close.

'What makes you so sure that Ash regards you only as a brother would?' Ty challenged.

'Oh, Ty, stop worrying,' Phinn said softly, knowing all Ty's concern was for his brother. 'Ash actually said so one day this week. Besides, Ash has someone new on his mind.'

Ty's head jerked back in surprise. 'You're saying he's interested in somebody else?' he asked, but was soon again looking as though he did not believe it for a moment. 'He didn't so much as glance at Cheryl Wyatt last Saturday, and I invited her especially to…'

'You were matchmaking?' Phinn queried, amazed, her mouth falling open. Ty had invited Cheryl on Ash's account! Phinn's jealousy of the beautiful Cheryl Wyatt eased somewhat. If Ty had invited Cheryl for Ash's benefit, then Ty could not be interested in her for himself. 'Er—wrong stable,' she announced.

'Wrong stable?'

'I don't think I'm breaking any great confidence—Ash has a date with Geraldine Walton tonight.'

It was Ty's turn to be amazed. 'He's…? Geraldine Walton?'

Phinn found she could not hold down a grin. 'So you've no need to worry that I'm going to let Ash down,' she remarked lightly. 'I just don't figure in that way.' Looking at Ty, loving him so much, she truly did not want him worrying any more about his kid brother. 'So you see, Ty, Ash truly sees me as a kind of sister.'

With her glance still on Ty as what she had revealed sank in, Phinn felt that he seemed to visibly relax. As if what she had just said was somehow of the utmost importance. As if a whole load of concern had been lifted from his shoulders. And it was only then that Phinn realised just how tense Ty had been.

Her grin became impish, and she just had to add, 'Sorry, Ty, that sort of makes me your sister too.'

But his reply truly jolted her. Shaking his head, he told her flatly, 'I don't think so. I don't want you for a sister.'

That hurt, but somehow she managed to hide it, and as casually as she could she got to her feet, tears again threatening—but this time tears from the hurt that he had just so carelessly served her. 'Well, that puts me in my place,' she commented offhandedly. And, head up, pride intact, 'Well, if that's it—if that settles your concerns about Ash—I'll be off.'

She did not get very far! To her surprise, she did not even get as far as lifting up her suitcase before Ty was standing in front of her, blocking her way. 'That,' he clipped, 'in no way settles it.'

'It doesn't?'

He moved his head slowly from side to side. 'No, it does not,' he said firmly, to her further surprise. Adding, 'I've a more special place for you than that.'

More special than a sister? Hardly! 'You've heard how good I am in an office? You're offering me a job?'

'There *is* a job for you—if all else fails,' Ty replied.

'What sort of job?' A job where she stood a chance of seeing him again? No, thank you, said her pride. Oh, please, said her heart.

Ty looked at her for long moments, and then stated, 'When Ash goes to Honeysuckle Farm it will be more than a full-time job for him. I shall need an estate manager here.'

'Me?' she exclaimed. But, on thinking about it, 'You won't need anyone full-time,' she denied. 'You're selling Yew Tree Farm, I believe. And while it will take a couple of years for Ash to lick Honeysuckle into shape…' Her voice tailed off, guilt smiting her.

'Honeysuckle will be fine—with your input. Presumably with your local knowledge you know of someone who will show Ash the ropes?'

'Er—I do, actually,' she admitted. 'Old Jack Philips—he's worked on the land all his life. He retired about a year ago, but he's finding retirement irksome. He was saying, that lunchtime Ash and I went to the Cat for a drink, that he's itching to have a few days' work each week.' Ty smiled, and that was so weakening Phinn had to work hard not to wilt. 'But that still doesn't make an estate manager's job here full-time,' she stated firmly. 'Besides, I've no experience of being an estate manager.'

'Sure you have. You take a stroll through the woods and spot exactly which trees need taking out—know which new trees should be planted. You've an in-built sense of country lore. Not to mention you can deal with office work with both hands tied behind your back.'

Phinn had to smile herself. Yes, she could do all of that, and she would love to stay—would love to walk the estate, love to be his estate manager—but there wasn't even a couple of days' work here.

'And don't forget there are a couple of tenanted cottages that would have to be kept up to date—their upkeep and running repairs to be contracted out.'

Phinn shook her head. She didn't want to go, she knew that she didn't, but… 'I have to go,' she said decidedly.

Ty stared at her, not liking what he was hearing. 'It's me, isn't it?' he challenged. But before Phinn could panic too much that he had guessed at her feelings for him, he was going on. 'You've had enough of my grouchy attitude with you on too many occasions?'

'Ty—I…' She was feeling out of her depth suddenly.

'Will you stay if I promise to mend my ways—apologise for every unkind word I ever said? Every—?'

'Oh, Ty,' she cut in. 'You weren't awful all the time!' She laughed lightly, ready to forgive him anything. She guessed that was what love was all about—forgiving hurt, real or imagined. 'Sometimes you have been particularly splendid,' she added, quite without thinking.

'Truly?' he asked, and seemed tense again suddenly. 'I wasn't very pleasant when I kissed you this morning, but—'

'I don't think I want to go there,' Phinn rushed in. 'I—er—was meaning more particularly your thoughtfulness in putting Grandmother Hawkins' table in my room. Getting Mr Timmins in to tune the piano. The—' She broke off. She had been about to say the replacement watch he had bought her—but she did not want to remind him of how her own watch had become waterlogged.

'Do the good times outweigh the bad, Phinn?' he asked.

'Yes, of course they do,' she replied without hesitation. It wasn't his fault that she had fallen in love with him. 'I just don't know what Ruby and I would have done if you hadn't come along and offered us a home.'

'It pales into insignificance when I think of what you did for Ash, and in turn for me.'

'We're going to have to stop this or we'll end up a mutual admiration society,' Phinn said brightly. And then, because she must, 'Thank you, Ty, for letting Ruby end her days in comfort and peace.' So saying, she took a step towards him, stretched up and kissed him.

It was a natural gesture on her part, but when she went to step back again, she discovered that Ty had taken a hold of her hands in his. And, tense still, he asked quietly, 'Am I to take it that you—quite—like me?' looking down into her wide blue eyes.

Phinn immediately looked away. 'You know I like you!' she flared. 'Grief—you think I—' She broke off. 'Time I went!' she said abruptly.

But Ty still had a hold of her hands. 'Not yet,' he countered.

Just that, but there was an assertive kind of firmness in his tone that Phinn found worrying. 'You accused me earlier of not ever talking to my brother. I think, Phinn, that you and I should start talking to each other—openly.'

Phinn was already shaking her head. 'Oh, I don't know about that,' she replied warily.

And Ty smiled a gentle smile, his tension easing as her nervousness increased. 'What are you afraid of?' he asked softly. 'I tell you now, all pretence aside, that while I may have unwittingly hurt you in the past, I will never knowingly hurt you again.' Her throat went dry. She tried to swallow. 'Come and sit down with me,' he went on. She shook her head, but found that Ty was leading her over to a sofa anyway. She still hadn't found her voice when, seated beside her, Ty turned to her and stated, 'Given that I was such a brute to you when we first met, you have a very forgiving nature, Phinn.'

'Brute doesn't cover it!' She was glad her vocal cords were working—thanks largely to Ty going off the subject of her liking him.

'I agree,' he conceded, his grey eyes steady on hers. 'To recap, and in my defence, Ash was doing so well here on his own, and I was going through a busy time in London. The obvious thing to do was to leave matters down here with him. The alterations were going well, with no need for me to try and find time to pay a visit, but when I did find time to come home I was shocked to my core by Ash's appearance—at how ill he looked.'

'You must have been. I was myself,' Phinn volunteered. 'He told you about Leanne?'

'I got most of it from Mrs Starkey. I supposed I grilled her pretty thoroughly. When she'd told me all that she could, I was in no mood to be pleasant to any member of the Hawkins family.'

'You ordered me off your land.'

'And to my dying day I shall ever be grateful that you ignored me bossing you about and came back again.'

Phinn had an almost overwhelming urge to kiss him again, but reckoned that she had done enough of that already. And in any case, he already knew that she liked him without her giving this clever man more to work on.

'I think you first started to get to me that day by the pool,' he went on when she said nothing. 'I could see you were upset about something, for all it didn't stop you being lippy, but I had no idea then that you were in shock.'

'I—er—started to get to you? You—er—started to like me, you mean?'

Ty stilled. 'It matters to you that I like you?' he enquired quietly.

She shrugged. She was getting good at it. 'Everybody likes to be liked,' she answered—and thankfully he let it go.

'It was more a personal thing for me,' Ty said carefully.

'Oh,' she murmured. Oh—heavens!

'And the more I got to know you, the more I got to like you,' Ty went on.

Her throat went dry again. 'Oh—really?' she managed, but her voice was quite croaky and unlike her own. She coughed to clear it, and was able to offer an offhand kind of, 'That's good.'

'Not from where I was seeing it,' Ty answered. She refused to say *oh* again. 'From where I was seeing it,' he continued, unprompted, 'that's when the trouble began.'

'Trouble?'

'Trouble.' He nodded. 'There was I, getting to like you more and more each time I saw you. And there were you, my dear Phinn, excelling in the job I hired you to do. Ash was coming on in leaps and bounds. So much so that you, as his companion, were doing things with him that I—I found I wanted to do with you.'

Phinn blinked. Open-mouthed, she stared. 'Really?' she gasped.

'Believe it,' Ty replied. 'I found I was coming back here every chance I could.'

'Because of Ash, of course.'

Ty smiled. 'Of course,' he answered. 'So, if it's all about Ash, why do I want you to take me fishing too—to teach me to tie a fly—to take me with you sketching? And why, heaven knows why, do I feel so cranky when Ash tells me that you think he's gorgeous?'

Phinn could only stare at Ty in amazement. 'You wanted me to think—you—were gorgeous too?' She didn't believe it.

'I think I'd have settled for kind, or nice—or even for half of the smiles you sent my brother's way.'

Phinn stared at him, feeling somewhat numbed. Her brain seemed to have seized up anyway. 'You—were…?' The words would not come. She dared not say it—and make a fool of herself.

'Jealous,' Ty supplied. 'The word you're looking for is jealous.'

'No!' she denied faintly, not believing it.

'Yes,' Ty contradicted.

'I—er—expect that—um—happens with brothers. A sort of brotherly—er—thing,' Phinn said faintly, not having the first clue about it, but still not believing that Ty meant what it sounded as if he meant.

'I don't know about that. I've never been jealous of Ash before. In fact, I grew up with it being second nature for me to look out for him, to protect him if need be.' Ty took a long-drawn breath then, but continued firmly. 'Which is why it threw me when I realised my rush to get home as soon as I could was not so much to check on how he was doing, but more because I wanted to see you.'

Phinn's eyes widened, and her throat went dry again. 'No,' she murmured.

'True,' Ty replied. 'You always seemed to be having fun

with Ash. I wanted to stay home and have fun with you too.'
And, while Phinn stared at him stunned, 'Work was losing its
appeal,' he confessed.

She found that staggering! She had formed an impression that Ty lived, slept and dreamed work. 'You...' she
managed faintly.

'I,' he replied, 'knew I was in trouble.'

'Trouble?' she echoed witlessly.

And Ty smiled a gentle bone-melting smile for her as he
explained, 'At the start I wanted you here in my home for Ash.
But the more I had to do with you, and the more I knew of
you, the more—dear Phinn—I wanted you in my home not
for Ash, but for me.'

She swallowed, her insides a total disaster. 'Oh,' she
said huskily.

'And it was *oh*,' Ty said gently. 'Because of how Ash was,
he had to be my first concern. He liked you, the two of you
got on well—which was fine. What was not fine was that the
two of you should start to care for each other. That,' he said,
'was not what I wanted.'

'You were protecting Ash when you were anti me?'

Ty looked at her steadily. 'Where you were concerned,
Phinn, I was losing it.' And, as she stared at him, 'I was as
jealous as hell where you two were concerned,' he owned.
'Logic fast disappearing.'

'Logic?' She suddenly seemed incapable of stringing two
words together.

'Logic,' he agreed, explaining, 'I knew, logically, that
there was absolutely no sense at all in my not returning to
London on a Sunday evening—but there was no space in my
head for logic when it came to my persistent need to want to
be where you were.'

'Oh, Ty!' Phinn murmured. He had delayed his departure
because of her! She found that staggering, and had to make

one gigantic effort to get herself together—she owned she was in pieces. 'Look, I—um—know you're a bit averse to me leaving, but you don't have to—'

'Haven't you been listening to a word I've been saying?' Ty cut in sharply. 'No, I don't want you to leave. But that's only a part of it. You're in my head, in my—'

'No!' she denied—but that was when her memory awoke and gave her one mighty sharp poke. 'If you're going on to—' She broke off, running out of steam before she began. But, gaining her second wind, she snatched her hands out of his grasp, the better to be able to tell him, 'You had your chance with me once, Tyrell Allardyce. If you think you can sweet-talk me—only to reject me again—you've got another—'

'Reject you?' Ty cut in, staring at her, thunderstruck. 'When did I ever reject you?'

'You've got a short memory!' She had an idea she had gone a bit pink, but had to have her say. 'Less than a week ago, up in your bedroom, I wasn't sophisticated enough for you. You—'

'For God's sake.' Ty chopped her off. 'I was off my head with desire for you!'

Her colour was definitely pink—high pink—and she began to wish she had not brought the subject up.

'Oh, Phinn, you idiot. Not sophisticated enough? Don't you know I treasure your innocence?' She shook her head, but Ty caught a hold of her hands and hung on to them when she struggled. 'Listen to me,' he urged. 'That night—last Sunday night,' he inserted, to show he had not forgotten a thing, 'I was already in a situation where I was more feeling than thinking. And then you go and throw a bombshell at me, and I've moved on to a totally new situation. I needed to be able to think clearly—but, dammit, I couldn't.'

'Hmph!' she scorned. 'What was there to think about?'

'Oh, Phinn—*you*, my love.' Her spine was in meltdown again. 'If you'll forgive me, we were both highly emotionally charged. I needed a few moments of space to think what was best *for you*.'

'For me?'

'Sweet Phinn,' Ty said gently, 'I knew I had to be away by four in the morning. Was unsure of exactly when I'd be back. I needed to be able to think, to judge—was it too soon to tell you how much you mean to me? How would you react if I did? I didn't seem to know very much any more. What I did know was that I wanted what was best for you. But did I have enough time to hold you in my arms and make you understand how very special you are to me? Fear gripped me—would I scare you away if I tried?'

'Special?' Phinn whispered, her throat choked. She gave a dry cough. 'Special?'

'Very special,' Ty answered. 'You were at your most vulnerable—I didn't want to go leaving you with any doubts. But before I have the chance to think it through, you and your massive pride are up in arms, and you're more or less telling me to forget it—and thereby solving my quandary for me.'

Phinn's head was in a whirl. 'Er—as you mentioned—we—er—should—perhaps—have talked a little more openly.' And, getting herself more together, 'Though since you went away there hasn't been any chance to…'

'I wanted to phone you. On Monday. On Tuesday. Countless times I had the phone in my hand—' He broke off to ask sharply, 'Has Will Wyatt been in touch?' And, when she was not quick enough to answer, 'I'll take that as a yes. He's been angling for an invite here all week. But…' Suddenly Ty halted. Abruptly—as if he had just reached the end of his rope. 'I'm done with talking,' he said impatiently. And then, taking what seemed to her to be a steadying breath, he said, 'Just tell me straight—if I promise not to roll in the aisle laughing, will you stand up with me in church and say "I, Delphinnium Hawkins, take you, Tyrell Allardyce"?'

On the instant, searing hot colour rushed to her face. She could not think, could not breathe. Though as Phinn recalled how Ty had said he did not want her for a sister, that he had a more special place for her than that, so her brain started to stir. He wanted her—not as a sister, but as his wife! Feeling stunned, for countless seconds Phinn could only stare at him. She had never for a moment dreamt that that special place was this! And, feeling winded, she was not even sure that she could credit having heard what she thought she had just heard.

Had Ty, in effect, just asked her to marry him? She felt trembly all over, but with her heart beating wildly she could not just leave it there. Staring wide-eyed at Ty, she saw he looked tense again—seemed to be waiting. He had asked a question and was waiting, tensely, for her reply!

Phinn took a deep breath. 'What…?' she began. But her voice let her down. She swallowed, and found her voice again. 'What sort of pr-proposal is that to make to a girl?' she asked with what breath she could find—and waited for him to roar with laughter because she had totally misunderstood.

But no! Looking at him—and her eyes were fixed solely on his face—she saw that he was looking nowhere but at her either. She saw him take another steadying breath, and came as near to fainting as she had ever done in her life when, after a moment of searching her face, Ty solemnly answered, 'Hopefully, should I be able to clear away my fears over you and Ash, the proposal I wanted to make—the one I rehearsed in ten different ways, but feared that you might laugh at—goes…' He paused to take a deep pull of breath. 'Goes: Phinn Hawkins, I love you so very much that I cannot bear to be away from you. I…'

'You—love—me?' Phinn whispered.

'I love you so very much, my darling Phinn,' Ty confirmed. 'Love you so that you are in my head night and day. You fill my dreams. Everywhere I go, you go too. You are there in every-thing I do—and it is my most earnest wish that you marry me.'

Ooh! The breath seemed to leave her body on a sigh. Numbly, she stared at him. He loved her! Ty—the man she loved—loved her. She stared at him, her breath taken.

'Well?' he asked when she said nothing, his hands gripping hers tightly. 'Have you no answer for me?'

Oh, Ty. Didn't he know? She tried to speak, but no sound came. She tried again, and this time managed to answer, 'I'm—not laughing.'

Her words were faint, but Ty heard them. 'That gives me hope,' he said.

'You *are* serious?' She started to have doubts.

'Loving you is not something I would joke about.'

'I'm sorry,' she apologised, her voice gaining strength. 'Your—er—what you've just said is such a surprise.'

'Is it?' Ty seemed surprised himself that she had not seen how things were with him. But his patience was getting away from him; tension and strain were showing in his face. 'Please, Phinn, give me an answer,' he urged.

She smiled at him, her answer there in her all-giving tender smile as she replied, 'If you don't mind if I whisper the "Delphinnium" bit in church, there is nothing I would like better than to take you, Tyrell Allardyce.'

Ty did not wait to hear any more. Joyously he gathered her into his arms and tenderly kissed her. 'I didn't make a mistake. That *was* a yes I heard?' he pulled back to ask—and Phinn realised that Ty, like her, could hardly believe his hearing.

'Oh, yes,' she replied softly.

'You love me?'

'I was afraid you would guess.'

'Say it?' he encouraged, with love for her in his eyes.

'Oh, Ty, I love you so,' she whispered.

'Darling Phinn,' he breathed, and, drawing her closer, he

kissed her lingeringly. For a short while he seemed content to just hold her like that, close up to his heart. Then, 'How long have you known that you didn't just hate me, as I deserve?'

'You're fishing,' she accused.

'Why not?' He grinned. 'I've been a soul in torment.'

'About me?' she asked, her eyes widening.

'Who else? I asked you to stay here partly because there was nothing I would not do for the woman who saved my brother's life, and partly out of concern that Ash would brood on his un-happiness if I left him here on his own. Only to soon find that, when I should be rejoicing because Ash is staring to pull out of it, I'm a bit put out at the closeness the two of you seem to be sharing. I denied, of course, that I was in any way jealous.'

'Oh, heavens!' Phinn gasped.

'You noticed I was out of sorts?' Ty asked, kissing her because he had to.

Phinn sighed lovingly. 'I thought you were anti because you'd seen how well Ash and I were getting on and were afraid that another Hawkins was getting to him.'

'It wasn't so much you getting to him that was concerning me, but that he might be getting to you.'

'You *were* jealous!' she exclaimed.

'I acknowledged that on the day I found you in the music room. I held you in my arms—and wanted to hold you again.'

'You did hold me again. That same night—in the stable,' Phinn recalled.

'I was ready to grab at the smallest excuse,' Ty replied.

Phinn smiled at him. 'That was the night I realised that I was in love with you,' she confessed.

'Then?' Ty exclaimed.

'I tried to hide it.'

'You succeeded. Although…'

'Although?' Phinn queried, when it seemed as though Ty would leave it there.

'Last Sunday—in my bedroom—when you were so unbelievably giving to me…well, it gave me hope. All this week I've been tormented by visions of you, wanting to phone, afraid to phone. Had I read too much into your unawakened but eager response to me? Was it just some sort of awakening chemistry on your part? Or dared I hope—did you care for me?'

'What did you decide?'

Ty smiled. 'That was the problem. I couldn't decide—and it was driving me mad. I decided to get back home as fast as I could, the sooner to find out.' He gently stroked the side of her face. 'It was inappropriate for me to say anything yesterday, when you were in such distress over Ruby.'

'I'm sorry I hit you.'

Ty kissed her. 'Given that you pack a powerful punch, I thoroughly deserved it. I was as immediately appalled by what I had said as you were,' he revealed. 'I knew I had to leave matters until the morning—this morning—when I would try to gauge how things were and then, if the signs were good, put myself out of my misery by telling you how things were with me, hoping against hope that there was a chance for me with you.'

'It all went sort of wrong,' Phinn put in.

'You can say that again. I wanted to come to your room last night—and again this morning—to check how you were. I wanted to hold and comfort you. But, knowing how you in your scanty pyjamas can trigger off physical urges in me, I was unsure. Having managed to stay away, I was a little short of incensed when I saw your bedroom door was open, and as I look in as I'm passing, there's my brother, kissing you.'

'He was just being his lovely self.'

'I know, and I'm ashamed,' Ty confessed. 'Ashamed that I was for an instant jealous of him. And oh, so heartily ashamed of my behaviour with you afterwards.' Phinn leaned forward and tenderly kissed him. 'Forgive me?' he asked.

'Of course,' she replied, smiling, loving him, her heart full to overflowing.

'Ash knew in your room this morning that I was jealous—the wretch,' Ty said good-humouredly. 'I can see that now. Now that I know his interests lie in other directions, I can forgive him that he went off whistling, not a care in the world—leaving me stewing when I sent him off to Yew Tree Farm with some paperwork.'

'He took your car.'

'He can be very aggravating when the mood's on him,' Ty complained indulgently, his love for his brother obvious. And Phinn knew that Ty was heartily glad to have his brother back to his old self, no matter how occasionally aggravating he might be. 'So—having got Ash out of the way, having got the house to myself—I'm left waiting for you to come down, knowing that I want to marry you, if you'll have me, but still with concerns about how Ash feels about you and how you feel about Ash.'

'And I came down with my case packed.'

'I wasn't having that,' Ty answered, smiling. 'Whatever the consequences. I knew my timing was off, knew you were upset, but I had no more time to wait. I've loved you too long, darling Phinn, to be able to let you walk out of my door.'

'Oh, Ty,' she sighed, and loved and kissed him. She pulled back to ask softly, 'When did you know?'

'That I loved you?' He looked at her lovingly. 'I suppose you could say that the writing was on the wall when I ignored the social events I normally enjoy in London the sooner to get back here.'

'For Ash?' she inserted.

'Of course for Ash.' Ty grinned. 'Then, as Ash began to surface from his feelings of desolation and I saw that a bond was growing between you and him, I found myself thinking that if Ash was ready to join the dating circuit again, I'd find him somebody to date. I realised then that I had begun to think of you as *my* Phinn, and that in fact I was actually in love with you.'

Her heart was so full, Phinn just beamed a smile at him. 'Oh,' she sighed. And was kissed. And kissed in return. 'You—um—mentioned inviting Cheryl Wyatt…?'

'Much good did it do me!'

'It didn't do me much good either,' Phinn owned. And, when Ty looked a touch puzzled, 'Being jealous is not your sole prerogative,' she confessed.

'Honestly?'

'No need to look so delighted.'

'I'm ashamed,' he lied with a grin. 'Anyhow, that backfired on me, didn't it? There am I, hoping Ash might show an interest in Cheryl, not knowing that he was keen to date Geraldine Walton…'

'I almost mentioned how well Ash had been getting on with Geraldine that night I asked you if it was all right if I took a part-time job—only the moment passed.'

'I wish you *had* mentioned it,' Ty commented feelingly, and Phinn, realising that he must have known some mighty anguish over her and his brother, wished now that she had told him too, and Ty went on, 'Anyway, with Ash so much brighter than he had been, I invited the Wyatts—only to find it's not Ash I've paired up, and if I'm not careful my friend Will will be marching off with you.' Ty broke off, and then, taking her face in his hands, 'Oh, sweet love, have you any idea what I feel for you?' There was such a wealth of love for her in his tone that Phinn felt too choked to be able to speak. 'While you charmed everyone at dinner last Saturday, I looked at you, could not seem to take my eyes off you, and I have never felt so mesmerised.'

'I had to keep looking at you too,' Phinn confessed huskily.

They kissed and held each other. And then Ty was saying, 'So why do I find you entertaining Will Wyatt in Ruby's stable? You don't mind talking about Ruby?'

Phinn shook her head. 'I don't want her forgotten. She's been a part of me for so long.' Swallowing down an emotional moment, she said, 'Will Wyatt was outside smoking a cigar when I nipped out.'

'Cursed swine,' Ty said cheerfully. 'He stuck to you like glue as much as he could—Saturday *and* Sunday.'

Phinn laughed. 'I—er—take it you didn't give in to him angling for an invitation to Broadlands again?'

'Too true,' Ty answered ruefully. And, after a moment, 'Though I shall be delighted to invite him to our wedding.' Her breath caught, and Ty's expression changed to one of concern. 'You *are* going to marry me?' he asked urgently.

'Oh, Ty…' As if there was any doubt. 'I'd love to marry you.'

He breathed a heartfelt sigh. 'Good,' he said, but added, 'And soon?'

'Um…' was as far as she got before they both saw his car sail past the window.

'Right,' Ty commented decisively. 'First we'll tell that brother of mine that I'd like him to be my best man.' He looked at her to see if she had any objection—she beamed her approval. Ash was her brother too—that would be cemented on her marriage to Ty. 'Then we'll drive to Gloucester to see your mother.'

'We're going to see my mother?'

Ty nodded. 'My PA got married last year. Her wedding, with her mother's help, was eighteen months in the planning. I'm afraid, darling Phinn, I can't wait that long to make you Delphinnium Allardyce. We'll go and see your mother and hope to get her approval for a wedding before this month is out.'

'Ty!' Phinn exclaimed, her heart racing. Ty wanted them to be married in less than three weeks' time! Oh—oh, how very, beautifully wonderful!

'You're not objecting? You don't mind?' he pressed swiftly.

Phinn shook her head. 'Not a bit,' she answered dreamily.

'Good, my lovely darling,' Ty breathed. 'Ash may not need you any longer, but I cannot live without you.'

And with that he drew her closer to him and kissed her.

He was still holding her close when the door opened and Ash stood there. He at once saw them—Phinn in his brother's arms, Ty with a look of supreme happiness about him—and a grin suddenly split Ash's face from ear to ear.

'What's this?' he asked, grinning still.

'Come in.' Ty grinned back. 'Come in and say hello to your soon-to-be sister—by marriage.'

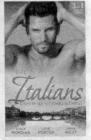

MILLS & BOON®
By Request

RELIVE THE ROMANCE WITH THE BEST OF THE BEST

A sneak peek at next month's titles...

In stores from 16th October 2015:

- **Ruthless Milllionaire, Indecent Proposal**
  – Emma Darcy, Christina Hollis & Lindsay Armstrong

- **All He Wants for Christmas...** – Kelly Hunter,
  Natalie Anderson & Tori Carrington

In stores from 6th November 2015:

- **In the Tycoon's Bed** – Maureen Child,
  Katherine Garbera & Barbara Dunlop

- **The McKennas: Finn, Riley & Brody** – Shirley Jump

Available at WHSmith, Tesco, Asda, Eason, Amazon and Apple

Just can't wait?
Buy our books online a month before they hit the shops!
visit www.millsandboon.co.uk

These books are also available in eBook format!